1

THE
LOK
A BOOK IN THE PARTHA WARS SERIES

Dedication

To my wonderful family for always being there for me, you have been the greatest support.

The people that I have met in my life, thank you for the inspiration.

-

Bill and my editors, I couldn't have done it without you.

My late Grandfather, for making me strong, and my Grandmother for the love always.

A thank you to our countries wonderful service men and women.

This book is for my father Tom, we did it. I miss you.

Old hand drawn Map of the Confederates, hanging in the back of Han Fords

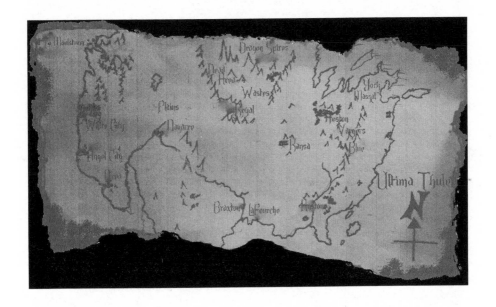

TABLE OF CONTENTS:

II

III

THE
LOK
A book in the Partha Wars series

Tommy Rice
Copyright © 2017

PROLOGUE

Present Day

It is seven years after the assassination of the King, disappearance of the Prince, and scattering of the Spartan Paladins. From the fortress Massal of York, one of the northeast's most powerful cities and once capital of the northeast Confederate States. The Razium Warlord Nemsor Vaul has led a series of campaigns of dominance over all the continents of Partha Terra.

The advance has recently stalled due to the heroics of surviving Spartan Paladins, being able to bolster the Confederates allied forces. With this help, the Razium have been held in check on the northeastern Confederate border of Ultima Thule.

The Confederates leaders have grown in disarray after the King's death, infighting and greed has poisoned and corrupted loyalty. A meeting has been called for the High Council's senior members and Governors. Discovering this, the Razium have seized their chance with the weakness of the Governors leadership. Bribes have been given, deals have been made, and the Razium are secretly moving more of their power into the continent of Ultima Thule.

War is still fierce overseas, where fighting in the Isles has stretched the Razium and their Aun Ka allies thin, but in tel gathered by the Confederates says the tides are changing.

Razium spies may have found information that may end the wars and destroy the Confederates and their allies once and for all. They have found the location of the King's last son, the Prince. He is the only one who can unite the people of the Confederates and open the full Labrynthian to them. They have found, the Lok.

I

"Why are humans different? What makes us special?

Why that is easy, anyone can learn tricks and spells, but what makes us special is our soul.

Our soul is what makes us who we are, defiant, proud, never giving up, and hopeful.

These qualities of our soul make us, Humanity, different; and that is what makes us great."

-MASTER LOK ORSON-
THE YEAR 962.13 APT

CHAPTER 1. INTRODUCTION:

The Saygar Mountain Range outside of Yourkin, Razium controlled providence, eastern continent of Ultima Prime

The large frozen mountaintops of the Saygar Mountains pierced the heavens with their razor sharp peaks. Peaks that were covered in snow from the assault they had taken during the winter storms. What these amazing peaks might have been or could have grown into had been washed and worn away from the weather to leave nothing but the cold rock. The same could be said for all this land. Now a cold desolate place where only the few or the faithful could struggle to make a living. The only thing here now was death and pain. Even the people that had tried to live here in the high peaks of Saygar had been forced out of their mountain monasteries, to move on from the death brought by the Razium army; who now occupied them.

The raven flying over the snow covered peaks could see the land from its perch high above, floating on currents that couldn't be seen. It twisted in the air as it was battered by the wind, catching the currents and falling with them as it traveled home. Its cybernetic eye rotated and clicked, recording as it watched and monitored the white landscape moving past beneath its pitch black wings.

The raven flew through the falling snow, toward the black of night. It flew over the Jotunn giants that lived and guarded the ice passes, and other monsters that lurked in the crevasses of the Saygar. It flew over the snow and ice below that now covered the once amazing road that lead to its destination. Its midnight feathers sliced through the frigid winter air as it sped toward a huge object in the distance. It could see it clearly in the night, only bird's eyes could. It flew to Ice Well.

Ice Well was a colossal fortress built within the Saygar Mountains centuries ago. The young people of the valleys of Yourkin say that Ice Well came from the mountains, and has always stood to remind them that there is always something worse than deaths cold embrace. Those who say that are wrong. Not about death, but about Ice Well's original craftsmanship and what it was initially meant for.

Ice Well was actually a monument to a different time, a better time. Its vast walls could be seen by travelers and knowledge seekers from miles away, its spires and large circular roofs rising out of the surrounding mountains, reaching into the heavens. The people that came here long ago would follow a long, wide, and amazingly crafted road. As they walked or rode down the freeway they were greeted by amazingly carved statues of heroes of the stories on each of its sides, and amazing contraptions that guided them. The road lead to runic steel doors so massive, they once had to be pulled open by teams of large stock Shire and Clydesdale horses. The runic wards alone made its huge walls almost indestructible with the magic tied to them. They were impenetrable to all but the strongest forces.

Ice Well was built by the greatest craftsmen the world had ever known, the race of Ulthwan, or Ogres as most know them. A race that was in their prime when it was built, before the wars of nations. When the travelers would arrive at the gates, they were greeted with smiles, knowledge, and warm tea from the Ulthwan.

It was a time of enlightenment, when the Ulthwan were the rulers of this once peaceful land, their knowledge was a treasure overflowing to those who would travel to listen. Centuries ago, the Ulthwan worked with and learned the art of the Runes from the Dwarger, and in turn they taught the Dwarger the use of steam power.

Using runic knowledge and their amazingly crafted steam equipment, the brilliant Ulthwan engineers carved the walls of Ice Well from a natural cave network in the great mountains. Over the years it grew until it was extended for miles beneath the base of the mountains as well. The crafting of this structure was an achievement of masonry to all the races on the planet. Then however, the wars came to them, and after being conquered by the Razium, the Ulthwan were scattered and enslaved. The time of enlightenment was no more. Now Ice Well is a prison, a place of death and torture, and is used to deal with the dissidents and political prisoners of whatever faction of the Razium army is stationed there.

The Razium torturers under guidance from the Zajust Warlords have modified Ice Well with their own equipment and devices. Installing things from other worlds and mechanisms that can touch the mind. Ice Well is known for its array of creative and skilled torture contraptions. Now though, these contraptions are powered by Razium technology as well. Huge pistons that groan and hiss open the massive doors, a hydraulic mechanism doing the work of a thousand men. The once proud statues and amazing automatons that lined the enlightened road, have been defiled or reprogrammed to kill any too close. The defenses of the walls have been upgraded with the best ballistics and the cells of the prisoners are now electronically controlled as well.

Legend states that the cells of Ice Well could hold any prisoner and even the Dragons couldn't escape its lower cells. Rumor holds that only one man has ever escaped its rune covered walls, and it seemed this story was to give the prisoners false hope. Hope that the torturers would take away, day after day.

Though all the items added to the Well were made to tame or to teach fear, the most dangerous items in the hell called Ice Well were created exclusively for the remnants of an army. An army that was nearly rendered extinct by the betrayal of the Razium and the continuing wars. When one of these survivors was captured, they were brought here. For only here could they be held and broken. They were too powerful anywhere else. When these prisoners are brought to the prison, orders were not questioned and security was at its tightest. Even the slave labor of the Razium talked when one was captured, the rumors of the power and danger of these warriors made the hardiest soldier weak. Though a prisoner like that hadn't been seen for quite some time, and rumors fade without proof.

However, it was rumored that they had yet again found one of those soldiers. That he was imprisoned now, in the cells below. It was rumored that they had found another of the Spartan Paladins.

booster, but as with all rumors it wasn't as bad when there was no proof and the man was already in chains.

Normally the Legionnaire guard stationed at Ice Well would be on high alert, with the rumor of a prisoner of such caliber. But they had heard many rumors, and they were tired and already on edge from the wars with the Isles. The recruiting of the soldiers here to bolster their forces was lessening the strength of the prisons guard, and tired men were careless.

* * *

From above them the raven sat on the rail and watched. It hopped down the length of it to the edge, looking down; its servo eye whirled and clicked as it adjusted its vision. Its head turning to follow the small procession walking down toward the Slab.

The prisoner's sight had adjusted and he had finally been able to see who was taking him to his new home. There were five leading him to his cell. Two were large flabby jailers; their un-shirted light purple skin marked them as Razium Task Masters or jail sergeants. They too wore the same dark pants and boots of the Legionaries, and had pistols strapped on their legs. However instead of the wool coats or uniforms of the soldiers covering their upper bodies, they only wore crossed leather straps of their position as jailers. Hanging from the straps were various instruments and tools of pain easily accessible for them when necessary.

The instruments jingled as the jailers tried relentlessly to push or pull the large prisoner toward the huge steal door of the Slab. Beside them were two others, Razium guards, one on each side of him. They were dressed in the dark attire of Legionnaires of the Razium army, and he couldn't tell if they were human or Razium. Their thick coats had black shoulder armor and they were helmed. Their faces were hidden behind the breathers covering their mouths and eyes, the lenses reflecting the light. They stood off to the sides, their guns raised, the large cylindrical ammo carriers protruding from the side of the wood stocked weapons.

The Legionnaires were there to make sure nothing out of the ordinary happened with this transfer. Normally there would have been more, but at this time of night, with a loss of so many men capturing the brute, most didn't want the job no matter the extra pay. Besides, they thought he was just going to the Slab to be tortured like so many others before him.

So, these four were doing the job that usually took many others to do. Whether assigned or volunteered who could say. The four underlings were being supervised by a slender, cocky Razium Sergeant. His Skin was slightly darker purple than the jailers, and he was dressed the same as the Legionnaires only with a short jacket. From his single black belt hung a sword, and his medals were on full display on the left breast of his too tight jacket. He was young, maybe in his late twenties, and his dark hair was short on the sides and combed slickly over with a large part. He was pointing and ordering around his subordinates, putting them in their places and bullying them with his commands.

The raven was losing sight of them and suddenly realized it was not alone. It flapped its wings, its cyber eye optic adjusting as it looked at the newcomer.

A very old hooded man appeared from the shadows, his long bony dark purple fingers reaching to stroke his black feathered friend.

"There you are, my pet. Why are you here?" He asked the bird. It cawed a reply. "What have we here that has piqued your interest, hmm?" The raven blinked and the servos in its optic clicked as it skipped toward him. The old Hold Master gently picked up the raven, and looked down onto the optic. With a touch of a button it produced a screen of blue in midair; playing back what the raven had been watching. The old man watched the flight back and saw the glowing rune and then the prisoner. The old man's eyes widened as he saw what the bird had seen. He mumbled and nearly tripped as he took a step back.

"It's true," he whispered as he turned quickly, almost stumbling, and dropped the raven on the ledge. Limping up the passage way, he hurried back to his chambers. The raven croaked twice, as it watched him shuffle away; the noise of it leaving an eerie sound that echoed into the prison before it flew after him.

* * *

The jailers were trying to secure the prisoner. "You big piece of," the flabby guard grunted as he struggled to hold the huge covered steel clasps that had one of the prisoner's muscled arms folded behind his back. They were struggling to attach the prisoner's restraints to the apparatus on the floor. "Dees fings weigh a ton," the sweating jailer stated in accented labored tones. The other was fairing no better with the weight, but was able to lock the prisoner's arm in place.

Instead of the conventional bars or cells, the Paladin was shackled to an apparatus atop the Slab. The Razium had added the device to the prison. A Zajust torture device. It was a gold bronze color and had many levers and latches that could be attached to shackles, cuffs, or any other number of restraints. It was made for torture and cruelty to break those they put in it. It was what the Razium were known for, cruelty, and the device had helped them achieve some of the cruelest acts imaginable. They planned to do the same to the prisoner they had now. He however, didn't look the part of a normal prisoner, nor even a Spartan Paladin.

He was a large man, and heavily muscled; even shackled he looked menacing. His legs were attached to the device that was latched to the stone floor, his neck and bull like shoulders set in a brace of covered iron connected to the device that pulled his head down allowing his dark hair to spill over his face. His arms were pulled out horizontally from his body, each pointed toward the edges of the chasm, and his shackles had been attached to huge chains that hung ten feet over the edges. At the end of each chain hung a massive rounded boulder.

The gigantic hanging boulders barely moved as they were set in place, the long links of the chain on rollers that were holding the rocks off the sides. Above the Slab stretched miles of networked prisons, girders, bridges, and buttresses built in to the stone that led to other torture chambers and worse. While around and below him was nothing but an endless dark chasm. Once they had locked the Spartan Paladin into the contraption, the jailers released the leaver and the full weight of the stones pulled his large shoulders and thick arms taught with stress. Most Spartans would have to use their power or be ripped in half by the weight of the boulders, and that would weaken them quicker and make it easier to break them. This prisoner didn't, though he grunted in pain. Then he spoke. "A little more to the left and it will be perfect."

The fatter jailer's head whipped around flinging sweat on the prisoner. "Be silent, dog!" came the barked accented reply from the fat Razium. His sweaty purple skin jiggling as he locked the last rivets of the device, linking them in place with a clack and hiss of alien machinery.

The jailer wiped the sweat from his clammy purple skin, flicking it at the prisoner. The dark leather belts crossing his chest were barely able to hold the flabby purple flesh that had grown to flow over his clothes, his thick arms hanging down over the straps and his fat. The other jailer didn't look much different, but was a bit more powerfully built. The first let out a sigh as he stood, and turned away from the device holding the prisoner.

The prisoner looked at his jailor through his dark wet hair. "Seems to be a lot of effort for just me. Are you expecting trouble, Razium?" the prisoner asked in a calm low but hoarse tone. Weight that would tear a man in half pulled down on each of his arms, but this prisoner seemed calm even with the strain on his corded muscles. The jailer was surprised he was speaking, but smug. He knew the rocks would take their toll soon enough.

"It is always the same wiv your people. Wagging your tongues too much. You will lose that tongue, or we will cut it out," the jailer said as he touched a cleaver attached to his belt. His accent coming through as he was clearly getting irritated by the banter of the prisoner. "I know it 'urts, you're not the first Paladin Izz put here."

A voice interrupted the jailer. "You'll lose your mirth in no time, when your interrogation begins!" The cocky Sergeant snapped, as he walked past the prisoner to the edge of the slab, looking off into the nothingness. He dusted his uniform off. The Sergeant had been content to watch, but now, with the prisoner's defiance, he felt he needed to show his power. The fact that the prisoner was now chained to the apparatus helped as well. The others backed away from the Razium Sergeant. The man was known for his violent temper and seemed to be getting close to losing it. He gathered himself, folding his arms behind his back then looked toward the prisoner. Then back to the other fat jailer to assure the prisoner was latched. The jailor nodded to his Sergeant, who continued. "Yes, we will teach you, you will see." He finished, emphasizing the last word. The jailers stepped toward the bridge, ready to leave this man to the torturers and get out of his presence as soon as they could.

The Legionnaires in the room lowered their rifles and walked toward the bridge as well. The Sergeant stepped back from the chasm walking toward his men, but stopped in his tracks. He was a cocky one, and wanted to put on a show to impress them. Putting a finger on his young pointed purple chin he said, "I figured it would have been harder to catch a legendary Spartan Paladin. You know, I bet you're not even a Spartan, and that you're just some giant half breed from the valley that got caught stealing food from the pig trough your mother ate from." The Razium chuckled. Smiling at them, the Sergeant wasn't finished. He turned toward the prisoner. "Oh, do be sure, we will cut you, and gut you, and throw you away when we are done."

The Sergeant paused as he moved closer to the chained Spartan, still grinning, his men watching in the background. "Do you hear me, boy?" The Razium Sergeant bent down looking at the chained prisoner through his lank grime encrusted hair, and then paused as he saw the Spartan's features. The Spartan had raised his head as high as it could go with the collar, a glare of defiance on his face.

The Razium was not able hide the look of shock that he had on his slender face as he looked into the man's eyes. They were haunted eyes. They were brown with a green rim, and looked as if they had seen many things, and much death. Then suddenly they flashed to a bright golden color.

The Sergeant snapped back, his eyes widened in terror as he realized this was no rumor! The man really was who they said he was. He really was a Spartan Paladin. The Sergeant had stopped talking standing quickly and dusted his uniform again, hoping the guards didn't see his face as he spun on his heel heading for the door. The Spartan smirked at the Sergeant's reaction, but couldn't savor it as he truly felt the immense strain on his arms, back and chest. It hurt. He was doing all he could to push the pain aside and not pass out as he spoke.

"Of course, if you were going to wine and dine me, you could have brought me to a room first," the Spartan said as he let out a strained groan of a chuckle.

The biggest jailer, the powerful built one, spun around at this mocking statement and started toward the prisoner, raising his mailed hand to cuff him on the head. "You dare to speak to the......," he trailed off as he was stopped by the Sergeant grabbing his raised forearm.

"Hold your hand fool. Don't let the metal near him, you'll get us all killed." He shoved him back; the jailor's face that of embarrassment. "You have heard the legends," the Sergeant continued scowling at him. The Sergeant pushed the fat guard back further and turned to the prisoner. "You will get your cell warrior, but first we have someone you need to meet." He said finding his confidence. "Oh yes you will meet the torturers of this place and we will see who is laughing after their whips tear your flesh. Well, you will get a cell if there is anything left of you. The last one of you didn't, he died like a gutted pig, bleeding out." The Sergeant sneered as he taunted the Spartan, the other guards joined in laughing with him. "Quiet, idiots," the Sergeant said scolding them. They slumped and stopped laughing. "Paladin, your time is over," he spat, as he turned to go.

The large prisoner spoke again, "My name is Walker."

The Sergeant was back to him in an instant. He smacked him in the mouth with the back of his hand! "I will tell you who you are, and what your name is!" He yelled, his temper and the chains Walker was in, giving him his fake confidence.

"You are nothing, and your people are dead. We have hunted you all, and none are left!" His voice was high pitched and furious. He was breathing heavy with flushed cheeks as he stood. Feeling he had gotten the upper hand, the Sergeant smoothed out his uniform, straightened his hair and wiped himself of invisible dust yet again as he brushed off his shoulders. Then he rubbed his gloved hand that he used to hit the prisoner. His hand ached.

He acted as if he had just quelled a rebellion the way he walked away; puffing his chest out to show that he was the victor. The other guards got out of the way as the Sergeant paraded through them crossing the chasms rock bridge. They followed him quickly, leaving the Spartan behind them. One of the Legionnaires was placed outside the door of the bridge to keep guard until the torturers arrived, and the other of the pair was sent up top to the observation deck to maintain the prisoner's whereabouts, looking down at him from the viewing room above. The jailers followed the Sergeant to another part of the prison as he continued to brag.

CHAPTER 2. BEGINNING AND END:

<u>Summit of Armistice, Gimralta Castle, Neutral Meeting sight between</u>
<u>Continents</u>

The Island of Gimralta was an enormous mountain of rock jutting like a jagged tooth from the sea, with a small stretch of land being the only connection the island had with the mainland below it. A large castle had been etched into its side, the grey hued slabs of rectangular block ran from walls around its edges tracing a path around its face to its summit. Landing platforms filled with different flying crafts displaying banners of different nations hung from the sides of the castle. A white fog had rolled in from the ocean covering the lower half of the monumental stone edifice, and only the massive grey face of the mountain and tall towers of the fortress stood out from the white beauty consuming its lower half.

Gimralta Castle seemed a floating fortress, its foundation made from the clouds of white around its edges, the banners of all the nations of the planet fluttering in the wind. Its tall spires looked through the cover of the clouds, reminding all who looked upon it of what the place was and why it had been built here. It was a place to mentally fight through and rise above the bad and corrupt that had become of the once great peoples of this world, just as the towers and walls rose above the clouds that tried to cover them. It represented what all those nations wanted; peace, prosperity, and freedom.

An explosion ripped through the outer wall breaking the serene scene of the castle. Dark smoke poured from the gaping wound that had just been created in its side, the dark smoke mixing with that of the white clouds, creating the grey fog of war.

"Matias with me!" King Agesilaus yelled to his commander as they raced down the smoke filled corridor of Gimralta castle. Explosions from where they had just come still echoed within the grey stone walls, the sound chasing them as did the dense smoke from the fight they fled. Matias and the dozen Spartans with him had turned to follow their liege and friend. Matias, Commander of the elite warriors of the Spartan Paladins was tall with short brownish blonde hair, shaved closer toward the bottom of his neck. His large sideburns looped into his thick handle bar mustache, and his chin was clean shaven. He was muscled in the arms and shoulders, and adorned in his armor he looked like he walked from the stories of knights of old. He was still young, being in his mid-forties but looked as if he had seen too much in that time; however he still retained a calm gentle appeal that made people trust him. He followed his King as they ran down a passage of Gimralta.

Gimralta, the meeting place of the planet's kings, governors, and dignitaries, was neutral ground. It was a place where all were safe to discuss differences and find ways to stop war, create peace, and innovate with fresh ideas. The Kings chief advisor and member of the council, Lok Master Orson, had just given his speech laying out the new treaties guidelines, and the King was stepping to the pulpit to sign the treaty first, signifying the merger of the nations of Partha Terra. The signing of the Armistice treaty would have kept the peace for the next century. It would give the Alien Razium more land and the same freedoms that the citizens of Ultima Thule had. It was supposed to align the forces of the Razium, the Confederates, and their allies, and continue in the sharing and growth of all who had agreed. It was then when all were at their most vulnerable that the Razium chose to enact their coup.

Lead by Nemsor Vaul, the Zajust Warlords, leaders of the Razium had been vicious in the attack, slaughtering all in the treaty room. High ranking officials from all sides had been killed and even the Razium dignitaries in attendance had been cut down like fodder, betrayed by their own. After his first dealing with the Razium the King had never truly trusted them; and had taken precautions. Now leading his guard, they had fought their way out and against their own teachings of battle had run. The King ran, ran to save his family and kingdom.

Continuing through the castle they had already met with other resistance, and the King's dark gilded ceremonial armor was streaked and scarred from a short but fierce fire fight in the Hall of Peace. His white short cropped beard was covered with the sweat of battle, his old eyes hollow from the encounter he had just escaped from. He was thinking about what had happened. There should have been no violence here, it was a vicious act of war and treason not to keep one's word at a time like this, but to kill your own and spit on the vows and sacred trusts of combat was unforgivable. His anger was boiling at the thought of the betrayal, when Matias interrupted his thoughts.

"Sire!" Matias yelled from behind him as they went, sweat rolling down his face as he looked at his runic wrist communicator. "The coms aren't working, we can't contact the Paladins; or the Palace. Dominus isn't answering our hails, either. We don't know what they are up against or how far this betrayal goes."

"I agree, but we have to make it to the Palace Matias, to my family. The Labrynthian is the only way," the King said as he slowed his running. They came to the end of the corridor with passages leading off to the right and the left. Looking at the large banner of peace hanging on the wall in front of him, the King readied to invoke the Tempest and open the Labrynthian gate, his guards taking up watch around him. "Orson?" he asked Matias as he programmed the gilded runic wrist com he wore.

"I don't know sire, I saw him make it out of the hall but he won't respond to my hails either. We are dark, no one is answering." The King paused. "Alright, we don't have time to wait, Orson can take care of himself. We'll have to come back for him if we can." Facing the tapestry the King touched his golden wrist band and the runes on the amazingly crafted device flared to life. A small black sphere appeared in front of him moving outward and taking the light away from the area, small lightning bursts played around its edges. A collage of colors rippled into being on the wall, the multi-colored hues turning into an oval large enough for an armored man to pass, the ripples of the opening showing a world beyond. Then the colors blurred to reveal a different place, then another appeared inside the opening. The places switching until commanded. The King motioned for Matias to lead the Spartans through the gateway of the Labrynthian gate, but before Matias could take a step, the end wall of the left corridor exploded outward. Razium Legionnaires spilled through the smoky hole, their black gas mask lenses catching the lights under their Stahlhiem helmed heads, weapons raised. They looked more like beetles than soldiers, with dark coats, reflective armored shoulder guards, and other various instruments in pouches and on belts. Tubes running from their masks went back to breather packs on the back of each soldier. Some Legionnaires were laying down heavy fire as others charged down the corridor towards the King and his warriors.

The Spartan Paladin's reactions were immediate. They were adorned in red caped golden ceremonial armor, their nose bridged helms visors currently open, as was the Kings, though his crown was mounted on his. Their armor was ceremonial, but that didn't mean it wasn't effective. "Phalanx, protect the King!" Matias bellowed. The Spartan warriors had already moved, the gauntlets they wore on their left arms crackling to life. The Spartan closest to the advancing Razium, a squat man with broad shoulders took lead. "Point!" he ordered as he took position in the front of the formation. He raised his armored gauntlet as the circular disk rose from the top of his gloved hand. He pulled a two foot spear from his side holster, a Daru. Half gun and half spear, he flicked a button with his thumb and the weapon lengthened to six feet. Down its length was a barrel and at its tip was ten inches of pointed death. The arcanium disk that had risen from his gauntlet was getting bigger as it spiraled around itself, the sound of it clacking together to form the solid shield. The shield was what the Spartans were known for. The layers of metal had turned the six inch disk in to a forty inch shield with the chevron of the capital of Lyconia marking the front of the newly formed weapon. All the warriors had done this and in less than five seconds from the order of Matias, they had shelled up creating a perfect pointed wall between themselves and the intruders. The Spartans opened fire.

"Commander Matias!" the sergeant of the troop yelled. "Go, sir we have this situation under control." The sergeant was a thick built man, and mounted on his helm was the small crest of a Centurion. His eyes were calm but deadly. Matias saw the feeling in that look, and knew the man would die for his King. Matias extended his hand and the Centurion grasped his wrist as a warrior. Matias looked to the King as he nodded his approval to the Sergeant, Steerpike was his name. "The honor is yours Centurion," Matias said putting on his helm. Steerpike looked at the commander and then back to the King. "I will leave an opening for you, with it or on it," he said, holding his shield up. He was referring to the Spartan phrase of battle, "Come home with your shield or on it." The King nodded, and turned from Steerpike. "Matias get two others, we need to go."

With a flash the Labrynthian portal reopened. The King, Matias and the two chosen Spartans went through the gate, the multiple colors and crackling of light closing behind them, leaving the others to fight the hundreds of Razium troopers swarming their position.

Steerpike rose from his crouched stance as he flexed his neck, then hurled his shield into the oncoming press; hitting two of the troopers killing them both, the shield ricocheting to another knocking the rifle from his hand. The shield then flew back to the Sergeant's hand and he clicked it back onto his gauntlet.

"For the King and Confederates!" He yelled, and they attacked.

The Labrynthian portal opened, Matias lead them through, shield up. Through the gate they had traveled over five thousand miles in a matter of seconds, from one continent to another. It was a powerful weapon and the true reason that they had been attacked. The King knew that the Labrynthian was what the Razium had always craved, and he had to keep it from them. He stepped through the gate and into his home.

All was quiet as they walked in to Sparta, the Lion's Den, and Palace of the King. Nothing was disturbed and the royal palace seemed at peace. He looked to Matias as the other Spartans flanked them.

"They might not be here yet," he whispered. "We must get to ...."
An explosion and gun fire echoed through the corridor beyond cutting him off. "No!" he breathed running toward the noise. It had come from the

direction of his chambers. As the guard followed the King, Matias heard a crying from the children's rooms. The Prince! He thought and broke off toward the boy's room, signaling for the others to stay with the King. Arriving, he saw that the door of the Prince's room was destroyed, blackened, and charred. Shield up, his spear shrank as he clicked it to his armor and drew his short blade kicking in the already broken door. The royal room was dark, as if a fire had burned it and it smelled horrible. The Prince was on his knees in the middle of the room sobbing. Dead Razium troopers were scattered and strewn around the room, and what looked like a burnt twisted husk of a figure was in the corner. Matias recognized it, or what was left of it, a magic siphoning creature called a Void. He shuddered. "What could have done that to it?" he asked himself.

He went toward the Prince, his shield folding down as he sheathed his sword. The boy looked up at him and started to scream, light coming off his hands. "Easy," Matias said, as he took his helm off and locked it on his belt. "Lincoln, it's me, don't worry." Matias held his hands out and slowly moved to the boy on the floor. The young Prince stopped screaming, the light slowly fading from his hands and eyes. He looked around, terrified. He didn't know what was going on, his brown hair a tangled mess. It fell over his eyes and into his soot blackened tear streaked face.

Matias looked at him and wiped the soot from it. "There, it's me," he said as he held him hugging him close, rubbing his head to comfort him. The power finally left the boy and he fell into Matias arms passing out. The boy was drained. Matias looked him over; he had a cut on his head but seemed otherwise unharmed. Matias picked him up in his arms and checked his way, then headed back towards the King. The signal on his wrist com was strong, making it easy for him to follow it.

He heard fighting in the same direction and hurried down the corridors to where it was taking place. He turned the corner to see the King cut down the last of the Razium Legionnaires. The King scanned the room, and seeing Matias holding his son, sheathed his blade and ran to his Commander. The King touched a rune on his helm and the faceplate retracted. Matias could see he had been crying, long tear streaks covered his face running into his short cropped beard. Only one other of the Spartan Paladins was with him.

"My Lord." Matias said, walking to him. The King held up his hand to stop him from talking. Instead he spoke. "We found the things responsible for the attack. We left none alive, though they didn't either." He paused. Composing himself, he grit his teeth. "They were not here for me; they didn't think I would return. They wanted to sever my line." Looking to his son in Matias arms, he reached for him, taking the soot covered boy from Matias he hugged him tightly. "What happened to him?"

"He was defending himself from a Void, sire." Matias said with pride in his voice. "He stopped them my lord." Matias paused. "He has power, his room showed that." "I know he does," the King replied. "They wanted him, they know what he is capable of, and they need me dead so they can use him. That was why the peace meeting, it was all a lie. We can only guess what the rest of the Paladins are facing," he said stating the obvious; more to talk out his grief rather than inform his second. His face softened, looking to his friend. "Matias you have to get him out of here. You have to go, I will meet you after this is over." "I can't leave you," Matias pleaded, stunned at what he was hearing.

"You must take him and go!" Agesilaus yelled the rage and hurt inside him boiling over. "You must my friend." He lowered his voice as he tried to compose himself, "They have already taken the others and my Queen." He stopped talking, pain and grief filled his face as he barely managed to hold back the tears.

The King looked at his son, rubbing the boy's head, kissing it, then looked back to Matias, he whispered. "He is a Lok. The Lok Matias, the most powerful ever born. He is the only one that can help us and save our people if I fail here." He stopped and swallowed hard looking at his friend, then handed Matias the Prince. "Go now." The King said softly looking at the boy, Matias took him carefully. Taking off a special part of the gauntlet from his forearm, the King touched a series of Runes on the jumper device and latched it to Matias' gauntlet, clicking it into place. The small touches to the bracelet opened the Labrynthian door behind them. The King looked at the rippling gate and then to his friend, clasping him on the shoulder. "You know what to do. That is what the plan was for, in case of something like this. I have to shut it down, and only he can reopen it if I die." Matias nodded. The King kissed the Prince on the head and moved back. "You must go."

Matias turned to look at the gate then stepped reluctantly toward the Labrynthian worm hole. The last of the Spartans stood guard while the King had talked to his Commander. The noises of battle had been getting closer and it was only a matter of minutes before they would be on them. "We will talk again, my friend. I will see you soon," the King said, as an explosion ripped through the outer chambers toward the throne room rocking them all. "Go!" the King yelled to Matias as he stepped away from him toward the intruders. "He is our future," he said pointing to his son. "You know what to do my friend, now do as I ask of you and go!" He rounded the corner and headed to the throne room, the Spartan guard in tow.

The King exited out of a secret passage under the dais of the throne, and hurried to the higher ground to make his stand on its top. Smoke was in the air and debris from the explosion had covered the floor. Part of the wall was crumbling where it connected to the large doors leading in the room. Once beautiful wood and gold inlays decorated the area above them. Now the large doors lay black burnt and opened, the locks destroyed. The King readied to meet whatever came to greet him, standing proudly by his seat of power. The remaining Spartan stood beside him, his shield open, his spear in hand awaiting his fate with his Liege. With a stomping of boots, they stormed into the throne room, the lenses of their masks reflected in the light. The Legionnaires of the Razium came through the destroyed doors with weapons drawn. The dust hadn't settled yet, the new disturbance only strengthened the swirling white debris. The steel shod boots of the black and grey clad forces thumped through the breach knocking over the tables and tearing the tapestries as they came. They kept their distance, as rifles and other larger laser weapons were aimed at the commander of the armies of the Confederates, and the leader of the free world. As they neared the throne's dais they slowed, making a semicircle fifteen yards in front of the

King. Behind them the more elite and heavily armored Grenadiers came through the breached doors, reinforcing the hold they had on the room. Standards of the Lion and Chevron emblems of the capitol fell to the floor, the Razium stepping on them dishonoring the ground they walked on as they came.

A large figure in dark jutting armor followed them in as they finished surrounding the King. The figure was covered in spikes, fetishes, skulls and war totems. Trophies from his kills and a beast pelt cape draped off his large rounded shoulder armor, flowing to the ground. His large muscled green scarred arms were unarmored, though he was helmed with a closed angular shaped face mask with tusk like points coming from its sides. He spoke though his helm, sounding like a mix of machine and deep seated anger.

"Well, we were wondering where you were hiding, your majesty." He threw his cloak over his armored shoulder and bowed mockingly; his sarcastic accented tone carrying through the room, echoing off the ruined walls and turned tables. The Zajust Lord rose from his bow and looked at the King. "You left the Armistice so quickly. What no retort? I am waiting." He stood in a relaxed stance, his hands falling to his sides. "It appears my cousin's trap didn't work after all, because here you are. I shall have to amend his mistake." His thumb touched a hidden button to release the blades he had in his gauntlets. They flashed out with a *snikit* noise.

"I was just waiting for you to finish your rant, Zajust. You proved me right once again." The King said. The Zajust looked at him, a quizzical turn of his black armored head. "Only this time I won't let you live. There is no treaty to stop me, or place you can hide. I will destroy you all for this outrage. Well, all of your kind that are left anyway."

"How dare you bark at me this way dog!" The evil warrior spat back, raising his hand pointing at him. "We have defeated your guard, and are inside your castle's walls, there is no way you can win, and." The King cut him off, pointing to the Spartan Paladin beside him, and roaring, "These are Sparta's walls, and there is no way you can breach them!" The Spartan Paladin acted on cue, thrusting his spear through the nearest Legionnaire before any could move. Then he darted to the middle of the press with the King, they were a blur of motion. As the King moved he opened his hand.

The power of the Magnus flowed into him with the currents of magnetic power. Then he closed his hand and five of the Razium slammed together, their metal packs crushing them with the force of the impact. He threw others away from him with another gesture and launched the troopers in front of him backwards with a flick of the wrist, the metal of their weapons turning against them as they smashed against the walls of the throne room with impressive force. The other soldiers didn't know how to react, they couldn't move their own rifles, the King's Magnus power locking them in place. Before they realized what had happened, he had pulled his sword and was among them. He and his Spartan fought through them like a whirlwind of destruction. None could stand against them in their battle fury. The Zajust warlord joined the battle. The Zajust was of the brutal Orc or Yrch race, and normally a match for any foe, but on this day and with this power the King wielded, he was unstoppable. The skirmish was quick, and brutal with the Zajust warlord falling beneath the King's blade.

After the conflict, the King stood defiantly over the fallen Orc lord, his sword drawn ready to deliver the killing stroke to end the creature. But he stopped. Something wasn't right, there was a crawling in the back of his mind. He felt something, something that could pull his gaze away from the hated foe he stood over. The only thing that could have pulled him away from delivering death to this monster, had just entered the room. Slowly he looked up at the huge figure standing in the doorway, and his heart sank. "Nemsor," he whispered.

Nemsor Vaul, the Iron Knight, Lord of the Zajust and commander of the Razium walked into the throne room, his cape flowing from his armor. The armor resembled that of his dying lieutenant, only slightly lighter in color and more embroidered with silver arcanium and gold lining. The runes and jewels that were etched into the battle plate were glowing faintly as he walked. The armor's color seemed to eat the light of the room as he strode to the middle of it. New Legionnaires filed in behind him and the few that had not been killed, immediately snapped to attention, holding their rifles in front of them and making an opening directly to the dais on which the King stood. Nemsor took in the scene through his helmed faceplate. It resembled a visage that was riveted from steel pieces, in the mockery of a stone face, a patchwork of contoured metal that oozed evil.

The King was spent from using so much of his power, and Nemsor knew it. Nemsor studied him with cruel eyes, the hatred burning from them. He had waited for this moment for a long time, and he was going to savor it. The King seemed unprepared, and that is when Nemsor struck.

* * *

Matias woke with a start, gasping for air. He was panting and covered in sweat. The chills of his dream, his past, still clung to him like the thick fog that was pooled around Anstone fortress in the early morning. He sat for a moment, then reached for a towel that was lying on his night stand and wiped his face. He rolled off the sweat soaked sheets of his bed and walked to the window undoing the latch and opening it. The cold air hit him and he gulped it in as he looked out at the darkness. It was early morning and the sun hadn't crested yet. The dreams had been like that lately he thought, as he tried to gather his wits. He didn't know why he was thinking about the past. Before two weeks ago he hadn't had any dreams like this. Something was coming, it had to be, and that's why they had to move quickly. But the dreams, they haunted him. He hadn't shaken this one yet. It was too vivid and he always woke at the same part. The worst was he knew what came next.

Nemsor killed the King with his own sword. Matias had never forgotten the final confrontation between them. Though he had tried to put it out of his mind, but even seven years later he remembered it as if it were yesterday.

The King had fought hard, but finally fell to both knees; his power spent, the anger he had was gone, flowing out of the wound he had just received. Nemsor Vaul stepped slowly toward him savoring the moment of his triumph. Nemsor raised his hand and opened it. The King gasped, breathing in quick ragged breathes. He grunted, wincing as his own sword was magically pulled out of him, flying to Nemsor's hand. The King spat a gob of blood, looking up at Nemsor. "I knew it would be you, I always knew," he coughed. "Why?"

There was a pause and complete silence. Matias remembered as if the air itself knew what this moment was. Nemsor walked around the King, to stand behind him. He bent close to his ear. "Where is he?" Nemsor whispered, with the deep metallic grind.

"He is gone." The King chuckled, then coughed and slumped slightly; blood dripping from his lips and spattering as it hit his armor. In a bloody whisper the King asked again, "Why?" Teary eyed, he looked to the sky, before lowering his head.

Nemsor stood and cocked his helmed head, as he stepped around to face the King. "You, of all people dare ask me why! I am a master of all I want, and now of all you hold dear. I will never go back to living the life I had before, I will never go back to living that lie, your lie.

You think you can enslave me? You think you can enslave my Zajust and Razium and keep them as you have all the others, you feel that these lies keep your people safe. These lies you tell, they will show themselves. I will ask one more time only."

"Where... is ...he? Where is Lincoln!" he yelled. The tone was harsh and accusatory, the hate in the voice making it all the more evil.

"You will never get him, and now," the King said, pausing as he held up his broken gauntleted wrist, the band the King had given Matias missing. "It is closed to you."

The King smiled closing his eyes, and whispering a prayer knowing his life had come to an end.

"When I find him I will reopen it, and if you won't tell me then you can go to hell!" Nemsor yelled as he moved behind Agesilaus spinning the blade in his hand and bringing it down on his shoulders.

Matias hadn't left the castle; he had been under the dais by the secret passage. He listened from the shadows hearing it all. He remembered the King's Helm fall to the stairs, the crown breaking from it. He remembered how it all felt, the warmth of the boy in his arms, the sounds of battle in the background, the smell of gun fire and above all, his heart breaking. He heard the ting of the metal as it fell. It seemed as if time itself had slowed as the crown fell bouncing down the stairs that lead to the throne. From one stair to the next it bounced, as the realization of his King and friend being killed hit him. The crown hit the final step and spun, and spun, round and round; it seemed to go on forever, before slowly coming to a stop on the tiled floor. The ting of metal resounding in its finality. Matias blinked, coming out of his thoughts. He knew he couldn't save him.

A large single tear rolled down his cheek and into his mustache. He remembered hearing other Razium moving closer, and then touching the band the King had attached to his wrist. The Labrynthian opened. Matias and the Prince slipped into the shadows of the newly created door; then he and the boy were gone.

* * *

Matias snapped from his thoughts with a start, as he heard commotion from outside his door, and a knock. "Commander, we heard something is everything alright?" The guard asked. "Yes," Matias croaked as he walked over to the door...."Yes, yes," he said again finding his voice. "I am fine just stubbed my toe, I am fine. Thank you." "Are you sure sir?" The guard asked again. "Yes, thank you, you may carry on, it's not a big deal it just hurts," he said with a fake chuckle.

"Yes sir," the voice replied. Matias listened to them walk away from the door. He walked back to the window and looked out overlooking the soldiers of the night watch. They were changing their shifts in the courtyard below. The cool air hit him and he closed his eyes breathing deeply as he tried to steady himself, his breath misting in the cool morning air. It was too much to think about, he had tried to put that past behind him but it seemed to have found him again. It was going to be a long day he thought, and then he remembered it was his birthday.

CHAPTER 3. BREAK OUT:

The Prison of Ice well

The Hold Master had made it back to his work chamber, panting and breathing hard. He lowered his hood as he entered the dim room. The white of his wispy hair was a stark contrast to the old and sweaty purple skin he wore. Immediately he closed the door then paused, panicking as if he had lost something. Reopening the door he looked back and forth in the gloom. He watched with relief as his raven flew down the hall and in the room landing on its perch, then he shut and bolted the door. He hurriedly walked to his table where upon it sat a view screen and control keyboard. The raven skipped over to it, studying the screen. The master went to the large oaken bookshelf on the wall and was about to take a book. He stopped himself, and went back to the table sitting down looking at the screen. He let out a sigh and ran his finger across the bottom, invocating it and waited. Staring in to the vid screen, he picked up his raven and started petting it nervously. The bird cooed as it was being pet, turning its head to watch its master, the optic focusing on him with a click. The screen came to life, the colors lighting the dim room in a bluish hue, and a strange voice asked, "Yes?"

"My lord, the prisoner we have captured has been awoken. He is a Spartan, as we thought, and he will escape, it is eminent, the runes...." the man said quickly, nervously, gulping as he let the words out, unsure of what to do.

"You have every right to be nervous my friend, and you did good to tell me, though calm yourself," the man in the screen replied. "So it's started then." He said aloud to himself.

"My Lord?" Asked the old Razium.

"It is sooner than I wanted, but I hear the best laid plans do go awry." The face in the screen said, wiggling his pointer finger in the air as if scolding a child. "Do be careful Hold Master. Make sure the Emissary is aware and contact me when you have been secured. I should have found him long ago." He signed off. The old Razium Hold Master slumped in his chair. What did that mean he thought? The raven cooed and looked at him sideways. "Yes I know," he told the bird. "We need to go."

He stood, and started to look for things to take with him. He jumped as a knock at the door startled him. He clutched his chest, breathing hard. "Yes, what is it?" The old man asked, trying to keep the breaks out of his voice. "My lord, the Emissary is here to see you," was the reply. The Hold Master looked at the raven. "Don't worry my friend, we will be leaving soon," he whispered to it as he walked to the door.

* * *

The man that had talked to the Hold Master sat in his dark chamber. He was sitting in front of a 3d view screen of his own. It had changed from the old master to show a holo pic of Ice Well floating above the desk inlaid screen, slowly turning giving a blue 3D picture of the entire mountain fortress. He looked at the fortress floating in front of him, his features hidden under his cloak's light colored hood and the darkness of the room. He lowered his hood, his features still hidden by the darkness and then touched a control key on the arm rest of his chair. Ice Well turned into a hologram of the masked metal face of Nemsor Vaul.

"You may start your attack, Warlord Vaul." The helmed face nodded back to him. "Very good," was the deep reply. The 3D image clicked off leaving the man in the dark.

The Front line, north east border of Essex. Northeastern Confederate and Mid Confederate of Meridion, Continent of Ultima Thule, Stalemate of the Razium and Confederate forces.

The green rolling hills of Essex were cold and wet. The mid-morning air was thick with the smell of gunpowder and dew covered grass. The fog had just lifted but still lingered around the muddy posts and trip wires that ran the length of the trench network on the battle line. The trench itself was an amazing achievement. It stretched five miles from the deep thick woods of Heston to the base of the small blue mountains of the Vargers. It was a perfect spot to hold an offensive as both flanks were covered by the topography of the area. The Confederate army had used this to their advantage. The trench system they had created was made of elaborate trip wires, barbs, mines, and assortments of weapons that lined its length, and so far the Razium hadn't been able to make it across the no man's land to the Confederate line. It had been a battle of attrition for the last few weeks but not much more. Early on in the engagement the Razium had been throwing men and older Warbot Gears at it with little affect, but recently they had stopped for some unknown reason.

The Confederates had proved stout in the defense; luckily the Razium hadn't attacked with any of their larger warships, probably because they didn't have many left to waste. As long as they didn't bring those craft in, the Confederate troops could hold.

The soldiers of the Confederates were dressed in their fatigues, high laced combat boots, light armor and rounded M1 helmets. Most were in the trenches holding their rifles and looking across the way for any sign of action. Every few minutes a shot would spark a mini fire fight along the line that would die down after a few moments. It wasn't raining but it was a grey day, and wet.

A few soldiers where helping a large white nosed Clydesdale out of the muck as its team pulled a massive Howitzer cannon through the mud. It was the last and largest of the battery that had been set on the hill. The huge 155 mm gun had gotten stuck in the mud and they needed it moved and working for air support, as the last Razium attack had left them open. The large guns took out the smaller aircraft but they had taken heavy damage in return, and if the Razium had pulled their troops back there was a reason for it. Something big was coming. The men needed to get the anti-air guns set before the Razium came at them again.

The Sergeant in charge, a broad man with a large scar down his face and a partly used and wet cigar in his mouth, watched as the soldiers set the huge ballistic machine. "Get the trajectory on that gun men, it won't shoot itself ya know!" The man bellowed, laughing and looking down the line as he pulled out the unlit cigar, spitting. As he looked down the line he spotted two soldiers who were intent on a particular place in the enemy line across from them.

They sat staring at the spot, one holding magnifiers. Neither had talked for the last few minutes when finally one broke the silence. "I haven't seen him for 20 minutes. Do you think they caught him?"

"No, not Nate, he is too slippery for the likes of them." The other replied. "I hope." The first whispered, a worried look on his face. He looked at the other and then went back to waiting, seeing the Sergeant staring at them. Gunfire from the other side broke the quite of the morning.

* * *

A black coated Razium grabbed for the dark skinned Confederate dressed soldier as he ran. The Confederate dodged the Razium, then hurdled over an ammo crate and ran. He didn't stop running the length of the makeshift wood wall, the trench and barbed wire not doing any good keeping the Razium from chasing him, lucky for him his speed did. They were chasing him through the maze of trench network but so far hadn't been able to catch the young man. He kicked a Razium out of the way and jumped onto a box of supplies as a shot went over his head. Then he vaulted to another box, over one of the soldiers in black and almost falling, but catching himself as he landed on to the trenche's edge. He was at the edge of their lines and looked up as he caught his balance. Before him stretched the open muddy ground between the trenches. No man's land! He heard voices behind him. He startled, and then he ran. Nate didn't stop to look, he just ran.

"They have stopped firing sir," one of the two soldiers said looking at the Razium line. "And!" yelled the Sergeant as he started towards them. He bit into the wet cigar, then pulled it out of his mouth. He looked disgusted as he stared at the limp tobacco. He frowned at it, like he was mad then tossing it to the ground he stomped over to the men. The two soldiers looked at him. The soldier that had spoken was holding magnifiers. "What do you see?" The Sergeant asked gruffly as he picked his teeth of the extra tobacco. "Ahh." The soldier chuckled. "Well it's Little Nate sir." Was the man's reply. "There." He said pointing. The Sergeant followed his finger toward the line. From across the expanse of no man's land, a skinny boy that looked barely eighteen, and young for that age was running. He was in the open and running as fast as he could toward the line of the Confederates.

The Sergeant bellowed, "Open the door for 'im, give 'im some cover!" One of the soldiers grabbed his helmet as he scrambled to the lock to open a hole in the line so the boy could pass, as down the line Confederate soldiers opened fire at the Sergeant's order.

Nate ran as fast as he could, he was scared out of his mind and expected to see lines of tracer fire zipping past his head, or hear the whine of Razium laser weapons aiming at him, but there was no sound except the beating of his heart and his boots hitting the mud. He ran through the wet dirt, ducking the cover fire coming from the Confederate's side and sliding into the open space in the lines, the other soldier quickly slamming the gate and setting the barbed wire back in place.

The Sergeant walked over and stared down at him. "Catch yer breath son," he said, "Dang boy, your fast. What were you doing over there Nate?" He laughed. Nate smiled a big toothy grin, as he tried to catch his breath.

"We were bored," he got out between pants, "I.... just wanted to know... what they were doing." "Well?" Asked the Sergeant. "They are just there sir, it don't make since." Nate said in a gasp trying to suck in air from his run. "They're just waiting sir." The Sergeant looked puzzled, and he looked back to the line, as Nate continued. "Every few minutes someone will shoot at a different location on the line, but not seriously. It is like they are just sitting there on purpose, to hold us here. I tried to get close, but was spotted before I could get to the command tent." He finished, still trying to catch his breath. "Before they saw me I heard them say something about a boy, an Emissary. Didn't know what it meant, but sir, there wasn't many of them that I could see. Only older Gears guarding the area."

"Sergeant!" The soldier looking through the magnifiers yelled. A noise like a roar of a lion only magnified ten thousand times rang out overhead. As soon as he had spoken it, the soldiers were diving for cover, and grabbing their ears. Only the Sergeant stood, hand shielding his eyes as he looked up. The wind whipped around them as the sky darkened. There was a huge object above them, but he could still see the sky. At least it looked like the sky, but it rippled slightly. A huge shadow crossed over them, the soldiers in the trenches looked around and above them, weapons at the ready, but seeing nothing. Something was there however, and the noise it made was almost unbearable. A huge something was there, somewhere. The sky didn't look right, and the wind whipped uncontrollably. Then it passed and was gone. Nothing was around them, and everything had gone back to normal. The Sergeant yelled, "Get me command!"

"Yes, I understand, I will deliver the message, yes. Thank you." The clerk put down the phone communicator and stood. His superior listening in on the conversation walked over to him. He lowered his small monocle glasses, and asked, "What was that about?" The clerk looked annoyed. "Well sir, a Sergeant on the front lines of Essex seems to think that we have been breached by a Razium warship or device of some kind. After scans we show nothing. Is it war imagination sir? Shall I send someone?"

"They do already have a Spartan in command sir." Finished the clerk. "Yes, they do." The officer said. "Is that the Sergeants report of what happened?" "Yes sir," the clerk replied, and handed him the paper describing what the Sergeant had claimed to see. The officer scanned it over. "Yes, your right, those boys just want something to do." He said smiling at the clerk. "I'll take care of it, thank you." The officer finished. The clerk nodded and went back to work. The officer walked into his office, looking down at the paper. He paused before entering his office, looking up and down the hall, the entering. He closed his door and picked up his phone communicator making a call.

* * *

43

Violin music was playing in the back ground as a butler walked to a man in beige and cream robes, handing him an ornate phone receiver. The man glanced at it, almost annoyed then picked it up. "Yes?" the man asked into the line. "It has started sir," the officer said. After hanging up the phone the officer looked around his office anxiously.

The man in the robes heard the click of the receiver and handed the phone back to his butler. "Anything else sir?" the butler asked. "No thank you, you know what to do." Nabis replied. Turning away from his butler he looked out his huge window, viewing the sprawling city below his fortress as he held his hot morning coffee.

The Prison of Ice Well

Walker heard the soldiers leave, listening to them laugh. He stayed alert until the door was shut, and when he was alone his head fell toward his chest in exhaustion. He lay there and closed his eyes. He awoke with a jerk, startled! Looking around he was not sure if or how long he had passed out. Then he remembered where he was. Whatever the case, the small respite had helped him, though he ached, and he groaned with the weight still on him. He closed his eyes again trying to focus and rid himself of the pain. The strain on his arms and back was intense. He breathed deeply trying to find a place of calm and then let out his huge breath, his training helping him fight through the pain. He felt his powers stirring though he felt weak. He breathed deeply again. The air was cool in his lungs and the slow breathing made him feel cleansed. After a few moments Walker felt ready to begin. If he didn't go now, he might not make it. Though his powers had been returning they would be a tax on him, it was now or never.

He tested the chain, finding he could get a bit of slack. One of the links had caught on the edge of the chain's holders. He pulled again crunching down, trying to move his hands toward the stone ground of the slab. He struggled, grunting. His hands searched for the stone floor and the metal in the mountain as he pushed his hands down. The Magnus was stronger when near an ore of some type, it made focusing easier. He concentrated, searching, it was there. Walker's fingertips darkened as they touched the floor. He felt the power that this place was giving off, it was giving him strength; he felt the vibrations and could hear voices all through the rock.

Focusing, clearing his thoughts he pulled on his powers, he pulled on the Magnus. The magic that made him so dangerous, that let his kind use its magnetic power. The dark marks of the Magnus coiled around his arms like tribal or Celtic tattoos. He searched and the stone began to speak to him in trembles and carried sounds. He heard mumbles of prisoners, the heavy footfalls of brutish guards, and the sharp taps of the boots of torturers and other guests of the prison, their screams of pain and agony echoing through the stone. It was a sea of sounds; he opened his eyes with a gasp pulling his hand off the floor exhausted. He was breathing hard. He rested, his body drooping like a rock in water, letting the apparatus catch him. After a few minutes he was able to control his breathing. When it was almost normal, he tried again.

Only the years of training to hone this gift was allowing this, and even after the training it was still a monumental talent that allowed Walker to hear the stone. But it was there, the strict, regimented footsteps of what was unmistakable, an armed escort. He let out a strained breath. His body ached and he hurt, but he had to ignore the pain. He had to do this; he could not let himself fail, not again. Cold sweat ran down his face, he screwed his eyes shut, reaching out again slowly taking in the power. He breathed the cold mist coming from his nostrils, concentrating.

No one needed such an escort in this prison, unless that person was important, and a prisoner of his caliber was an important thing but that's not why they were here. He knew why the man was here, that was why he allowed himself to be captured. To be closer to this man, this Razium Emissary who had something he needed.

He focused his thoughts on the metal ore, the metal that ran through this structure. It could enhance the power of any warrior capable of using the Magnus. All Spartan Paladins including Walker had this capability. The Magnus allowed its wielders to manipulate magnetic fields of things and items around them. Wielders could control weapons, crush armor, and some talented ones even hear through the rock; a gift of the Magnus. There were stories that Magnus wielders could move tanks and even stop bullets.

The giant warrior had to use this gift now. Ironic that the runes throughout the structure that were used to stop magic from the outside were allowing him more access. They were giving him more strength, helping him in his task.

He needed to concentrate, and listen. Readying himself he pulled on the Magnus, and listened. With all his being he listened, as if he were picking out particular currents from a raging pool of water, the complexity was astounding.

His long dark hair hung limply over his face, the sweat running faster down its length dripping on to the floor. In this temperature most would be bundled or huddled to a fire, but Walker was sweating. Steam rose from his prone inclined form, and he looked as if he was burning with all the hot air rising off of his massive frame. Dark almost black marks had appeared on his body and around the triceps of his arms, shoulders, and back. It was as if he was pulling the metal on to him as the living tattoos swirled to their spots over his body. He sought the words, through the depths. He could only recognize small pieces and phrases, but slowly their words became clear. They had found him, a jumper, getting ready, an invasion. Walker had found the man with the information he was looking for, he opened his eyes. They were golden. "My Prince!" he gasped.

CHAPTER 4. THE FORTRESS OF ANSTONE:

Atlantioc, the southeastern most Province of the Confederates, the Continent of Ultima Thule

The Sun was shining bright in the midday afternoon of the Southern Confederate of Atlantioc. The ground had been freshly tilled; the smell of dirt and honeysuckle was in the air. A cool breeze blew from the west over the beautiful meadow a few miles off. Farm hands were finishing gathering the feasting crop, loading their carts with the fresh harvest for the night's festivities, as the perfect day was slowly coming to an end.

A raven flew overhead. Dipping lower, slowly gliding on the air currents as it came closer. It was watching the scene play out below it, turning its head back and forth, the wind whipping around its purple tinged feathers. Then movement caught its eye. The dirt beside a cornstalk broke, as a grub worm popped its head out of the fresh ground soil. The raven swooped down grabbing it in one fluid motion, gliding up to a branch, landing to enjoy its meal. The worm's world was gone in a flick of his beak. Zooko, the raven of the Master Mage of the house of Anstone, had the habit of flying to the field and eating a worm or two while the men worked, and today was no different. "So it is, Zooko, your breakfast was served after all." A laugh came from the man standing off to the side holding his rake watching. "That's the way of the world, the early bird gets the worm." Matias smiled. He was tall with grey streaked brownish hair that was messy on top. His graying hair was shaved closer toward the bottom of his neck and ears that matched into his sideburns that his thick mustache looped into, though his chin was clean shaven. He was still muscled in the arms, and had a slight taper at the waist, though a small potbelly poked at his tattered and very used overalls.

His lean muscles bulged under his shirt as he picked up his rake shovel and a few other tools scattered throughout the garden. He looked as if it he had been through a lot in his 50 some years but still had a calm gentle appeal that made most people want to trust him. He tossed his tools in his bag and threw it over his shoulder as he walked toward the cart. He waved to some of the hands to stop for the day. They had to hurry, there was still more to do for the festival later. He looked over his shoulder by the big apple tree at the top of a small hill twenty yards off.

"Lincoln let's go, we have a party to get to!" He shouted, then signaled to the rest of his men, waving them to the carts with a grimace. "Oh," he said reaching up feeling his achy shoulder, then moving it around rubbing it for a second. "Linc!" he yelled again, still rubbing. "Coming uncle!" Said a voice shouting from behind the tree, as a tall skinny boy came running out from behind it holding a bag full of apples. Matias rubbed a bit more, he loved coming out in the field with the farmers and growers; though it was very rare he did anymore. Even though he was a commander there was something relaxing about working in the crop, well that was until he pulled something. He smiled to himself and stopped rubbing as he watched the boy run. His mind wandered to his dream. He didn't know what the dream had meant but he wasn't going to let it ruin the day.

"Maria can make apple pie with what I found. Wait up!" Lincoln yelled.

Matias shook the dream away and smiled. The boy caught up to the tall man as he had stepped to the cart. "Uncle are you ok?" Lincoln asked. "What, oh yes," he replied faking a smile and then changing the subject. "Oh, you brought the good apples, didn't you?" Matias asked, as he tossed his bag into the back and then helped the boy on to the seat. Zooko flew to the back of the buck board and landed with a click. "We'll take those to Maria and she will know what to do with them." Matias finished. As he snapped the reigns of the wagon the large horses started to pull. The others had made it to their carts and wagons and fell in line following Matias.

"Yes sir, you are going to have a great birthday Uncle." Lincoln said looking at the sky, "We should have left a while ago though." "Yeah, yeah," Matias shook his head, always my birthday, I should have never told that woman she could plan a party." "Look at it this way, enjoy it." Lincoln said. Matias nodded looking at him, "I might," he responded. "You know what I am excited for?" Matias asked. "For you!" He practically yelled it before the boy could answer. "A Prince's celebration and all, you will have some fun my boy. I talked to Master Zen; the White Tower is very excited to receive you. You don't even know what is in store Lincoln." Matias was smiling obviously proud of the boy. Lincoln's eyes were wide at hearing the master's name.

"Really, the Master Zen! I thought it was just to learn."

"Yes, it's still very hush hush, only a few I trust know, but it is time for you. I am so proud of you." Matias winked. "Uncle that's amazing, I am so excited," Lincoln paused. "Hey don't change the subject on me." "What?" Matias asked innocently. Lincoln smirked. "That will be next week but the party tonight is for you Uncle, it's not every day you turn fifty...fifty, what is it again?" Lincoln asked chuckling. "I forget," Matias replied back shrugging his shoulders.

"Oh, you know." Lincoln said elongating the last word. "Let's keep it at fifty," Matias replied, "and don't remind me, these women have been at me all week about that. Who I'll be taking to the dance. Can I go with you tonight? What I'll be wearing." Matias paused and thought about it. "Ya know, I guess it isn't so bad, girls fighting over me huh?" He smiled. "No I guess not," Lincoln replied, "Especially Helga, she has it out for you."

"Oh not her," Matias said wrinkling his nose and they both laughed, causing Zooko to take flight off the back of the cart. "Oh, speaking of changing the subject, tell me about this girl you like. I hear she's a looker." Lincoln laughed, his brown hair falling in his eyes. Matias sighed, admiring the boy beside him. "What?" Lincoln asked. Matias grinned. "Nothing, so who is she?" he goaded. Lincoln shook his head. Matias stared at him, looking at him hard, then harder...squinting.

"Ok, ok," The boy laughed. "Her name is Leena, she's..." Matias interrupted, "Oh you mean Smith's daughter, yes she is pretty, be careful about that family." He joked as Lincoln's cheeks flushed. "I'm sorry, I'm sorry, really, go on," Matias said. Lincoln's cheeks were still red. "Really go ahead." Matias insisted. Lincoln stared off into the sky. "Well her eyes are so pretty, and we can talk about anything." Matias could tell he was excited. "Last week I showed her a trick, with a flower." Lincoln smiled as he recalled the story. "I floated it in midair and then made it sparkle, her face lit up." He was cut off mid-sentence. "What?" Mathias asked, looking at him with a confused and frustrated look. "I thought we talked about this. No one should know what you can truly do, not yet, not in public, it's too dangerous. It brings attention to us, with the things I've been hearing, the fighting up north getting closer," he puffed. "The Confederates in disorder way they are, you shouldn't be showing off like that."

"But uncle!" Lincoln protested. "I can't help it, my powers are growing. The Master Mage can't teach me anything more. Even this morning an apple fell from the tree and I caught it three inches from my hand, it was like I knew what was going to happen and then, willed it to." Matias' expression changed, hope came to his eyes and his face softened. "Well, that's good." He said nodding. "I know your power is part of you, and you're getting stronger. That's why we are going to the White City, but Lincoln, you must be careful. Everything has to be kept between us." His deep voice carried off as he looked in the eyes of his young nephew. "My Prince, nephew." It was as if the air had gone out of him when he spoke. "You don't know who could have seen, that's all, and you are the only one of your line left and I will not lose you too."

"I don't even know why I have this power if I have to be so careful." Lincoln said. "I am the Prince, I can save the nation, I have the power." The boy looked down, his eyes tearing up. Matias put his hand on Lincoln's shoulder and pulled him close.

"Linc, I understand, it has been hard on you." Matias stopped talking, and looked in the young face staring up at him. "You know what, let's go home, get ready for this celebration and have some fun. How about that? We will put this behind us for now. Ok?" Lincoln, looked at his Uncle, and lowered his eyes. "OK," he said. Matias still looked at the boy. "Lincoln, don't get down, I am proud of you. You will save the people and unite us again, it is your destiny." Lincoln looked up at him with a smirk on his face, "Do you believe that?"

"Yes, with all my being." Matias replied smiling clapping him on the back. "I just want you safe, you know. I love you boy." Lincoln smiled and nodded, "All right uncle sounds good, you too." "Alright then, let's go home," Matias said. "Oh...and I hear that Master Gunner Wilhelm, has a fireworks show tonight. He better be careful or he will blow us all up the crazy man." They both laughed, the mood more cheerful as they rode over the hills and headed toward the large fortress walls in the distance.

The day was in its mid stages and soon the night would be upon them. Above them the Zooko circled around searching for another meal, the breezes carrying it up and down as if an invisible hand held it in place. It surveyed the scene below it, seeing apple trees, crops, plowed fields, and all the work carts being pulled by huge Shire horses or steam trucks, on a road running away toward a walled fortress city. The fortress city of Anstone on the hill in the distance. Not big like some of the larger metro cities, but it was a very secluded and well defended place. A place that was easily hidden, or easy to hide in, just another fiefdom with a rich family in the south. The bird turned, circling the carts below it still searching for another grub or something else to eat. As the currents caught it, it laid eyes on a shape in the sky. It croaked as its eyes widened, and it burst away from the thing. It flew as fast and as quickly as it could from the new danger.

Off in the distance, many miles from the raven was a dark shape in the sky. Not much to see and it looked more like a dark patch of clouds than anything else, but if one looked hard or had the eyes of the raven, one could make out the shape of the enormous flying monstrosity coming fast from the northeast, and it was heading directly toward Anstone.

Ice Well

Walker's blood was pumping, the thought of his goal so close gave him strength. He felt the adrenalin of excitement flow into him. He had found what he was looking for. His intel was correct, an Emissary of the Razium was here and he had the knowledge Walker needed to find the Prince, and a way out of this dreaded place as well. He closed his eyes harnessing his power and concentrated to focus his energies. He pulled on the Magnus, the tattoos that had faded returned stronger and darker.

The guard posted outside the door was half asleep from the long night. His watch was overdue and he was ready to hit the sack, his head drooping. The other Legionnaire in the observation room above had made himself comfortable and had taken off his breather, but still wore his helmet. He was a normal looking Razium man in his twenties, light purple skin and a longer nose. He had sat and was sipping his coffee, the steam coming off it in whiffs, the cool air blowing over the top. He took a sip enjoying the hot liquid. It was nice and quiet. He paused and listened, then took another sip. There it was again, had he heard a grinding noise? He looked up, his eyebrow cocked listening. He heard nothing; he dismissed it and sat back letting his shoulders relax. He was settling back in the chair when he heard it again, this time with a bang at the end of it. He looked around trying to find where the noise was coming from. He was hit in the helmet with small rock chips that had fallen from the ceiling. They rolled down the sides of his helm and landed on his leg, a piece falling into his coffee. He held his hand out and another piece of the ceiling landed in it. He looked up, confusion on his face. The noise intensified. He stood slowly and walked to the view port of the room looking over the edge. He peered down at the prisoner and realized what was happening; he did a double take, fear in his wide eyes. "What is he doing!" he cried out.

Walker heard the yell, but to him it was as if the voice were as distant as the voices from the stone. He had been able to move the chained stones he was locked to, slowly at first but they had been gaining momentum with each pull of his massive Magnus laced arms. His sweaty dark hair covered most of his face, the tension on his body causing the beads of sweat to run down his back, that like his sides and arms were covered in the black tattoos of the Magnus. He grunted, using his might to rock the boulders back and forth. They swung openly; each one picking up momentum grinding the sides of the slab, two boulders of death using him as their fulcrum. He was aching and sore from the rubbing on the device but he couldn't stop now, he was almost free. The guard above broke from his trance of watching the mythical come to life, in front of him. He ran to the alarm, slamming his hand down on the button. It sounded, blaring through the subterranean prison. Walker continued to swing; his powers enhancing the magnetic field around him allowing him to get more momentum and in turn more power. With the extra power, he lurched, rising up breaking part of the apparatus from the floor. He was almost standing now, though his neck was still locked in the collar. He squeezed his shoulders together, swinging the boulders forward then back again, he continued until the once shackles whipped back and forth like the pendulum of a grandfather clock, only without the confines of a darken oak box to keep them in check.

52

The stones were close to hitting each other, and Walker knew this was the moment. Straining with all he had and with a furious shout that shattered eardrums and cracked stone, he brought the swinging boulders together, smashing the stones apart in a cataclysmic roar of crumbling stone and shattering iron. He slumped slightly, allowing his body to recover from the weight, the blood pumping in his massive veined shoulders, but without it pulling on him he felt light.

His closed fist moved to his throat stopping inches from the shackle, he opened his fist. The shackles lock crumpled and opened, dropping to the floor with a thump. Walker flexed and the flimsy shackles on his wrists and feet popped, falling to the floor. He ripped his legs free, the Magnus crushing the metal locks, then stood, rising to his full height for the first time since he had been pulled into the prison. He was dizzy and hurt, almost falling to his knees from the exertion. His head was swimming, but he was able to steady himself on what little remained of the apparatus. Freed, but tired, he had to go on. He was too close to stop now. He looked across the bridge to the door, no one had come yet.

The guard outside the door had dozed. He was leaning on the outer door frame and fell out of his chair when he heard the huge boulders explode. Gathering his wits, he peered through the looking slit of the door seeing the prisoner was free; there was a moment of silence, then shock, then fear. The stunned recognition of a complete tempest unleashed. He looked the monstrous warrior in his glowing golden eyes, seeing that he wore black tattoos that were not there before. He couldn't fathom what he saw. Rage, a terror of legend stood before him. He ducked back down, flinching as he slammed the looking door shut.

The alarm blared behind Walker; the guard upstairs was alerting the entire prison. The prisoner is freed, bring the Ogres, the slab is compromised!" Walker heard this over the intercom and looked at the guard in the room above him. A quick surmising of his location, he realized the best way off the slab was through the door. But he had another idea. "Shard arrows!" He heard the call in the background. He needed to hear better than this, the alarm was deafening and annoying; he pointed his Magnus covered hand toward the broken collar. With a gesture the metal was launched toward the speaker, using his power to guide it. It sliced into the speaker, the metal cutting it in half as it stuck in the mountain. There was still noise in the background, but at least he didn't have to suffer through the blaring of the siren. Walker looked down; around the floor then up the walls of the slab. Judging his trajectory he started running toward the bridge. Midway across, he jumped, launching himself to a protruding ledge below the observation room. He reached out for the ledge, slamming against the wall and grunting with pain as he caught it with his fingers. His muscles hadn't recovered from the ordeal of the weight of the boulders, but he held on pulling himself up. There were jutting edges and footholds in the rock, he grabbed one and started to scale the wall toward the observation room.

The Legionnaire above couldn't see where the prisoner had jumped to, only that he had. He tried to look over the edge but couldn't see without leaning his head out over the chasm. He waited, holding his rifle at the opening. He was nervous and shaking. A Spartan had escaped! He waited, sweat running down his purple face, thoughts of fear and doubt crept into his psyche. The masters would be furious that there was an insane tattooed giant outside the window. He froze in fear. His heart pounded for what seemed like hours. Then he listened. He hadn't heard anything for a few moments. A few more went by and slowly his fear keeping him locked in place eased. He crouched down as he moved toward the lookout window, listening. Still nothing. Maybe he had fallen, he thought. Yes, he had to have fallen. The Legionnaire found his nerve and leaned over the edge sticking the barrel of his weapon over as a warning and firing a shot, still nothing. He leaned out slowly looking for the giant, eyes wide wondering if he really had fallen. He fell, he thought as he let out his breath. A huge tattooed hand grabbed him by the collar, he yelped as he was pulled out of the room.

Walker tossed the soldier into the abyss, pulling himself up over the ledge; he leapt into the observation room landing lightly for someone of his size. He made his way to the control console and hit the button that silenced the alarm in the rest of the prison. Ice Well became silent, except the mustering of guards outside. He released his hold on the Magnus and his marks slowly dissipated back into his skin. He took a moment of respite. Looking around the room, he found a map of the prison on the wall. He studied the rooms, walls, and jail outside it seeking the best way out. There, he pointed to himself. Looking out a small window of the room, down to the outside entrance of the Slab's cell door he noticed Legionnaires were pouring down the corridor. They hadn't known he had made it off the Slab yet. He saw outside the Slab door was a vestibule that the corridors lead into. It seemed the Razium were planning on holding their position in front of the entrance letting him come out to greet them. Walker watched from the small window of the room, as the Legionnaire commander walked through the press. He stopped and hesitated, then talked with the frightened guard at the door. The Legionnaire talking seemed like a line commander or some rank above the others, and he was yelling at the door guard, who refused to stand up still holding his rifle tight in a fetal position by the door. Walker opened the observation door, quietly slipping out to the small landing. He looked over the edge and scanning the Razium below, found his target. The Legionnaire commander put his finger to an earpiece, and was giving orders; then stopped talking as he felt eyes on him. Walker watched as he turned to look up directly at him.

"Stop him, there!" He yelled pointing, "Bring him down, he is weakened!" The Legionnaire commander moved behind his men, pointing yelling in his ear piece as he did. "He is out, bring out the Ogres, we must protect the Emissary!" The Legionnaires around him looked up at the commander's cry for alarm.

They saw Walker and froze with the look of surprise and utter cowardice on their faces. The Commander yelled louder and their training kicked in. As one, they lifted their weapons toward the warrior above them. The barrels erupted in gunfire, but it was too late. Walker had already started moving. He leapt off the landing above them, the dark tattoos returned to his skin. Now instead of merely a guide or ear, the Magnus flowed into him, skin hardening, the tattoo marks returning on his skin in their usual patterns. Turning from flesh to ink black as they set on his muscled body. As he flew he repelled their bullets with his left hand, pulling his right fist back as it became alight with a blue nimbus of power! The bullets he couldn't stop were bouncing off his hardened flesh, as he hurtled towards them. The Legionnaires started to lose their nerve and scattered realizing the weapons were having no effect as the tattooed giant came flying towards them. The Commander tried to maintain control by bullying and threatening the men as they started to run, cries of panic rising from their voices. Walker yelled a battle cry as he flew through the air and with a defending sound of one hundred simultaneous thunderbolts striking, he landed in the middle of them slamming his powered fist on the ground releasing the Magnus into it. The blue power pulsed through the stone floor exploding outward with concussive force. The impact creating a crater that threw the guards, dust, and debris in every direction.

It was over before it had begun. Walker was on his knee in the middle of the crater. Slowly he stood, as he checked for anyone still standing. Dust from the blow floated around him gathering on the prone shapes lying on the floor. He flexed his hand checking it for injury then back to the floor. All were sprawled or smashed about; even the Commander that had spotted him was down. Walker shook his head to gather his wits. The release of the Magnus had taken a lot out of him. The marks had dissipated back into his skin as he checked a few more of the downed Legionnaires. He was satisfied they were not a problem and he needed to move. The prison must be going into lock down he thought as he hurried through the corridors. He jogged the way that the soldiers had come ducking under the metal door that was closing. He continued down the corridor mentally following the map from the observation room, as he headed towards the main area of the prison.

A few floors later he stopped to gather himself. Leaning against the rock wall, he listened to the yelling voices and thumps of boots that joined in the collage of sounds, making the commotion he was hearing in the area above him. He hadn't been able to gather his power back after the jail break. It had taken too much out of him and he needed rest, but he couldn't yet.

He took a breath, steadied himself, and then continued moving. He knew he was getting closer to the top as he made his way through the next door. It led to a long carved hallway that was sloped, cut from the rock of the mountain and leading upward toward an open door, the light shining through. All the other doors he had tried to go through had been closed or locked and it seemed he was being guided toward a certain destination. It was a trap, and he knew it was. The Ulthwan know how to build 'em in case of escape, he was thinking as he slowed at top of the incline.

Walker looked out in to the open area that had guards running across bridges and gantries above. Looking from the threshold's shadow he saw the first line of Legionnaires. They were Human and Razium well over thirty strong, all bearing wickedly barbed crossbows. The crossbows held Shard arrows. On the tips were jagged heads that would puncture most flesh and stay put firmly in the epidermis of the creature they hit. They wouldn't kill but would weaken the individual, slowly letting blood until there were no more struggles. The tormenters used these in most prisons of the Razium. Why kill it with bullets, when you can torture it with blades, was their reasoning. The mention of Shard arrows was enough to calm most prisoners, but he wasn't most prisoners. He rolled his shoulders, feeling the Magnus in him. He sat for a few minutes, watching them. He could feel his power returning. The runes of this place were helping to heal him quicker. It was a good thing too, he wasn't sure he could manage this much power in his condition. He sighed, blinked away his tiredness and thought of his duty. The Prince. That his freedom was at hand, gave him hope. After a few moments when he felt ready, he slowly stood and stepped out from the doorway into the open. A Razium Sergeant spotted him. "There!" He yelled, "Take aim!"

Walker jogged to meet the arrayed battle line, "LOOSE!" the Sergeant howled and bolts filled the air before him. Moments before they struck, Walker's body hardened. The Magnus swirled across it in their patterns. The flimsy tips snapped and shattered against the Magnus wrought stone hard-skin. Concentrating to keep himself impenetrable, Walker lunged with a surge of speed into the now panicked line of archers. With no weapons but his fists, he barreled into the troops, smashing them and knocking them into each other as they fumbled between drawing blades and lining up another shot. He punched, kicked and smashed any who were too close to him, ending the disorganized soldiers with ease. With no one to lead them, and no orders being given, the fight had ended in seconds, fear leading to panic.

The last of the Legionnaires turned and ran. Walker was holding a crossbow that another guard had tried to hit him with. It didn't work and had left the guard on the floor unconscious. He took the crossbow slightly aimed and threw it, guiding it with the Magnus; it hit the running guard in the legs crumpling him to the ground. Walker trotted over grabbing him by the back of his coat, lifting him up. It was the cocky loudmouthed Sergeant who had brought him to this god forsaken place. The Sergeant was in shock at what he had just witnessed; his men had been dismantled in a matter of seconds. He was struggling to get away from the warrior he had no hope of besting, and the same look of dread crossed his face that he had when he had seen him on the slab earlier. His taunts of meeting torturers and pretending the false security of control were over. Walker stared at him through his matted hair.

"I am sorry, I didn't," the Razium was saying as he started to cry. Walker didn't let him finish, "Where is my belt?" He asked harshly shaking the man.

"I, What?" The Razium asked, pleading back. "When you brought me here, where did you take my things, where is my gear, my belt?" "The, the armory." The Razium stuttered, it's through that passage," he said pointing to a door in the wall. "It leads up, you can't miss it." He looked back to Walker grimacing. "Are you going to let me go?" Walker looked at the sniveling wretch, his purple skin was covered in sweat. "Yes."

Relief flooded the man's face almost to a grin, the fear replaced it just as quick as Walker carried him over to the crevasse that lead down into the prison. "What?" the Razium exclaimed trying to get away. With a toss Walker cast him down into the pit, his screams lost to the inky blackness, until he hit a ledge with a thud, stopping his fall.

Walker was breathing hard, the Magnus was taking its toll and he felt dizzy, he knew he needed to rest. The Magnus receded. Even after all this time, he realized he still hadn't fully healed from the weapon of the Aun Ka. The betrayal, he thought to himself, it had taken a lot from him. He pushed the thought of losing his friends and powers from his mind. They will pay, but first I need to get out of here, he thought. Hearing more guards moving in the corridor above, he left jogging through the passage door.

CHAPTER 5. ICE WELL PRISON:

Saygar Mountains, Ultima Prime

Walker had moved quickly through the mountain fortress. He wasn't sure how old his intel was, though he knew he was close to running out of time on whatever it was the Razium had planned.

Finding the armory, he entered carefully and started looking around the room searching for his items. It was stocked well enough to outfit a small squad, but most of it was mundane weapons and armor. He didn't see his weapons, coat, or hooded cloak, but continued to look frantically. Then he felt it. Set on a hook across the room under other such belts and straps, Walker saw what he was looking for. His utility pouches. He picked up the dark leather belt almost nostalgically checking the Arcanium plated pouches over. As he got to the largest one, he entered a quick code on its rune covered plate, then opened it. He reached in and smiled. "There you are old friend," he said aloud, a relieved look on his features. Walker patted the large pouch, and then closed and latched it, pulling it around his waist. He found a couple of old pistols, and a shot gun with ammo, loaded them, and tucked the guns in his pants. He kept looking for someone to come in on him, thinking it was strange that no one had found him yet, but knew that they would be mustering their strength. Let them prepare as much as they'd like, he thought. He also found a shirt that fit and changed, then checked the hall as he left the room.

On his way through the maze that lead to the entrance of Ice Well, he had met with some resistance. In the quick engagements he dispatched several small squads using the guns from the armory, as he tried to conserve what energy he had left. He only used the Magnus when needed, saving his power for the main battle he knew was to come. He was now out of ammo but the weapons had helped. He hated using such dishonorable items, but his lack of using the Magnus had allowed him to heal slightly and he was feeling better, more like himself. He finally reached the huge upper chamber that held the Emissary. He was a Razium, a traitor. Though this one was a diplomat with both vital information and the whereabouts of the Prince. Walker needed that information, he would have it. Now the Razium power seeker was in his reach, and Walker would not let him get away again.

He had made it to the main hold of the fortress and crouched just out of sight in a corridor off to the side, slightly hidden in the shadows. He surveyed the amazingly crafted domed and pillared chamber. It was monstrous. He didn't think something this big could be constructed inside a mountain. He knew of whole fortresses that could fit in the incredibly high vaulted ceilings and large thousand yard spaces hewn from the stone. Large intricately carved pillars were situated every hundred yards or so, roads for hauling weapons and slaves had been built running through them. He watched from his hiding place, trying to gain information on the warriors he was about to engage. In front of him was a chasm. The only way across was a wide steel bridge that extended from either side of the chasm and tapered down connecting in the middle, of which there were no rails. There was a mechanism to open and close the bridge so that either side could be pulled back toward its own edge, disconnecting the bridge and taking away the only way out if on the wrong side, which he was. Walker thought it strange that it had been left connected. He pulled a pair of field glasses he had in his belt, and looked across the crevasse. He saw small trucks delivering weapons, and soldiers running from orders of their masters. Then he saw what he was to face, and wondered why the bridge was closed no more. They wanted him alive. He watched the torture masters whipping the Ulthwan to task, arranging the huge brutes in lines in front of the bridge.

Looking past the Ogres, he saw other soldiers and behind them in the distance were the crow's nest gun emplacements of the main hall. They were built on either side of the huge doors that lead out of the prison, a few hundred yards behind the small army. There were also tunnels leading to the gun emplacements by the doors. These tunnels allowed the Legionnaires to move freely from inside the cavernous hall, to the outside ramparts, giving them the freedom to use their weapons on whatever threatened them. It didn't matter if it was an army attacking outside or a prison riot within, they could deal with either. After sizing up his opponents, Walker glanced to the middle of the battle lines behind the Ulthwan and it was there he saw the Emissary! Beside him was the commander of the prison. A fat Razium who was bellowing orders, to others as he looped his thumbs in his large belt. The arrogance of him stank, he seemed like he was going through a drill rather than fighting a warrior, the way he carried on with the Emissary.

The Emissary could have left at any time, but had wanted to stay. He was confident in his safety, standing behind three lines of the Ogre berserkers, as the commander continued showing off barking orders to his Legionnaires. The Emissary seemed to be enjoying himself as if this was a battle to watch for fun, like the wars of the old southern stories.

The Emissaries light purple skin was shiny and in contrast to the deep amethystine wool cloak and the dark uniform and armor he wore. Walker scanned back to the Ulthwan Ogres. Brutish things, each one over seven feet tall and bulkier than four muscled men. The poor creatures had been lobotomized, turned into slaves and were not the regal thinkers and craftsmen they normally would have been. Walker pitied them, they were Ulthwan no more. They were slavering things having been turned into berserkers, drooling and braying, the once proud creatures debased and shackled. Each wore bracelets and headgear that pumped toxins and strength cocktails into them, making already formidable creatures into unstoppable monsters.

Walker knew what he had to do, but fighting these creatures would not be honorable, and it would take much of his power, maybe too much. He had to push through, his people and his Prince counted on him and he would not let them down, not again. He paused as he thought back to how he had gotten to this place and the events that had led to it. His face grimaced as he thought about it. His eyes teared slightly. Walker bit his lip in a snarl of frustration, and battle rage took its place. He wasn't about to let this stop him now, he had come too far and he would not die here. Walker grit his teeth, stood and walked out of the shadows.

CHAPTER 6. THE COMMANDER'S BIRTHDAY:

Anstone fortress, Atlantioc Provence of the Confederates, the Continent of Ultima Thule

The carriages and wagons came over the hill toward the city as the sun was just starting to set; beautiful reds and violets made the clouds look like floating gold lined cotton. Lincoln looked out over the dream world scene toward the castle fortress. "Home, and it looks as if they are almost ready for tonight Uncle!" He could see the people of the huge city on the ramparts hanging banners and balloons. As they drew closer they could tell everyone was in a hurry. There was music in the background as the bands were readying their instruments, chefs and bakers were bringing out their delicacies, and others were waiting for the newly arrived caravan to deliver the vegetables they needed to finish the meals. The shops of the city were closing and all were moving fast trying to get ready for the night's extravaganza. Even the normally stern portcullis guards had big grins on their faces for the upcoming party. Though it was a fortress, balloons, party accessories and the flags of the surrounding cities had been hung on the walls welcoming the neighboring peoples to the joyous celebration. Of course the normal .60 caliber guns on the wall's battlements were still out; and the huge 419 cannons on the back towers and on the walls looked as ominous as always, but the atmosphere was different. Even the Tryonic force fields were down as they rode through the gates. Lincoln didn't remember the last time he had seen that, the fields were always up. They were Razium technology, apparently what the aliens used on their ships for space travel, but a modified version for large or rich castles. They kept the city safe from ordinance and ballistic fire, and could detect incoming objects strengthening to stop them before impact. It was an amazing piece of technology. Master Mechanic Bor had told him about it in his studies of alien electronics, but he hadn't listened fully. Still it was cool to see in action.

Lincoln looked at Matias, "The Fields are down." He stated more than asked as they rode through the main gate. "Yes, it's easier for visitors to arrive. I don't like it, but I think we have enough security." He smiled at Lincoln, "For anything to get near here it would have to be invisible." Matias chuckled. Lincoln smiled back as they entered the Fortress. It was the Commander's birthday, and Matias had not been ready for his 55th. He didn't look that old anyway, Lincoln thought as he studied his Uncle. Matias said that he made too much of his birthday and that it was time spent that should be about getting himself ready to take the mantle of his birth, going to learn from the council in the White City. Though that had to remain a secret for a while longer.

Anyway, no one, especially Lincoln, was hearing Matias wasn't celebrating this birthday. They made arrangements and all in the four immediate cities were invited, including soldiers from the large southern staging armory of Fort Pain. The large gathering would also give the neighboring leaders a chance to meet, and discuss the future of the region the next morning, but with the drinking tonight the meeting might have to wait until the afternoon. Next week would bring about his departure to the White City to train with the master Loks there, and Matias thought it would be good for him to attend this meeting and learn some diplomacy before he went.

Matias was a respected hero, and head of the council for the major cities in the area. He was going to be elected to the Mayoral council and a possible Governorship, though he had resisted the post originally, thinking it would draw to much attention to them and Anstone. However, the people of the area loved Matias and the higher ranking leaders wanted to get behind the old Commander. This party was a great way to do it, and give him the push he needed for election. Matias had finally relented, with Lincoln leaving the next week he wouldn't have to worry about anyone finding out who the boy really was. Also, he thought Matias knew he could help with the leadership of the southern area, with the war drawing closer.

Lincoln's attention switched back to the movement around them, the people of the city going to and fro. He loved coming home after a day out, whether hunting, gathering, or playing it was always fun to return to the city; and the fortress, his home almost as long as he could remember. The walls were huge almost wondrous, though Lincoln had read about and seen pictures of the large metropolis Capitols, but he couldn't fathom them being bigger than this. He loved to look up as they rode through the fortress watching the walls go by overhead, and seeing the towers in the background. It made him feel safe. As they road down the cobbled streets Lincoln saw that the rounded street lamps hadn't come on yet, but would soon as night was getting closer.

They made their way down the streets of the citie's inner walls and then past the market area, by the tallest buildings and apartments. As they neared the inner castle Lincoln could see the huge zeppelin style warship Skylance, docked by the air bay. He was excited, because he would be riding in it next week when he went to the White City. The airship was amazing to look upon, the grandeur of it exhilarating. Especially now with the huge streamers that had been attached to it, a classic Carrack battle ship outlined in gold that had been transformed into a sleek airship.

Young children ran beside them and waved as they rode through the city, and up to the front of the huge main entrance of the castle. They were greeted by the royal retainers, who helped unload materials from the wagons. Lincoln hopped down saying hello to the younger kids, tossing them a few of the apples he had and smiling as their faces lit up from the gift. Matias started talking and directing the men. Lincoln watched one of the smaller girls tear up when she wasn't able to catch an apple. He went to her and bent down. "Don't worry," he said to her, and an apple appeared in his hand. Her eyes widened at the trick. Lincoln winked handing the girl her own special apple. "Shhh," he put his finger to his lips. She smiled and nodded, turning and running off holding her prize. Lincoln stood watching her run and was greeted by a very round woman, pretty in the face, but rounder in the hips. He nodded cordially, handing her the bag of apples. Her small hand pinched his cheek. "Thank you sir," she said and turned to Matias yelling something.

Lincoln reached up to his cheek, Ouch, he thought, man she has a grip. He turned back to the festivities. It was busy. He looked through the crowd and back at the rest of the caravan that had pulled up behind them. Lincoln saw his friend Eric jump out of the one of the trucks in the rear. He

64

waved; Eric waved back and nodded his head toward a side alley. Lincoln nodded back. Matias had handed the reins of his huge horse to the stable hand, and saw the exchange. "Well get it out," Matias said. Lincoln looked embarrassed. Matias' eyebrow went up expectantly. Lincoln looked to his friend and then back to Matias, "I know I was supposed to help you with your speech but we have a little time and I wanted to hang out with my friends for a bit." Matias looked over seeing Eric waiting for him. "OK, go ahead." Lincoln turned to run, "Ah, ah, ah," Matias halted him, "I want to talk to you before I finish my speech, you come to the study. Deal?"

Lincoln's face lit up, "Deal. Thanks," he said running off toward Eric. "You got forty minutes!" Matias yelled after him. "Set your wrist com and use it to find me before this thing starts, and wash up!" he yelled after him. Lincoln swatted at him with his hand. "Hey don't make me send the dogs after you." Matias said laughing. Lincoln turned and looked over his shoulder as he grinned. "All right uncle, enjoy yourself, you're 55!" he yelled back. Matias had a huge smile on his face and it drooped at hearing his age broadcast for all to hear, but as he watched Lincoln run off it came back. "Silly boy," he said under his breath, then looking away started giving orders telling people what to do for the party.

Lincoln turned down the side ally after Eric, and ran to the barn where some of their other friends had been waiting. The barn was massive. It really wasn't a barn so much as barn machine shop and storage facility. It also acted as a classroom for Steam, Electro, and Agriculture classes. The young kids of Anstone knew the inner workings of it and used it as a clubhouse while not at school. It was a grand place, a make shift hideout for them when they needed, or a place for quiet when they wanted to get away. Lincoln had used it a lot for that. Especially recently, he was having dreams about things. He didn't know what they meant, but his powers were getting stronger and maybe that was it. A lot was changing for him, and this place always seemed to be a nice refuge to get away. It was one of the best places to go in the compound.

The boys ran up stopping at the front, catching their breaths. "It's about time you got here," another voice inside the barn said. A tall boy came out to greet them, smiling. "Come on lets go." He said and they turned to run off. Lincoln looked back toward the keep, then brought up his rune covered wrist com. A present from his father; Matias had told him. He missed his father; he didn't remember him as well lately. A feeling of remorse touched him and he started to reminisce, although he couldn't quite remember what he wanted to think of. It was as if the thought was right on the edge of his mind but just out of reach. So he thought of his parent's faces and the few memories he had of them.

He heard Eric yell for him and shook the feeling, looking back at the large strap on his wrist. A piece of exquisite design. It was gold and very ornately crafted, with runes, cogs, and other devices on it. He touched invisible keys on its side and it began to glow around the edges, as he set the device to find his Uncle. The blue lights inside illuminated for a second. He locked it into place and took off after his friends.

CHAPTER 7: AMBASSADOR NOW

Ice Well Prison, Continent of Ultima Prime

"I said get in line!" One of the taskmasters shouted to the Berserker Ogre in front of him, cracking his long barbed laser whip. The beast flinched, with the knowledge of the pain that device would bring and yelped, but listened and got back in line. The skinny black clad task master was taking great satisfaction in the pain he could cause and the power it gave him over these huge creatures. The taskmasters were gruesome things. They wore dark leather outfits, with masks, covering the upper half of their purple faces. Their suits covered with hooked barbs and weapons that were attached to various places on the suit, for easy access. Small hoses ran from vials, coiled around their arms attaching to their chests and waists the red or green liquid of some type of stimulant seemed to lend them strength, much like that of the Ogres. Each task master held a whip in one hand and some type of hooked blade in the other. They were the torturers of this place, and the sadistic nature was evident in the attire and weapons they carried. The closest one to the chasm pulled his whip back to him coiling it, as he surveyed his creatures. A surprised look followed by a nasty grin came to his face when he saw Walker step from the shadows and into the open across the chasm.

Walker breathed deeply, the rage pooling in him. He concentrated closing his eyes briefly. He pulled as much of the Magnus into him as he could, the power surged into his body, and he loosened his neck rolling it around his shoulders as he did. His Magnus marks swirled on to him and then as the power increased they started to glow. He slowly opened his eyes and they turned gold, then slowly he raised his hands toward the snarling berserkers before him, closing them into fists. Waves of power surrounded them in a bluish light. He was at his limit pulling all he could for this final stand. The lead Ogre that saw him snarled, his raged brain treating the action as an insult to his superiority as he alerted the others to the warrior's presence.

The Emissary was in shock at what he had just seen and pulled his magnifiers away from his widened eyes. "They really are still alive," he whispered, the fear from the last time he saw a Spartan Paladin in action creeping back into him. "CRUSH HIM!" He howled at the commander. "KILL HIM!" The commander looked surprised but gave the order over his com piece, as he looked to the crow's nests behind him and pointed toward the warrior. They opened fire with the slides of metal chambers and then the barks of hot steal. The machine guns tore through the ground between the Ogres and Walker but little else.

Walker sprinted. He moved like a great cat, the Magnus enhancing his speed. He ran ducking and dodging the tracers, frustrating the gunners that weren't able to hit him. Any bullets that got close Walker repelled with his power as he charged toward the bridge. The berserk Ogres couldn't be held back any longer. One bellowed slapping a taskmaster out of the way and charged right toward the gunfire. The others followed, their berserker's lust for pain and the toxins in their bloodstreams making them uncaring maddened beasts. "Yes, kill him!" The Razium Emissary screamed with evil delight as he watched the Ogres run on the bridge to meet the Spartan.

"Rockets," ordered the commander. One of the Legionnaires in the crow's nest fortifications stopped firing the huge .50 machine gun. Nodding he looked to the other Legionnaire with him; the man hefted the weapon beside him, setting a very ornate looking tube on his shoulder. Cogs and coils ran along the outside to the scope of the rocket launcher. He hit the buttons on the side priming it, then going to his knee; he looked over the rampart down to the scene playing out below. The soldier paused, the Ogres were running to face the glowing Spartan. "Sir, we will hit our own," he said as he watched the Ogres. "Fire, fire now, don't let him cross the bridge!" The commander bellowed back over the com. "Yes sir," the Legionnaire replied taking aim, as did others above the doors.

Walker was on the bridge, running to meet his fate, his anger giving him focus, the Magnus powering him. The Ogres had made it to the bridge as well, and ran toward him with reckless abandon. Walker glanced over the horde that was only hundreds of feet away; he caught flashes in the distance coming from the fortifications above and beside the huge runic doors. Rockets were flying right at him. He saw them coming, and he realized he wasn't going to make it across before they hit.

He threw his hands up using the Magnus, as the rockets streaked towards him. The rockets sputtered flipping backward the way they came, with a swipe of his hand he sent one of the explosive devices into the top of the ceiling above the huge gates, detonating. Part of the ceiling came falling down crushing loading trucks underneath. He curled his hand and with another gesture two others flew directly back toward the gun nests, another spinning out of control flying through the opening of the weapons bay. It hit the wall ricocheting and landing in the ammunition and weapons caches located in the crow's nest inlets. Walker had stopped most but there was one rocket he hadn't been able to halt!

It hit the bridge exploding, the force of the blast throwing him sideways and sending him sprawling toward the edge.

A few of the lead Ogres had gotten caught in the blast as well, blowing them from the bridge; a howl of rage was brayed from the others. Seeing Walker almost fall angered the berserkers as they hadn't yet reached him. They wanted to fight, to kill, to rip him apart and it made them run faster. Others fell off the sides of the tapering bridge, their fellows running into them from behind in their eagerness. Walker had almost gone over the edge, but had been able to slow enough that only his legs had slipped off. He pulled himself back and was on his feet instantly. He spit blood, holding his ribs. His Magnus skin had protected him but he had felt the explosion, and was hurt, his blueish light was gone.

Thunder boomed across the inner sanctum of the stronghold. The rockets that had landed in the ammunition of the crow's nests detonated, causing a chain reaction to the weapons cache igniting the full complement of cartridges, munitions, and powder. With a deafening rumble the munitions exploded with enough force to level the mountain. The huge explosion rippled through the rock and into the doors mechanisms, blowing them outward and off the walls. The impact killed any too close, as the blast surged out; the force of it knocking the commanders, Emissary, Legionnaires and even some of the Ogres from their feet. It leveled everything in the main hall, in one huge catastrophic detonation.

The Emissary was on the ground, trying to get his bearings. He spit dirt and debris as he looked around. He couldn't hear, the ringing in his ears was deafening. He felt a cold gust of wind and looked back to the fortifications. They had been ripped outward by the ammo exploding. The huge once impenetrable runic doors lay half hinged on the mountainside, fires still burning in the background. The huge pistons that had held the monstrous runic metal in place were broken and disjointed. They had been snapped like twigs at the hydraulic joints. Most of his forces lay dead or unconscious on the floor and he tasted blood in his mouth. He tried to stand, but couldn't as his head swam.

The Ogres in the front of the maddened horde had been out of the blast range, and had continued on not knowing the destruction that had just happened behind them. Such a charge could sunder an entire battle line with almost no losses, but on the confined middle of the bridge only a few of the beasts could get to Walker at a time. Walker used this bottleneck to his advantage and braced himself as they came. The explosion might have broken a rib, but he knew he had to make it to the Emissary before he was able to escape. He clinched his fists and charged meeting the Ogres head on.

A battle cry left his lips as he ducked the first punch barreling in to them and throwing his first blow as the Ogres got into his reach. Clad in the magic of the Magnus waves, his steel hardened fists smashed into the torso of the first Ogre, killing it outright as the punch pulverized bone and anything beneath with the strike. The Magnus force knocking others aside as it launched the Ogre through its maddened kin. Lost in a killing frenzy, the others simply pressed in, stamping on the fallen, each one of the beasts straining to bring down the warrior for the pleasure of their masters and to ease the pain in their heads. Walker darted and swayed between the mass of bodies, delivering brutal, yet surgical blows to the gang that surrounded him. Knees, elbows, and other joints were hammered into paste as he was slowly stopping their press. When possessed by such violence, Walker did not concern himself with small wounds or honorable blows, each strike was a blow intended to violently break bones and end lives. Magic hardened fists pummeled the first and second waves of Ogres before even their dim senses realized that they were in a losing battle. Caught between the desperate whips of their masters, the edges of the bridge and certain death of the warrior smashing through their lines, they started to panic. Their toxins were running out of the maddening effect that they had while in full frenzy. Some tried to flee, only to be driven back into the raging Spartan warrior, while others were pushed from the edges by their own dim witted brethren to fall into the depths of the chasm below.

The alpha of the brutes, a hulking muscled beast, had gotten stuck in the middle of the press and had been knocked aside from the earlier explosion. He had finally gotten back to the maddened mob and was bellowing at its lesser kin to fight. It had been caught in the blast and had been hit hard, but that had only angered it, and he was taking it out on his kin. The beast was noticeably bigger than the others; it wore a steel armor chest plate, boots and had wires that ran from his helmet to a pack on his back. His tree sized thickly muscled arms were covered in huge mace like metal fists. Its muscles jerked as the wires pulsed, lending the huge monster even more strength, its veins pulsing from the shocks he was receiving from the apparatus on his head, the armor barely containing the muscle beneath. The thing bellowed its frustration at not being able to kill anything yet, its chest rising and falling with his angered labored breathes. It could take no more; a guttural yell erupted from the thing as it crashed through its kin. The yell cowed the Ogres as they parted for their alpha. Walker, realizing the Ogres were backing away, turned to face the beast. It watched him through the eye slit of its helmet as saliva filled its mouth and drool ran from its lips. The beast beat the floor with its mace hands, snarled and charged toward Walker through the mass. It threw the others aside knocking them out of his path as a fitful child would its toys! Walker yelled, and readied to meet it.

The Emissary had finally been able to get to his feet. He was woozy and holding his head. He looked up hearing the thunder crack of metal and dove out of the way as a huge armored Ogre sailed passed him, landing with a clang and thud as it hit the far wall of the prison slumping to the floor, its steel armor plate was buckled, and its head gear was fizzling. The Emissary looked at the armor, a hand print was indented in the chest of the Ogre. Then he looked back to the bridge and the battle, the Ulthwan were running.

Walker had delivered a Magnus strike to the Ogre brute, the steel armor enhancing his blow, the power of it throwing the Ogre against the wall! With the alpha down, the Ogre's fury waned. The taskmasters that hadn't been killed from the blast had regained themselves. They saw the Ogres run and tried to stop their retreat, but their whips did little now and most were crushed with the creatures batting them aside running for the doors, their brains realizing they were finally free of the dreaded place. The Emissary watched his army dissolve, as the last of the Ogres went running into the snow outside.

Walker was standing in the middle of bodies and debris. He looked up, his tired haunted eyes catching the Emissarys. A bluish light had receded into the floor pulsing out around him as Walker released most of his power, though the tattoo type marks remained. He was bleeding and breathing heavily, hurting and bruised. The Ogres had taken a toll on him, but he was almost free of this place as well. There was nothing left between him and the Emissary, though he was still on the bridge.

The Emissary was on his face after almost being flattened by the Ogre Alpha. He raised his head seeing the warrior on the bridge. How was he still alive, he thought? He was in shock as it hit him that his forces were gone or dead. Sweat ran from his purple skin, his dark attire was soaked with it. He didn't know what to do as he looked around. His death was in front of him, on the bridge. The bridge, yes, he thought. He managed to get to his feet, staggering, then found his footing and ran to the control mechanism. When he reached it he slammed his hand down on the button. With a clack the middle sections of the bridge unhinged and pulled away from the other, condensing like a trick sword at a carnival, as they closed toward the walls of the chasm.

Walker lurched as it did, he had to hurry before he was too far to jump. He reached out with his hand, using the Magnus he held the furthest side of the bridge open, the gears and servos whining as it pulled against his invisible magnetic power. He ran to the edge and then leapt floating magnetically toward the other side; hand stretched holding the bridge against its will, its gears ground under the pressure as they groaned, about to give from the pull.

Walker released his hold and with a clang he landed head down, then stood as the bridge pulled him toward the Emissary. Walker raised his head, looking right at the alien and watched the man's fear swell. The ends clacked in place, the echo resounding around the emptied prison.

The Emissary didn't know what to do. All around him was in ruins, he had allowed one of the mightiest fortresses on the planet of Partha Terra to be taken from the inside. He hadn't listened to the Hold Master when they had talked, the old man had been right, and with despair in his eyes he watched the Spartan come for him. He knew he was dead, either this warrior or Lord Nemsor would be his end. One would have him, and he knew it. He could have run, he had a head start, but it would have been for naught. Better this than the dread of waiting for his master. He knew the Spartan was weak, he had fought them before, and he could tell this one was fading and injured. He thought he might have a chance if he took him by surprise, but he had to gain an advantage.

The Emissary walked toward Walker, clapping his hands acting as if he was amused at the man who had just crushed his army single handedly. Walker looked like death, his Magnus mark still covering him. To the Razium's credit however he did not falter, even after seeing Walker up close he kept his act up. Though he didn't feel nearly as confidant as he acted. As he neared he drew his slender double edged fencing blade in a grim salute of the Razium.

"You think this is over, Spartan? You want me to hand you my sword in surrender? This has only begun, you don't know what comes for you!" He spat. "I will watch you die and then I will deliver your head to my lord for show. I will get a promotion for this." He said chuckling, though his voice was starting to give his fear away.

Walker was exhausted and in pain. He felt the broken ribs from the rockets, and his arm and face were a bruise of purple from fighting the Ulthwan. Holding his hand to his side he winced, blood was on his lips. He was weak; he hadn't broken anything for years.

"You are going to die here." Walker said calmly, walking toward the Emissary, trying to fight the pain he felt. The Razium sneered at the huge warrior in front of him, spitting at him, and moving closer leaning toward him. "If I do, I will be remade, but your line is ended Old Guard." He hissed, the conviction of his feeling coming through his false words. He moved closer to Walker, continuing his monologue. "We have already won, we found your last hope and by now it is done, and he is ours." Walker's jaw clenched. Did they really already have the Prince? Is that why the Emissary hadn't left yet?

The Emissary felt he struck a chord, he saw the doubt on Walker's face, and this was his moment. "My race is superior!" He yelled, and then lunged! The move was fast, as he thrust his quicksilver blade out towards Walker's throat. Walker caught the quick but telegraphed strike with one hand and the Emissary's neck in the other. He had moved so fast the Emissary didn't realize what had happened.

"Perhaps, but this is what awaits your return," came the simple reply before Walker collapsed the Emissary's wind pipe in a single squeeze of his hand, dropping him to the floor. Walker let out a breath. He paused looking at the Razium's wrist, on it was a gold bracelet with what looked like some type of clock mechanism, an inner light shown inside. The jumper, he thought. Groaning he bent, unbuckling the device from the wrist of his fallen enemy. He looked it over then tapped the runes in a quick succession and they glowed. "Good." He said aloud.

If he could get to him in time he might be able to save the Prince. He turned it off tucking the jumper in one of his belt pouches, and holding his side he limped toward the doors as the cold wind blew in.

He was pale, the power of the Magnus had drained him of all vitality, and Walker knew he had to release it. His marks were gone and a bluish essence of light left his body pulsing outward dissipating back into the rock. He grunted as it passed by his ribs, starting the mending process before flowing out with the rest. He was dizzy, and fell to a knee; his world swam as he collapsed to the floor.

Light, beautiful light, and a cool breeze, was what he felt. Walker was standing with his brothers at arms. He had just heard a speech; the men around him had arms in the air. He was in his muscled Zeus mark I, Spartan armor, and was holding a weapon. Looking to his left he saw one of his Spartan brothers smiling, a dark skinned man with golden eyes. He clapped him on his armored shoulder, and said something. It was indiscernible. Walker couldn't hear him. "Kree, what did you say?" Walker had tried to ask. They had been in a battle. The sun started to fade, his vision blurred and it started to get dark and cold...

Walker awoke with a start, he didn't know how long he had been out, only that he had been. He was cold and he ached, his ribs most of all. He felt tired and didn't think he could move. He was very stiff. Slowly he contracted his muscles and after a few seconds, he tried to move. Wobbling slightly he was able to get to all fours, then after a minute or so he stood, taking in his surroundings. He was just inside the huge runic doors. The snow had continued to fall and the inside of the huge doors was under a sheen of white. Slowly he made his way toward them, walking better with each step. Some of the prisoners below must have been freed, he could hear cheering, and sporadic gun shots; the prisoners overrunning the jailors that were left.

He surveyed the wreckage. Only the original Ulthwan architecture still held, as it was arcanium laced. Ironic, the wards used to keep others out let him in and destroyed the place. Ulthwan can build them, he thought. He studied the huge runic, half hinged doors and looked at the scope of ruin before him. The munitions and ammo caches had done more damage than he had realized. It was a fitting tombstone for a centuries-old place of pain and torture, he was thinking as he walked over the threshold to the road leading out its entrance. He stopped outside the doors and looked off at the blackness down in the valley; the snow still falling, gently landing on his shoulders. He was warmer now that he was moving but he knew he would be getting cold fast and he was still breathing heavy from the battle wounds he suffered.

His breath was misting in the early morning air, and he closed his eyes realizing how weak he really was. Walker flexed the fingers of his hurt arm. The use of his power was a drain on him, and he still needed to rest. He hadn't used that much power since the Thermic War.

He sat down for a moment listening to the perfect stillness, bent over and took a handful of snow. Then bit it, and swallowed. His mouth was dry. The snow tasted good, he needed water after the ordeal his body had just been through. There was no noise accept for the last rumblings of the rocks behind him inside, and the wind gusts in his hair and through his beard. He sat on some rubble and calm washed over him. Glancing up he saw the day's first light was coming, the sun about to crest the mountains to the east of him. The sun wouldn't warm much though, and he poked at his clothes, realizing the holes and tears. He looked around for something to wear, glancing at the rubble inside the exploded mountain face. All around him was broken armor covered by rocks and dead Legionnaires. A flapping caught his eye by the entrance under one of the large golden runes. Walker stood and slowly walked over to what looked like an officer. He was face down on the floor just inside the huge door's opening of the prison. He was wearing a cloak that had been caught on a piece of rebar like pole jutting from the wall, the wind blowing it back and forth.

My cloak! He walked over and looked down at the man who wore it, realizing it was the commander of the force that had originally fought and captured him. Well that's convenient he thought to himself, as he pulled the man from the rubble. The man had taken his things earlier when they had brought him here. He remembered him briefly before going unconscious. He checked for a pulse and felt nothing. He set his head down carefully then unlatched the cloak, unhooking it from the rebar, almost tripping as he did. He was still so weak, and grabbed the bar to steady himself, a cool wind hitting him in the face. He held the cloak and continued looking around for something more to wear. Going back inside he found a fine chain mail upper hauberk, a leather shoulder holster with pouches that fit over the mail, and fur lined coat with the sleeves missing. He also found a newer pair of steel toed boots that one of the smaller Ogres had been wearing. They fit well enough almost matching the ones he had. They would be good to keep the elements off. He found gauntlets, some ammo for the shotgun that he strapped to his thigh, and a sizable sack of coins that the commander had on his waist. He picked up a long bladed polearm that had been strewn in the blast, looking it over noticing its craftsmanship, Eldra or Elven. It had a small button on the side of the shaft. He pressed it, and the shaft shrank to a haft. He swung the weapon. It felt good, balanced like a sword. He set it down with the other items and then dressed, sheathing the blade on his back strap when he had finished. The wind whipped a frost cold on his face again, and he looked around himself; managing a small laugh at the destruction he had created. He walked back to the Emissary and checked him, finding a broken com that wouldn't turn on, but he did have a few sealed papers with information. They had started an attack, though not the one he needed. Not exactly what he had hoped to find, but it did give him a place to start looking for the prince, and a hint of the attack planned against the Confederates in the south; though the Intel was old. Walker folded the papers stuffing them into one of his pouches.

He headed back to the doors, and noticed a ration pouch by one of the soldiers. He hastily picked it up; opened it smelling the contents, and hungrily wolfed down the tack meat and then did the same to another. After he ate most of the ration, he opened one of the utility pouches on his waist and took a pin from it. Then placed the ration in it latching its top. He held up the pin studying it. He huffed a breath on it and rubbed it till it shined. Then pinned it on his cloak. It flashed slightly in the light, the chevron of the Spartan Paladins glimmering. He packed snow in his canteen, then left the carnage of the prison, walking out the huge broken doors. The rising sun was coming up behind the fortress as he pulled the jumper from his pouch. "Time to go home." he said as he walked into the dark, the snowflakes still falling. With a flash the Labrynthian portal opened, he stepped through and was gone.

CHAPTER 8. THOUGHTS IN THE SKY:

Anstone Castle, inside Anstone Fortress City

Lincoln was late. He was supposed to have already met his Uncle before his speech, but hadn't realized the time while he laughed with his friends. Once his wrist strap went off however, he knew what time it was, and panicked. "I gotta go, see ya guys," he yelped as he jumped up, tripping over the equipment in his hurry to go. His friends laughed. Great, good job Linc, he thought, his cheeks flushing with embarrassment. Once he was out of sight he ran.

He ran from the barn as fast as he could, through the walkways and past the guards up to the study of his Uncle. He stopped only long enough to straighten his hair and grab a shirt from his room. He had noticed the lack of people in his way and was grateful; it had allowed him to make much better time. He was tucking his shirt in as he rounded the tower corner, giving him a nice view. He looked over Anstone City. It was a beautiful place. The outskirts of the city were quiet and dark save for the lamps that had recently been lit, the homes and farms outside the fortress had their lights off and the shops were closed up for the night. All were making ready for the party. It was so peaceful he thought and he looked up at the stars. Lincoln smiled to himself then started toward Matias' study.

The castle however was a different story. The laughter and noise could be heard for miles. The tables were covered in food, ready for the feast. There was a huge skewered hog that was roasting in the middle of the square by the big bonfire, and small sausages and pork loins were being handed to the people to try. The smells of the succulent pork, beef loins, cakes, tarts, and all the other delicious food were amazing; and making the crowd hungry. The finest keggers and Dwarger wine merchants in the areas had brought their best stock too. They had tapped the kegs and the place was erupting in fun and games. Children ran through the cobble streets and the older folks sat with pipes in their hands, as the light men had come earlier lighting the street lamps while the sun was setting. The low lamps put the whole castle in a soft glow.

Lincoln had made it to Matias' study and knocked on the door. "Come in. You're late," the Commander said without looking up. "Sorry Uncle," Lincoln replied, as he walked in watching his Uncle looking down at his speech. Matias was wearing his dress uniform his many medals and awards displayed on his breast. "It's alright boy," Matias said looking up at him over his glasses. "I understand the needs of youth. Well, come here and tell me what you think." Matias said waving him over. Lincoln walked over. "You look great," he said as he looked at Matias medals. Pointing at them. Matias was dressed in officers dress blues, and had cleaned up his mustache and sideburns. He looked the part of a commander. "Well thank you, and you as well." He pointed to Lincoln's untucked shirt. Lincoln smiled, tucking it back in. "Now read this," Matias held up his papers. Lincoln looked it over, reading a few lines and nodded. "Pretty good, but..." "But what?" Matias asked. Lincoln smirked. "Let me help," he said bending over. "I was hoping you would say that," Matias replied. "I'll get us something to drink."

After a few adjustments and changes to punctuation, they were heading to the party. They walked on the upper bridge walkway that surveyed the revelry going on below them. Both had pints in their hands and were laughing as they walked down to join in the festivities. "I think that bit you added in the end will be a hit. Thank you, your Highness." Matias said making a slight bow to the boy. Lincoln stood tall his hand on his hip, "Yes, I know, thank you, thank you." He sarcastically said back. Matias sighed. "You are going to be a good King you know." "How do you know that?" Lincoln asked his young face unsure. Matias pointed at his chest, "Because you have this. A good heart." The venerable Commander looked up at the sky, "Your father had it, and so did your brother. You have it too." "I have it, you think so?" Lincoln asked. "Yes my boy you do," Matias replied. "I have power too." Lincoln said matter of factly, "Enough to help our people." Matias cocked his head and looked at him, "Yes, yes you do, but you have to have the heart to wield it, and the head to use it," he said pointing to his chest and then his temple. Matias sat down on a small stone ledge not too far from the study; he patted his hand on the spot next to him for Lincoln to sit, and he did.

"Lincoln, your father and I sat looking at the sky many nights, the awe of the stars and power that it must have taken to create them. Power, is a very big thing. Who do you think had the most power of the races we have on our planet?" Lincoln thought for a moment. "Loks, or Dragons," he said with a smile. "Although the Spartans might be the ones, they are my favorite." "Yes you are right, Loks are powerful, like yourself, and I am partial to the Spartans myself, but only the Dragons had ultimate power." Matias said holding up his finger. "Only they had it. The Dragons used to be the masters of the sky, and the ground." He took a drink from his pint before continuing. "They used to be helpful to the people in the old days before the fall, long ago. They were so amazing and so unique," he added with a sigh. "But power corrupted them. Not all at first, but after a time power has a way of turning and sometimes corrupting even the best."

"You liked them, Uncle?" Lincoln asked. "No, but I respect the power they had, and the power they lost." "But Uncle it doesn't have to be that way. If one masters the power they have, they can make others do what is best."

Matias interrupted. "That is what I mean Linc, that is what the Dragons thought, that's what the Razium think. Power has to be used not to make people do what you want, but to help them find what they need in themselves. The Dragons turned evil because of their desire for more power, same with the Razium and they have already lost it once."

There was a pause and Matias let what he said sink in. "Do you understand what I am saying? The Creator gave us power, gave you magic power. You can't use magic to unite us, but you can help us to unite ourselves, that son is great power." Lincoln nodded. Matias grinned, and took another sip of his pint. Lincoln heard footsteps and looked to see his friend Eric coming from the other tower over the bridge toward them. Lincoln perked up, "Eric!"

"Hello, Commander," he said to them as he nodded to Linc.

"Eric, how are the festivities?" Matias asked. "Good sir, but I think they are waiting on you," the brown haired boy said. "My uncle was telling me about Dragons," Lincoln added.

"Really," Eric asked, "have you seen one Commander?" The old warrior stood with a grunt. "Oh." Matias said letting his age show as he stood. "What?" Matias asked and then remembered the conversation before his old injuries hurt. "Oh yes, I've seen one, fought one too." Both boy's eyes got wide in awe. "I'll tell you the story some other time, now though, I have a party to get to."

"You know you like the attention," Lincoln said.

"Yeah thrilled, now you boys go run along and stay out of trouble," Matias said chuckling. "I have a speech to give and a date with some pork loin." The boys laughed. "We will catch up later," the old Commander said to Lincoln. "Go have some fun and watch me make a fool of myself during this speech." He finished as he shooed them with his hand. Lincoln and Eric went back across the bridge and down to the party, laughing as they went. Matias watched them go. When he was alone, he looked at the sky and smiled.

CHAPTER 9. HOME:

<u>Upper Northwest Confederate, The Palace City of Sparta, Laconia the ex-Capitol and once home to King Agesilaus</u>

The portal sphere opened with a swirling flash of multi-colored etheric light. Walker emerged from its smooth surface snow covering his massive cloaked shoulders and his hood pulled low over his face. He paused and listened, then lowered his hood cautiously observing his surroundings while he gained his bearings. Rain was all he could hear. He had arrived in a thickly wooded area, the smell of pine filling the air. He gazed upon the thick canopy of the forest. From what he could tell it must have been later in the afternoon but with the grey clouds and light rain there was no definite answer. After all, it was always grey and raining in the northwest, at least that's what they told everybody.

After he was sure his arrival had gone unnoticed, he checked his jumper, the name for the strange wrist mounted device he had taken from the Razium Emissary. The device allowed the wearer to make micro jumps using the Labrynthian gates, without the use of arcane abilities. Seeing as how the Labrynthian couldn't be opened to its full strength these devices were rare, and valuable, which is why Walker needed it so badly. He had been trained on the inner workings of the jumper and could send it on slightly different routes. Like a Labrynthian Key, though not nearly as powerful.

Only a few had the knowledge to use Jumpers, much less make them and those people were very hard to come by, especially now. Most Arcanium craftsmen had been taken or killed by the Razium, used for their knowledge of the Arcanium metal and then discarded like trash. Many people he knew had died for the secret of Arcanium Runes. The ones that hadn't, had been given safe haven in the White Tower and were under the protection of the Council.

Walker pulled papers from a belt pouch compartment while he studied his surroundings. He was back on Ultima Thule, in the northwest corner of the Laconia Confederate, close to the City of Sparta. Walker frowned; he was losing time and needed answers. He looked at the papers he had taken from the Emissary. Reading them, he had discovered that the King's youngest son had been located, and that the Razium were going to move against the young Prince. He also knew they had attacked the Confederates in the east, keeping the battle a stale mate to hide their true intentions. The Razium didn't want the Governors of the Confederates uniting under the Prince. He was rumored to be a Lok powerful enough to open and control the Labrynthian again. If they were able to capture him and use him to unlock the Labrynthian, then the Zajust masters might not be able to be stopped. They could attack from anywhere at any time, and with the technology they still possessed, nothing could combat them. Walker didn't know where or how to find the Prince, but he knew a man who might, if he could find him.

Pulling his hood up, he started toward Sparta. The ex-Capitol was a huge metropolis, and many claimed the King's Palace in the middle of it was the grandest palace ever constructed. Most thought that the walls of the fortress and the mountainous landscape couldn't be penetrated by any normal army, and the magical defenses of the mighty palace untouchable, even by the Lok Wizards themselves. That left a mystery as to how the Razium had been able to occupy the fortress to assassinate the King. To Walker's knowledge it hadn't been uncovered why or how the Razium had been able to gain access, only that they had. On that night they had almost put the royal line to an end. Walker tried to dismiss the dark thoughts, he needed to stay focused.

He was glad to be home and started to take in the scenery laid before him. The look and smell of the trees all around him brought back memories of his youth, he and his friends running through the forest as children. It smelled so fresh here. He had made his way through the thick green woods to the main paved road that led through the mountains toward the city. As he studied the scenery he noticed it was very similar to how he remembered it during its time as Capitol. The area had been slightly rebuilt, the watchtowers and small outer walls somewhat bigger than he remembered. It seemed that most of the roadways, buildings, and walls on its outskirts had been refurbished. Smoke was coming from the refineries over the edges of the trees and it made him reminisce. When he was younger he would ride his horse on this very road to the city gates. He loved when he was close to the fortress, riding through the gates on a cold day; and the smells of Pantheon Square as he went to the market. When he smelled those smells, he knew he was home. In his youth it had been one of his favorite spots to mess around with his friends.

He was thinking about those days as he was rounding the bend, remembering the way the city looked from this spot on a sunny day. Nothing could beat the view when the sun came over the mountains hitting the walls of the city. The huge metropolitan that was Sparta was built into the mountains, with a carved port and snow coved caps of the mountain range behind it. To see its grandeur in the morning sun was one of the things he had truly missed.

The top of the main peak the city was constructed on had been leveled by Dwarger and Ulthwan engineers. Working with Sparta's own Green Artificers they had been able to create towers and walls of such structure and magnitude that some of the designs couldn't be duplicated, even with the greatest Razium technology. The structures boggled the mind in complexity. Sparta was a bastion of what the King stood for. Hope, that anything could be achieved.

Runes of protection were inscribed on the ramparts and any defendable position, which he thought, was another reason why the mystery of the Razium attack was so strange. There was no way they should have been able to breach the huge walls, by magic or by technology. Sparta's Tryonic fields had been the most advanced, saved for those on the largest of the Razium Cruisers. The city should have been sealed to any intruders with the way it had been constructed.

It was an amazing achievement to be sure. Usually it had air ships flying over the walls, with goods or dignitaries to see the King, and banners flying high for some festival or ceremony. Walker remembered when he was a guard there, how they would land the air ships on the King's View, showing off for the guests in grand displays of aeronautics.

The King's View was the large landing that jutted from the throne room, a two hundred yard span that allowed the King to walk out and greet his guests as they landed, giving him the ability to look on the city below as well. It was where rulers of the Confederates were given title, and every elected Governor had celebrated their inauguration there.

Even below the King's View, the inner courtyard was amazing. The walkways around its base had been lined with the statues of the greatest heroes and scholars of the Confederates, all were perfect likenesses of the people they represented. Every block had been perfectly laid, a breathtaking achievement of the amazing architecture of the edifice. Walker remembered how amazing it looked every time he saw it. He couldn't wait to see those walls again.

He rounded the bend at the scenic look off and stopped dead in his tracks, a look of horror on his face. He was in shock, having come around the pass thinking he would see the once amazing metropolis, the huge Spartan Palace behind its walls. There was the city, amazing as always, but of the palace there were only ruins. The jewel of the northwest had truly fallen. His heart sank, he hadn't realized it had been so bad. He had heard the rumors but to see such a once untouchable majestic place in such disrepair. He didn't have the words, he just stared. The cities huge buildings and towers reached in to the sky like great titans that they still were. Only now where behind them had stood the King's Palace, The Lion's Den of Sparta, the greatest structure that had been built at the time; now there was only a hollow ruin.

Walker stared blank faced, clinching his jaw as the place he knew as home was now only a blackened husk. He took his field glasses from his belt, and looked through them to study the palace. Some of the towers still had holes in them, and the colonnades, statues, and some of the bridges had been toppled. It was a place of war and death. The banners were not flying and it seemed no one had lived in the massive palace for years.

The city around it seemed to be flourishing, its lights twinkling in the grey gloom. The palace itself was a dark silent thing, a shell of its former glory like a shadow that wanted to be forgotten. It stood only to haunt the people that still lived under its dark door, a reminder of the events and tragedy of one of the nation's darkest times. The Blood Night. He hurt thinking of the name, and he felt the guilt for not being there by the King's side. That night was a tragedy and the pain it caused was still being felt to this day. He should have been able to make it back, he thought as he continued walking, trying to get his head right. He had his mission that was what mattered now. Seeing the palace like it was put him in a bad mood, though as he got closer he could make out some small repairs. Mostly patch work, though it seemed as if it might be inhabited after all. His stomach hurt, and then growled. He was famished, the rations he had found had run out hours ago. He needed to find some food.

It was the busiest time of day for Sparta, the afternoon crowds in for trade, shipping, and business as usual. It was also a perfect time of day to try and get in unseen, or as unseen as a man his size could. Walker had made his way down the pass, mingling with the crowd to go through the guarded checkpoint that lead to the bridges granting access into the city. There were three main bridges, monstrous things that lead down from the mountain passes over the chasms or port, to the main city gates. The bridges tying the mountain and massive city together in a spider's web of steel, iron, and concrete.

Walker had made it through the press and stood at the main entry to King's Gate or Lion's Gate, depending on your taste; as the King's symbol had been the Lion. It was covered in travelers, steam cars, and carriages, moving to and from the city. He looked both ways at the traffic, finding his spot, then stepped around one of the newer looking motor steam cars, as he walked to the mouth of the gate. The bridge was enormous, he had forgotten how big it really was. The Bull Gate was the second of the three. It lead in from the harbor. The Sound as it was known was a masterful dock yard, built in the huge chasm behind the city. The chasm lead to the fjords, protecting the rear of the inlet, leading out to the sea. The fjords were always garrisoned and had long guns to protect its borders from pirates, which is why it was one of the best harbors in the Confederates. It was safe. It was called the Sound on account of the noise the echoes of the fjords created.

The Sound wasn't visible on an overcast day like today as the fog had rolled in; though normally one could see the tops of the loaders, cranes, and elevators that were built into the mountain chasm. These amazing devices would lift and lower goods from the city above to the ships at anchor below. The system was so ingenious that it could lift the ships themselves, pulling them from the water for services and repairs. The cranes would take them out of the water, pulling them up until another lift would slide them into docking yards built in the chasms face itself. The Bull Gate was the best way to travel from the port area, into the city.

Eagle's Landing, was the third of the large bridges. It extended from the landing platforms where huge zeppelins, bi planes, and other air going vessels docked; and lead to the public transportation depots. The landing area itself had recently been enlarged and Walker thought it looked close to being finished, with all the construction and steam equipment arrayed around it.

Walker stood in front of Lion's gate looking up at the large carved lion head statues and support beams that held it aloft. The bridge itself was ninety feet wide, and a little over one thousand feet long, with suspension supports in the middle that reached to around four hundred feet, at the highest points. Though it wasn't as spectacular as the Golden Bridge leading to White City, it was truly a work of genius, and an amazing miniature version of the floating walkway none the less. The Green Artificers who built it should be proud, he thought. Walker rubbed the corner stone as he walked by, the chevron perforated on its sides, symbolizing the home of the Spartan Paladins.

He crossed Kings Gate Bridge, and as he approached the entrance of the city he stopped. Looking up at the huge golden Lions head that loomed over it, he grinned. Home, he thought and his heart quickened, it was surreal. People passed him as if there was nothing special about this place, no one said anything to him for blocking the walkway, but he did get some stares. He watched the people pass, then looked back to the Lions head. He had walked through this gate before, with his soldiers, his brothers. He studied it, the lampposts and their ornately crafted light fixtures, that lead through the walls lighting the way into the city. How many times had he come through this gate he wondered?

He shook his head and made his way toward the massive steel and Arcanium laced double doors that lead through the walls and into downtown. The doors were opened as they usually were for traders and visitors to come through. They were so big however, they had to be pulled back with hydraulics and steam machines, another testament to the Green Artificer's ingenuity when they built them. Each of them had a large golden rune of protection inscribed in its center, and it was said when the mechanism was locked the doors could only be opened by the magic of a master of the Tempest.

After coming through the doors that lead under the walls, Walker realized he hadn't been stopped or checked since the main gate. That could have been because there were not many soldiers here and only the local police garrison protected the city. Not that there was much to protect against, as the war was still in the east, and they still had the guard that was trained here if they needed. The city seemed to be doing well despite its losses, and the commerce seemed undaunted with the fishing and industrial craftsmanship of the Green Artificers still booming. There was always money in metal work, arms, and armor, especially in this time of war. The Artificers supplied the Confederate armies and their allies, and were some of the best metal craftsmen alive. They were made up of many races that taught and learned at the Artificers guild school, and it was good to see they were still in the trade.

Walker had stayed to the outskirts of the city, walking down to the old stores of the Pike, close to the pier and the Sound. The aroma of the salt water delicacies in the air and workers tossing fish to the customers made for a nice atmosphere, and when the smells hit him, it reminded him how hungry he really was.

He bought some fish and chips from a quaint eatery called Dukes, and devoured it while he made his way to the inner parts of the city. It was delicious though he didn't taste much of it. Walker slowed as he entered the middle of the city, away from the press and vendors. He had forgotten how clean it was here. Awnings, shops, and large umbrellas covered the street stores in colors; the greens, reds, and blues vibrant even in the gloom. People were not sitting outside as they normally would be if the weather was nice, and Walker was glad of that. It made traveling easier. Some people were out however, enjoying the cool air, and those on the streets were giving the big man plenty of room as he walked by. As amazing as it was, the city was still gloomy, and looking darker still from the shadows of the tall buildings, clocks, and towers. Though not everywhere.

The Street of Lights, was bright as always with energy. It pulled him in and he made his way down its length. The lamps leading down its sides were always lit, though they were turned down at night to create a relaxing atmosphere. The posts were intricately designed by different artificers. It was the first job they received when they had been elevated from apprentice, as a test for the Green School. Which was why the Street of Lights was so popular to visit. All the lamps were original works of art. People came from all around the Confederates to see their workmanship. Walker was glad it was still intact, who would destroy this he thought. As he walked he observed people under the glass top that covered the walk, sitting in chairs and on benches drinking hot beverages; while others were reading books or talking about life. Of course there were people just looking around in awe of the lights craftsmanship as well. He kept going, out of the district and continued through the middle of the city. He passed the schools and parks where the kids of the city were playing games, past the armory, and the Green Artificers huge factories. As he passed them, Walker looked at their amazingly designed air bridges, leading to different parts of the schools above him. He continued past to the inner city, and to the one place he knew he could get the information he needed. The taverns at Motts Layer. He had to see what exactly had changed and who was in charge of the city now, and it seemed the good drinkers of the city always knew. Walker continued making his way down the business district and left the nicer part of the huge city, heading toward Motts Layer and the taverns. He was getting close when a smell hit him. Pantheon Square! How could he have forgotten it?

He made his way through an alley, across a street, around the corner of a building, and there it was. Pantheon Square. It was just how he remembered, a small wind bringing the smell to him again. The crowded streets were choked with the residents, steam vehicles, and travelers out to enjoy the city and continue with their daily grind. Though right now there were no events at the Pantheon itself, the area was always busy. It was the food that kept them coming back. The smell of fresh bread and sweet rolls mixed with, beer and coffee beans, hit his nostrils. His stomach growled again.

The small fish he had earlier hadn't done the job and his stomach rumbled letting him know it! The taverns can wait a bit longer he thought, and his stomach agreed. Walker made a detour up a side street and then another following his nose that took him right to the square. It was busy, people walking across the streets, and in front of the small cars or steam powered carriages that drove by. Some of the autos were stopped at light lamps or were parking on the side of the street.

Walker noticed some kids playing with a ball by a small park in front of him. They were running and laughing all different in their own way, a memory crept into his mind and it made him smile. It was gone though before he could grab it as something caught his eye. He noticed one of the kids had an apron on and was standing off to the side. He walked over to him.

"Hello," he said, gesturing to a skinny midsized boy with the apron. The boy hesitated. He looked about ten years old and had a dirty face. Walker lowered himself, elbows on his knees to look less imposing. "I'm not going to hurt you," he grinned. "Do you know where the best place to eat here is?" He asked as he pointed to the apron. The boy frowned while he was concentrating on the answer. The other kids stopped playing and walked over to the pair. "You're big," said the biggest one of the kids, a large red haired boy of around 12. Walker looked at him, stood to his full height and replied, "Well you're observant. Now who knows where I can get some good food and drinks around here?" The second closest child, a brown haired girl, eyed Walker up and down nodding. "Are you a soldier?" She asked. Walker was surprised by the question but before he could answer, the one with the apron finally spoke up. "My Da has a place, I'll show you, follow me." "Bye," the boy said to the others and turned to cross the street, Walker waved to them as well, and followed the boy. "See ya later," the girl called out as they left. The kids started talking about Walker, if he was a soldier or not, then one of them threw a brown ball and they started playing again.

The boy led him toward a building that was behind them, down a side alley and out into the nicer part of the Square. Then they walked out from the shadows of the ally and crossed the stone street toward a tavern café. It was a tall building wedged between two others. It had white walls with wooden boarders and it had green awnings out front. It was built in the old style, with excellent wooden craftsmanship and the entrance had an oaken door that was very large. There was a picture of a mermaid carved on the front of it. Which was common, as mermaids were a sign of good luck; lots of shops had them it seemed, most of them on corners. There was a sitting area outside of the window, with a fire pit built into the wall, and chairs around it.

Walker followed the boy, entering the small tavern to the amazing aroma of fresh bread, coffees, and hot tea, his stomach rumbling again. He stepped in to a quaint room with tables and chairs in the middle, and a few booths around the edges. Though the café was empty at the moment. A small fire place was in the wall; it still had embers in the bottom as if it has recently been in use from the morning rush. The boy ran to the door behind the counter to get his father. When his father came out his eyes widened in shock. "Oh, oh hello." "Hello," Walker said back pulling his cloak over his shoulder exposing his huge arm. It was awkward for a few seconds, as the shop keeper seemed surprised at something, but it passed. "Welcome, welcome, I'm sorry for my manners please sit." Martin, go and get tea for our guest please." Martin, the young boy just stared at the hulking new addition to their customer base, mouth hanging open. His father looked back at him, "Martin! Go boy," He said shooing at him with his hands, as the boy ran to the back.

After watching his son run in the back of the café he looked at Walker, "Nice kid, takes after his mother, Creator rest her soul, please sit." He gestured with his hand. Walker sat at the table that had been pointed to. "My name is Bally, and I see you have met my boy Martin." Walker was smirking, "Yes, he seems like a good kid." Bally nodded. "Ah, what...ah might you like?" Walker studied the old man, and how he had smirked as he watched him. Bally was averagely built and older, with a slim but rounded head and nicely cropped mustache. He had on a pair of round seeing glasses over a larger nose and a beige apron that tied at the waist, with flour smudged on the front. Walker looked up at the menu, then back to Bally. "What do you suggest Bally?" The man's face lit up as he answered. "Well everything is good; it depends on what you are in the mood for. I would say ...an herb tea, ah yes, of course," he stated putting his finger on chin. "It's good for regaining ones strength after traveling, and you seem to have been traveling, so maybe that and some sweet bread and,"...Walker cut in. "Tea and bread sounds good, for now." Bally's face drooped a bit not being able to share his entire menu with the man. Walker had seen the change.

"Actually, the bread had my attention as I walked in the door. It smells wonderful," he finished with a small smile, lightening the mood.

"Very good," Bally stated almost hopping while turning to go get the bread, and continuing to talk. "You look like a warrior; did you fight in the wars? Not the ones now by these idiot leaders we have now," he said waving his hand, "But the old wars?" As he said it he glanced at the warrior, raising his eyebrow, quizzically. "Am I that obvious?"

Bally nodded. Walker grinned then continued, "Yes, I have seen action in my time, I could tell you stories," Bally was interested and leaned in to listen. "But I'm just passing through right now."

"Sure you are" the old man said. 'That's what they all say. What's your name?"

"I go by Walker."

"Well Walker, do you know about this city now? " "No, why don't you tell me about it." Walker said as he watched with amusement as the man's excitement rose. No doubt because he hadn't talked to someone in quite a while, either that or because he liked to gossip. Either way it was of no consequence.

Bally started, "Well you need to watch yourself unless you want to get caught up in the war." Walker looked at him for an explanation, so Bally continued. "Well, after Governor Garners passing, the new Governor has been recruiting for the war in the northeast, anyone who can take up a weapon, he wants. Male, female, it doesn't matter." Walker interrupted, "Wait, Governor Garner passed, that's too bad, when?" "Not long, a few months almost a year I would say, and then the Council appointed the new Governor, his name is Crouse. He is from a large family to the east." Bally dismissed that part, waving his hand. "He was to be temporary until the elections this next year. But, with the war on he might stay for a bit longer. He has been appointed by the Council so naturally he wants to look good. So, after he arrived most of the soldiers we had here were shipped out, and the small garrisons you have seen are all that are left. Something tells me though, that you sir would be a great commodity for this Governor."

Walker looked at the man, puzzled. "Why do you say that?" "Oh you're big and all, I see that, but," he lowered his voice and looked right and left as if there were someone else in the room. "You're Old Guard, aren't you, you're a Spartan? I know that emblem anywhere," he said pointing to the pin Walker wore on his cloak. "You know, there are still some of you left too!" Walker perked up at the news, "Really, where?" Bally continued not stopping to listen. "Oh yes they're scattered, I'll tell you. Some still serve as leaders in the army, though none here that I know of. Not since the House of Swords was attacked. There are some scattered still though, you know," Bally didn't miss a beat and kept going with his tale. "Once I saw your general. No really, I saw the Bull of Sparta! Once I did. In person. He was the best, he was bigger than you I'd say, though you're pretty big," the man eyed him and continued his hands in the air explaining the story as he talked. "He was in his armor and had his mighty sword drawn." Bally was excited and looking at the ceiling hands up, as if the warrior he spoke of was right in front of him. He looked at Walker, who was just watching the spectacle. "Sorry," he said. "My excitement has gotten the best of me." He sat down and continued. "Better times you know. Did you serve the palace? It's in ruin now, a shame really. Though as big as you are you probably served in the Royal Guard, or you might have been a Paladin, only the best you know." He said with a smirk. Walker's expression didn't change as he listened to the man. Bally expected something, waiting as he stared, but then continued as he realized he was getting no response from the big man.

"Don't worry your secret is safe with me." He winked at Walker, putting his finger on his nose. "But if it's all the same to you, I'd rather you just up and leave, we've already got enough trouble. The city looks nice, but it has gotten bad. Not like Royal mind you, but bad. With no order except the police, and I think some of them are as crooked as my back." He stretched his back out, popping it. "Oh, see. That's better," he said chuckling.

"Well what about the standing garrison or the soldiers I saw when I came in, what about them." "No, they do help, but they are usually only training, and then they ship out leaving here and heading toward the battle lines in the northeast. Or they go to strengthen our allies in the war overseas. They go where the Council says. Heck with the Governors fighting amongst themselves it's up to the Council to keep control, and it's been taxing on them. They are supposed to direct other matters, like budget and economy. It's getting bad here, I tell you."

"Well if it's so bad why don't you and the boy leave?" Walker asked. "No. Some of the other cities are worse off than we are," he said holding his chin in reflection. "Since I lost my wife, Martin is all I have and we do well here." Bally continued, waving around the shop. "They usually leave us alone. Except for the taxes," he said with a frown standing. "Always the taxes, but at least we are protected."

"From what?" Walker asked. "We are too close to the Jotunn of the north, and the giants are very warlike. These walls well, they stop 'em, I believe they are mixed up in this war too. I have heard they have allied with the Razium. They have been coming closer to the borders lately, at least that's what I hear. I feel it's just a matter of time before they decide to start acting up. It's like the old days." He finished and nodded to the picture of the mountains over his fireplace. It was a depiction of an old castle on snow covered peaks, holding off a siege. "The Dragon Wars of old," Bally said with a bit of amazement in his voice. "Wow, that's cool, I haven't seen that picture in a long time." Walker replied as he looked at it.

Martin had come out of the kitchen door and was bringing a plate with dried meats and fresh bread. Bally watched with a smile as he set the plate on the table. "Well let's eat," Bally said holding his hands up, "and thank the Creator for the blessings." Walker looked at young Martin who was already chewing on the chunk of bread, crumbs coming out of his mouth spilling on to the table. The boy smiled a large happy smile. Walker chuckled and reached for a piece, as Bally started to pour the tea. Walker took a big bite, then looked at his host. "Well back to what you said earlier, I am going to be leaving soon, but I do have business here first. Do you know who I can talk to about getting information?" Bally was holding his cup in both hands blowing on the hot tea. He set the small cup back on the table and looked up. "I do yes," he finally said putting his hands together finger tips touching as he talked. "Though I don't think it will suit you, and to get real information it might cost you." Walker nodded as if he knew that. "Or, maybe I can answer a question you have," Bally stated eyebrow raising. "I don't know if you can." Walker replied back and Bally shrugged his shoulders. "Ok then," Bally said clearly put out. Walker sighed; "Ok, since you seem to know about the Old Guard, I need to find a Wizard, a Lok. He is known throughout these parts as a healer, or conjurer, he will try to stay out of the main stream though, his name is Orson."

Bally had picked up his cup and was just starting to sip his tea as Walker was talking. Hearing the name, he choked and almost spit it out.

"Orso..." he said gagging. Martin ran behind him and started hitting his back as he coughed. Walker stood to help him, but they were both shooed away as Bally caught his breath, hacking a little more. "Fine, I am fine," he said between gasps and coughs.

When he finally stopped coughing, he put his hand on his chest to catch his breath. "Orson, the Orson, the King's Lok master."

"Yes the same."

Bally had calmed himself. He stood and walked across the shop locking the door flipping the, be back soon sign over. Coming back he looked at Walker, "I knew you were Old Guard," he said wildly. "I myself used to know him," he said standing taller, "Let's say he is an acquaintance. I'll tell you what, I would be happy, and honored to give you a place to stay while you're here." Walker looked at him. "Really you knew him, well thank you. You can help me then?"

Bally nodded. "Yes I will tell you what I know. You have been led here to me for a reason, thank the Creator, and I will make sure you are taken care of if you remain here. Are you going to stay in the city long?" Martin was staring at the giant warrior again, mouth open. Walker smiled at him. "Thank you for your kindness; but as I said no, I am leaving as soon as I find out about Orson. I have lost too much time as it is, unless he is here." Bally closed his eyes and held up his hand. "No, he is not unfortunately, though I might know where to start. Though there are things you might find helpful here."

Walker nodded. "Well, I need answers and I have other questions, maybe you can help me with those as well." "I will try, but first I'll pour us some more tea." Bally said, a twinkle in his eye.

They sat and talked about what had happened after the Blood Night, and about why the Royal Palace had gone to ruin. Bally also told him about the restoration. That it was started but the project was put on hold, though continued slowly. Bally told him about the Jotunn attacks, the goings on with the Council and the year it was now. The information seemed to take Walker aback and he had to gather himself before he asked more. Bally answered his questions though, and continued about how the Razium had fought and the city had been a war zone after the Blood Night. He told him of other things he felt were important, and elaborated about the Capitol being moved to Angel city. That was supposed to be only temporary at least until the restorations to the palace could be finished. Though Bally wasn't so sure of the truth of that. It had only been patched up enough to hold it from decay. Walker could not believe it. This had been the Capitol since the founding of the Confederates. He was saddened to hear so many had perished, the attack on the House of Swords the Spartan Paladins headquarters, and what it had taken to get the Razium out. Bally talked a little longer and they ate their fill as Walker listened. When they were done, Bally packed some food for Walker to take with him.

Walker studied the old man, he seemed different, younger than when he had first met him, more of a twinkle in his eye. "Thank you for your hospitality, but I am losing time. So can you help me find Orson?" "Yes, but on one condition."

"Name it." Walker said. "When you find him make sure you give him my best regards, but tell him he still owes me money." Bally said frowning, his finger in the air. Walker was surprised, "What?" He asked.

"The old fool thinks he won last time we were at the track, but he didn't. My pony was fast, and Orson, the old dodger, left before I had a chance to collect. I think he knew he was going to lose. Never was good on telling the future that one," Bally finished. Walker didn't know what to say. Bally shook his head, and laughed. "Will you tell him?" Walker was thinking he was crazy, but nodded. "Yes, but what..." Bally interrupted with a smile, "My large friend, I will explain at another time, all will be revealed. You will see, we will see each other again." He finished with a sly grin. Walker didn't know what to say, but knew enough of wise men and wizards to say anything more about it.

"So let's get you where you need to go," Bally said thinking. "Now I talked to him, well it's been a while now, and I am not sure where he is exactly. He won't be back here until a few months from now, but he should be in one of two places. Martin, bring me that map in the back." The boy jumped off his chair, and grabbed an old rolled paper from a desk in the back of the shop. Bally looked back to Walker. "It isn't safe for Orson, with the Razium and their mercenaries still hunting down the King's council. They are more active than I have seen in a while. I hear they are looking for something."

"You are well informed, master Bally, I don't know how, but you are." Walker said to him, the old man grinning over his glasses. Martin handed the paper to his father and Bally spread it out on a table. Both the men leaned over it as Martin tried to get a peak from the side, Bally was still looking at Walker. "Well?" He asked. Walker looked up. "The Razium are acting weird, I know it as do you. So what are they looking for?"

Walker looked at him hard, not sure why he felt he could trust this man but he felt calm around him, similar to the way he had felt with Orson. "The Prince," he said.

"What, I knew it, he's been hiding. Oh this is great news!" Bally said as he pranced around, holding his hands in the air, then looked at Walker. "Oh, right, the map, what's the month?" Bally asked thinking out loud. He leaned back over the map with a pencil. "Ah, yes. Ok, he is either here, or here. In Royal or Navarre. I know he will be at one of them, best info is at those two holes, and the taverns are always the best places to look. Hans Fords and DeCeasers are good places to start," he finished. Walker stood; well it's better information than I have now." Thank you Bally, you have been a great help, and you too Martin." the boy smiled at him and took a bite of a cookie. "Well how do you plan to get there?" Bally asked. Walker grinned, "Jumper." Bally smiled back at him. "Good, now go, and good luck. May the Creator protect you. Oh, and don't forget to tell Orson what I said." "I won't." Walker told him.

A second later, a customer knocked on the door; looking in the window pointing at the sign. Bally went to let her in and Walker followed him to the door. "Be safe, I will see you again, for now though, you need not waste time." Bally said unlocking the door. Walker wanted to find out more about this man, he felt different than when he had arrived there. Like he knew or had known Bally from another time. He waved back at Martin who sat stuffing his face, then shook Bally's hand and moved allowing the lady to come in. "Thank you again Bally," he said and closed the door behind him to the sound of Bally yelling for Martin to grab something. Walker smirked and looked at the sky. It was still grey dark and dreary, perfect for a walk he thought.

Walker made it out of the city easy enough. As he made his way back up the pass he turned to look at Sparta, not knowing when he would see home again. The clouds had opened, and a small ray of sun had broken through the mist. A good sign he thought. The light shone across the city and Walker could see across to the inlet of the ocean, and the port. The view from where he stood was beautiful, as the sun shone through lighting the Lyconian Mountains around it. He had been back on Confederate soil less than a day, and had found out little he liked. He was still baffled that the Capitol had been moved to Angel city. It was a lot to take in. He looked at his jumper, it was getting weak, and he knew he couldn't use it many more times without it shorting. It still had a little left though. "Let this thing hold up," he said as he looked at it. He wished it were a key. At least one of those would allow him access to the gates, but there were only eight of those, and they were gone or hidden. One key had been given to each of the Governing lords of the Confederates and one to the King's house. True they could only use certain doors unless the full Labrynthian was unlocked, but they were far too valuable to let go unguarded. Bally had told him that the Key of the King's house had been lost during the battle and no one knew its true location. Walker needed to find Orson; he hoped the Lok Master could help him. It would be good to see him after so long. He took one last look at the proud city, gazing at its grandeur. "I will see you restored." As he said it the rain started falling around him, and the thick grey clouds covered the sky again. He pulled his hood up as he started walking.

Finding his spot he activated the jumper. The small gate opened and he slid through, the Labrynthian portal taking him.

* * *

The rain hadn't let up in hours. Cool and cleansing, it poured in buckets thumping the ground with a steady crackle. It gave off the smell of fresh dirt that any farmer or country dweller on this side of the continent would love. The big man walking in it wasn't a farmer though; no he was not from these people. He knew work, but the calluses on his hands and the weapons on his sides marked him as warrior, and this warrior had been in the rain the last two hours ever since he had come through the small Labrynthian gate.

"I'm drenched," he said aloud, just talking to hear some sound other than the thudding of rain in the mud. Walker was back, walking down a muddy road he had been down before. He knew these mountainous lands.

Lor was what is was called, and this road called Hard Road. It was the main road between the fortresses and towns of this area. The road was a well-used path of mud and wheel tracks that flowed through the mountains and out to the open plain. It was dense and even though it had been used thousands of times it kept its firmness. This dirt was why the area could be used as farmland this high in the mountains and why the roads were so well traveled. Hard dirt they called it. It was a fitting name, because it was so dense. It had twice the amount of minerals that most soil could contain. This resource allowed it to thrive through so much use, its minerals feeding generations of Lorlanders and regions beyond for years. On both sides of the road there were huge patches of oaks and every twenty to fifty yards was a thicket of reeds and tall grass, the only place that had them in this mountainous area. He studied these patches as he walked, noticing the bugs and frogs gathering by the puddles in each.

His cloak was a flap of water that kept the rain off his shoulders, but even it had started to feel the dampness as the water looked for ways to chill the warrior within with its cold embrace. His mind started to wonder. It could be worse, he thought. Then paused, as he felt the ground start to shake. Walker knew that sound, horses.

He had felt them a good hundred yards before they came around the bend behind him and into view. There were five riders and they were in a hurry not bothering to stop or slow as they raced passed, spattering mud and gunk all over him as they went. Only the rear rider spared a glance, the others acted as if he wasn't there. "Well I guess it can get worse," he said to himself as lightning flashed and thunder boomed behind him. The rain intensified and he raised an eyebrow, looking at the sky. "Really?" He asked it. He pulled his hood tighter and kept following the road, watching the horses get smaller. As he watched them go he noticed the lights of a huge fortress metropolis in the mountainous distance. Royal.

CHAPTER 10. ASSASSINS IN THE NIGHT:

Anstone City, South Confederate of Atlantioc, Anstone Fortress party for Matias

Matias had given one of the best Speeches anyone had heard in years. At least that is what the guests had told him when he had stepped down from the stage, greeting everyone and shaking hands. He had thanked them for coming and for their support for the area. Then moving on to dinner he had given the order to slice the boar to joyous shouts from the crowd. After the food it was on to the fun, and fireworks. As the guests drifted around, the activities started and the party was in full swing, the music and revelry giving the whole compound a wonderful atmosphere. The cool night breeze had set in rejuvenating the guests, the large bonfire was stocked and the music was getting louder, as the city was in full celebration.

Outside the gates two of the guards on duty were talking. The younger man, new to the castle guard, was waiting for his fellow guard and partner for the shift to come out from checking the Aux. The Tryonic field was down, and so the guards at post were using the Aux, or Auxiliary Unit X-sensors. These were devices from the wars that could track movement and body signatures. It was easy to use and mostly reliable for tracking around the perimeter.

Robert, the older of the two had been in the guard for a couple of years and had seen some action on the outskirts of the realm. His action was mostly against highway thieves or the occasional bar fight, but he was respected by his peers. He had been brave in those showings proving he was a capable soldier, and was gaining status in the Anstone army. Some said he might have his own post soon. Robert checked the Aux readings, then grabbed a hand held version of the device and stepped from the small gatehouse to the cool air outside.

Leaving the gatehouse he walked toward the younger guard Micah. Micah looked up as he heard him coming and with a sly grin said, "It's about time, I'm off in 20 minutes and when I am, I am going to get a drink, talk to one of those girls, and when I do...."

Robert stopped listening to him, he had heard him talking about the party all day, bellyaching about not being at the start of the celebration, and he had heard enough. He looked out in the night shaking his head as the other blathered on. The stars were out and the night was perfect, the moons were crescent but both visible and the stars were out overhead. It was an amazing view of the sky above. Robert looked from the sky and something caught his attention, about twenty yards off to his left. He looked at the Aux, it had picked something up, but it wasn't there now. Robert shook the device, tapping it on the side. Something felt wrong, and he held up his hand for silence. The other guard Micah, just kept talking. "I am not going to hold your hand wanker!" Micah practically yelled.

"STOP talking, SHHH," Robert said... "Quiet!" The aggravation in his tone coming through finally silencing the other guard. "Did you hear that?" Micah put his hand to his ear acting as if he was listening, then pulled his hand down and sarcastically said, "Yeah a celebration and were not in it." Robert rounded on him "Be quiet you imbecile!" The other guard looked as if he had been slapped in the face. "Something doesn't feel right," Robert finished lowering his voice. "Ok ok," Micah said. "I just wanted to have some fun, sheesh you could have just asked." Robert just looked at him annoyed.

* * *

From his impossible high vantage point miles away, Nemsor Vaul looked down on the fortress, watching the lights and fires of Anstone. He was standing on the bridge of his flagship Lords Wrath, watching the celebration waiting for the right time to give the order to start the attack. He wore a look of cruel satisfaction under his mask. The screen beside him was alight with the action of his crew and the preparations he had made for the capture. The light from the screen illuminated his runic suit of armor in strange blue shadows, as the instruments changed courses and operations. His outward demeanor was hiding the grim satisfaction that he was about to have a prize. The prize that counted the most, his prize. Nemsor surveyed the area in the upper portion of the large screen that was showing him Anstone Fortress a few miles away. The fortress he was about to take, and the small army stealthily advancing on it. The time was now. "You may start your attack, Shadow Lord," Nemsor's deep rasped voice had just given the order of death.

"Ah, you're no fun," Micah said sighing as he turned away from his fellow guard. They had listened a few minutes and there had been no sound or movement on the Aux. Robert turned to Micah. "I'm sorry, I shouldn't have yelled at you. It's the Commander's birthday and I just want to do a good job, you know. I know you're excited, soon we will be in there with the girls." He chuckled. "Ha, I knew it! It's cool. It will be sweet is all I can say." Micah finished. Robert smiled then looked at the Aux. There it was again. He looked out into the night.

From the right of where the guards were talking what looked like a large shadow came to life. Micah had started to dance, acting as if he had an invisible partner in his arms. He stepped and then twirled and turned right into the shadow hand that caught and gripped him by the temples; with a quick twist of the shadow wrist he was dead. The hand let go, and he fell to the ground, landing with a thud. As Robert heard he turned toward the noise, he was pulling his weapon and trying to see what happened, only seeing the prone form of Micah on the ground. "Micah?" He was greeted with a black blade that was shoved through him. Evil eyes stared at him through a white skull face mask, one that hadn't been there less than a second ago. The eyes of the evil being watched the life slip away from the young man, with apparent joy. With a gasp and gurgle the young guard slipped from the sword and onto the ground his blood flowing over the cobbles and into the dirt. The black armored assassin stood over him. His suit and mask flickered. The contoured armor, and trophies barely catching the light of the Fortress. He studied Robert until he passed, watching his end with grim satisfaction. The assassin looked right, then left, cocking his head to listen, pausing to see if anyone had overheard. No one could have, with the unnatural quiet of the assassin and the Celtic dance music in the background, it was a flawless execution.

He blinked and the lenses of his white skull battle helm became a lower resolution, giving him night vision more adapt at this level as he prepared to enter the fortress. His head was still cocked listening. He lowered the blood covered blade to his hand wiping the blood on his forefinger. He then wiped his finger across his own white mask, giving a streak of crimson across his skull face. A ritual he did after all his first kills. He enjoyed it – the death he had just delivered, the smell, the feel, it kept the beast in him in check. He was a master assassin, an artist of his craft, and he was about to deliver his Picasso. All around him shadows came to life, his minions moved and jumped. Just as their master, they came out of the shadows, climbing the walls and entering the gates too fast to be human. Some of the fowl creatures had already made it in the towers. They began opening the portcullis, as Lord's Wrath jammed the Aux system. The rest of his force was coming to life and moving to join their master in the art that was death.

Astrals, shadow warriors, death merchants, and specters, all were names of the dreaded alien figures that the Razium used against their enemies as assassins. The mention of one of them usually made most shudder, but to have an army of them in full display here was terrifying. Pale, the Shadow Lord of the Zajust, looked at the serrated edge of the black blade he had just wiped the blood from, staring at it until he heard the first scream. His head shot up, and with the speed and grace of a panther he bounded through the gates, his weapons drawn ready to cause pain, to deal death, and to find the prince.

* * *

Matias walked toward the noise of the band, taking in the amazing celebration. The sounds of music and laughter were echoing all about the outside court, and all who attended were dressed in their finest revelry. Tall boots, spats, vests, and large pea coats with medals and buttons, were on display from the men; while the women were in extravagant dresses with parasols or jeweled corsets. Some of the men had boutonnieres on that matched their date's outfits. While others including the children wore goggles, which was the fashion and with steam power still a mainstay, a necessity to some. Other gentlemen wore simple top or bowler hats, while the ladies wore smaller hats or feathers, and all were wearing their best showing off for the party.

As the adults talked and drank, the children were dancing and playing, though most were watching the master gunner put on his lightshow, the fireworks exploding above their heads. Even the oldest or grumpiest were having fun as the fireworks popped, courting and carrying on as if they were children themselves. As more people had arrived, the party got louder, the atmosphere was amazing and it was turning out to be one of the best parties the area had seen in quite some time, though that could have been because of the drinks.

Matias had noticed some of the guests had snuck off to get a kiss or cuddle, others were playing cards or shoes, telling stories, or watching the fireworks. Unfortunately for him, a couple of the women he knew had had too much to drink, and he had quelled a fight more than once tonight. He opened his thick collar to let out the heat of the uniform, then drank the rest of his stein, and enjoying the buzz he was getting, went to the beer cart to fill it back up. He saw Helga one of the women by the cart, and quickly hid behind the tent in the beer garden hoping she hadn't seen him.

Lincoln and his friend Eric, had been dancing and playing as well, but had slipped away with the rest of their friends. They had another agenda and acting as if they were watching the lights above their heads, they eased toward the tent that kept the fireworks.

While he was hiding Matias took another drink of his stein, and out of the corner of his eye he saw the boys heading toward the tent. After a few seconds, they snuck to its edge and tried to untie the flap. The Commander watched then looked around making sure Helga had gone. When he didn't see her he let out his breath with a sigh of relief. He finished his ale, then watched as the boys made their way around the tent, the flap had been compromised he guessed. Matias checked the area again and stepped from his hiding place. He was about to walk over to the beer cart, but another of the women had seen him, yelling his name. He jumped as she yelled. There was no hiding this time, and he stood with hands open as she came huffing up handing him a fresh pull of ale. He wasn't paying attention to what she was saying as he took the drink and looked over her head, continuing to watch for the boys. They were gone from sight. Rascals he thought. Then he got swept up by the woman grabbing his hand and pulling him to the dance floor. He took another drink as he allowed himself to be taken away.

After not getting in through the back flap, the boys had moved around its edge steering clear of most everyone. They were at the entrance of the tent when they stopped cold. A huge shadow came to life, turned and monitored them. The other boy Eric let out a breath; he had never seen the Gear so close. Agrius was its name. Agrius was one of the two Wargears, robotic constructs, and sentinels. They were the guardians of the Castle Anstone and usually were kept inside the inner sanctum to protect the prince. The riveted magical metal beasts had mostly been destroyed during the wars, and it was rare indeed to see one of its caliber in such good condition, much less two. Lincoln thought it was weird that both were outside tonight stationed on either side of the compound, but Matias had insisted, so it must be needed he thought. The robot construct looked down at them through its Spartan like helm, its green lit eyes piercing the night. It made a growling noise like a chuckle. His shoulder mounted Roto-cannon turned and locked in place with a hiss and the sounds of its ammunition gears turning. The boys were in awe. The machine was huge. Over nine feet tall, its chassis was that of a bipedal, and it looked almost like an armored human, albeit a very heavy extremely larger than life armored human. It had two huge legs, arms, and a small helmeted head that looked sunk into its armored gorget. Its shoulders where huge rounded things like large ball joints, and they had armor plates on top which made the head look even smaller. Agrius was covered in weapons with small lights and lit runes all over, a true construct of war. Looking up, Lincoln smiled at the Gear and patted its leg, then ran in the tent. Eric followed, stumbling behind him as he watched the huge machine monitor them.

Lincoln had known this Gear for as long as he could remember, it was never too far away and that always made him feel safe. Agrius tracked their movements as they went, and when they were gone went back to monitoring the compound. The machine looked over the area, and steam released from its back vents as it started to walk, the large thuds of its steps taking it back on patrol. Talos, the other of the Wargears was at the front by the castle portcullis, standing like a statue monitoring the goings on. Every few minutes walking to another part of the castle front and scanning to make sure all was secure. He looked similar to Agrius only his helmet and shoulders were different styles. Talos received a signal from Agrius all was secure, and then he was back to patrol as well.

"This is gonna be great," Eric whispered as he and Lincoln ran around the corner of the tents opening, holding armfuls of fireworks. They ran past the beer garden and through a crack in the wall that led to a courtyard where their friends waited. Tossing the fireworks to the ground the boys started tying the huge rockets together, their friends gathering around. Lincoln was getting ready to launch them when Leena, the girl he liked came up to him. "This looks exciting," she said. "Hey Leena," Eric croaked. "Eric," she said back, though she was looking at Lincoln, and he looked back not realizing how close she was. Losing his voice as he locked eyes with her, he tried to talk. All that came out was a squeak as he looked into those pretty eyes. Her long hair fell over her face, and she giggled as she pulled it back behind her ear. Lincoln nodded finally, and she and the two other girls that were with her laughed, smiling at the boys. Leena was dressed in a pretty red and cream skirt with a small corset around her already tiny waist. She like the other girls had on knee high boots that matched her reddish brown over straps. She smiled nodding at the tied fireworks. "Is it ready?"

Lincoln smiled back regaining his confidence. "Ah, yes, yeah, of course it is." You look nice," he said, looking at her. "Thanks, you also." He looked down at himself, he like most of the boys wore some sort of khaki baggy pants, with suspenders, and cool spat like boots, which were the latest craze. He also had on a red button up shirt that had the sleeves rolled up. "Thanks and, yeah it will be great, watch this." He told her as he looked over to his buddies to make sure the candle was ready. Eric nodded, as the boys backed away, "Go ahead Linc." "Get behind me." He said to Leena.

Lincoln stretched his arm out toward the rocket candle and concentrated, or at least made it look like he was, but this trick he had done many times and his concentration was for show. He levitated the fireworks they had tied together, his left palm out holding it two feet above the ground, as he smiled at all of them. He loved showing off his powers for his friends, and with a snap of his fingers the fuse lit. Lincoln moved to get back, but with the fun he was having and the girls there he didn't notice his wrist com was glowing. The huge Roman candle was tied with other poppers, cats, and fliers, waiting to explode lighting up the night. With a fizz it screamed and took off flying skyward, exploding in a beautiful cascade of colors and pops, making a noise so loud it could have shook the castle. All of them were in awe and started to cheer. "That was awesome," Leena said and she kissed Lincoln on the cheek. "Let's do another one," She said excitedly. Lincoln blushed, smiling at her, a dumb grin on his face. He felt so amazing, what a night he thought to himself. His friends where readying another of the super bombs, when he heard a commotion, it was loud and the only thing that could have stopped him from looking at Leena. Lincoln listened closer. "Do you here that," he asked. The music had stopped. One of his friends looked up, "Was that a scream?" he asked the rest. Lincoln ran over to the hole in the wall and bent down to peer through, he focused in the dark and his eyes widened in terror.

* * *

Matias watched the fireworks and was getting quite tipsy as another of the ladies he knew brought yet another round for him. "The master gunner has really out done himself this year!" he yelled as a huge bright flare went skyward exploding stunning the crowd with the noise. All cheered except Matias. He shook himself, stood up from his chair looking to where it could have come from, remembering the boys running off. Lincoln, he thought. Then something caught his eye, something big and dark in the night sky. "Oh no, Lincoln!" he yelled right before he heard a scream.

"Lincoln!" He heard his name and saw a soldier run to the wall beside the court yard, he was looking for something. He had his rifle in his hands and his helmet on. From behind him a shadow seemed to solidify cutting the soldier down with a blade that didn't seem real. It looked like a shadow, and moved with an eerie fluid motion like smoke rising from fire. The soldier fell to the ground as the shape turned completely solid standing above him. The thing was clad in tight fitting black and grey like body suit with wrist gauntlets and it had a strange shaped helm that he could barely see, it turned its head right and then left, looking for something. As it moved Lincoln saw light playing about its suit or body, which now he couldn't tell which it was. He thought it was a suit but he didn't know where the suit ended and the thing began. The light moved in patters like runes but it was hard to look at them. Then it faded, he watched as it looked toward him. He pulled back from the stone wall, looking at the terrified faces of his friends. "We are under attack," he told them. "WHAT?" One asked. "Shhh. The castle is under attack," he repeated. "I saw something," he paused. Thinking quick he said, "It was bad, we have to move, those things." He was interrupted by his friend. "What do you mean, what did you see?" Lincoln looked at his friend, he had to tell them. "I think it was a Ghost Assassin. An Astral, like we were taught in war history class." The other boy looked at him like he was crazy, but Lincoln could see that he was scared. Another spoke up. "But, but they haven't been seen in years and anyway they are stories made up about the Razium." "Don't say that word;" Leena said, then looked at Lincoln. "Linc, what are we going to do?"

Lincoln was scared himself, but stayed calm. "Don't worry. We have to get to safety. Matias will know what to do. We will split up, you and you with me and the rest of you stay with Jeffrey." He pointed to Jeffrey Han, a young round faced boy who nodded to him. "Meet me at the armory courtyard, the back door we always use by the tanks." "Alright?" He asked. "Alright!" He asked again. The boy Jeffrey got himself together and looked at Lincoln. "Yeah, alright."

"Good, stay down and go fast," Lincoln added. The group lead by Jeffrey snuck out the back leaving Lincoln and his four friends to go through the gap. He carefully looked into the walkway and saw nothing, all was clear. In the background he heard screaming and then gun fire, as the unmistakable sound of a Roto-cannon erupted fifty yards to his right causing the small group to jump. "Let's go," he said as he led them, staying low around the small walls of the walk garden. Keeping to the plants and rose bush walls, they moved through the walk. They were getting close to the docking bay and the armory where the tanks, artillery, and biplanes were located. It was also the place where the mighty airship Skylance was docked. Skylance was one of the last ships of its kind, a greatly armored sky ship of the Confederate armada. Most of the zeppelins or other sleek style steam craft of its type were destroyed during the Affinity wars, and the others in the latest conflict with the Razium, but this ship persisted through it all as a testament to the will of the Confederates and her people. Lincoln looked at his friends, "Stay low we are almost there." The Roto-cannon was red hot as it spun, killing the magical assailants in droves from Agrius' rune etched bullets, the smoke creatures not able to withstand the magical laced ammunition blasting through their forms.

When the attack first started the Astrals had been fighting the drunken soldiers and civilians of the fortress, but as it had persisted the defenders had started to make a valiant stand, and with the help of the Gears, Matias had rallied his troops. His officers had the rest of the citizens head to the safety of the inner castle. The start of the defense had been the Gears, Talos and Agrius, the two hulking construct robots reacting to Matias and his sergeant's commands. His sergeant, Grankon Bor or Bor, was a short but very wide man with a bald head and big beard with fetishes and golden talismans braided into it, the master of the armory and a good man to have in a fight. Some joked he was half dwarf as technically inclined as he was. He laughed it off as he did most things, though it wasn't far from the truth.

Agrius had moved to the back of the castle to find Matias as Talos stayed in the front fighting off the threat of the assassins. Servos whined and gears clicked as Agrius had found the Commander fighting for his life against the creatures. Agriuss Roto-cannon opened fire blasting any that were outside of combat threat range. The heroic construct barreled into the press of bodies knocking them off his Commander. He smashed the closest of the attackers to the ground with his huge fist, his Roto-cannon stopped its firing as its ice lock compressors cooled it. The Gear crushed another with the barrel of the gun, and then kicked the last into a wall spattering the vile magical creature into mist and thick black goo as he did. Matias had taken up fighting on its flank and had cleared as many himself; his two handed axe and short sword blurs in his hands. He was bleeding from his head, half drunk and was still in his dress uniform, though he had tossed his over coat that had been ripped by one of the Astrals blades. Wiping the blood from his face he tapped his wrist com to give commands to his soldiers that had sobered. He waited a second and then asked, "Where is the Prince, where is Lincoln!"

"We haven't found him sir." was the reply of his Sergeant Bor, who had just run up beside him. He nodded to him, listening to the com, waiting to hear from the others.

Bor and the squad he led looked as if they had already seen action, one was bleeding and it looked as if Bor's beard was singed. After hearing from his men Matias looked at Bor. "No one has seen him. What is happening?" "We are taking heavy casualties on the east sir, we can't hold much longer and I have already lost sixty percent of my force. It's the Razium" The sergeant stated. "Same on the west," another of Anstone's sergeants voiced through the com. "Alright fall back, fall back to the armory," Matias said into the wrist com, "And find Lincoln or this will be for nothing." He clicked the com off. "Bor, go to the west side and help them, then meet me at the landing pad."

Bor nodded, and turned addressing the soldiers behind them, "You four with me, the rest stay with the Commander." Matias watched his Sergeant go leading his small force toward the safety of the Armory. Then he looked at Agrius. "Follow him, and then return." He commanded the Wargear. "Yes sir," it answered and turned, stomping off after Bor. A few seconds later Matias heard Agrius's Roto-cannon giving support fire, hearing that made him happy. They would be close to the Skylance and the docking bay of the armory soon. Matias didn't know where to look for Lincoln, he could be anywhere and heaven forbid anything had already happened to him. He had to find him. Hearing a scream behind him he turned at the sound, running toward it followed by the rest of Bors squad. It had come from the low garden walls. He came around the corner of the wall, and was relived but horrified as he saw Lincoln. He was backing away from one of the Astrals as it advanced upon him.

CHAPTER 11. THE WARSHIP, LORD'S WRATH:

Outskirts of Anstone

The fortress was alight with fire and tracer flashes. The party was in ruins, the guests running for their lives as the Astrals attacked them. From high above, cruel eyes watched the carnage play out below, carnage he had created to fulfill one goal and now he was going to get his prize. Nemsor Vaul, the Iron Knight, stood on the bridge of his cloaked flagship Lord's Wrath. He saw another explosion and fire in one of the gun towers. Turning from the window of the view port, he walked through the bridge of the space vessel. Lights reflected off of his dark runic armor, his long cape flowing in his wake as he walked from the view port to his command console. Nemsor watched the hologram vid screen of the battle below. The novite monitoring the screen beside him glanced up. "They have air capability?" Nemsor asked.

"Yes my lord." "Good, connect me to Pale." The communications officer nodded and opened the frequency.

"Pale, what is stalling your advance?" asked Nemsor. After a few seconds a raspy whisper of a voice came over the com. "The Gears my lord, they have two Runic heaviessss. We can't break through them. The ex-Paladin leading them is proving to be a capable opponent, although I have not engaged him personally." Nemsor slowly turned and nodded to the deck officer behind him, watching as he hurried to carry out the unspoken order. "I am sending Sinagog. He should help your... predicament." "Thank you, my lord," Pale said and the com clicked off.

"My lord, your line is open." A huge mass appeared on the holo screen, with eyes the color of molten lava, his breathing heavy like an uncontrollable fury resided in him. "Sinagog, go help your brother," is all Nemsor said and then the screen blinked out.

"Connect me to the forces on the ground." The novite communications officer nodded to his liege, touching the screen, opening the channel. Nemsor addressed the commanders of his now advancing soldiers one last time. "I want the Lok Prince found. This is the Castle, I can feel his power inside, and I have looked for too long to be denied this now. Find him!" With that the link was cut off, and Lord Nemsor Vaul walked back to the viewport to watch the chaos below him.

Lincoln could see a clean path to the courtyard. He looked over his shoulder at his friends behind him. "On me," he said, "We can make it, just be ready to run." He turned his head back around to go and staring him in the face was one of the assassins. Leena screamed, and Lincoln jumped falling back, startled. The Astral solidified and he saw the blade in its dark hand. Leena ran but the creature was faster. It transformed into its smoke form and went after her. "No," Lincoln cried, jumping to his feet. His cry alerted other Astrals to his presence, and like a pack of wolves they descended on their prey. Lincoln yelled as he saw the thing knock Leena to the ground, pulling at her dress and standing over her. He didn't know what to do. His head started swimming, images of his past raced into his mind, he didn't know what they were or meant; and was confused. His confusion led to anger. His temper flaring and his anger started to take over. He liked the feeling, he grabbed it. It made his power grow, he could feel it as he focused on it. He watched the thing grab for her. "No, you will not take her from me!" he yelled throwing his hand out releasing the energy in him, not holding anything back!

The vile creature reached toward Leena, bluish green light flew from Lincoln's eyes and outstretched hand, encasing the Astral Assassin in a field of aqua colored energy. The thing released an ear piercing shriek and exploded in a puff of smoke and ichor. The Astrals froze. They backed away from him transforming into solid black creatures, each carrying black blades in their unnatural runic burned hands. What Lincoln thought to be a suit was actually flesh, their bodies' oily black. It disgusted him, made him sick looking at the revolting creatures. These things don't deserve to live he thought, as his hate infused him. His eyes alight, he channeled his power to his fists, the light growing around them. The Astrals were mustering their courage, and were going to fight but stopped, realizing the power this boy had, and that they were going to die. Lincoln realized too, he felt their fear and smiled.

They tried to flee, but they couldn't. He unleashed the light upon them destroying them, vaporized them the way the morning sun destroys the darkness of the night. He was releasing blasts of energy, in waves off his body. The Astrals exploding as the energy encasing his form rushed out over them, catching all, leaving a charred black semi-circle area in front of him. In less than a few seconds the Astrals were no more.

The power sucked back into him and was gone. Lincoln was sweating and breathing hard. Looking around he saw Leena was safe, then his eyes rolled back into his head and he fell to the ground.

* * *

The instant Lincoln released his power, Nemsor tracked him. "That is the boy, lock on to that signal and bring the one attached to it to me!" The communications officer immediately repeated the order, quickly tapping the screen in front of him, not wanting to incite the wrath of his lord. Opening another channel to his favored warrior Nemsor spoke, "Sinagog, go to these coordinates and find the boy. Be mindful his protector, he is still a danger." "Yes master," was the deep gritted reply.

Lincoln was dazed as he lay on the ground, smoke was coming off him in the night air, but he was alive and coming to. Matias seeing what had just happened ran over to check him, another squad of Anstone soldiers led by their Sergeant Macguyar were close behind. "Set a perimeter," the tall sergeant yelled, still dressed in his formal attire and an intricate sword at his waist. The sergeant was muscular, clean cut with short black hair, and blue green eyes that knew much of war. The large Gear Talos had come with him and moved to stand by Matias. Its weapon systems clacked together, as it switched its offensive capabilities and adapted a more defensive scan mode. Matias was holding Lincoln, carefully picking his head off the ground.

Lincoln coughed a bit and opening his eyes tried to look around. "Are you alright boy?" Matias asked pulling him close. "Yes, Uncle I am fine," He coughed again, sitting up looking over Matias's shoulder. Standing above them watching was Talos. The huge machine cast a black shadow over them in the nights light. "Good," Matias said back. "Can you stand?"

Lincoln nodded. Talos was moving to step past them as Matias was helping Lincoln to his feet. A flash of light from the left smashed into Talos side, spinning the four ton construct almost knocking him from his feet. He went to a huge armored covered knee, falling into the small wall beside them.

Matias put Lincoln behind him as he tried to figure out where the blast had come from. He watched in astonishment at the thing that had shot it appeared across the courtyard. It was a monstrous thing. An eight foot tall hulking mass in jutting black lacquered armor, with chains around his wrists, legs, and waist, stepped from under the bridge leading from the castle to the armory.

The monstrous warrior stared at them through the visor of its closed tusked skull faced helm. Teeth, talismans, and fetishes hung from the chains, trophies from other battles that the beast was obviously proud of, and in his robotic hand he held a brutal single edged archaic looking blade. On his shoulder was a smoking cannon, a Lancer cannon. It was one of the many advanced laser type weapons that the Razium still had in their arsenal. The weapon was an unstable but a very powerful short range gun, which at the moment was being pointed right at them. It was this type of weapon that helped turn the wars.

Matias knew who this being was, and that in the condition they were in it was no use to try to fight him. His name was Sinagog, the Monster, a different species than the Razium. Sinagog was one of the Zajust, Yerch, or Orc warlords that commanded and ruled the Razium soldiers, another hierarchy in the alien force. The Zajust were ruthless killers. Their warlike race had enslaved the Razium and took over as their Overlords, leading their people against other races in battle to further their blood lust. There were not many of the creatures left. They were very powerful, and battle only made them stronger. To make matters worse, the thing had brought more Razium Legionnaires with him. As he stepped over the wall the Legionnaires were filing through the already lost castle, smashing what was left of the party and capturing any others they found.

Seeing Matias then Lincoln, Sinagog smirked under his helm. A deep metallic rasp formed from within. "There you are pup," he said gazing at Lincoln, "And your master too, today will be a good day for me." His deep voice was followed by a scratching sound that could be taken as a laugh. The monster walked towards them, chains clinking against his armor as he strode with purposeful strides. "Hold men!" Macguyar commanded as he drew his sword, black marks of the Magnus crossed his face and hand. Matias pulled Lincoln up, "Mac!" He yelled to the sergeant. "Sir," The warrior asked, holding his sword at the ready. Bolstered by Sinagog, the Astrals started to reform coming back for Lincoln. Matias knew he had to get the young ones to safety before they left.

"Get these children out of here!" Matias said pointing to the others that had been with Lincoln. "What!" Lincoln yelled. "No uncle I am not going anywhere!"

Agrius smashed through the wall close to them, twin shoulder mounted blazerbeams aimed at Sinagog. Sinagog turned to meet the new threat right when Agrius opened fire blasting the huge Orc. The Zajust stumbled back under the onslaught, the shots glancing off his armor, but driving him back none the less. Agrius's weapons came to life sending tracer fire at the Legionnaires or anyone else foolish enough to be within twenty yards of the construct. Agrius sweeping the wrist mounted Roto-cannon around him as he ran. With a rumble of dust and mortar, Talos rose to his feet joining his brother Gear. Both laid down fire cutting Razium soldiers and converging Astrals to nothing, the runic weapons laying waste to any armor in their path. Even Sinagog the huge Zajust, was blown off his feet, smashing through a small wall behind him as they poured it on.

Matias reacted, turning to his sergeant, "Mac you know the fall back plan, listen for my instructions, and help control the people." "Go, now. Get them out of here, go!" Lincoln will stay with me!" Matias yelled. "Yes sir." The Sergeant replied. He and his small unit led the children away behind the Wargears cover fire. Leena waved to Lincoln with tears in her eyes, he waved back. To his left a Lieutenant came through the breached wall holding a runic long barrel rifle. He was handsome with long hair that was pulled back and was in his officer's uniform, though it had been torn and rent in a few places.

He had come shortly after Agrius, and had a small group of soldiers in tow. They ran low toward Matias, watching for the Zajust or any other surprises. The garden court had been a fire fight, and more Legionnaires were on their way to reinforce the huge Zajust. Talos opened fire, cutting down Legionnaires that tried to enter the court. He stepped toward the opening to stop any other advance, while Agrius stayed with Matias and Lincoln.

"Commander!" the Lieutenant shouted above the gunfire in the background, "You must leave, I have initiated evac procedure 44, all the families that are left are getting out to safety. We are overrun." Matias heard the sounds of the castles long guns over his Lieutenant. The huge 419 howitzers were firing. The Razium were attacking from the air, and that didn't bode well with the defenses the way they were.

"I read your coordinates and was able to get Agrius here, but the castle is lost, the assassin leader is a Zajust as well. He has no respect for protocols or for parlay, he is butchering any he can find, we must go Sir. Sir!" The Lieutenant yelled. Grief was the mask that Matias wore as he listened to the man. He was thinking, the noises around him gone, the grime and blood of battle was on his face as was the decision he had to make. He looked at Lincoln, the boy's eyes told him everything. He was scared, and didn't know what to do. Matias would protect him at all costs. They had to go, and no matter what, Lincoln had to be saved. Then realizing he had no other choice, nodded.

"Confirm it, Le!" Matias yelled over the gun fire of the constructs. "Yes. Get everyone out, scramble any pilots we have left. Get them to their planes. You know what to do Lieutenant, follow the fall back plan."

Le Kai, nodded and ordered the small unit he had with him back toward the castle. "Talos!" Matias yelled over his wrist com, "To the armory meet at docking bay four by the lance. Talos stopped firing and scanned the area. "All threats contained Commander. Copy orders," the metallic voice crackled back over Matias wrist com. Matias watched him go, his guns lighting up as he met interference on his way.

Matias quickly looked around the area for Sinagog. "Damn," he said, "Agrius with me." "Let's go Lincoln, that big thing is still out there." "What is that thing uncle?" the frightened boy asked. "Something we don't want to meet Linc, we have to hurry, I will explain later."

Agrius was getting peppered with small arms fire. He stepped backward his cannons roared to life again, covering them as they made their way toward the armory, and the Skylance. From there they could go to the tank levels or board the ship itself, which was the best way they had to leave.

No one followed as they made their way to the armory, Agrius made sure of that. The sky was getting brighter, morning was close.

The door slid open and Matias entered bringing Lincoln in the cabin; Agrius was standing outside beside the Skylance airship and Wartrak tanks, behind him the crane was readying to hoist him to the vehicle hold. Agrius was giving cover fire to any that needed it, as the remaining guests were running past him to enter the MV armory. Matias' officers had given orders on procedure 44 and how to break out of this death trap they were in. All available were to go to their fliers, carts, cars, and tanks; anything that could move fast, and wait for the signal.

Matias had taken Lincoln into the ship, looking down at him Matias smiled. "Buckle up and get ready, we will outrun them." He nodded as he stood, trying to calm the still rattled boy. A young blonde soldier had come in with Matias, Lincoln knew him. Saul. He was one of the twins that had recently been inducted into Matias's guard. He sat down as well. "Hey don't worry everything is going to be alright," Saul said seeing Lincoln's face. Matias nodded, "That's right, you rest here, ok." Lincoln nodded. "Saul here will keep you company and check your vitals." Matias nodded at the soldier. He was about to leave when the alarm went off, and over the com Bors voice came on. "Sir they have launched hover blades we need to move." "I'll be back." Matias said to Lincoln griping his hand. The boy didn't want to let go. "Don't worry, I am not leaving you." They locked eyes. "Ok," Lincoln said, letting go. Matias touched the control pad mechanism, and the door slid open. "I'll be right back." He said as it closed.

Talos's Roto-cannon slowed as the barrels were once again red hot. The Anstone soldiers standing next to the huge Gear waited to see what, if anything was left. He and the squad with him had gotten held up by a Legionnaire counter attack before they had reached the armory. They had taken casualties as they fought their way out, but they had made it to the armory setting a defensive perimeter as they received orders of evacuation. The rest of the castle had fared no better, though the soldiers of Anstone Fortress had fought valiantly through the carnage and surprise. They barely had enough time to get their weapons, and most still wore their uniforms or dress clothes from the evening. The Razium had the ground now and the air was swiftly being taken by them as well. The thick armored planes of the Confederates had scrambled earlier, taking the fight to them in the air. They were few in number but were trying to buy some time for the ground vehicles to escape.

The rampart long guns were helping as well, but the Razium technology was too great and they had countered, sending Hover Blades to stall the retreat. Hover Blades were small one to three men hover craft that had the capability to close on a target quickly over land. They had small caliber ballistic weapons, but the long port and stern blades used to rend armor and flesh, were what they were known for. They could fit in most places on the ground, and that in itself allowed them great use. These small craft had already taken a toll on the populace of Anstone and had begun harrowing the armory vehicles, though the docked Skylance was using its deck guns to lend support and was keeping them at bay.

Matias sat in the command chair, his Sergeant Bor at the steering consol. With a flip of a switch, Matias opened lines to his officers. He could hear the rumble of Skylance's engine start, and the battle tanks below it revving their engines readying for the break out. Matias knew that Procedure 44 was an action that no one had wanted, but it was a necessity. It would break them up in to small units that would lead the enemy away from them in different directions, hopefully allowing the prince to escape. He wanted to fight these interlopers, to kill them all, but knew the future of the kingdom, of all kingdoms of Partha Terra rested with the boy he had with him. He paused looking at the intercom button, knowing his soldiers and his people were listening. Gathering himself he held the button down as he spoke.

"My friends, comrades, brothers, and sisters. If you are hearing this get to your designated areas. Please hurry." He paused. "I want you to know I have enjoyed this privilege of serving with you all. The time we feared has finally come and the Creator has seen fit to start us on our journey. We have trained for this; you know what to do, and where to meet. The biplanes will give us cover fire from the air as we go, and listen to the howitzers. They will cover our paths until we are clear. I will see all of you again, tomorrow or in the afterlife. Be careful, be safe, and run fast. May the Creator protect and guide you. This day will be remembered forever, as the day we took our country back! Commander Matias Layne, out." He turned off the com, "Bor get us out of here." He said to the big sergeant at the helm. Bor gave the signal.

The Razium had them surrounded, the Armory was being closed in on all sides. Most of the rest of the fortress castle had already fallen. Only minor pockets of resistance remained and those were dwindling quickly. The Razium had made a charge for the Armory but hadn't been able to crack its defenses. The huge construct Talos was at its doors and was still repelling them, buying the time that Matias needed to get most of the people to safety. Talos had unloaded most of his payload and his ammo was running low. He launched the last of his rockets, blasting a Hover Blade from the sky, the thing crashing in the distance, while a howitzer for the ramparts took out another. Talos had fought valiantly stopping the Razium from completely overrunning their position, none of the Razium weapons being able to stop the huge machine.

The last few seconds had been quiet, the fighting stalled, and the now completely sober solders of the Confederates crouched down behind the small walls waiting for their Captain's orders. They were tasked to hold another minute and then to withdraw to their vehicles, Talos with them. The Captain leading them looked at the smoke filled castle, he couldn't see anything. It seemed unnaturally quiet and the thick smoke from the rockets, cannon fire, and churned earth was obstructing his vision. "Talos, scan the area." He ordered, "What do you..." Before he could finish he was blasted from his feet, landing dead beside the Wargear, a smoking hole in his breast plate armor. A huge sword cut the air slicing three soldiers to the right of the large War Construct. "Attack!" the new comer bellowed, and the Razium closed in from the flank. Talos started the Roto-cannon aiming at the monster holding the blade, but was rushed by him. With three mighty strides, Sinagog barreled in to the huge machine with a crash hitting him under the arm, knocking Talos off balance. The huge black clad warrior continued on running over the brave men he had just slain like they were worth nothing. When he had hit the Wargear its Roto-cannon strafed the area, mostly hitting the Razium Legionnaires as they came in, the tracers shooting in the air as he fell back.

Sinagog had led a small group around the confederate position and had now taken the initiative, and their flank. It had been crumpled as he himself had taken down the one thing slowing them, the Gear, Talos.

The huge robot shook him off, throwing him to the ground. But the damage was done and the rest of the Legionnaires were closing from the front. Talos corrected himself, aiming his Roto-cannon at Sinagog's head as the beast was destroying the soldiers, but the Zajust was too fast. He turned, lashing out as the weapon went off, his sword knocking the Roto-cannon up in the air as it started to fire. Tracer shots flew skyward, hitting a Hover Blade as it flew over; the engine exploded pulling the blade from the sky. It crashed behind the oncoming Legionnaires, flipping and exploding behind them, the blast knocking the rest to the dirt.

Talos swung at his assailant, but the giant robot was blocked and countered by the monstrous Zajust. With a double handed swing, Sinagog brought his powered archaic blade in an overhead arc, its serrated edge glowing. It severed the Wargears fighting hand, the heat of the blade melting the end of his arm. The Zajust spun and chopped through the armored shin greave, cutting a piston inside Talos metallic calf. The cut toppled Talos taking him to his knee. Talos managed to push him back with his cannon arm, and open fire but it wasn't enough distance, and it caused only minor damage, as the weapon was batted aside.

* * *

The engines of Skylance where humming a softy electric whine as the thrusters underneath propelled the ship and it slowly started to rise from the platform. Sinagog heard the whine of the engines thrusters, "No, not too late," he said pushing away from the robot, trying to disengage from the fight with the Gear. He was smacked in the back with the gun arm of Talos. "You will not get them this day," the construct bellowed, in his calm deep robotic voice. Sinagog was furious lashing out with his blade. He cut through the other arm the Roto barrels falling clanking on the stone walkway, and then took a chunk of shoulder with another swing. Sinagog was mangling the irreplaceable machine. "We will kill all your kind Gear," Sinagog spat as he hacked off another piece of Talos. Talos mechanism runes and warning counters were blinking inside his helm; he was overheating, his systems freezing up. The Gear slid his hand from the sliced gun and tried another swing but it was easily blocked by the mighty blade. Sinagog realized he had beaten the machine, and was wasting time, but he was too late.

He watched with smoldering rage as the Skylance pulled away out of his grasp. Sneering through his tusked face mask helm, he raised his head to the sky and bellowed, but his rage was short lived. The ground shook with the sound of a thousand horses, and he dove aside as the tanks of Anstone blasted their way free of the walls of the armory, crushing all in their path. Legionnaires were blasted apart by the weapons of the tanks and steam engines, and any Astrals left puffed to the dark smoke forms not to suffer the same fate. The bulk of the Razium force had followed Sinagog to the armory as the soldiers of Anstone had fallen back. The Razium had been pulled into the trap set by Matias and his men.

The breakout was working. The tanks and steam carriages, rode out of the armory and through the fortress city, over walls down streets, any way they could escape. It was a complete breakout and there was no way of countering the undisciplined routes the vehicles took. The Skylance had taken flight and the other smaller ships of the Confederates were giving an escort for the Prince. As the ship pulled away. Sinagog picked himself up off the ground, he was cursing in his native tongue as he did and smashing anything close in his anger; including his own men. Talos was crawling trying to grab the leg of the Zajust warrior, even though he had no hands to grip, swiping with his mangled arm at him. The Zajust stepped on the arm, the metal creaking under his armored covered foot. He looked down at the mangled construct, the light in its eyes flashing, the power supply dwindling, and its servos whined. Sinagog raised his blade and sent it through Talos head. The lights died, and Talos was no more.

CHAPTER 12. GANGSTERS AND INFORMATION:

<u>Metropolis of Royal, Outskirts of the Dragon Wastes, above the
Confederate of the Pallence, the Southern Flat Iron Mountains</u>

Royal was many things. Some said it was a pirate city, some it was a
mercenary palace, some a gangster hole, and others an escape from the real
world. But all beings and all races on the planet knew of the city of Royal.
The huge city of sin it was. Anything you wanted you could get, anything that
was for sale, it sold. Any race you hadn't seen you could see, or sometimes
buy. You could do or get anything you wanted but you had to watch your
back, or else you might be the one got. Royal was corrupt, and had no real
government. It was controlled by two factions, the Kissar, human gangsters
of the north and the Outcast Elves of the Dru Nar.

The Kissar, were northeastern human warriors who had migrated
down many centuries ago to make a home away from the Ice Glacier of the
north and the wars with the giant Jotunn. These men wanted to make a living
away from fighting the Ice Giants and Trolls for control of the nothingness
that was the north. They wanted to make life easy for themselves and they
knew they could by giving the southerners the evil they wanted. Then there
were the Sea Dru Nar. Elven gangsters, for lack of any better term. For
reasons known to very few, the Prince and his retainers had been disgraced
and cast out of their home lands far to the east. They ended up here as their
best resort, though they were still Elves and still secret. Anyone who wanted
something done in this city needed to know one these two groups, and
usually it meant that person would be in the debt of one of them as well,
which one would not want to be in. Royal was also a recruitment center, if

not the prime recruitment center, for mercenaries, outcast, and no good doers. The Razium had poached some of its finer trash from it.

Royal was located on the outskirts of what had been the Dragon Lands in the range of the largest of the mountain chains on the continent, The Flat Iron Mountains. The mountains outlined the area around the now Dragon Wastes, an area that after the wars had been declared desolate and not fit to live in. It didn't used to be this way though. It was once an amazing city, a huge trade city between the kingdoms before the wars. It had been a conduit for the traders of the Dragons, old Kissar, and the Southern Confederates long ago. But now the city had grown fat on its gluttony, becoming a monstrous edifice to the grime of the world. Though being so close to the Dragon Spires meant a territory divide. It had been in many conflicts and in many battles and its people had to fight beasts, monsters, and other nightmares most thought only myth. It had become more efficient and sufficient during those times. It had even managed to remain neutral during the wars, selling weapons and ammo to the highest bidder. Though now it was a mercenary hole that had seen its best days, but it still clung onto its last glory like a dying breath.

Most cities and towns were protected by their lords and governors but Royal had become free space. The government of the city having no real allegiances, with the Bosses being the real law of this area it was up to them to run things. Technically it was in control of the Regent Governor of the Pallance, the Confederate to the south. Though he washed his hands of it, declaring it too polluted an area after the battles fought by its walls. The main factions that had controlled it paid tithes to the government of the Pallance to leave them be, so they did. Even though it was considered a dead land, it prospered. For some reason or another it just did, and Walker was walking right toward it.

* * *

The riders that had passed Walker minutes ago slowed as they neared Royals huge grey walls, the rain coming done harder as it pattered off their cloaks. The horses were tired and run out as they reigned them in, cantering up to the huge grey walls, the city behind them surrounded by fog and mountains. The riders made their way to a small outlet on the side. It was the rider's entrance to the city, where they were waved through by guards in similar burgundy cloaked uniforms. They rode under the huge arched walkways and through the large streets of the city toward Six points. Six points was the area of Royal that the Kissar made their home, a meeting place of all things vile and detrimentally fun. With large, older, but well-built buildings that met where the six main roadways of the east side of the city came together. It formed the place where the Kissar could share their ideas of fun with the world. The riders continued through the points and headed to a walled fortress on the edge of the inner city boundaries. The huge rock wall wasn't out of place, most of the large estates in the city were walled off for the protection of their owners. Many rich people lived or visited the city, and they had the money to be protected. The huge steel gates were swung open where four armed guards waited at the entrance of the estate.

The first waved the riders through. They rode in, the turrets guns on the walls were trained on them until they had ridden completely through the gates. The gunman walking the wall above watched them through his steam goggles, giving the signal to lower the huge mounted machine guns as they passed. The riders dismounted, handing the reigns to the servants that greeted them, and walked to the main house. Their horses were escorted to the stables by others that were dressed in the burgundy of the house. The lead rider passed the others walking hurriedly to the huge main house, through a side door and into the large waiting room where three guards sat at a small square table playing cards. Across the room a man dressed in the loose fitting garb of a monk was watching them intensely. He sat on a very ornate rug, legs crossed and hands resting supinated on his knees. The rider walked in, and snapped her fingers. The monk quickly popped up and walked over to stand off to the side of the others. The other guards seeing him did the same.

The rider lowered her hood. She was extremely attractive with pouty pink lips and long blond hair, though some of it had been died dark underneath, and tied in a small braid on the side. She was tall and had an air of confidence about her that said she was used to being listened to. She was mostly covered by her cloak but her build couldn't be hidden as her boiled armor was high up on her chest. She addressed the monk. "There is a man about to enter the city. He is rather large, wearing a rain cloak, soldier attire, and he is armed. He looks like he can handle himself." She paused looking at each fiercely then stopping on one. He was bald and had a large mustache; he had the look of someone that was not to be messed with. Then she looked at the man standing next to him, he looked similar. She continued, looking back to the monk and nodding her head towards the pair. "Go, take a few men and monitor his movements. Use Earl if you need to, but only if you need to," she said focusing on the word need. "Now go, I will be along when time permits," she said finishing sternly. The monk nodded, and turned waiting for the similar looking guards. The guards that had stood put on their burgundy cloaks and left the room followed by the monk. The other riders had finally entered and she looked at the tallest one. "Still raining I see." She said, her voice sweet even though she was poking fun. The man named Dahl looked at her with a wolfish grin. Her smile was dazzling. "See if Lord Dillion can give me an audience, there is someone he might want to meet." Dahl nodded.

Walker passed small outposts and ravelins that were abandoned, or made to look so as he neared the walls of the immensely large city. As he neared Royal, he noticed it was anything but royal, but it made up for its lack of artistic décor in its sheer size. Its dark well used walls rising out of the white fog, like a whale breaching the surface of the ocean. The large buildings behind them were lit up and huge sky towers poked their heads out of the fog. Older style air ships, large Zeppelins, and others of newer Razium design, flew over the buildings. Search lights guided them, their lights barely visible in the white mist. It was amazing to see a city so massive, it seemed to go on forever as he ran his eyes over it, noticing the architecture. It could have been magnificent once, he thought, but now it looked run down and used like the people in it.

Save for a few, the buildings seemed to be built on each other, the towers were tall but dirty, and the wide cobbled road that led to its gates not quite kept up. The fog around its walls made it look more like a scene from a painting than a real place. On each side of the huge walls, the Flat Iron Cliffs jutted out like the horns of some great hidden beast. From his vantage point they looked more like the jagged teeth of a monster, than a mountain. It was a stronghold for sure, the mountain buffeting it from the outside world. Still as he looked he thought there was something quaint about the old fortress city, he liked it. Now that also could have been because he was soaked and hadn't had a hot meal in a while, but he wasn't so sure. Luckily the city never slept, so he could get a meal and some shelter somewhere. He felt the money pouch in his belt, then, looked at the city walls one more time as he made his way to the gates. He was thinking about Orson, and hoping he was in there.

More people and other creatures had been coming in to trade for the day and the city gates had gotten busier in the last few minutes, Walker noticed as he walked towards them. He purposely strode toward the east gate of the city. The walls that he passed through were very thick huge structures and looked as if they could take a pounding. He had heard this city was always ready for war, it seemed he heard right. Royal was known for holding against armies of Dragons during one of those great battles of long ago. It was said that the walls had stood for hundreds of years, and were Dragon Fire proof. It was also said the huge walls had been created with a special element that was hard to find, and lost to legend.

Walker took in his surroundings seeing the guards and Kissar soldiers looking down from their positions on the walls, watching him come through. One spit over the wall turning away from him to look at the lines of people that had started to come for the daily trades. Studying the walls as he walked, Walker saw they had murder holes every 30 or so yards, and around the entrances. Also, the front gate house that looked like a mini castle itself was protected in the same way but had electronic gauges that attached to steam hydraulics just inside the entrance. The vents led to steam shooters, weapons that shot the heated air in a 30 foot area in front of them. The heat so intense, it could melt flesh or cook one inside their own armor in seconds.

Around and between the emplacements, were weapons and of various sorts and swivel guns on the ramparts. The biggest of these were the bastions drum towers, on a lower wall he had just noticed. They were armed with the huge cannons. The long barreled weapons were dripping with the rain of the morning, looking more like huge spikes jutting from a rock than a projectile weapons, but these howitzer style guns could shoot as far as one could see and were perfect for defending from air attacks. Walker guessed you had to have that type of fire power when you lived this close to the

Dragons. However the fire beasts hadn't been seen in over five years, and he had heard that the one seen then hadn't been very big anyway.

The gate had an entrance for wagons and vehicles on one side and foot traffic on the other. He walked toward the latter and as he got closer saw the guards checking any travelers on foot, answering questions before they entered the gates.

"State your business," the first guard was saying as he walked past a steam powered carrier car as it drove through. The guard was dressed in the burgundy Walker had seen the riders wearing, and he was looking down at a schedule in his right hand while scratching his head with his left. The guard hadn't noticed the size or look of the man in front of him yet. The other guard had though, and tried to grab his partner's sleeve.

"What?" He asked looking at him, the rain making him squint. Seeing the others face, his eyes wide, he looked up to face the huge bearded warrior. "Hello ah," he stepped back. 'Yes sir anything to check?" He asked slightly startled surprise in his voice. "No, not today," Walker replied smiling. "Alright, well do you know about this city?" Walker nodded like the man was wasting his time, though he wondered why people kept asking that. The guard got the hint. "Papers." Walker handed the other guard his papers, and he looked them over quickly handing them back, as the first started talking. "Ok, well to let you know we have recruiters right inside the gate, three shops down. You might want to join. Good money, let me tell you. Your weapons will remain sheathed at all times, or you will be arrested, possibly shot. You have no goods to barter, so there is none of that." He told him as he looked at his chart. "Also, today is half price on the shops on third." "Thanks, I'll keep that in mind," Walker said back, nodded and stepped passed the guards, under the huge raised portcullis, and into the city. After Walker was gone the second soldier made his way to the guards shack inside the wall. He picked up the receiver. "He just came through," he said into it.

East gate was very large, large enough to drive five wagons side by side at the same time. The gate opened into a huge shopping area with people walking, merchants yelling, and general chaos. Some were trying to sell their goods, and services, others looking for food to buy from the fresh market stands and shops, and then some just there to see the daily craze.

The rain had slackened a little, and the Lorlanders and other visitors were coming in the city for trade. The market seemed to be getting busier as he watched.

As Walker continued through making his way into the city the first thing he noticed was the size of the place. It was enormous. It looked bigger inside than out, and was a bit more modern from the inside as well. There where lights everywhere, and advertisements of what they sold.

It was still early morning and the light rain had given way to a slight fog. The paperboys where running through the streets tossing the news to the few shops that read it, others were handing little flyer cards to the new comers as they passed. They had all sorts of pictures and advertisements on them, from food to women and everything in between. He held his hand up and shook his head, as they slapped the things on their legs trying to hand them to him. A paper boy ran past and Walker caught one of the informational guides he threw; it almost hit him in the face. The boy smiled, "Good catch." He said running off to finish his job. Walker watched him go. Rascal, he thought, and looked down at the paper. The fighting over seas and the meeting of Council or The 12, were the front page headlines. "If they only knew," he said aloud. The tall street lamps hadn't been dimmed yet, and they cast a collection of glowing illuminated shapes in the crisp wet morning fog. This part of the city was amazingly built with an old style and seemed very sturdy. Inviting, though busy shops were on one side, while the other opened to plank wood sitting areas that lead to a park in the middle of the city. He continued walking noticing the buildings here were perfectly aligned. The large points of the towers and the gargoyles of the taller buildings started to take shape as the early rays of the sun lightened the area. He guessed, when scum of humanity were off the streets one could really take in the architecture of the city.

The streets were well built, and wide. Not as nice as Sparta, but they were wider than most cities with cobbled and paved roads, alleys and streets. Most of the buildings had arcading on the way into the shops, a classic but elegant design, with the tall buildings stretching high over the city and estate walls. The city was coming to life as the chimneys puffed white smoke that seemed to mix with the fog as an artist would paint grey on a white canvas. He remembered seeing them in the distance as he walked toward the monstrous mercenary den. He could make out a buttress like object poking out from one of the buildings on the other side of the city but the fog hadn't cleared fully so it was hard to tell. As he walked he noticed awnings of an assortment of bright colors over the entrances and the lower windows of the shops and structures. The streets continued to get more traffic and he stopped looking at the tall buildings so he could transverse the crowded streets. They were starting to get choked with the day's residents and travelers.

The city looked rough, and choked as it had gotten busier. The people here were rough too, and knew what they were doing especially when it came to bloodletting and surviving. He could tell, as everyone walking by him carried arms and wore armor. Who could blame them, being on the outskirts of the Dragon country. Since he had come in he had already seen all kinds of people and things. From Ulthuan, Trolls, Razium and a Dwarger, to steam cars, robots and even a Razium hover craft. The people of Royal were used to many types and races here, and they seemed not to care that someone of his stature was in the way as they bumped passed him. It had made him relax a little to think he didn't stand out as much, though in the back of his mind he felt as if he was being followed.

Walker was starting to get more looks from the people as the day progressed, and figured he should get inside and start to find out if Orson was in this cesspool. He remembered where Bally had told him to go, the taverns. As he looked for a suitable place, he spotted men who had been following him. He knew he had felt eyes on him. Three Kissar soldiers had been watching him from across the street. They looked similar to the riders that had passed him outside the city, and wore the same style burgundy cloaks. This was the third time he had seen them in the last 30 minutes. Two were talking and glancing at him. The taller one, bald with a mustache, looked like the other he was talking to, a twin perhaps. He stopped talking and turned to the smaller man behind him who was dressed the same, telling him something. Looking at Walker, the eyes of the smaller man widened and with a nod to his superior, he left jogging down a back alley. The bald men stood and continued watching.

Great, he thought, trouble already. He knew this type of town and needed to get information from it quick. Until then he needed to keep his head down. Besides that he was hungry and thirsty again. I wish I had kept more of Bally's food he thought. Yelling caught his ear and he looked to his right to the street corner opposite him. There by a lamp post a young man was yelling the news and selling papers to any who walked by. "Extry extry, read all about it, the Council meets to end the war, the 12 are in session, extry, the Razium are close to the border...Paper here!" he shouted. Walker looked back toward the Kissar following him. He glanced back and forth but didn't see them anywhere. They'll be back, he thought. He didn't want trouble but if it came to that he would give them all they wanted. He paused and then made his way across the flat street, passing a carriage pulled by two huge horses, a keg brew looking device in the back. He moved behind a stalled armored steam car, and came out on the other side close to where the young man was yelling the news. The young man had seen him, and watched him close the distance. "I'll take one." Walker said to the teen tossing him a coin. He caught it and made to get change. "No, keep it."

"Really?" The boy asked, his teenage face lighting up, then he paused looking at Walker suspiciously. "What's the catch," he demanded. "You have to tell me the best place to find some food and get out of the morning air, and stay out of it," he added to the young man. "How long you want to stay, out of it?"

"The longer the better." Walker replied. "Ok, are you looking for someone then or them for you huh?" A man walked out of the crowd and picked a paper from the stack, handing the boy a coin, he thanked him. Walker watched him go and then looked back to the paper boy. "Maybe both, but now I want to sit, and eat." Walker winked. "Alright," the teen said, smiling flipping his coin and grabbing it out of the air. "I know just the place."

"Han Fords, a tavern of notoriety." The younger man said holding his hand to the large lodge tavern as they neared it. "Nice." Walker nodding, remembering Bally mentioning it might be a good place to look.

The Victorian looking building was huge. How could one describe the best worst place to be, if you wanted to hide or get caught? But that's what Han Fords was and it was busy, and filthy in a quaint sort of way. No one talked except that everyone talked, just not to any one new that had come to the nasty dreg hole. The paperboy had led him to the place, telling him it was the best place to find out any information, or just to get out of the weather. Walker laughed, watching as cute servers were bustling through the crowd to serve the many patrons. When they had made it through the front crowd, the paperboy had taken him to the back and introduced him to the second of the place. He was in charge of security, an old but incredibly thick set man named Pork. At least he might have been a man, but could be an Ogre the way he smelled.

Pork had immediately asked if Walker wanted a job bouncing, a man his size and all. Walker had his cloak pulled over his shoulders to try and hide some of his bulk, but he still looked big. Walker thanked him but declined. Pork said that he being a friend of Paper- the nickname of the paperboy Walker guessed, he would give him a few minutes of his time. They walked through the press as with most bars and taverns; the patrons sized up the new addition. Most did and most moved, but some he could tell wondered who would pay for the information about this man. These people would sell their mothers for some coins or drink. Walker stepped passed a man with a monocle and top hat. The man's left arm was a steam contraption that seemed to augment his strength, the way the wires and metal pitons were strapped around it. He inclined his head to Walker as he passed, the man's entourage making sure their Boss had more room than most; each of them had some type of similar mechanical augmentation as well. All of them were armed to the teeth. Walker moved passed them keeping his head down as he followed Pork to a table in the corner where they sat down.

"So you sure you don't wanna work at this primo establishment?" Pork asked, holding his hand up toward the room as he slid in a chair beside Walker, his eyes following one of the more attractive serving girls. She walked over and took the glasses that were left on the table, winking at Walker before she sauntered off.

"It is tempting," Walker replied with a little sarcasm, which was lost on the idiot he sat with. "Aye, it is ain't it." Pork said smiling back at him, looking at another girl, a little drool coming from his mouth and catching on his 5 o clock that was starting to look like a 6 o clock shadow.

He chuckled for a second and then leaned close. "I like you, and Paper tells me you're looking for someone. He mentioned you pay well,

Eheee?" The fat man asked eyebrow up. "I do, but it depends on the information you give me." Pork looked annoyed at him for a second then leaned back. "Ok, so you're a business man, I respect that," he stated in his flat Isle accent. "So I tell ya what." Pork never got to finish, a small man with an augmented arm landed on the table bouncing his head off it with a thud and falling to the floor. "What tha!" Pork yelled and was on his feet, smashing any one close out of his way. "I'll be back," he said before charging into the melee. Walker dodged another tossed patron and watched the heavy man storm off smashing people as he went. As he did he thought he saw someone in the corner of his eye. Slightly glancing over he saw no one was there. Damn, I'm probably made, he thought, remembering the men earlier.

The brawl was dying down and the place was getting back to being loud and drunk. Walker still waited and it seemed Pork was off doing what he did, so he stood and headed for the bar. When he got there he looked for the bartender, after a second of looking he spotted him. He was barely over five feet of shoulders and a thick beard, walking from the back holding a huge keg that Walker wondered if he would have trouble lifting. The Dwarger, Glorn or Dwarf, depending on where you hail from, was massive. He had a huge beard with talismans and gold trinkets braided through it. He tossed the XXX marked barrel by the counter, popped a tap in to the metal laced top, and slid it back underneath. After he finished, he walked up his small ramp to stand looking at Walker.

"Well?" the dwarf asked gruffly. "What you want lad?" Walker smiled. "I want some of that finest you threw under there." The Dwarf squinted at him and then smiled back with a crooked toothy grin, a large gold one shining as he did. "Ha, I see ya have a good palate, for a man, aye?" He took a mug and filled it up. "How will ya be paying?" He asked sliding the golden contents across the Span Cedar bar counter. Walker slid a golden coin to him. The Dwarf looked at it then him. "Well with this you should start a tab," he said picking it up. Walker looked at the gold barely protruding from his thick fingers. "Keep it." he said. The Dwarf stopped and squinted, looked at him hard. "Ok, for this much I'll bite, go on ask." Walker grinned as he sipped from the mug. "Alright. I am looking for a healer, a medicine man or hedge wizard, going by the name Ol' Hedge, Olson or Orson. Ring any bells?" The Dwarf looked around then yelled to a bar hop along the wall, breaking him from his trance of watching a server girl. He startled, and the Dwarf waved him closer. "Watch the bar," he told him. The hop nodded. Then looking at the patrons around them suspiciously, the Dwarf waved his hand. "Follow me."

They went to a table close to the back of the tavern, as he went the Dwarf grabbed some bread and meat from a small ice box behind the counter. They sat. "Can't talk sabotage on an empty stomach can you," he said to Walker. Walker held his hands up in defense. "Don't look surprised," the Dwarger said. "I saw that pendant you're wearing, lucky too. I know some who wouldn't mind selling that information, but me an mine have ties to tha crown. Rest the King's soul." He finished as he looked above the table, a painting that would have gone unnoticed was hung above them. It depicted the city and a Dragon flying away from it, the King's banner of the Lion and Chevron in the background. Below the painting was what looked like an old hand drawn map of the Confederates. "I'll help ya." He said tossing some ham and a biscuit to Walker. The Dwarf took a bite of his.

"Thank you." Without missing a beat, or chew, the Dwarf started talking, crumbs falling out of his mouth. "The names Rulik Goldfinger but you can call me Snorri, and you are, mister pendefff?" He asked with a full bite of ham in his large mouth. Walker looked puzzled and then realized what he had said, Mister Pendant. "Snorri. Nice to meet you. I'm Walker, guard to the throne, well long ago I was." The Dwarger nodded to him. "Nice to meet you as well Walker. I don'a know who you're talking about," he said thinking. "Can't say tha I have, and there aren't many healers around, with the Razium here and them tracking them down and all." He took another bite. "But, my cousin would. He owns a small tavern in Navarre. Now I have heard that there is a healer or two there, safer for them ya know. If so, and tha one who your looking for is there, my cousin can tell you and set you up. Especially if you don'a find him here."

Walker was eating a slice of ham and listening to the Dwarf when he stopped and stood, looking across the tavern. There was some commotion at the very front of the tavern. A large Ogre and a few thugs dressed in the colors of the Kissar had walked through the doors. Snorri grabbed him pulling him back down. "Listen," he said, "get out of town quick or you'll be in it with the locals. You know about this city right?" Snorri asked. "Why does everybody ask that?" Walker asked frowning. "What?" Snorri asked.

"Nothing." Walker said, nodding. Snorri continued, "The Kissar and the Elves, ah filthy Elves," he spat. "They each own half of this place, lucky you're on this side of the wall. Don'a get caught up. You look like somebody they would hire right away to turn the tide, and even you can't fight them all." "Anyway," he continued. "When you get to Navarre ask for Glorin, Glorin Goldfinger. He owns the Fat Pig Tavern. Tell him, Snorri sends his love..." Walker looked puzzled. "I know, I know," said the Dwarger, hands up. "Inside joke. Best of luck to ya, soldier," he said with a wink and extended his hand. Walker shook it. "Thank you again, one last thing. Can you direct me to a church; there is something I need to do." "Aye," Snorri nodded.

The Dwarger gave him directions and told him to leave through the back door. Walker stood to leave, took the last drought of his stein and made his way to the very back of the tavern. He was about to walk out the door when the Dwarf called back. "Hey, now don'a go steppin in it." Walker nodded and was gone out the door and down the alley.

CHAPTER 13. THE RAZIUM HUNT:

Above the Fortress City of Anstone a mile east of the city

The monstrously large flagship, Lord's Wrath, sat hovering above Anstone like a grey cloud of death, just waiting to unleash its torrent on the fortress city below it. The huge ship's shields flickered from the bombardment it was taking from the howitzers of Anstone. The green energy fields static running down its length from each hit, though none of the projectiles penetrated. Its thrusters were spurting in short bursts, holding it aloft as its small weapon's batteries would fire sporadically at any of the Confederate aircraft that got too close. Nemsor Vaul stood on the bridge surveying the battle below.

"My lord Nemsor, all crafts are maneuvering at high speed. They are coming around as an escort for the larger craft. It has the mark of the Prince, and the energy signal we tracked earlier was last monitored was from that ship." Nemsor turned to the officer behind him. "Open a channel to Captain Xylor." "Aye my lord. He is on sir."

Captain Xylor appeared on the touch display in front of Nemsor. "My Lord," he addressed as he saluted. Xylor was a big Razium. He was dressed in the dark colors of a fleet officer. His double lapel coat had 8 golden buttons that ran up the front, and his many medals of battle were adorned on his left breast. He also wore golden epaulettes and a red arm sleeve that showed his status as Lord Captain of the Fleet. He was commander of the Dark Hand, the second greatest of the Razium spacecraft left after the wars. His light purple skin was clammy as he listened to the armored Giant on the screen in front of him.

"Captain Xylor, send a squad of Spear fighters in pursuit of their flagship, and give the order to recall the forces. I want us out of the castle, it is no use to us now."

"Yes my lord. And the people, prisoners?" "No, leave them; I don't want them to slow us. I want all our forces in pursuit now." Nemsor finished. Xylor bowed as the screen disappeared.

Nemsor addressed his navigator and helmsmen. "Set our course to intercept, we have tarried here too long, and I will not lose him now." With the order given the bridge was a burst of movement and action. Nemsor turned from the command bridge and slowly walked to the window of the ship, his patience fraying as he watched the Confederate craft descending out of view. The other armored black cloaked Zajust that had recently arrived to the bridge, followed and watched as well, though said nothing. Lord's Wrath, the command ship of the Razium forces and Nemsor Vaul's personal transport, decloaked itself.

The sun had finally risen, and the Lord's Wrath now cast its immense shadow over the fortress city of Anstone. The space vessels cloaking device was not as powerful in the daylight as it would have normally been in the darkness of space or at night, but it was not needed now anyway. Lord's Wrath was enormous. It was around 1000 meters in length and half as wide. Its grey smooth hull seemed to eat up the sky as it slowly appeared out of nowhere with the cloaking vanishing away. The large Desolater style battleship started turning, the huge thrusters on each side of the large craft giving it a nimbleness that wouldn't normally be associated with a craft of such size, no matter what field of battle it was on. The small hover thrusters on its sides had kept it floating in the air waiting for the moment it had needed to reveal itself. Its main engines were preparing to activate, the spooling of the engines deafening as the air around the openings heated. The ship would track its prey, as it had in the wars, so it would be the same now. It had enough fire power to destroy mountains if it needed, and if it weren't for the boy below them the ship would have destroyed the fortress with little trouble. The cannons and weapon systems used to fight some of the Razium's most important wars were trained on the city, and the reinforced walls of the fortress below were of little consequence, even if the Tryonic field was up it wouldn't have taken long to have brought it down.

Ships like these were instrumental in defeating the Dragons in the air. It was what had corralled them to their spires. Though the Razium had lost many of the ships in the process, the beast's fire able to melt through even their advanced metal hulls.

The giant mass that was the Lord's Wrath, continued turning, the thrusters burning in short bursts on its sides guiding it. Inside the crews were readying, setting coordinates to follow the small ship that carried the prince. The Wrath, shook as it turned. It was taking direct hits from the long guns that were still operational and the few Confederate planes that had remained behind for the rearguard. The valiant, if trivial effort was wasted on the colossal superior engineered space vessel. Its armor was too thick to penetrate with their weapons.

Heavy plated Confederate biplanes had starting strafing runs on the Wrath when it started moving, the 50 caliber machine guns and port missiles firing on its armor trying to get its attention. Attention that needed to be drawn from the escaping Skylance, tanks, and other smaller vessels trying to leave the fortress. The air had just become the Razium's field of war. Though the Confederate pilots were winning the battle of skill against the Razium, the war was lost to them already.

The Confederate pilots were magnificent in the art of aeronautic warfare, but were outclassed by the superior technologies of the Razium fighters and it was becoming a losing effort for the cumbersome planes of the Confederates to continue. The Camels, newer metal steam engine bombers, and untested electro fighters, were no match for the speed of the advanced ships of the Razium. Their armor was holding up, but it was only a matter of time before the superior weaponry would pierce their hides and bring them down. The biplanes flew toward the Wrath in a V formation opening fire, their weapons making marks on the hull armor of the monstrous warship, but little else.

A Razium Spear fighter shot by them, and one of the middle biplanes exploded, debris clinking on the exterior of the huge vessel as it passed, clattering over its bridge. Confederate planes were flying around the Lord's Wrath like flies on a horse. Their intent was distraction and maybe getting lucky and cracking the outlook bay. Nemsor was immune to it as was his crew, he watched the ships dog fight each other as the crew continued about their business. Lord's Wrath had almost completely turned to follow the Skylance, and Nemsor knew they would have the Prince soon. An explosion erupted on the bridge, and warning sirens went off. The Wrath had taken a direct hit on the flank, it was little consequence of getting through the armor, but it was slowing the ship's advance and pursuit. One of the crewmen fell from the impact and even Nemsor had to steady himself, holding his hand out using the Magnus to do so. The 419 howitzer cannons on the walls were still firing. They had kept the villains at bay for a while and now they had turned their attention to the small air battle.

Nemsor looked at the Captain, annoyed. The Captain Stren Norn, a Razium man of average height and look with dark close cropped hair, was standing straight as a statue proudly, almost arrogantly. He was dressed in the dark coat of a ship master, his epaulettes and medals of office displayed proudly. He looked at Nemsor noticing his displeasure. "Sorry sir, I will take care of this." He said as he hurriedly stepped to the con behind the helmsmen. "Well let's see if we can get these ships out of way. Tell the fighters to engage." "Yes sir," the helmsman stated flatly, having already processed the order.

Anstone Fortress still wasn't silent, and Pale the Zajust Lord that had started this war was still on the ground sating his sick twisted desires. The few soldiers and civilians that hadn't made it to safety were screaming and trying to run. Pale and his Astrals where killing any survivors they found for the joy of it.

Pale pulled his blade from the soldier on the ground, looking up from his kill as his second approached. He was garbed in similar dark attire with armor under his cloak, a cross design covering his lower face mask. He bent to a knee in front of his lord. "We have been hailed twice, Lord Pale." He said slowly. "The spoils of war are ours, Anx." Pale replied sickly. "Who dares infringe on me?" "Xylor." The other answered. "The fool, he is a lapdog," Pale sneered standing.

On the bridge of the Dark Hand, fleet master Xylor was watching the fall back of the troops. "Pale not responding?" he asked. The communications officer looked unsure what to say. "Get him now." The Fleet master slowly said. "This is the Dark Hand, to Lord Pale, Lord Pale?" The wet raspy reply was unpleasant to hear to say the least. "What do you want boy?"

"This is the Dark Hand, you are ordered to withdraw." "Do not order me," the sick voice came through the com, "Or I will kill you!" The deep voice of Xylor made him pause. "This is Xylor, I told you to leave them. Lord Nemsor commands it. Why are you still on the ground?" There was a pause on the com and then the answer.

"I am sssorry my lord," the sickness of his voice appalling. "We will return. I was." Pale was cut off in mid-sentence, "I know you will, I don't care if you are Zajust, Orc! Next time you slip your leash Pale, I will allow Phalayon to talk to you."

"Yes Fleet Master." Pale spat, releasing a phlegm wet laugh.

The channel broke. Xylor waited, arms folded behind his back. He looked at the radioman; the man nodded answering his unvoiced question. "Yes sir, he is withdrawing sir, the Astrals are returning, and ground forces have finished the sweep there is nothing of worth left. A few battle tanks, carriages, and the main ship where all that were allowed to escape and they are being tracked." "Good, and the Lance?" "We are to rendezvous with Lord Nemsor; he is closing in on it as we speak sir." "Lord Xylor," another communications officer interrupted. "The Wrath is hailing us sir." "Proceed," Xylor said.

"Lord Xylor this is Captain Derus." "Captain," Xylor commented. "Sir," the captain continued, we are taking fire from the Howitzer cannons, could you see to their stopping?" "Yes, tell Lord Nemsor it will be done. Xylor out." The screen blinked off. "Get me Pale now, before he gets too far away. I have a job his sick mind should like."

A few minutes after Xylor gave the order, the guns stopped and all was silent. The war on the ground was over and only a few scattered pockets remained of the once mighty city of Anstone.

Skylance

The Lance was a beautiful ship. Some would describe it as a classic sea carrack with its smooth sweeping sides and rigging. It was made at the height of the steam era and had been commissioned by the King himself. A replica to honor the old ships of the past with its look but to be a ship of the future with its technology. It had been re-outfitted for royal transportation during the truce with the Razium, before the wars. When the Razium had outfitted the air force of the Confederates with the armor and engines, they had created a ship that had speed and power to match one of their own. Though the Razium didn't share all their secrets during the Affinity wars, what they did was enough to make this ship one of the toughest ships in the Confederate air armada.

It had the latest in aero flight gear installed, and a Razium thruster drive engine. It was an amazing technological achievement. Its armored prow was smooth and tapered, the rivets almost hidden within its craftsmanship. It was made with Arcanium Alloyinum, the same material that the Razium had used for their space vessels and had given them the ability to withstand most weapons and even reentry heat. The Lance stretched back to a gun port of six of the large Laser Pulsers and had other ports for smaller arms fire as well. Lastly, it had a Nova Dev cannon that could be used to fire blasts that would destroy most ships with one hit, though it took a lot of energy to use and it had to recharge. The solar sails of the zeppelin could be pulled down and its outer hull folded over the deck as the bridge rose through the floor to create a command deck for off surface exploration. It had never been tested outside the atmosphere though, but the scientists and Arcanium Artificer engineers that built it were sure it could handle the extreme conditions.

As amazing as it was though, it was far outclassed by the bigger, more advanced ship coming up behind it with astounding speed. The Lord's Wrath had already closed and started its attack run, firing on the Lance.

The Lance jerked but was holding up under the bombardment it was taking on the rear and side panels. With its Tryonic energy fields and Arcanium armor it was capable of withstanding most weapons, and even the heat of Dragon fire. But the superior weaponry of the Wrath was taking its toll and it wouldn't be long before the Lance would come down.

The Lance was trying to out maneuver its pursuer, to no avail, the smaller Spear fighters were harrying it on its sides so it couldn't take countermeasures to out maneuver the larger ship.

The Razium flagship was a monster of a ship, almost as big as one of the Typhos class Warbirds that had been destroyed against the Dragons during the Affinity Wars of Unity. It was capable of spaceflight, but it wasn't in space. The behemoth was flying close to the ground and closing as it bombarded the quarry that only minutes ago eluded it. Blue and red beams flew from its exterior hull, as it was raining laser fire upon the smaller warship to knock out the shields. The lower grey armor panels of the massive ship were pulled in to give a swifter gate over the gravity of the planet, and it had worked, having caught up to the Skylance and was now almost right on top of her.

They were being chased. Matias had hoped they would get out with less resistance. With so many options and with so many targets to choose from, but it seemed they would still have to fight their way free. Lincoln looked out the observation port; to see laser beams almost hit the window, the rumblings of taking shots to the rear and trying to evade capture in his ears. He pulled his head back with a frightened yelp. Matias ducked his head through and walked in the cabin, Lincoln looked up relieved to see him.

"Let's get you to a safer area, it's getting dangerous." "Ok." Lincoln said, and stood up to go. Lincoln had been thinking of the people they had left behind since the attack. He was worried about them. This whole thing was horrible. This was supposed to be a party for his Uncle. Now it was all gone. He had been ripped away from what he knew. He had a sick feeling this had happened before, but couldn't remember when or where, just that he had had this feeling before. He had been having feelings like this for some time now. Memories, and it was only getting worse. As he and Matias walked through the next door Lincoln asked, "Uncle, what about the people, will Eric be okay, Leena and our family and friends?" Matias looked at him and placed a reassuring hand on his shoulder. "The Creator will protect," he said, "Don't worry; now get strapped in, it is going to get bumpy."

Lincoln jumped in a seat and pulled his seatbelt tight across his hips and then his shoulders locking the mechanisms into place. There was a rumble and blasts all around. Matias smiled after he had made sure Lincoln was buckled. "It's just like racing back from the field after drills, don't worry." Matias winked and walked out the door, Lincoln looked up as Saul came in, closing it behind him in the small side hatch. "Don't worry Linc, we will get out of this. The Commander never loses, you know that." Saul said smiling, buckling in beside him. Lincoln gulped, and nodded. He looked down at his hand. It was glowing slightly.

Matias ducked and walked through the door to the weapons room, he looked at the gunner. Ian, Saul's brother, the younger of the twins. "Well, what are you waiting for an invitation, get that gun up there." Ian smiled, as he had it primed and ready. The top hatch opened with the clank of gears and the big cannon rose to the top of the vehicle ready to deal death. The huge weapon was called a Dragon Cannon, and like its namesake was a massive force of destruction, and one of the few things that could hurt those legendary beasts. As the weapon port opened the wind whipped in the opening bringing with it the smell of ozone and gunpowder. "Now that's a sweet taste, you got a love that smell in the morning son," Matias said laughing. The port closed around the base of its stand and Matias looked to Ian sitting at the control panel. He gave the thumbs up that the gun was locked onto its target. Matias nodded and the weapon roared to life.

* * *

On the bridge of the Lord's Wrath, Stren Norn Senior Captain of the ship awaited the news from his communicator. "Sir they have taken out two more of our fighters." The Captain looked at the helmsman beside him for answers. "They are fighting hard sir, but now we are in range." After a few seconds Captain Norn looked down. "What is the trouble?"

"The magno beam is not holding them, the design of their vessel is compromising it sir." "Well then," Captain Norn raised his eyebrows, standing ramrod straight. "We will have them, use the Nails." He said. The helmsman looked up alarmed, wanting to ask if he was sure, the nails could damage the vessel considerably. "Commence pull in and capture. We want them alive after all." Norn said slightly tipping his head, his smugness oozing from him. "Yes sir," the other replied nodding.

"Oh do be careful, with that ship," the Captain added, "we don't want to damage the prize. I will give the good news to Lord Nemsor myself, Carry on." Norn stated as he left the bridge of the ship.

Lord's Wrath had closed on the Lance and looked as if it was about to ram the other ship, but thrusters ignited when it was less than two hundred feet from it. The flaps on its sides and rear opened, front thrusters igniting to slow it as it descended upon the smaller ornately crafted vessel. The Wrath was now one hundred yards off the aft of the Lance and closing. The forward lower section of the larger ship started to open like the mouth of some metallic air predator, readying its titanic maw to suck its prey down in the dark of its belly. The metal of the large ship shuttered, the gears and hydraulic mechanisms operating and groaning as the front opened wide enough to engulf the Skylance whole.

The crew of the Confederate ship that had been watching in alarm and seeing its lower prow open, started yelling. "A monster, shoot, run, it's going to swallow us!" The Captain of the Lance, Quince, a scrappy veteran of countless wars and one of the few men Matias trusted, knew they were caught. He watched the ships close on the screen, and the weapon inside its hull lower. Seeing the huge harpoon like heads of the weapons they called the Nails gleam as the sunlight hit their sharpened heads; made him feel sick. His stomach lurched. Those things would destroy his ship. He moved across the bridge to the speaker, and grabbed the mic, knowing it might be his last flight. "They have us men, get ready for a fight. We do our duty for the Confederate, and our Prince." He looked around the bridge at his crew and nodded. "Get ready boys, be brave, we are gonna give them all they want. They can come at us, but they will be pulling back nubs after what we give em." He stated, his rough accent coming through, laughing as he did. Though it wasn't much, it was able to calm the crew until they lurched as the larger ship took them.

With the magno beam on them they had a chance of getting away, but the Nails were a different story. Huge spikes 30 feet long, with grapples that extended into the armor to the ship when the tip of the spike breached. The spikes were attached to huge chains and coils made from the hardest metals of the Razium. Once in the armor of the ship no matter how fast you were, there was no getting away from them as you were pulled in. They were crude but very effective, like the Zajust, and one of the Zajust warship designs that the Razium had adopted. Clanks and rumblings sounded as the concussive force of the Nails boomed. Three were launched and two ripped in to the armor to the lance smashing into its aft. The third glanced from the shield and armor plating, falling from the mouth of the Lords Wrath like a lolling tongue. It was raised back with the others as the Lance was pulled toward the larger craft. Lords Wrath moved forward over the Lance, engulfing it and pulling it inside, like a bass eating a minnow. The magno beam had them as well and now there was no escape. A large metallic arm from the rear of the vessel moved toward the Lance. The bang and clanks of the cables and the force of the magno beam now holding it bucked the Skylance, sending shudders and groans through it.

The huge arm reached from the inner belly of the open Razium warship, the large blunt pincher shaped claw reaching for and grasping the Skylance. The claw pulled and the Lance jerked backward, sending its crew and passengers sprawling. The Lance was being pulled further into the bowels of the Wrath, the shadow of the others prow casting ominous darkness over the royal vessel. As it was drawn in the hanger, smaller bolted arms were moving in patterns toward it. Patterns that had meant death for countless other ships, and now were doing the same to this one; soon the Skylance would become another trophy for the Zajust. The Wrath had them completely inside, and it grew dark, the prow closing shut.

Smaller mechanical arms were moving down from the gantries on both sides of the Skylance. They had hand like mechanisms, and on the end of those digits were screw drivers, levers, and all sorts of tools that would be found in the most advanced mechanics box. First the small Zeppelin and sails were cut, and then the metallic hands grabbed the armor of the thruster drive on the back of the ship, dismantling it from the rear in a few seconds of whirling gears, tools, and noise. The pieces were carried to the walls and placed on the racks there.

Next the arms grabbed the sides of the warship. The Nails were removed and the damaged plates were pried from the sides of the ship by other various instruments, then the undercarriage and so on. The veering noises of drills and tools working, flooded the area.

Captain Norn had ordered it and so it was done, the Skylance was being completely dismantled. Large flood lights had lit into being, as the gantry cranes were furiously working. After the front doors of the mighty ship had been shut, the Razium Legionnaires came flooding in the cargo bay. They surrounded the Skylance that was now hanging, suspended from the upper sections from large cranes, the mechanical arms having withdrawn. The Legionnaires stood down the walkway like statues with a close interval between themselves. They were holding their carbine rifles at port, arms two count position. A team of breachers had moved toward the hatch of the Skylance and after a few seconds of checking the doors backed away. The team leader turned to his subordinate pulling up his goggles, "Go get me the..." He stopped in mid-sentence and quickly snapped to attention. His purple skin marked him as a full Razium and he knew his Zajust Lord when he saw him. "My Lord," he said as all straightened in unison, the clack of boots heels hitting each other sounded through the cargo area.

Coming down the walkway flanked by two massive Anusiya Cyber Guard was Nemsor Vaul. The other black armored Zajust that had been with him on the bridge followed them. The Anusiya monster machines with him were clad in black armored plates that fit their bodies, leading to cables on their armor that were full of unknown toxins and steroids. They wore breather masks attached to their smooth helmets; they were armed and incredibly muscled.

CHAPTER 14. RUNNING IN THE SKY:

Ten miles west of the fortress of Anstone, Atlantioc

Matias bucked as the vehicle shuddered. He pressed a button on the cockpit console opening a channel into the hatch holding Lincoln. "Soldier," he said, "Protect him with your life." "Duty and Honor sir," Saul replied. "Duty and honor." Matias said back and closed the channel. Lincoln knew it was getting rough and just as he was about to ask Saul about what to expect, the whole cabin spun as he heard metal clanks and explosions outside. It sounded as if they were getting taken apart. He could hear the whine of the turbo engine revving toward full speed and the guns blasting at their pursuers. Another jerk, and he felt sick as he came to a sudden stop not knowing fully what had happened.

* * *

The bang and clanks of the metal buckling rocked the Skylance sending shudders through the craft. The Confederate soldiers inside looked around as they heard the strains of the armor, the force of the magno grapple pulling the ship to its extremes, as they were jerked from their feet. The ship lurched and started to slow, the engines howling with the pressure. Then it moved backwards. "What is that?" one of the soldiers asked the fear in his face giving doubt to those around him. A grim scarred warrior wearing the badge of a Chaplain stepped through the soldiers. He was the commander of the men, their most senior officer in the hold. He looked at the soldier that spoke, his gaze moving to meet the others as well. Seeing the looks on their faces, he knew he needed to rally these people or they were done for. The Chaplain was dressed in the dark colors of his station with his vest robes over his shoulder armor. He was older in years having been in countless battles, but his eyes still gleamed as that of a young man. "What are you looking at, it's nothing but war boy," he said with a smile through his grey mustache. "Now get below. All of you fall back to the middle of the ship; get your weapons and courage ready, I think we are going to have guests." The soldiers and civilians in the hold started moving and the Chaplain emphasized the point as he held up his large tri barreled handgun, "Move!" He spat.

The Chaplain had moved them to an area in the middle of the ship, setting soldiers on either side of the corridor the Razium would have to come through. The remaining people and crew were in front of the Royal room of the Prince and the Razium only had one entrance or exit to get to them. The Chaplain knew it was going to be a rough fight, and he wanted to give them a chance, also the bulkhead hatch of the Skylance was well protected and would be hard to breach. The Lance stopped moving with a bang, and he looked up and closed his eyes as he touched the small cross covered book locked around his neck.

The soldiers in the corridor were waiting, ready to give their lives for the Prince and the Confederates. The Chaplain had explained to fight then fall back, using granados to seal the way and stall the advancing forces. The soldiers that had volunteered had gone to their respected positions and waited. They had been there for what seemed like forever since they had stopped hearing the noises of gears and machines outside the ship. The men were brave; they sat, sweating in their fatigues and M1 helms, waiting. Now there was nothing. It was quiet. It seemed even the noise from the outside had stopped like there was no activity at all, as if they had been freed and were just floating in silence.

The side of the corridor exploded, ripping open the ship blasting the soldiers from their positions, any who were left alive were lying on the floor tone deaf from the explosion.

Before the smoke cleared a huge black armored form entered, the smoke swirling around him bringing the nightmare to life. It was the Zajust Lord that had been by Nemsor's side, and his name was Vangel. Vangel was helmetless, but only the massive silhouette, huge green jaw, and red eyes could be made out in the smoke. The monster held twin axes that were alight around the edges with a sinister gleam. With a roar upon his lips the creature charged.

Of the vanguards plan to fall back sealing their way, there was nothing left as all had been killed. The soldiers that were alive in the corridor tried to fall back, firing their rifles sporadically desperately trying to hit the monster. They watched in horror as the bullets bounced off, the weapons of the Confederates no match for the Razium armor. The creature stalked the corridor eliminating all threats, his axes flying in whirlwinds of gore, any opposing him being cut to ribbons. The Zajust Berserker seemed to be feeding on the killing, getting more enraged with each death stroke he landed.

After the initial wave there was little to no resistance. The Confederate soldiers and crew in the next corridor had already fallen back to the center of the ship for a final stand. The Chaplain was in the middle of the battle line, trying to calm the horror struck people. He was chanting verses of a book he had clasped in a chain by his waist, and trying to rally the troops with rousing oratory. It seemed to work as the soldiers stopped their panicking and slowly started joining him.

"We can hold. They are nothing to us. The Creator guides your hands this day, and will deliver these creatures to us. We will win or we will be proud when we meet him in the afterlife, do not be scared for fear is in your mind. We don't fear, we are fear, we are soldiers of Anstone. The memories of our families go with us and we will make these Razium pay!!! Are you with me?" he roared. The soldiers listened realizing they could only fight. They had to fight. The Chaplin started the Battlehymn of the Paladin.

"For this day, I have my shield, to return with it to my mother."

Slowly the soldiers started singing with him and as he grew louder they grew louder. He had convinced them, they believed! He gave a yell, and they cheered with him as he turned to meet the monster advancing around on them.

The Chaplain bellowed, "Hold." The singing came to a stop as Vangel came around the corner, weapons raised. Seeing the creature the Chaplain aimed the tri barrel .44 caliber Blazer hand gun and shouted, "Now men fire, for the Prince, for the Confederates!"

It would have been a glorious end for them, shots firing and bullets tearing through the Zajust. It would have been honorable and if the Berserker would have made it to them, it would have been a hero's death straight out of the story books. It didn't happen that way.

The Chaplain gave the order and as he did the Zajust, stopped advancing. The huge panting beast stopped his rampage completely and slowly stepped backward.

The soldiers had their weapons raised but they wouldn't fire, as if the weapons had minds of their own. Something, a force was moving the rifles the soldiers held. With dread they realized the weapons were slowly turning. They were turning them, to point at each other. The men cried in panic, only the Chaplain, through sheer force of will was able to keep his large blazer pistol raised. Sweat dripped off his brow from the effort, the runes on the weapon alight with the power that was being used to control him.

Vangel was still panting from the battle, and watched the soldiers weapons turn on them. He cared little for the magic and was reluctant to stop, he wanted more slaughter, more war. However he knew his master's wishes and feeling his presence behind him, he had stood aside as the huge shape of Lord Nemsor Vaul walked past. His cape billowed behind him as he came, his cloak hiding his dark face shaped helm covering him, allowing only his burning eyes and flat v nose piece to be seen through the shadows of the corridor. The dark armor he wore matched the gauntleted hand he had raised and moved, controlling the last defenders of the Skylance. They couldn't fire without killing themselves. Nemsor walked toward them, seeing the Chaplain fighting his power; he was fascinated.

He watched as the Chaplain gritted his teeth, a small bead of sweat rolled down his face. He was winning, with supreme will the Chaplain shrugged the Magnus power from him and pulled the trigger firing his pistol. He let out a breath of triumph, his eyes wide in jubilation. The shot was deafening as there was no other sound in the ship. The bullet flew toward the dark lord, but as it did it slowed and all watched. Nemsor Vaul, squeezed his pointer finger and thumb together, slowing the shell as it came toward him. It had almost stopped as it reached him suspended in front of him, still spinning from being shot from the grooved barrel of the tri blazer pistol. He held his gauntleted hand under the floating bullet, allowing it to float, spinning a few inches above his hand. He looked through his mask at the soldiers. They were terrified. Sweat rolled down the faces as they still tried to fight with the weapons they pointed at each other, pleading with themselves not to pull the triggers.

The Chaplain whispered, "Old power," as the realization came into his eyes of who this man was. It crushed his heart, for he had known him. Nemsor looked at him, their eyes locking. "Traitor, Demon!" The Chaplain roared. With a flick of his middle and forefinger Nemsor sent the bullet back at him, directly into his chest. It punctured the armor plate he wore. The grizzled man looked down then back at the evil warrior before him. "I know who you are," he whispered, and collapsed on the floor. Nemsor moved and Vangel launched himself at the rest.

The soldiers, crew, and other passengers of the Skylance were being rounded up as Nemsor and his Anusiya guard entered the area marked with the Chevron and the Lion, the royal seal of the Confederates. The whole ship had been searched and they had found all who remained taking most prisoner. Only the Prince was left and he was locked in this command room, of Matias there had been no sign. One of the elite Razium grenadiers was standing outside the Prince's door, his helm, armored coat and mask breather on as he stood guard. A mechanic was on his knees by the door working on the lock. Nemsor walked through the corridor. "Is it unlocked?" The mechanic nodded moving back from the mechanism. "It is unlocked Lord, and there is only one person inside. He is yours." He said tapping the lock pad as he stood. The door was pulled back with a whoosh of hydraulics. Nemsor walked in. "Hello my Prince, it has been too long," he said but stopped, as he saw the young man before him. Eric, Lincoln's friend looked at the Lord of the Razium with contempt in his eyes, and smiled saying, "Oops, you have the wrong boat?"

* * *

The tanks of the Confederates were fast. Wartraks they called them, for the speed and maneuverability of the more advanced stabilized track system they had been built with. That and it was hard to follow them unless you could see them. Their track indentions being engineered to cover themselves so they couldn't easily be followed. Also, most of the vehicles had been fitted with mini cloaking devices. It was a design created so the enemy at the time, the Dragons, couldn't spot them from the air. A smaller version of the ones on the Razium Cruisers. The Wartraks were track amphibious vehicles built for the King's Spartan Paladins and used during the Affinity Wars. Built with the best Razium technology and Green Artificer know how.

They had been used to deliver the warriors of the Spartan Paladins into the caves and Spires of the Dragons, the Ice fortresses of the Jutonn, and the Layers of the Krakens of Lagosha, to name a few. These tanks were all but impervious to harm with the armor plating reinforced with Arcanium Alloyinum. A few flakes of this precious magic metal were dropped in each batch of plates. It made them extra durable. The metal was able to be heated differently, making it lighter which allowed them to keep speed and maneuverability without losing durability. They were outfitted with a large caliber weaponry, but main Dragon Cannon was its true power. It was a very powerful weapon that could pierce the hides of the Dragons, and most anything else for that matter. They were large vehicles and had transport capability to hold a squad of soldiers, with various other rooms, such as a mess, and small bunks built in.

In the breakout Matias had sent the commanders of his armies in different directions to save lives and hopefully throw the Razium off the trail of the Prince. Unfortunately, the scout ships, Cannon Trucks, and Hover Blades of the Razium had been able to tail all of them while the Lord's Wrath followed the Skylance. They had fought at first, the superior armor and weapons of the huge Wartanks seeing them through the hardest of the fighting. However, the Razium had kept too many reinforcements to deal with, and in the end they had to flee. Of the two left from the battles, one was already damaged from their most recent fight, and both were being chased.

The Wartraks had been weaving and dodging cannon fire as they drove west through the mountain regions of the southeast Confederate. They had lost one of their number already but had taken a heavy toll on the Razium as they fought their way past the blockades. Their Dragon Cannons taking out all the Razium air support that had pursued them. They had made good time at first, but now the Cannon Trucks were closing.

Cannon Trucks were a type of vehicle, made from a stripped down t-300 truck chassis, with a large motor that put out 600 horse power, and a wider base that allowed them to maneuver faster than normal and still hold the large cannons on their beds. Though they were mostly engine and cabin, they also had a large flat bed with small sides and foot holds so troops could jump on and off with relative ease. They were cheap but effective shock unit delivery systems, and each could carry fifteen or so of the Razium mercenaries. Mercenaries were a flattering name for the men. They were more like Razium lackeys and stooges, basically pledges that were in it for the spoils of war. They looked like rag tag dirty things, wearing scraps of other army's clothes, weapons, and broken goggles. They weren't bounty hunters like the Cowboys, Hounds, or Rogues of Erach, no they were common trash. Some were from other races, and some just turncoat humans. Either way they were all scum and easy to pay when out so far; and money scarce.

The furthest tank back had been hit in the side by their powerful cannons, and had taken damage to the hull. With the damage it had already sustained on its thick caterpillar tread, it was all it could do not to spin out of control. The driver evaded another blast, and his luck was holding so far, but it was about to run out.

The Razium knew they had weakened the tank and poured it on. The last swerve allowed the driver to outmaneuver the blast from the truck on his flank. However, it was a ruse. The Razium truck that had been following directly behind the Wartrak had locked on to it. A direct hit from the Beam Cannon on its bed ripped through the tread of the wounded vehicle. It spun out of control as the treads went flying causing the huge irreplaceable machine to crash into the mountainside. Its core cells ruptured, and it exploded as two larger Beam Cannon shots penetrated its cracked armor. It detonated in a small mushroom cloud. The force of the blast causing the trucks to swerve, almost tipping one. The last tank was still going, but the Razium picked up the chase again. Now, there was only one of the revered machines left, and the Cannon Trucks were right behind it.

The trucks were running hot getting closer to the last of the venerable war tanks. The tank took an evasive maneuver; spinning on a dime it turned to face the oncoming horde of scrap metal and guns. As it did it raised its Dragon cannon and the front mounted .60 caliber machine guns in its side compartments folded out. The huge guns opened fire. The mercenaries weren't ready for the sudden change in tactics and the spray of metal death and noise made the driver jerk the wheel of the lead truck. The shot from the truck's cannon went wide, the beams bursting harmlessly over the battle tank. The leader of the mercs yelled and hooped at them. "Go, go!" he yelled, "Shoot them now!" The leader was in the cabin of the second truck. He was a cocky ex-soldier turned mercenary named Ike. Ike was average height with a close cropped blond beard that was covered in dirt, though his clothes were those of a man that worked for one of the city fortresses. Whether he stole them or bought them was another story. Ike realized too late he had just been outmaneuvered by the war machine. His soldiers wouldn't be much of a fight for that tank when it wasn't running from them.

Ike started yelling orders at his underlings. The first truck didn't know what to do as the Dragon Cannon of the tank fired, tearing directly through its cab and crankshaft. The explosion causing it to flip in the air as it was torn in two, throwing everyone from the bed. The Beam Cannon that had been mounted on it, hit the ground dislodging the fire mechanism. It exploded, creating a small mushroom cloud of its own, and the concussive force knocked the third truck off its frame, toppling some of the mercenaries to the ground. The truck was able to right itself just-in-time to have the .60 caliber guns tear through the front of it, obliterating the driver. The vehicle lost control turning sideways, flipping and exploding when it stopped. The last truck turned sharply and tried to maneuver around as Ike, was shouting orders. "Turn this thing around, you. Move, move they've got that Dragon Cannon on us, go, go!" he yelled.

Ike heard the silence of the air heating, and knew that sound. He jumped out of the cab, landing with a crunch and rolling. He scrambled away from the truck, looking back just in time to see it explode fifty yards from him, the wreckage going everywhere. He ducked his head, the dirt crusted goggles he wore protecting his eyes from the light of the explosion.

Ike kept his head down, hoping that the driver of the tank didn't see him leap off.

Moments passed and he waited, listening, as the tank drove close to the wreckage. Probably scanning for survivors, he thought as he kept his head down in the dirt, trying to keep from coughing and moving. The engine of the tank revved and it drove off, turning its heading west in the direction it was going before it was attacked. After a few minutes of lying in the dirt Ike stood up, coughing, hacking up a big dust ball. Dust was all that was left of his men as Ike stumbled toward his right, looking at the receding form of the tank heading into the sun. He surveyed his destroyed trucks, still on fire. "Damn!" he yelled, at no one in particular kicking the ground. He shook his head, and started walking.

*　*　*

Matias let out a deep breath as he sat in the cockpit. His plan had worked. While the Razium chased the Skylance, other ships and vehicles had gotten away in the tank, though at a great cost. He had wanted all three of the tanks intact. They were relics of the old wars and he thought they would need them. The men and women on those tanks were good soldiers, and people that would be missed. He paused. He hoped the crew of the Lance had made it, and he hated to put the others in harm's way but the prince was what mattered. "Bor," he said to his Sergeant. "Set a course and continue west." "Yes sir. Any heading in particular sir?" He asked. "No Sergeant, just watch for any interference and cloak us. Also, make sure you stay out of the mountain ranges. I want to stay away from the damned Dragon wastes and their Cowboys and Gangsters. We have had enough trouble for now." "I agree." Bor replied, setting the course then looking back to Matias sitting behind him in the cockpit. Matias looked at him, "What are you thinking?" He asked. "We need to get to White city," Bor said. "That is probably what they expect us to do though. It's just. I just don't know how that monster ship could have gotten past the blockades or the battle lines without someone realizing it. Matias, we didn't even know it was there, didn't even pick it up on our sensors. It doesn't seem right." He finished staring down. "I agree." Matias added. "Sabotage, and that hurts worse if it's true. So should we head to the White City, or look for someone to help us?"

"Most of the Loks are in the city readying for the meeting of the Council, and we aren't going to hear from Le or the others for a few days."

"What about one of the cities loyal to the crown?" Bor asked. "Perhaps, but the cities are... well I want to stay away from them. For now let's just stay with the plan, we will meet with Le Kai and the others and find out what they know and move from there. I know something will show itself." Bor agreed as the tank sped off into the sun.

* * *

Nemsor, stepped with menace toward the Captain, "You said we had them." Captain Norn was wide eyed, trying not to let it show how terrified he was. "My Lord," he managed but stopped. His Captains pins on the sides of his collar moved, he looked down and was shocked as he was lifted to the ceiling, hitting it with a loud clank. Nemsor stood under him hand raised waiting for the reply. "What was that?" Nemsor asked. "It seems your Captaincy is a burden on you, I can alleviate that." He finished. Only gargling could be heard as all the officers and command watched. Captain Norn couldn't talk as the metal pins and buttons on his collar were flat against the metal of the ceiling pulling on his throat. The small shoulder protectors and other metal items of his uniform holding him in place. With a smooth calm voice Nemsor said, "I cannot tolerate lying, and the boy here," he turned holding out his hand toward the boy the Grenadiers where holding a few feet away. "Is not the Prince we are looking for." His already deep voice had started to rise. "You have let me down Captain. If I can't trust my officers then who can I trust?" Nemsor asked. All the Razium around him felt his power, they felt the raw aggression and the dark energy he exuded, and most of the metal on their uniforms moved slightly when he flexed that power. Captain Norn tried to answer but couldn't, his eyes were red and straining and he couldn't breathe, a large vain bulged on his temple. Nemsor turned to a random trooper that was walking by carrying a metal chunk of the ship that had been blasted from the hull. Using the Magnus he flicked his fingers at the trooper, launching him back punching him through the wall to smack hard in the next room. He had kept the Captain frozen above them with his other hand letting him watch. The Captain gurgled.

Finally, Nemsor Vaul let him drop to the floor with a loud clack. He looked back and motioned for the armored Grenadiers to bring the boy. "This is not the boy, find the boy or his punishment shall be yours." Nemsor pointed to the downed soldier he had thrown in the next room. "Captain," Nemsor said turning and walking back to his flag ship, his Anusiya in tow. Stren Norn lay there gulping in air; a long drop of blood ran from his nose to his lip and dripped on to the floor. He was covered in sweat; his eyes had broken blood vessels and were horribly red. Wiping his brow he tried to stand, but couldn't. He was on all fours desperately trying to catch his breath. He looked around him, and in a hoarse voice said, "Go, you heard him, go."

As Matias sat in the rear quarters of the large tank with Lincoln, Bor came over the com. "Commander."

"Yes Bor, go ahead."

"Sir we are intercepting a coded signal sir."

"And?" Matias asked.

"Well sir its Royal frequency, it's looking for us. No one but us could intercept it sir." Matias looked at Lincoln. They both stood going to the cockpit. The door opened and they walked in. "I have it decoded, here." Bor pushed a small button on the right of the console. A hologram face of a man appeared and started to speak. His voice was soothing, just like a politician.

"Commander, Commander Matias, I hope this finds you well. My people intercepted a coded signal from a city in the Southern Confederates. It was cut off after a few minutes of broadcasting but I was able to intercept and decode it. I am sorry, my manners. I know you sir, you might not remember me. I am Councilor Nabis, Holder of the house of Aveion, and Acolyte of Lok Master Zen, one of the 12 as you know. I have heard that the fortress of Anstone had been attacked by a Razium Super Cruiser? How one had gotten through the Southern barricades was beyond me, but rest assured I will find out. I have information that they sought a Royal young man of the fortress there. I hope he is unharmed, I can only glean that it is him, the true Prince of our nation. I know this comes as and at a horrible time, and I am sorry for your losses, but I am also rejoiced to know the Prince of the Confederates is alive and with you now. I know you Commander and if you are with him it really is true. I support you as well, and want to lend you aid. I have encrypted this message and it will play for three days. Only one possessing a Royal seal interceptor can hear it. I would like to arrange a meeting, and then we can escort the Prince to the White city together. I assure you my men are quite adept and capable of stopping another attack. Use the code at the beginning and the end of this message to contact me and I can lead you to my manor. I will leave it up to you. At the end of three days I will have feared the worst. May the Creator Protect." The face disappeared and all was silent.

"This seems too good to be true," Bor said looking up at Matias. "I know, he just happens to find out, but that doesn't seem right either. I do know him, he was young and new to the council when I met him, an aspiring Councilor. Seems he has grown in power. His master, Zen, he was a member I wish we could have found instead. We don't have much of a choice." Matias thought about it. "Bor, get a message to Le Kai, tell him...." Matias was interrupted as the message started playing again. "Commander, Commander," Bor touched the button and the message went silent. "Sorry sir."

Matias nodded. "Send a signal to any of our warriors that are left. Try to contact Le Kai and any other Spartans you can, find out how far away they are from us. Give me an update when you know. We need to meet with them if we can, and I need to know who Le has with him, because if we do meet this Nabis, I want as many of us as I can get." Lincoln spoke up. "I have a good feeling about this Uncle. We will make it." Matias looked at him. "Always optimistic," he said smiling at the boy, "I pray your right."

II

"The only good Elf is a....Actually there is no such thing as a good elf, at all. "

-Boss Dillion to his guests-

CHAPTER 15. STEPPING IN IT:

City of Royal, Kissar owned Human side of the city, nicknamed the Kiss

The rain had let up and the fog had blown out, allowing the sun to show through the dark clouds of the monstrous metropolitan city. It was mid-day and the sky had lightened but was still mostly grey. Walker had left Han Fords, and was following the directions that Snorri had given him to find the church. He noticed the smell wasn't quite as good in this part of the city, and the further he was getting from the richer part of the city, the more run down it looked. The colored large awnings and buttresses disappeared in favor of grey brick and mortar; and low overhangs.

Bridges ran from building to building, and the shops were smaller, built on top of each other and looked more run down. Most had cracks in the walls and small dark side alleys. As he walked down the street, the people that were out looked at him and swiftly walked away or didn't look up at all. Even the shop owners were quiet here. Not like the hustle and bustle of the main gates or the middle of the city for sure. They seemed like they knew that he was trouble. They might be right he told himself, and a church here, it made sense. The poor needed hope.

As Walker thought about it he came upon a man, a thin shop keep that seemed not to mind him walking up to his store. Actually he didn't seem to even notice. The small man was sweeping and didn't even acknowledge the warrior looking in his shop. Walker looked in the windows and through the open door, trying to be nice. The store had trinkets and sculptures, little knick knacks, and herbs. After a few seconds the shop keep seemed to startle. He acted as if Walker wasn't a huge man looking in his shop and had just appeared out of thin air.

The little man gathered himself. "See anything you like there big fella?" Walker looked at him. The man looked half crazy. He was clean shaven except for a wispy white goatee and had wild brown hair with white streaks. His red faded apron hung over drab pants and a shirt that was too big for him. He was still sweeping, in the same spot as he waited for an answer. "Yes, actually. Do you sell herbs, and pills?" The man looked at Walker, his eyebrow rising suspiciously. "Yeah, but notin illegal I tell ya." He said quickly his accent making him sound faster than he was really talking. He stopped sweeping, holding his very used broom; still just looking at Walker. "No, I know," Walker said. "I'm not the authorities. I need a special pill, I think you can you help me out." Walker said, and as he did he showed the man a coin he had in his palm. "Oh, of course. Where are me manners, do come in."

Walker followed him into the shop. It smelled. Walker blinked his eyes. It was stinky. The shop keep jumped behind his counter and looked at Walker expectantly. "Cru Nak?" Walker asked. The shop keeper nodded. "Oh yes, I see, I haven't heard anyone ask for that in a while," he said and a crooked smile came to his thin face, "Healing something ehh, I have it rit ere." He laughed then scuttled away to the back of the store. Listening to the man Walker heard something break and something else roll across the floor. Then, well he didn't know what that last noise was, maybe a cat? He waited looking at the oddities in the shop, listening. With a little more rumbling and jumbling, glass hitting the floor, and some cussing that he couldn't make out, the man finally hooped in triumph. Walker watched as he came back dusting himself off. "Here you are sir, just the thing for ye." Walker looked at him and then smelt the odd looking pills. He nodded and handed him the coin. "Thank you." Walker said and turned toward the door. "No sir, thank you, and if there is anything else you need let me know," he added as he bit the coin and then tucked it away in a pocket on his apron. Walker saw something hanging on a support beam, and looked at the shop keep. He pointed at the item. The shop keep seemed happy, "Oh, yes," he said noticing Walker pointing at it. "I don't know if it works, been here for ages. Go ahead and take it, on the house. You more an covered it anyway." Walker nodded his thanks and slid the item into one of his pouches. Just as walker was about to go out the door, he stopped. Poking his head back in the shop, he asked. "Actually, can you tell me how to get to the nearest church?"

The older man walked to the door and looked out pointing toward the end of the road. "Yes, it's right around the corner. Just go to the end of the street," he was saying, then changed his mind. He thought about it again and told Walker it was just around the corner two blocks up. He finished and was about to say something else but stopped, as a shadow was cast over them. "Well I hope you find it sir." The shop keep hurriedly squeaked, practically jumping back in to his store, slamming and locking the door with a clunk; putting a closed sign up.

Walker had known he was being followed for some time and was happy the perpetrators had finally made themselves known. He turned, and was a little taken to see six guards moving to encircle him; one of which was an Ulthwan and a big one at that. They wore burgundy capes brown britches and dark tops that where tight fitting like an assassin, thief, or trained fighter. All were armed with holstered pistols and blades. Walker was in the middle of the semi circle the shop at his back, and staring straight at the Ulthwan. The Ogre was over seven feet tall and over half as broad, but slightly hunched. He wore a huge folded back cape with a burgundy and brown jerkin that barely covered his massive chest and gut. The buttons looked as if they would pop at any moment. He had a flat face and his hair was tied in a tail and pulled up behind his head. Only two others stood out as any threat. One to his left was decent sized with a mustache, and wore a holstered gun on each leg. One of the men following him from earlier. The smaller one behind him was dressed different. He had the traditional garb of a Soa Lin monk. He wore beige pants and slightly armored shoulder guards on his jacket with dark brown and closed toed sandals. On his head he wore a mask that was tight fitting and covered most of his head, but the eye holes were large and didn't hide much of his face. The mask was padded though, as to be able to give some protection. Walker knew this mask and had seen its wearers in action before, they were deadly at close quarters fighting. The monk's hands were tucked in his sleeves. The others were forgettable, and seemed to be this cocky only because the brooding Ulthwan leading them.

"I was wondering what you were asking that poor man to make him run so fast?" The large Ulthwan said in an Isle accented voice. He seemed to be panting and slightly snarling as he talked, his warm not so fresh breath hitting Walker in the face. "We don't take to no one oos causin trouble, no matter what he looks like. Savey?" Walker looked at the Ogre then the others around him. A short man to his left spoke up in an accented and slightly squealed voice. "Aye, Big Earl is talking to you, you better answer." Walker's face hardened, and the man shrank back as Walker's stare bore holes through him. The Ulthwan was getting anxious as he saw the look he was giving the men, and the way they reacted. He looked at the pendent on Walkers chest and saw the plain chevron emblem. "A war hero huh, well that don't go round my town," he snarled. "So you gonna answer me or..." Walker slowly turned his stone glare on the beast in front of him, and the creature almost lost his nerve, then he got angry and it was all over.

The Ulthwan grabbed Walker pulling him toward him, Walker reacted before any of the incompetents could move, slapping the huge Ogre in the face distracting him. As he did Walker grabbed his palm twisting his massive arm to the right extending it fully and pulling him down, then he thrust his knee in the middle of the Ogres elbow breaking the joint with a loud crack. It sounded as if a two by four board had just been snapped in two. The monster yelled and tried to get away throwing his other hand out so as not to fall on his face. Using its own momentum to his advantage, Walker twisted the limp arm turning the Ogre slamming him to the ground with a thump, the pain excruciating, leaving him barely conscious. The others started to react but had to jump out of the way of the falling Ogre. Walker lashed out with the back of his hand smashing the bigger one in the face, breaking teeth and sending him sprawling to the ground before he could pull his pistols. Spinning, Walker front kicked the other guard square in the chest, breaking bones as the man flew at the monk who hadn't moved since this began. The guard landed face first, smashing it on the road. The monk just moved to the side watching him hit. The rest ran, leaving the monk looking at Walker. He said nothing, his hands still tucked into his sleeves. He gently bowed; looking at the guards on the ground with disgust, turned and walked away. Walker checked the area, making sure no one else was coming and then stood tall and took in the mess he had made of these thugs. "I think I just stepped in it," he said shaking his head.

Royal

The people or lack there of had fled as soon as the Kissar had come upon Walker. He looked at the groaning thugs lying at his feet, and then around the immediate area. Some of the people were looking out their windows to see who had stood up to the Kissar. He knew he would have some more trouble coming soon. The Boss couldn't let a newcomer trash his enforcers without some type of action being taken. Walker shook his head; he needed to find Orson soon. With a shrug he started toward the church again. He felt strange though. He hadn't shaken that feeling of being followed even though the thugs were behind him still pulling themselves from the ground. He looked back over his shoulder, all normal activity had resumed and there was no sign of anyone following him. As the big warrior turned and trotted down the street, a shape came from behind one of the buildings.

It was tall and slender, the features hidden under its cloak. When Walker had left the store after the fight, it tapped something onto a receiver on its wrist, and followed him staying close to the wall and out of sight. It looked at its wrist com and followed Walker.

Walker hoped the shop keeper's directions were good, as the man had to tell him two different ways to get there, but as he rounded the corner there it was. The church was smaller than he had expected and not in the best state, but quaint in its own way. It seemed to have had little repair over the years. Its walls were a whitish grey and it had a red roof that had faded into a muddled orange. He walked up and was greeted by a clergy man in black.

"Hello." The Friar eyed him, noticing his weapons and girth. "We bring no war here stranger," the man said holding his hands up. "Hello Friar, none will be brought. I am here to pay respects." The clergyman's face softened as Walker introduced himself, and they chatted briefly. The Friar shook his hand and moved for him to pass. Walker stepped through the oak doors, and was hit by the scent of leather and old parchment, the fragrance giving him a warm nostalgic feeling; he inhaled the scent.

Its smell brought good memories to him and he started thinking about old times and loved ones. He closed his eyes and stood silent. For the first time in a long time, he felt at peace, his regrets and guilt gone. He felt cleansed. He stopped thinking and opened his eyes looking around. No one was there but it felt as if there was a presence. He continued in, walking down the short aisle toward the front, to the pulpit and the table that was on the floor beneath it. Walker bent to his knees looking at the pulpit, behind it was an alter with a plaque that read, "For the one Creator." There was no idol on it, or any other thing for that matter, only the plaque. Walker bowed his head and looked at one of the leather compartments at his waist.

Opening it, he removed a small dark brown cloth. He laid the cloth on the small table in front of him and started to unroll it carefully. As he did he started talking. "I know it's been too long," he paused continuing to unroll the last of the brown cloth; until it covered the table. He started again. "I, I haven't been who I have needed to be, all this time, all the power I had, I haven't been the man I need to be. I let the ones I care about down, I ...I." He stopped, he didn't know what to say. His mind flooded with things, his memories and his failures. He took a glass bottle filled with weapon ointment that had been rolled in the cloth and undid the top. Then unlatched the big rune covered pouch on his belt, the one he had been relieved to check earlier.

It was large, about six inches in width that could stretch to eight or ten and about that in length as well. Holding the ointment, he made sure the cloth was flat, then set the ointment on it. He undid the latch and opened the large pouch reaching in and pulling something from it. He continued to pull, the light catching the metal of the sword. The sword itself was massive, barely fitting through the opening of the Labrynthian pouch. It shouldn't have been able to fit it was so big.

The pouch or compartment was an enchanted item, a wormhole pocket of the Labrynthian that allowed him to carry things in the small space. It was a special item he had been rewarded with long ago and it had served him well over the years. It also kept whatever was there hidden, undetectable, unless one knew how to open it. Walker looked at the monster blade with familiarity and it reflected him in its massive silver spance. "Havoc," he whispered looking at its golden rune laden pommel, his eyes moving up to the design of his order. The Spartan Chevron on its middle guard. The chevron's tip pointed to the runes starting at the base and running up the length of the huge double edged blade. He laid the massive sword on the cloth with both hands. He was careful not to awaken its runes. It was an Arcanium blade after all, and could be tracked if its magic was invoked. Meaning he could be tracked and that was the last thing he needed. Since the runes on the pouch couldn't be detected, he wouldn't need to worry about it, as long as he didn't actually use the weapon for battle.

Taking the ointment he rubbed it on the blade, speaking low as he did, finishing his prayer thought from earlier. With his head bowed he anointed the blade with the oil, starting the Spartan ritual of cleansing. After he finished he wiped the huge weapon down. He gripped it, and it felt good in his hands. He didn't want to put the sword away, but knew he had to until it was time to actually use it. He returned the blade, slowly sliding it back into the runic covered pouch, the leather swallowing it up, and clicked its latched closed. He unlatched another of the pouches then started to roll the cloth to store it.

He stiffened, slightly looked over his shoulder to his left; hearing them before they entered. Still on his knees, he continued to roll the ointment into the cloth with this right hand and with his left he reached to the pistol grip on his leg. He finished rolling the cloth, tucking it back in his pouch on his side, buttoning it closed. He looked up and softly said. "Guide me."

"Guide you where warrior?" A voice from behind asked. Walker touched the stone floor where a piece of the carpet had frayed away. The stone underneath was old and he could feel the ore in it, his hand tattooing as he let the Magnus flow through him, feeling the vibrations. There were many behind him, five men and a woman about fifteen feet from him, and another five outside. "Who you talking to, don't tell me you believe in that religious hokey bull," the speaker said with a slight twang.

Walker lifted his hand from the floor. With the speed of a great cat he was up on his feet with the gun at his side drawn at the man who was in front of the crew. The barrel was three feet from his face before he could speak or move. Looking down at the frozen mercenary, he said, "I think that's enough out of you, back up." The man did. "Now what do you want with me?" He asked to all of them and the man with the gun in his face started to stutter an answer.

"You, don't talk!" Walker barked. "Who is in charge, cause I know it's not this piece of trash!" The man was about to pee himself. A tall man in the back walked through the mercenaries toward Walker. Walker studied the men. They were of descent build, none as tall as he or nearly as broad, but looked as if they could hold their own in a fight. They wore capes of dark burgundy and walker noticed, two of these were the riders that passed him hours earlier, mud still clinging to them. Also, the one in the very back was thinner. It was the rider who turned and looked at him as they rode by earlier this morning. A woman, watching me the whole time, he thought to himself. He felt something different from her aura but couldn't put a finger on it. She looked at him, the lower half of her face was covered with a scarf, their eyes met and she turned away. The man who had made his way to the front of the group, the supposed leader, spoke up. "Sir," he said. He was darker skinned and had a deep southern accent, Kajun. He was also nicely dressed, in a coat and white slacks, the make very expensive.

"You may lower your weapon. I could tell you were a good soldier, but I did not know that good," he smirked. "My employer would like a word with you, and I assure you it will be worth your time. Besides, I don't want to mess up the church with you blowing young, and stupid I might add, Billy's head off. What do you say; I give you my word as a gentleman of no further hostilities." Walker asked, "Where are you from?"

"Ah yes, where are my manners. Please call me Colonel. I am from the south of this here, let's call it hole. From the most amazing and fun place in this continent, you might know it, a place down south called Lafourche." Walker did know the place. Mostly good people lived in the back woods of the swamps, honorable people. It was a great place to visit, two months out of the year anyway. The rest of the time it was hot and overrun with the wrong kind of people. Some dabbled in the black arts, and that made him suspicious. As he looked at the man, Walker knew this man dabbled as well, he reeked of magic. Walker considered a moment. He knew he could take them, but he didn't know how good a wizard Colonel was, also he wanted to know more about the woman. He might be able to get some info about Orson as well. Either way it would be easier to see what this was about and not have to fight his way out of the city. Walker squinted, then smiled. "Well I know your customs sir, and a gentleman's word is good for me."

"Excellent we have an accord, follow me sir," Colonel said. Walker holstered his side arm and walked through the mercenaries, with the Colonel beside him.

Colonel looked at him, "Your name sir, I didn't get your name?"

"Walker."

"Well, ah Mr. Walker, I am sure you know of my employer by now. This is his city." "I thought the Elves had some of it." Walker added sarcastically. Colonel chuckled. "You have me there sir, but you see my employer, ah he wants you to help with that, turn this city around. I hear you know your way about a good scrap."

"So you know about my fight, not surprising."

"Yes it is my job to be in the know for my employer. Let me tell you about him." As they walked, Walker listened to Colonel babble on about this and that, asking questions, and telling bad jokes.

A figure in tight fitted black leathers and a cloak with the sign of a Dragon and a ship embroidered on the breast, looked down on the small procession as they left the church. She was situated in the shadows, on the top of a building that was across from the church giving her the best vantage point. She stayed in the shade of the building watching as the figures walked away. As the sun came from behind the clouds, its beams hit the shadow area, she was gone. She had other matters to attend to, on the Elven side of Royal.

CHAPTER 16. FRIEND OR FOE:

Kansa, Capitol of the Middle Confederate of Meridion

The large marble columns were resplendently white, as the morning sun shone in between them; casting long shadows over the length of the huge veranda. The sky was blue and the morning dew was still on the grasses and crop of the land that the Councilor looked upon. Lord Octon Nabonidus, or Nabis to his peers, which were few, stood on a balcony of his estate in his long cream colored robes. He was holding a hot cup of coffee as he normally did, looking down into the light brown liquid, over his hawkish nose. He watched the cream he had added swirl around in the cup, the steam coming off it in the not yet heated morning air. He closed his eyes and took a long sniff, taking in the aroma. "Aaah," he said letting out his breath.

He was looking out from his Acropolis at the huge surrounding city below, the roofs red in the rising sun. Another day rises he thought, and then he turned his gaze to the rows of crops off to the east. A knock on the door brought him out of his trance. A courtier had just entered his large estate room and walked around the circular dark varnished table in the middle. He stopped a few feet away from Nabis and waited. "Yes?" Nabis asked, looking back at his coffee. "My Lord, the transmission, we have received a reply." Nabis looked up from his coffee.

Outside Kansa, Capitol of the Middle Confederate of Meridion

The sun was setting on another day and Matias was getting anxious. They had lost or destroyed all their pursuers and he hadn't detected any new ones for the last day or so, but he was still leery. He was sitting in the cockpit of the Wartrak tank staring at the fuel gauge, it was getting low. He reached out and tapped it. Not for the sake of it doing anything or helping the situation. He just did it out of habit. Wishing that this gesture would make it go up again, full. He tapped it again. It didn't move. He looked at his co pilot the younger of the twins, Ian. "How much fuel?" he asked. "About a day and a half sir," the younger man said. "And the cells?" "At full power sir but," Matias interrupted him. "I know soldier. I know, we can't fire the cannon effectively without them." "Yes sir." The young man said back nodding and continuing to drive.

Matias studied him. He was clean shaven in his late teens, he looked green, and Matias knew he was. He was a good solider though, not a Paladin yet, but a good soldier. He followed directions, decent with a sword, and knew the right side of a gun, but had no battle time. The Commander feared his youth might be a detriment. No, he thought, we were all in that position when we were young. He would learn, besides, he was a great pilot. Both of the brothers were. Might be in for some learning soon with the luck we have had, he thought. Looking at him Matias felt for the younger man. He had left his family for the sake of the Prince, and the shot at a better life that he could give the Confederates. He hoped the young man's family had gotten to safety; he prayed that this was worth it.

"The controls are yours Corporal, find a place for us to stop for the night, get me some cover and let me know when you find it." "Aye sir" he replied. Matias stood and stepped to the door leading to the back area of the tank, and touched the control pad. He was going to visit Lincoln, and see how he was holding up. The cockpit door opened with a hiss from the hydro locks. Matias still marveled at the technology that it took to power this amazing vehicle and was saddened at the wars that had reduced it to only the few machines they had left. Even the factories of the northeast couldn't reproduce it effectively, and they were the most advanced of the Confederates. Even with what was left of the Razium technology, there were few who had gotten past the steam power that seemed to be most popular, and to reproduce the parts alone took an immense amount of resources. He hoped when they got to White City the Council could help with that.

He touched the next keypad and walked in to the main hull of the tank, coming upon Sergeant Bor playing a game of War Chess with Lincoln and from the looks of it, getting crushed. The large Master Sergeant, Grankon Bor was slumped over the table concentrating. Sweat was shining on his forehead, and his big fetished beard was flowing to the edge of the table, almost getting in the way. He was very jovial usually and loved to joke, that was until a job needed to get done, and then he turned into a raging giant of battle and one of the best soldiers a commander could ask for. That is the way he looked now, frustrated, only he couldn't hit the figures before him. Matias chuckled as the large man in front of him looked like a child, his tongue out, staring at the game board trying to figure what move to make. Bor was a master player and tactician, though as of late, Lincoln, who he normally would defeat, had been giving him fits. The chuckle brought Bor and Lincoln both around, and Bor looked at Matias. "What? I don't know what to do."

Lincoln looked at him, "It doesn't matter where you go Bor. I've got you this time," he said smiling reclining back. Bor let out a puff. "Yes, I guess you do," The Sergeant turned to Matias, trying to change the subject. "Commander?"

"Oh no, do not let me interfere with this beating." Matias said as he sat down grinning and then continuing. "So, we will be stopping for the night soon. Tomorrow we have to go to a fortress or city that has oil or electric resources. We need fuel to get closer to the White City, and to keep you safe." "What about Master Nabis?" Lincoln asked. Matias looked at Bor, then back at Lincoln. "Well that is a possibility. The fuel is low and we don't have a lot of options." "I should be hearing back from Le Kai soon, he sent a coded transmission earlier." Bor stated.

"Can Councilor Nabis teach me how to better understand my powers?" Lincoln asked. "Yes, I imagine he could," Matias stated, his eyebrow rising as he looked at him. "Linc, I am unsure of the whole thing, let's see if we can contact Le Kai in the morning." The tank bucked causing

Bor to bump the pieces. "Oh, I'm sorry," he picked up the fallen piece, "It went there I think." he said restoring the piece to the table. The tank slowed, the turbine engines humming down in the background. "It can wait until tomorrow, let's gets some sleep. I think we've found a place for the night." Matias finished. "But the game." Bor said. Lincoln laughed. "Too bad Bor."

"But, I had a move." Bor complained, as Lincoln and Matias chuckled.

"I had a move too, see." Lincoln moved one piece and then said "Gotcha." Bor looked at the board. "But, I." Then he just stared at them, and they all broke into laughter.

The morning came quickly and Bor woke Matias. "Commander," he said over the intercom. "Yes Sergeant, what is it?" he asked from his cot. "I have talked to Le, sir."

"Alright, I'm coming." Matias said, sitting up and scratching his head. He didn't have any dreams he could remember and that was nice. He had a good night sleep, which in itself was a blessing he thought as he stretched. After he dressed he followed Bor outside the tank. The Morning was just upon them and still cool, the sun hadn't crested yet. "I could have kept sleeping; any coffee made?" He asked looking at Bor in the morning air. Bor nodded and handed him his cup. "Well, what did you find out? What did he say?" Bor didn't answer, looking off in the distance. "There," the short Sergeant said pointing. Matias looked to where he was pointing. In the distance, coming fast was a flyer. "Razium craft?" he asked. "Yes Sir," the Sergeant replied smiling. Matias grinned as well. "Well you seem happy about it." Bor laughed, "I want to hear the story," he said excitedly.

The small skiff came on them in a cloud of dust; the air blowing around its thrusters as the engine snorted and cracked in spurts of flame. Turning above them, it landed a few hundred feet away from the Wartrak, the dust blowing over them.

"Where did you get that thing?" Matias asked as he walked to the first one out of the small ship, the wind still whipping around him. "From the Razium, where did you expect?" The Lieutenant, Le Kai answered with a sly grin. Le Kai was tall and lean with perfect brownish hair, though a strand had broken free and hung in his face, flipping in the wind. He wore dark pants and boots and was covered by a mid duster with armored shoulders. On his back was what looked like a wrapped long gun. Lincoln had been looking from the tank and trotted out from the rear entrance of the lowered cargo door, running down the ramp that lead-out of the small bay of the massive tank. "Le!" Lincoln exclaimed as he ran towards him. "Lincoln!" Le replied back. Agrius lurched up from his dormant spot on the west side of the tank where he had been monitoring. "My Prince, do step back," the huge rumbling voice came from the Gear. Le laughed, "I see you brought Agrius," he said smiling, high fiving Lincoln in a special handshake.

Le extended his hand to shake with Matias, and Lincoln caught a glimpse of a bandolier of knives under his coat, one glinting in the new day's sun. Lincoln watched as three other warriors had exited the Razium grav troop carrier. All soldiers, all Spartan Paladins, some of the most powerful warriors on the planet were now standing before him. Lincoln had seen them in Anstone and knew them from meetings with Matias, but they were recent additions and he had only gotten to know them in the last couple years or so. What he knew of them he liked. They joked a lot and what training they had given him was always hard, but fun. He however didn't know the monk Orion, until a few months ago. He had started helping him on honing his powers, teaching him how to draw on them and concentrate on the Tempest. That had been the best thing he hadn't taught himself. Le Kai was the first up, and behind him was Orion. A Sao Lin monk. He was very tall, lean, but very muscled with large scarred shoulders and arms. He was dressed in dark cream pants and a vest of armor. Leather belts crossed his torso and midsection the armor chest plate on top of them. He wore a large polearm on his back and had pouches on his crossed belts; actually they all wore the crossed belts with chevron symbol buckles. The interesting thing about Orion was his mask. Apparently all monks wore masks Lincoln had heard. It was tight fitting with ribbed armor on the back and it had eye holes that showed the face also, and a place for the nose and mouth. It didn't hide the chiseled jaw of its wearer, and Lincoln thought it was more for his rank as a monk than anything. The next was Sergeant Macguyar the swordsman. He was muscled, very tall, armed and armored; this included his elbows, his knees shoulders and shins. He was used to getting into the thick of things and his dark short cropped hair was messy. Last was Greal bringing up the rear, the dark skinned gunman. He had two runic blazer pistols at his side, with what looked like sharp pointed daggers on the back of them.

When they were drawn the long blades would cover his forearms, or could flip forward to use as bayonets for his pistols. His shoulders were armored and he wore goggles around his neck. His stark blue eyes were sharp, and his goatee was white and neatly trimmed. "Commander," Macguyar said nodding, Matias nodded back, then to Orion and last to Greal. "Brothers welcome," he said. Macguyar or Mac cut him off. "Sir, you got any food? We are starved." They all chuckled, and Matias slapped him on the shoulder. "Always hungry. Come inside and tell me the story of this contraption you are riding in." Le started the story, "It's funny really. See after we got out of the city...." he continued talking as they all walked inside.

After they had eaten and gotten their bearings Greal spoke up. "Well what's the plan?" Matias looked at them all in turn. "I have been contacted by a Councilor; he is not one of the twelve but is on the outer council. Nabis is his name, one of Lok Master Zen's pupils. I want to be able to trust him, if only to get Lincoln to White City sooner. Although, it seems too good to be true, this Councilor seemed to know to contact us when we really needed it. Apparently he intercepted an emergency transmission about the attack." "He would have the tech for it," Greal said. "True," Matias added. "But it does seem too convenient. Right now however, we don't have a lot of options. The Trak needs fuel and there isn't a closer place I want to go. Also, the Razium know we are running and if they find us out in the open it could get messy. They will seek at nothing to find Lincoln." "So what would you like us to do Commander?" Orion asked.

"I need you to accompany me to meet this Nabis; from there we can get to White city faster. But, if this goes south I need you to get us out. Also, the others will be excepting to meet us at the fallback as planned. So we need to be there for them, for any who made it." Matias finished.

"So that's what we need to do. Well ok," Greal said "We will go to protect you, and if it does blow up then we stay with the plan. I mean we have the Hole to fall back to, it's archaic but it's hidden, and safe."

"So where does this Nabis call home?" Mac asked. "Kansa," Matias replied. "I will go," Le Kai said, "I know some people there that may be able to shed some light on this." "Me too," Greal added. Matias looked at Mac and Orion, "You will both be needed at the hole anyway, just in case, and let the others that come know what is going on." They nodded and Matias added, "We will contact you to join us if we need or if we need to come to you." Orion hadn't said much but spoke up. "There is another option if this doesn't work but it's a long shot." Everyone looked at the monk. "Master Orson." The warriors looked surprised. "During my meditation I have been able to feel his magical essence, but he is warding himself, only letting certain people feel his power. I can't pinpoint it, but his aura is close to the mountain cities."

"The Master," Matias asked, "You know he is there?" "I believe so, but haven't felt him in some time after he sent his beacon. Though to come out of hiding and for him to be sending out that type of essence, something must be coming." Everyone was quiet for a moment. Matias had a far off look, and no one wanted to interrupt his thoughts. "Very good Orion," he finally said. "Keep us informed if you get anything from him." Orion nodded. Matias continued, "It is settled. We stay with Nabis for now and see where this takes us agreed." He looked at all the assembled. "Good, now finish up; we have some ground to cover tomorrow."

The next morning, Orion and Macguyar loaded in the Razium craft and flew southwest toward their destination; to meet with survivors on Antone at an old Spartan shelter called the Hole. It was a staging point used as far back as the Dragon wars, having been outfitted during the Affinity wars to support Confederate soldiers. Lincoln waved as the dust kicked up around them from the thruster of the craft. "Uncle it's strange but I know we will see them again." "Really?" Matias asked quizzically. "Yes, they are great warriors and we might need them soon." "I agree." Matias said smiling and hugged Lincoln with one arm as the skiff flew out of site. Though he tried not to show it, what Lincoln said had worried the Commander. Le Kai looked at Linc and then Matias He knew they were thinking the same thing. Bor broke the silence. "Alright lads, let's get moving." They made their way in the rear of the tank. Agrius was stored and locked in, ready to go. With a Rumble of the huge engines, they headed toward the fortress of the Councilor Nabis.

Kansa City, the Acropolis home of Lord Nabis

Lord Nabonidus had dressed, trading his long robes of leisure for ones that better fit his rank as Councilor. They were cream and brown in color, and he had on his sigil of Councilor. His over tunic was short sleeved allowing for his under tunic to tuck into his wristbands. Around his waist was a thick dark colored belted sash type cloth, with buckles. His pants, the same in color as the under tunic were baggy and were tucked into his tall shin boots. He walked back to a large window to look outside before his guests arrived. He watched as the morning was taking its final bow of the day, allowing the afternoon heat to flow over the lands surrounding Kansa.

Flat with small hills, was the topography of the region. The mass of the largest of the hills, a plateau, was the place where Nabis's Acropolis citadel was located, and the city spread out below it. Surrounding Kansa city were crops and scattered hamlets around the farm areas while the city itself was walled in. A lower curtain wall by normal standards but a fortified wall none the less. While checking over the domain, Nabis looked off in the distance to the small river that cut through the lands giving the life sustaining water to the crops. While he scanned the horizon a glimmer caught his eye. He spotted a shape in the distance. It was just entering the boarders of the area, and closing on the city gates. He summoned his retainers and went to greet his guests.

Matias saw the walls from a distance. "Low wall," he said commenting on the structures they were closing in on. "Doesn't matter with the guns on the top of it," Bor said reading the picts in front of him. "That's serious firepower," he finished looking at the weapons with a small hint of excitement in his eyes. As they closed on the walls they could see what Bor was talking about. On the walls every 500 feet or so was a small bunker turret with what appeared to be a pair of long guns on the main port and huge barreled machine weapons on the sides. The tops of the bunker emplacements were bolted on and the roofs where thick for hindering a siege attack.

"Sir we are being hailed," Bor said sitting at the helm. "Put it up Bor." A screen blinked on in front of him as he sat in his chair behind Bor. "Hello Commander, very nice to meet you." The man on the screen said. "Well you haven't yet Councilor Nabis, but soon enough," Matias replied. Nabis paused, "Yes ever the politician I see, excellent. I will have the gates opened for you; I look forward to our meeting." "Thank you for your hospitality." replied Matias. As they neared, the gates opened for them and a guard waved them through.

From a distance two miles off, Le Kai was lying on his belly holding his long rifle as he looked down the scope of the impossibly intricate rune covered Blazer weapon. He was a speck on a hill, his rifle trained on the guards and any around the vehicle as it slowed when reaching the gates. The gates opened and the tank slowly pulled inside. As he lay and watched, he smiled, while his ear communicator sounded quietly. He heard Matias' voice. "We are clear; make your own arrangements to enter the city. I will be in contact and letting you know anything of importance." "Aye sir," Le replied. He went to his knee, unslinging his pack to restore his weapon to its sheath, and made ready for the walk to the city. While he put his rifle away, the black arrow and crosshair shaped tattoo marks of the Magnus around his aiming eye and forearm receded, and then disappeared as the Magnus left him. He was a Spartan sniper. He could have taken out every soldier down there if need be, that was his skill. He was one of if not the best shooters on the planet, and his Magnus skills only made him deadlier. He wrapped and slung his weapon over his shoulder, then checked his pouches, belts, and bandolier. The Spartan Paladin Le Kai started for Kansa City.

Meeting a Vanguard a few hundred feet in and then making their way with escort, the Wartrack drove through the city streets, then up the hill to the top of the road that had been carved into the plateau. The city was very defendable indeed. It had a maze of streets through it leading past many entries and exits. The walls taking them to the top realigned them if they would have strayed. Bor noted any enemies would have a tough time fighting through this city, and Matias agreed, it was well thought out in design.

As the tank came through, the people wanted to see who had arrived, but moved back looking down and away as they saw the escort. Lincoln looked through one of the window holes as they passed. All the people they passed looked away or went about their own business, except for one boy. He was younger than Lincoln, his clothes marking him as a city boy, buttoned short sleeve shirt and suspenders with boots. He had darker skin and eyes, which locked with Lincoln's as he rode by. Lincoln held his hand up to the glass to wave, a small smile on his face. In reply the boy started to do likewise but his mother grabbed his hand and hurried him away. "Why are they afraid Uncle?" Lincoln asked Matias, who had been watching. "I don't know if they are, this might be the first time they have ever seen a Wartrak, they are scary looking. Maybe they don't want to meddle in government business. Come away from there, we are almost to the top." He said gesturing to Lincoln. Though deep down he knew that was a good question. He looked at Bor who threw back a glare.

They reached the top of the summit to the Acropolis, pulling up to the main palace. It was amazing. They drove through a colonnade of plants set between classic sculptures of Kings, Warriors, Paladins, and heroes. Matias laughed as they passed a certain one. Bor snickered, "Well Matias it appears you are well known." The tank rumbled by the marble statue of the Commander of the Spartan Paladins. Matias looked to Bor, "That was long ago my friend." "Not as long as you think." Bor said back with a grin. As they finished the colonnade, the tank pulled in the rounded drive stopping in front of the huge palace. It was designed as a temple of old Olympia, a beacon of hope to the people of the area. The place was a symbol of freedom for Kansa City the capitol of the Confederate of Meridion. The palace was a beautiful structure with large columns that stretched forty feet high. Its thirty columns represented the colonies that joined to create the Confederates. It was an alabaster white Marble that shown bright and glimmered in the sunlight. The staircase that lead down from the front of the Acropolis was very wide, its steps, representing the tribes that had lived in the area long ago. The place was steeped in tradition and the area had been a seat of power even before the founding of the Confederates.

The Wartrak had come to a stop in front of the palace steps. The rear hatch of the Tank opened, the ramp unfolding with the sound of hydraulics and release of air. Matias buttoned his leather coat and looked out from the rear of the tank to the staircase. He took lead walking down the ramp. Greal was next in line, hands close to the runic pistols on his hips, though the blades were hidden from sight and Bor behind him, armored and looking side to side, the talismans in his beard shining in the sun. The twins were still in the tank with Lincoln. Matias made it to the bottom to see a middle aged, averagely built man with a slightly hawkish nose at the top of the large stairs leading to the palace doors.

Nabis came down the stairs to greet them, he was flanked by four of his house security guards. He swatted them away as he hurried down the stairs. "Hello my friends," he said arms extended. "Welcome to Kansa, and to Kansa City to be exact. This is my realm. It is a pleasure to meet you," he said looking over their shoulders. "Is he here with you?" He asked excitement in his voice then corrected himself. "I am sorry, where are my manners." Nabis paused; he gathered himself. Then properly introduced himself. "I am Octan Nabis, of the 3rd tier, and councilor of the Outer Circle. Welcome to my home." His guards had slowly walked up behind him but kept their distance. "Thank you," Matias said watching them. Then back to Nabis. "I need fuel for my Trak and food for my men, if you would be so kind." "Yes, Commander of course. I also have a place to rest and bathe, please allow my men to take care of your vehicle." "Thank you Lord Nabis. Allow me to introduce you to my crew; the man behind me is Paladin Greal and my Sergeant Bor." Nabis looked surprised, "A Paladin well I am honored sir. I haven't seen one of your kind in quite some time. I shouldn't be surprised though, with the cargo you are guarding. Welcome." He finished slightly bowing. Greal returned the gesture. "Thank you sir." Nabis looked to Bor, "Sergeant," he inclined his head. Bor did the same with a small grunt, and jingles of the golden fetishes looped and tied in his beard. Greal's Magnus receded from around his eyes, and he nodded to Matias all was clear. Matias waited and then spoke.

"Allow me to introduce to you Lincoln, the last son of Agesilaus, and Prince of the Confederates." The young boy came from the cargo hatch of the tank flanked by two younger soldiers, one on either side. They were almost identical. They walked down the ramp with Lincoln and stood behind him as he went to meet with Nabis. Nabis was beaming. "Hello, young man, it is my pleasure to meet you." Nabis looked him up and down. He was tall and had brown hair. "He is the image of his..." Nabis stopped himself, not wanting to upset the boy, and then continued carefully. "He looks like his family." Nabis said. "Strong lad, I bet? I can see why you are such a powerful young man, big and strong." Lincoln smiled a little. "I am Nabis," he bowed and then reached his hand out to shake. "It is an honor your highness," he said as Lincoln moved to accept it. The moment was interrupted, loud clanks and servos whined into motion taking all by surprise, all but Matias. The construct Gear Agrius, had detected something moving into proximity with Lincoln and activated from his offline state. The huge gear moved from his holding area on the tank, large steps booming, guns popping from his armor, and sliding into place with clacks and clicks of gears and ammo. "Please step away from the boy," it said. The rough raspy metallic voice boomed over the courtyard. Its huge weapon was trained on Nabis, his guards not knowing what to do, stepping back. Matias was enjoying the cowing, but held up his hand. "Disengage Agrius."

The construct bots head swerved to look at the Commander, the eyes glowing fiercely. They turned from a red to a calm light green, the weapons clicking back into place, with a clack of sliding metal. Agrius powered down standing guard behind them. Steam from its coolant erupted from the back with a hiss. Nabis was in shock. Agrius stood beside them quiet but vigilant. "I am sorry Lord Nabis, protocols and all," Matias stated. "He is of course locked to protect Lincoln. It is his programming." Nabis was clearly shaken, but tried to keep a calm appearance. "Yes commander I understand, I do wish you would have told me you had brought a Gear with you though." Nabis casually dismissed the matter, clearly back in his role of Councilor. "No matter. Please come in, I will have the Trak washed and the Gear may accompany it. We can also clean your Gear, though I don't have anything as impressive as a Centurious Wargear. I do have some of the smaller steam bots and house guards to accommodate me, and you can use their cleaning systems. I thought the big ones destroyed, except for a few here and there. May I say that one is impressive. The Gear may use the appliances, to lube and wash." Nabis smiled looking to Lincoln. "I am happy you are here, Lincoln you will love the grounds. I have much to show you all. Come in come in," he said excitement returning to him as he ushered them up the stairs. Matias nodded and all followed Nabis. Bor told Matias he would catch up, after the tank was stowed. Matias nodded as the members of Nabis' house led the Bor to the area located behind the Acropolis designated the MV, Agrius striding behind him.

* * *

Le Kai had made it to the city. He watched the wagons and steam cars, as they plowed through the main entrance. The guards at the checkpoint walking casually up to them did not seem to interested in checking the carts. They did minor sweeps around and underneath the sides and let them pass. Le watched the next few carts coming; these had barrels of what looked like ale or mead, and were flanked by guards to protect them. He smiled to himself; he had found his way in.

Once in the city he slipped out from under the cart rolling between the wheels and then quickly stood. Pulling his hood up but hunching slightly, he joined the crowd, blending with the daily masses that were walking through the streets. He looked to the palace on the plateau, knowing he didn't have much time to find out any info of what Matias had asked of him, so he had to hurry. He needed to get any information he could, besides he was hungry too, and thought he would check out the taverns and see some old friends. Friends, he frowned at the thought. He walked toward the plateau, joining with the crowd going unnoticed to all around, just another person.

* * *

After they had showered and changed, Matias, Lincoln and the rest, had been invited to a lunch for the Prince. Lincoln had finished his bath, put on his robe, and walked out to his chambers where three teenage girls waited for him. They had his clothes picked out and placed on the bed. "Hello sir," the oldest said. "Hello," he squeaked back not knowing what to do; he was in shock, though he did think she was very cute. "Oh, don't be alarmed," said the second. "We are here to help you get dressed, if you want." "We have never seen a Prince before," added the third girl. They played to his ego, talking about how they had heard stories of him, and that he was magical and could unite the Confederates into a Kingdom again. By the end of the girl's stories and questions, Lincoln was relaxed and sitting on the bed with them. "Can you do any magic," the third girl asked playing with his hair. "Well yes," he said trying to sound confidant. "Watch." He sat up holding his hand out toward a bowl of fruit across the room. He lifted one of the apples, then the grapes, and then a banana, floating one to each of the girls. "Amazing!" they exclaimed, "Do another."

Lincoln was smiling and full of himself. He was about to do something a little more bold, when there was a knock at the door. Matias stuck his head in, surprise crossing his face, his mouth dropping. "Oh, ah sorry. Lincoln we need you, ah, downstairs. Can you get ready please?" "Oh yes sir, yes," Lincoln said embarrassed, as he jumped out of the bed.

"Awwww," the girls said in unison. "We will see you soon," the oldest said kissing his cheek, the others waving. They bowed leaving the room. Matias watched them go, faking a smile. "What was that?" he asked Lincoln after the girls had left. "I don't know, they were here when I came out of my bath, and they said they had heard of me, and my talents." Matias looked agitated, "And, what did you do." Lincoln didn't answer right away. "Lincoln?"

"Well I was showing them tricks." Matias interrupted. "Lincoln! We have talked about this!" Matias composed himself when he saw the boys face, the unwitting pawn to the girls affections. "Alright we will discuss this after we eat. I will meet you downstairs." Lincoln looked into his Uncle's face, "Yes Uncle."

"Good, see you shortly." Matias said as he tried to put on a good face, and left the room as Lincoln started to dress.

The journey through the palace while coming down to dinner was amazing. The fortress of Anstone was large and grand, but it was a fortress, this was something totally different. Lincoln looked everywhere, his head swinging back and forth marveling at the extravagance and architecture. He was looking up and down the halls, trying not to trip as he walked, watching the scenery instead of where he was going. The ceilings looked like marble, some painted with frescos, and all were vaulted beyond belief. The only thing stopping him from continuing his dizzying tour of the maze of extravagance he was in, was the artwork on the walls. The paintings depicted great battles and conquests; he stopped at one that caught his eye. Staring he realized it was his father. He was dressed in full armor, and Dominus was in the painting as well. It was after they united the Confederate Kingdoms. He stood there looking at it. Then tears started to well in his eyes. "It's a great painting is it not?" A voice asked behind him. Lincoln hadn't known anyone was there, he quickly wiped his eyes and nose hoping that whoever it was didn't see him cry. Nabis walked around him to stand on his left. "Yes," Nabis continued looking at the painting as if he hadn't seen Lincoln tearing up. "It is a great thing, the unity. Those," Nabis paused for effect, "Were brutal and amazing times. Prosperity came after them, hope came with them. Lincoln, may I call you Lincoln?" Nabis asked looking at him in wonder. "Yes Master Nabis." "Good. Lincoln, we believe, meaning the Council and I, we believe those times can come again that they are right around the corner. Son, we believe in you. You like your father and even your mighty brother, can lead our people to the best of times." Nabis glanced at the painting as he spoke. He could tell Lincoln was overwhelmed at what he heard. "You really think that?" he asked. "I mean I am just a boy."

"No," Nabis cut him off. "Not just a boy, you're a young man," he said emphasizing the words to make them seem more important. "And the power you possess can restore us all. I, we, the Council believe in you."

"I can teach you to control the Tempest, and you can learn the secrets of the Lok order. You can become a Lok on the field of battle, a War Lok." He said this and stood up tall and proud looking at Lincoln. The boys eyes were as big as saucers as he thought about it. "Do you want me to teach you?" Nabis asked. "Yes," Lincoln blurted excitedly. "I want to learn."

"I knew it!" Nabis said a huge smile coming to his face. "I can feel your power Linc, you will be a tier three before you know it, you will be the best of us." Hearing Nabis going on about him made Lincoln want to hear more. He knew he could help the people, and with Nabis teaching him who knew what he could do. All Lincoln knew was he wanted to hear more, and Nabis knew this as well, continuing. "Now come along, let's not keep the rest of your party waiting."

They walked into the banquet room, as most had started to sit, and as they did the assembled guests of Nabis house stood and started to clap. Nabis was behind Lincoln and whispered to him, "This is for you." Lincoln looked at the people at the table. They were all dressed in exquisite attire. He saw Matias, Bor, and Greal among them; he also saw the twins and many who he didn't know. Nabis helped him to his seat and Lincoln nodded to the assembly and all sat. The assembled stopped clapping as Nabis took his seat at the head of the table, Matias to his right and Lincoln beside him. The Councilor raised his hands for silence, and then he bowed his head as they all did and they were in silence for a moment. Lifting his head back up he said, "May the Creator protect. Thank you all for coming, let us eat." House servers brought the courses around and the assembled picked from the amazing display of meats, cheeses, fruits, and wines. Nabis started a conversation with Matias, "I must admit I was worried and excited when I received the distress call from Anstone. At first I didn't realize but," he took a bite of his food then continued. "The frequency was an old one and I knew only a few and none from the south would be on that line. When I put it together, I feared the worst. Matias I am relieved that you are here, we have kept it very secret." Nabis finished.

"You mean like meeting us at the gate?" Matias asked playfully. "Well you were in a Wartrak, very rare vehicle, I made it look like I would have with any of my guests visiting, do not worry Commander. You are very safe. As you know only my house and Governor Morain are here." Nabis paused and looked to his left at the Governor Morain. The man was older and slightly overweight, though he had good color in his cheeks. He was dressed in a fine dinner jacket, with leather on its shoulders, and a chain leading to his pocket watch. "My lord Commander, we are honored to have you, and you my Prince," the Governor said inclining his head to Lincoln. "Thank you for your hospitality Governor, it has been a wonderful stay so far. If all your land is like this I don't know if I want to leave." Lincoln said. The Governor and Matias for that matter seemed quite impressed. "Quite the diplomat isn't he," the Governor said smiling, and all chuckled. "You, young man, have a future in politics, I think." He continued laughing, wiping his mouth on his napkin. "Remember flattery will get you everywhere," he finished, chuckling with the others. Lincoln laughed with them. After a few more minutes of banter, Nabis leaned to Matias.

"Commander, I have been in contact with the Council and they have been informed of your arrival. After the attack, the Razium have pushed the line further in the east and there is much fighting there. I have heard that most of the Paladins that the Confederates have left have bolstered the Confederate lines, but if they break through nothing will stop the Razium from moving south. "I have heard," Matias said. "Have you heard any details on how the fighting goes in the Isles?" "That is a good question Commander. They have indeed pushed hard as of late, but have been held up in the mid territories. The Razium haven't brought any of their warships to the battle yet, and they seemed to be stalled by our efforts, though the Aun Ka have been idle. If we can hold them, and the Aun Ka don't join the war, the Council will be launching a counter attack to hopefully cripple the forces enough to push them back. We have sent a request to O'Cea, but have heard nothing from them, we can only hope that it might be able to buy us time to stop any major invasion."

Matias nodded, then asked. "Lord Nabis, I was under the impression that we would be able to have your aid and protection on our travels to the White City. We don't have time to dawdle and the more teaching Lincoln gets the better equipped we can be to stop an invasion when it is time. The 12 know we are coming, when will we be ready to leave?" "Yes of course, Commander, however I do feel that we cannot leave yet though I am afraid." "Oh?" Matias asked. "I have been made aware of Razium presence close to the city, it was a good choice for you to come here. They were searching for you and close on your tail I might add. I assure you, we are protected, but they are looking for a running Wartrak and I feel it would give us away if we left now. I don't want to risk him over a small battle, or skirmish. Besides we can tutor Lincoln here. I can start his training and get him prepared for schooling of the White Tower before we leave." "Yes," Lincoln blurted, and Matias looked at him not realizing he had been listening in. "Yes, I would love to train with Master Nabis. It would be greatly beneficial Uncle," Lincoln said his eyes full of excitement. Nabis looked at Matias when he heard the word Uncle, as if he realized something but quickly dismissed it for the moment.

Matias looked away from Lincoln back to Nabis. "I don't like this Nabis, it feels forced. If you will not help us we will need to find other means," he said calmly. "Commander Matias, I do understand your hesitation." Nabis' face softened, "I want him there just as much as you, he means everything to us as well," as he said it Nabis looked at Lincoln. "But we can train a week or so and then make our way to the city, Governor Morain leaves tomorrow and can make our way clear through the Pallance." "No," Matias said flatly. "We will need to leave soon. I see your point on not leaving yet, but we need to be on our way soon. I feel that the White city is the only place he will truly be safe." Nabis nodded, and thought to himself for a moment putting his finger on his chin. "Let us do two, possibly three days, and then we will make preparations. I can make sure it is safe by then, yes, Governor Morain?" The Governor nodded. "Yes." Nabis continued, "And until that time we can train Master Lincoln here." He smiled holding his hand out toward Lincoln, to put him on display. "To concentrate on the powers he has. I hear he is quite skilled." "Oh do you now," Matias said, as he looked at Lincoln. Lincoln looked down at his food. "Alright Master Nabis, two days," Matias said holding his fingers up. "No more." Nabis nodded.

* * *

The sun was out and the breeze was crisp as the boy looked out over the mountains. "Come you, get away from there," the voice behind him said playfully as he grabbed the boy by his sides and tickled him. "What are we doing today huh?" The man asked still tickling him, and both laughing. The man was tall with a beard, the bristles itching the boys round face as his father kissed him. Then he put him down and they were in a castle, a room, his room. His father was clad in armor now, not the tunic he was just in, a chevron and lions head emblem flashed in the light. "Papa?" What's going on, the confused boy asked, "Papa?" His father didn't answer; he smiled a weary smile and he left the room running down the hall. Then the boy saw fighting, a flash of light, "PAPA!!!"...he yelled.

Lincoln woke with a start. He was covered in sweat, the white sheets of his bed were drenched, even though the air was cool. Daylight was barely visible, the sun cresting the horizon of the plateau of Kansa City, taking away the dour night that was, and giving it new life. Lincoln looked around his spacious room, trying to remember where he was, what he had been doing. The dream, it was fading. He had been having it or a variation of it for some time, but it would fade away, now it seemed to be more real. He caught his breath and stood stretching. After a second he walked to the balcony window and looked out at the dark city below. A knocking brought him around. Matias walked in. "I heard, bad dream?" Lincoln nodded. "Your father again?" "Yes," he replied. Matias walked over and put an arm around the boy. They stared out the window up at the sky, the silence thick but pleasant. The sun wasn't out and the sky was still dark as they watched the stars disappearing. Lincoln broke the silence. "I miss them, and I want to make them proud." Matias listened, looking at the boy as he spoke his mind. "I know I can be a good leader. I think Nabis can help me, and then I can learn from the masters at the White City. I will bring the Razium to heel, and unite the Confederates."

"You sound like your brother." He smiled and Matias continued, "Those are lofty goals, Linc. I think attainable goals though. Your father and mother were proud of you, and I know you miss them, they miss you too. You will see them again," He finished and then turned to face the boy, turning him as well, his hands on both shoulders. "Lincoln your father was a very powerful man, he gave you that power, your birthright, but your power is very much a danger and a blessing." Lincoln looked at him puzzled, "What do you mean Uncle, I am no danger to anyone, only the enemies of our family and our people." He said his voice starting to tremble. "I can become a Lok Master, I can. I will make them pay." He said his eyes misty.

"I know you can, Matias assured him. I know you will, and I will be there to see you become the man you're meant to be." Matias said. The Commander smiled at Lincoln. "I assure you, you will be a great leader, but caution is what is needed now; and teaching. You will learn from Nabis, but the Tower, they can teach you what he and I cannot, the ability to truly wield that power you have. To control the Tempest like your father. You are already great Lincoln." Matias finished hugging him patting his shoulder. "Thank you Uncle," he said. "Alright now, let us not keep the chef waiting, get your clothes on, we have to eat and then get you to training."

Nabis was standing in the middle of the Dojo, the training area for himself and his personal guard. It had training dummies, punching bags, and weapons. It also had sparing bots of different colors on the wall, and other training instruments that Lincoln could only guess what they were used for. Lincoln was in awe as he looked at Master Nabis. Nabis was dressed in the same type of robes from earlier, but the cut was tighter, and looked like it was used more for battle. Or training. He also had the belt of his tier around his waist. Nabis held his hand toward the middle of the room. "Show me what you can do." Lincoln looked puzzled.

"Can you do anything magical?" he asked. "Yes." Lincoln replied confidently. "Good, so show me." Nabis said still holding his hand toward the middle of the dojo and the sparring dummy not far from Lincoln. Lincoln concentrated and threw his hand out, palm open. The force knocked the training dummy against the wall. Nabis looked at him. "Good, now aim it at me." Nabis instructed pointing at his sternum. The Master saw the doubt in Lincoln's eyes. "Do not worry, I will be fine but I need you to do this. I will be here I assure you. Now let me see your power. Do not doubt yourself, it will come to you. Focus, close your eyes." Lincoln did. "Breath," Nabis said. The air was cool as Lincoln pulled in his breath and it seemed to grow colder as he let it out. He felt something. "Open your inner eyes, grab the current, do you feel it?" Lincoln did feel it, he felt its embrace and it was cold to his touch, not the warmth he felt when he was showing his power off for his friends, though as he held it in his mind it became warm. "Do you feel it?"

"Yes," Lincoln finally said, "Good," Nabis praised. "I feel it in you, you're getting stronger. Release it." Lincoln, opened his eyes grunted and unleashed what he felt, straight at Nabis. The power was immense a red blast exploded from the boy right at the councilor, engulfing him in light. "Master Nabis!" Lincoln yelled and made to go help the man, but stopped, watching the color dissipate. A shimmering glow faintly resided around Nabis as he stood, hands together one with his pointer and middle fingers up, glowing as it sucked the power away. "Good," Nabis said, "I almost felt that. That was a powerful attack, if I hadn't had my defenses up it would have hurt. Lincoln it was very powerful," he reiterated smiling. Lincoln smiled back.

Off to the side in the observation room, Matias had seen the display. Watching as they started into another lesson. He looked to Bor, "I hope this is a good idea, I still don't trust him." Bor looked at the Commander. "I agree, but we will have to wait and see." Matias nodded. "I wonder how Le is making out?" Bor asked.

CHAPTER 17. OLD ACQUAINTANCES:

Kansa City, Black Market district, Meridion

Le Kai walked through the black market district of Kansa, trying to find information about their host and anything on the whereabouts of Orson and what, if any, Razium forces were close. Most didn't think that there was a black market district in Kansa City, but there was, if you knew the right people. If you did know the right people then you could find out many things about many people. Luckily for Le Kai he did. The Rogues of Erach, finest Fusiliers on this side of the Pallance, were the clan of thieves that ran the guilds in Kansa and other mid Confederate territories to the south. They were known for their long rifle marksmanship and really the many types of guns they could bring to a fight. They employed some of the finest marksman and pistol Loks on the planet. Le had been one when he was young. He had been trained by one, and when that man had gone against a clan ruling, the man Le Kai looked as mentor was gunned down, murdered. Le went looking for revenge and found it, but it left a rift between the Rogues and himself. A rift he hoped wouldn't get him killed now.

Le Kai walked into a larger tavern, Double Barrel was its name. The sign on the outside of the place showed a picture of a smoking two barrel shotgun. Le had his weapons hidden under his armored long coat and a scarf loosely hung around his neck. The place was busy, as it usually was in the early evening. Patrons were wandering the room after dinner, as were others. Mostly mercenaries who were back from a campaign or had nothing better to do then go looking for something to take their minds off the daily routine. They would go to their favorite holes to gamble, lose money, and get lied to by the nicest of people. This was one of the best places for that, and as he walked in he knew he was at the right spot. Earlier as he had entered the city, he had found out that this and another bar in the district were the best places for information and after talking to a few of the gun smiths in the area, narrowed it to here; which he had figured anyway.

He scanned the room as he headed toward the bar, noticing no one regarded him. That would be if you didn't count the gunner on the stoop above the bar, the man in the corner table with his hat low, and the back table where four others sat with a few ladies. The other patrons in the room he cared little for, the man in the corner was looking for someone, but it wasn't him. The shooter was a paid guard for fights, but the back table, they were part of the Rogues. They all had goggles, some around their necks others on the top of their heads, or top hats, one was wearing his over his eyes. All had special aimers on the sides. The goggles were a part of the Rouges attire. Originally they were used to shoot when hunting or tracking during the dust storms that happened on the plains, but after so many shooters used them they became custom and then part of the Rogues wear. That and they also shielded the face to make you look like the rest of your compatriots. This always marked them out easily, though a lot of people wore goggles in this age, just others weren't nearly as advanced. Plus, the group in the corner seemed too cocky for the place. The way they were acting and talking to the servers and other patrons. That made them stand out. Sloppy.

"What will it be sir?" the barman asked him. Le looked above the man at the drink selection. "I think I will have a Jonny Moss," he said. The bartender nodded. "Good choice," he replied turning to make the drink. The place smelled like beer and peanuts, why peanuts he wondered and then saw a bowl not two feet from him. He took a handful and tossed some in his mouth. The barkeep brought him the Jonnies and set it down. Le slid him a coin. "Keep it," he told him. The barman nodded his thanks and went to help the next customer. He took a long drought of the ice liquid and then set it down. Man that is good, he thought to himself, looking at the stein. Taking another he realized that it had quieted and he could sense something was amiss. Slowly he turned around. The table in the back corner was empty; all of them, minus the girls of course were standing behind him. "Yes?" He asked. "You're wanted in the back." The one closest to him stated, holding his thumb pointing toward a hall off to the side. As he looked at them he saw they were new in the order. He looked at the long tight fitting leather coats they wore, didn't have their stripes yet. They hadn't shot anyone from over 1000 yards. Only the best got the stripes. Le had ten. Le nodded and stood, he took another gulp of the Jonnies, looking at the glass, and then set it down. "Lead the way," he said. The one that spoke had his goggles around his neck. He turned and Le followed him.

They walked down the dark wooden hall passing under dim lights and turned right going down another hallway. At the end of it they stopped at a metal door. Le was ready if he needed to act; his knives were too easy to use this close. There was no one better in a close space like this, well no one that he wouldn't just tear it to pieces with the Magnus. The first Rogue knocked. The slit hatch slid back and the man behind it looked at them, slid the small slider back in place and unlocked the door. The front man went in. Le followed him.

The room was smoke filled and dark with a single light hanging from the ceiling. "Well, look what the dog dun dragged home boys, a true legend." A voice said sarcastically.

It wasn't easy to make out much but Le knew that voice. "Decker?" he asked knowing. "Well well Le you remember, how quaint. I should shoot you on sight you piece of." Le cut him off. "It wouldn't make you feel better and you know it."

"That may be true, maybe not true." Decker replied. "Let's find out," he said and the whole room filled with the clicks and clacks of guns being cocked, slides drawn. There were about twenty guns of various types pointed at him. Le slowly held up his hands, "Well, or not." He said giving up. Decker chuckled.

"Yeah, I knew you were smarter than you looked." Decker stood walking from the darkness of the room. He was average height but had a good build. He was a decent looking man with a five o'clock shadow. He wore a leather vest over a tight shirt with a pocket watch and suspenders holding his army type fatigue pants up. He had a holster on his hip that was empty and goggles around his neck. He stepped toward Le Kai, holding a huge .50 caliber hand held cannon. He leaned close the cigar in his mouth still smoldering. "You got a lot of nerve, coming here. I heard you been asking questions in my city, my area. You know what? I'm gonna find out why, cause your gonna tell me."

"Really?" Le asked hands still in the air. "Yep, have a seat," Decker said as he pointed the huge pistol towards the chair behind Le. Le moved towards it and sat. "Leave me boys." He said, Le heard the guns withdrawn and holstered. Slowly the Rogues in the room left, the smoke going with them.

Decker was standing in front of him the weapon pointed at his chest, the single light of the room casting shadows around them. With a flip of his wrist the gun twirled a few times; the speed and grace of a master, and he holstered it. "Well," Decker said looking down at him. "You gonna sit there or you gonna give me a hug," he asked arms open. Le awkwardly smiled and stood, hugged him relieved. "Sorry about the theatrics, gotta look tough you know." Decker told him smiling. "When did you become the leader here?" Le asked. Decker walked to the wall and turned on the lights. "Well a lots changed, with war and all, too much is going on. Penny got involved with Razium and the Dru Nar, and well, he got dealt with. We had a mini war and then me and one or two others formed the guild leadership again. We are on the up now." Le squinted at him, "Ok we still have some contracts, but we are snipers for the army. It's a long story, but I'm in charge for now."

"So, what are you doing here?" Decker asked. "I thought you were in the south, I had heard a lot of different things." "I can't talk about it now, we do need to catch up, but now isn't the time. I'm sorry to come asking, but I need your help." Le said grinning. "Man it really is good to see you, and I heard you were high up, but I thought Penny was still in charge."

Decker grinned, "Well it's good for you he ain't, and it's good to see you too old friend, well go ahead, ask."

"I need to find out some information about your Councilor, and maybe some info on the whereabouts of a Lok."

"Really, ok what kind?" Decker asked.

"I need to find the High Lok, Orson, the King's Master Lok." Decker looked at him, blankly. "I don't know, Le. After the fall they are hard to come by. Either recruited to help the war or the ghost hunters come for them. I know the Razium have been looking for the more powerful ones. They have sent assassins. The last I heard was a year or so ago, there was a healer close to that, and he had ties to the crown, but nothing since. The man I heard about was in Royal, or maybe it was Navarre. Those are the best places to look." "I can keep an eye out, and if I hear anything I'll get in touch with you. I hope that helps," Decker finished. "It does, thank you my friend." "It is good to see you again." "You as well, especially in a Rogue's Den." Decker said shaking his head. They clasped hands. "Let's go have a drink and I'll tell you what I know about the Councilor, and then I'll get you out of here. Oh, and Le, make sure you hide better next time, my people saw you immediately." "Well that's cause I wanted them to." Le said back and smiled.

Night had fallen, and after he had left the Den through a secret entrance, he pulled his hood up and scarf close as he made his way through the streets of the busy trade city. The information Decker told him about Orson, the Razium, and Nabis was helpful. He needed to talk to Matias.

Kansa City, Acropolis of Nabis, Confederate of Meridion

The first day of training had ended and Lincoln was beat, he walked into his room and flopped on the large bed. It had been a long day for him trying to grasp his power, and then controlling what he had learned. The last part of the day was study on the Labrynthian. Nabis was trying to get him to try and see it, but Lincoln couldn't quite grasp it. It was too big, and it felt forced or closed, he had told Nabis. "We will try again tomorrow," Nabis had told him. "Don't worry my Prince, you did very well." Though Nabis had told him that, Lincoln had felt as if he had let his new teacher down. He wanted to take the power by the throat. He would make it happen and would show Nabis and the other Loks of the Tower he could do it, he must. For now though he needed to rest, and he lay there exhausted. Matias and Nabis were discussing politics and Bor was in the motor pool making sure the repairs to the tank went accordingly. Greal was the only one close, sitting outside Lincoln's room in the small foyer. It was the suite for high ranking guests or whoever resided there at the time for Nabis to entertain.

Lincoln was restless and couldn't sleep. He opened his eyes and rolled off the bed, sitting for a second. He flipped his tongue up and down realizing he was thirsty. He knew dinner was soon, but his mouth was dry. He opened his door and walked across the foyer room to the decanter on a table on the far side. It was a tall and crystal clear, cold to the touch. Lincoln picked it up and poured a glass for himself. Greal flipped a card from the game he was playing and watched Lincoln as he did. "So have you learned anything?" Greal asked him. Lincoln nodded, and took another sip of water. Then walked over to Greal and dropped in to the soft chair next to him. It was large and grayish in color. It felt so soft and Lincoln just sat almost dozing off. Greal chuckled, "You look tired. That water should make you feel better. Do you know what type of water that is?" Lincoln shook his head no, as he looked at the glass. "It is Rangor water."

"Really!" Lincoln said surprised. "I have read about Rangors, but have never seen one." Greal continued, "Well a Rangor looks like a Puma, but with thick scales on its shoulders, an adaption to the harsh climate of the desserts in the Pallance." "Really?" Lincoln asked, "Have you ever seen one?"

"Yes," Greal answered. "They are very rare now I hear; the poachers have taken to them. They store water on pouches under their plate scales to help them survive in the desert. That water is the purest form one can filter, and the minerals and components the animal gives off are like a vital elixir. Some say it is so pure it can even give longevity and youth." Lincoln had taken a sip, it was very good. "The water is salvaged and pouched from the animals and sold on the black market of the trade cities. It is sad, Rangor are very interesting creatures." Greal could tell his story had dampened the mood so he changed the subject. "Enough about that, so tell me what you learned so far?"

Lincoln looked over at him, and sat up a bit. Sharing his experience gave him a small burst of energy, that or it could have been the water. Greal could tell Lincoln lit up at the chance of talking about it. "Well, it has been good, but hard. So first we started with me showing Master Nabis what I knew so far. He said it was good, raw but good, and he was impressed at what I had been able to do. With levitation and harnessing the currents. I didn't even know what it was, it just felt right. So next he tested my level with the ten Orbs of Asha, I had never knew anything could be so hard at first, but I started learning and got to five before we had to stop."

"Five Orbs?" Greal asked. "Impressive." Lincoln continued, "Master Nabis said it was too draining for me to continue. Then we did light sparing, I had the glow of power, it was amazing Greal."

Lincoln paused, his eyes glazing over as he remembered, and then thrust his fist out. "My whole body was a weapon that transferred energy through my limbs. After that, then we went to the control phase of my powers, which was draining." "I bet," Greal said. "Oh there is more but there has been so much to learn, and it's so hard." Lincoln's energy had slipped away and he was feeling the effects of the work he had put in as he slipped back in the chair. Greal had listened and was enjoying talking to him, his excitement had reminded him of his brother Dominus with his boyish energy, though Greal didn't voice it. "It sounds like a lot to take in." Greal told him. Lincoln agreed. "Master Nabis said I did better than most who have been training for a year in the White Tower," the spark coming back to him for a moment. "Really," Greal said enjoying their conversation and the youthful excitement of Lincoln. Greal had started snacking on the small fruits on the table. Lincoln slumped apparently done, then raised his head from his chest.

"Greal. I know you have power, is it like what a Lok has?" Greal thought for a moment. "Slightly, my power comes from Estomagnetics, or the magnetic energy of people and objects, not the magic of the Tempest. Though I feel they are intertwined somehow, as I can feel your power. I feel the waves of energy from things. The magnetic fields or auras that pull from things or people around me. I can become slightly stronger, by touching rock or a metallic object, but only for a very small time. Though we," He paused thinking of the right words. "Spartan Paladins have differences of power. I for example have most in my hands and eyes, and can control the Magnus through them, while others, like your brother Dominus could use his whole body. The magic of a Magnus user and a Lok is different but I think in many ways similar." Lincoln nodded. Greal continued. "I know I have worked very hard to make myself a master of the Magnus, and I still learn new things all the time. I feel both the Lok ability and the Magnus are gifts that we can never truly master, but can make ourselves the best that we can be over time. That is all it takes Lincoln practice and time." "That is good insight Paladin Greal." Lincoln stated. "Though I intend to master the Lok training," he said emphasizing the word master, as he looked straight into his glass of water. "I will be the best I can be, the best ever." "I know you will," Greal said nodding and they sat enjoying the silence of the room.

It was day four of their stay at Kansa City. Matias had grown weary of the delays, though it had been beneficial, as Lincoln had been able to hone his skills and learn more of the ways of the Tempest. It seemed the boy had taken to it and was a natural at adapting to the control of his powers.

Nabis seemed genuinely in awe of how fast he was learning and the ability in which he controlled them in just a few days of his tutelage. Matias however, had a bad feeling that they were being delayed on purpose, the things stopping them from leaving trivial though important. The first delay was the tanks coolant housing for the coils, it had been cracked. Bor told him he knew it might have been damaged in the fighting though. The second had been one of the deadly but rare, Kansa wind storms, and tornados. It had shut the city down for the whole day. After which Nabis had given caution that the weather was still fierce on the outskirts of the area and they should give at least another day to wait it out, especially when traveling by air. His propeller style air ship needed to be properly readied. That lead them to day four, and Matias was ready to go after preparations had been made. They would be leaving on the morrow, but the vehicles and supplies had to be loaded and Master Nabis' airship was almost finished being outfitted for the trip. It was the fourth day, and Lincoln came down the stairs to see Matias looking off the balcony of the great Acropolis, watching the loading of vehicle supplies and other items for the journey. Lincoln ran down, "Uncle!" he yelled. Matias turned. The frown replaced by the affection he had for the boy. He was proud of him for learning what he had and it showed.

"Good morning," he said, walking over to give Lincoln a hug. "How did you sleep?" "Real good, I was gone when my head hit the pillow." Matias chuckled, "Yes you looked the part, after the teaching session I saw you go through, I wouldn't be surprised if you were still asleep." Lincoln was smiling, "No I was too excited. Master Nabis said I would be able to learn a secret today or at least try." As Lincoln talked the excitement bubbling in his voice made him seem a little higher pitched than normal. Greal had come down the stairs and nodded to them. "Commander, Lincoln." Lincoln looked at him, "Linc is fine Greal, and good morning to you too. Armored I see." Greal was in fact armored. He had a tight stretchy chain type shirt on with metal shoulder and chest guards strapped around him, which his cloak usually covered but not today. He was of course wearing his pistols and blades at his hips. "Yes I thought it fitting, it just felt like a good day to wear it," he said back looking to see Bor below bellowing at some laborer of the area about a part for the tank. "Always Bor," Greal said and both he and Matias grinned.

"Hello all," Nabis said greeting them from down the long balcony. Nabis was robed in his normal morning attire, and holding a cup of coffee, the steam coming of the top. "Nabis", Matias nodded. "Master Councilor," Greal greeted him. "Hello master Nabis!" Linc almost exploded, causing Matias to laugh. "Sorry," Lincoln said, "Good morning Master Nabis. "Good morning to you Lincoln." Nabis stopped his eyes squinting at the boy. "Have you gotten taller?" "I don't think so," Lincoln said back, "Maybe." "Hmm interesting," Nabis continued. "Well I did promise a surprise didn't I?" Lincoln just waited, his wide eyes beaming. "Well young Prince," he said pausing for effect. "Do you know how to fly?" He asked taking a sip of his coffee, Lincoln's eyes got huge with wonder.

CHAPTER 18. THE TEMPEST OPEN:

The Plateau of Kansa four miles from the city

The air was dry, a slight breeze coming from the south. Lincoln was standing on the edge of the Plateau of Kansa City, a few miles away from the gleaming Acropolis Palace. Matais watched the boy pacing and looking off the edge. He was excited, he dripped with it. Ever since they had left the city to journey out to this small ledge, Lincoln had been smiling ear to ear. Matias was standing by the hover skiffs a few feet away, watching him. The boy was like his father, he thought, his mind started to wonder about the things he could do. Matias quickly dismissed the images from his mind. Then he smiled. Lincoln was more like his brother at that age. Lincoln was slimmer than Dominus, not the bull his brother had been, but like Dom, always optimistic and happy, very determined to succeed in what was before him.

The plateau area they were in was sectioned off from the populace as farm land, so the chance of being disturbed was little to none, and they were surrounded by Nabis's security. Even with the security Matias still was unsure of their host, and had made sure to bring Agrius in case anything happened. The large robot construct was standing behind him as he watched the boy. Matias turned to regard the metallic beast. "Anything Agrius?" "No Commander, nothing near." The metallic voice answered. "It is a nice day though." Agrius said unexpectedly. Matias regarded the Construct, smirking. "Yes it is." He answered back.

Lincoln looked off the plateau, he could see for miles around, it was a breathtaking view. He could see the main highway, small towns, hamlets, and mini castles in the distance, with miles of farm land and crops farther out. He saw his shadow and held his hand out, catching the breeze. He was on top of a ledge that dropped about 4 feet to another, and then six feet to another, and so on in intervals until the bottom of the plateau. It was called the giant steps, and now he knew why. The topography looked as if it had been made for a giant to walk to the top of it. He started day dreaming of a giant walking and stepping on the ground, pushing it down with its weight making the steps. Nabis walked over from his hover skiff, to stand behind Lincoln.

"Let us learn to fly, shall we?" Lincoln snapped from his giant dream, looking over to where Nabis was standing. "Are you ready?" The Councilor asked. "Yes." Lincoln replied the smile still glued to his face. "Excellent, let's begin." After a brief explanation of how to stand and turn using his power, Nabis began to show him.

Nabis swung his right hand down in a circular motion followed by his left. He was concentrating, his feet slightly spread when he made the movements, and then he started to raise, off the ground. The dust under him fanning out in swirls of invisible currents. He was off the ground and glided a few seconds, then floated fifteen feet or so landing gently. "Wow!" Lincoln yelled. "I mean, very good master," he said trying to control his glee. Nabis took a breath, "Thank you, Lincoln." He was sweating slightly, "It does take a lot out of you, and I must be out of practice." He said smiling. "Now remember, just as you did with the orbs, find the currents of the Tempest, it will open to you just calm the storm and guide yourself. Remember to grip it slowly, and allow yourself to follow it, don't jerk, or it will not take and you will fall." "Yes, I will." Lincoln answered. "You try," Nabis said.

Lincoln stood in the same stance as Nabis, his right hand flashed and then his left, both pushing downward. He started to move slowly, the dirt at his feet swirling. "Good!" Nabis encouraged. Lincoln concentrated harder, feeling for the currents of the Tempest. He pulled on them and leapt floating a few feet. It was a bound more than flight but it was something. Lincoln smiled; "Wow," he said breathing in deeply. "Excellent!" cried Nabis, "Again." Lincoln did it again, the same motions and this time he went almost as far as Nabis had. He was breathing harder this time. "Excellent," Nabis exclaimed. "You are magnificent."

"Again." Lincoln said. "Yes again, remember feel it." Nabis encouraged with more vigor. Lincoln let his power flow, he was gaining confidence and it felt amazing. He felt the storm, the power that was the magic of the Tempest, and then he grabbed it. He had it. Lincoln leapt right before he had left the ground and he soared into the air, he was literally flying. He laughed, landing a few feet away. "Watch," he cried as he leapt again. Nabis was in shock. "He is amazing," he said to Matias who had walked closer to them; while staring at Lincoln. "I have never seen anyone do this before, ever!" It has never been documented, he is the key, and he is the Lok we have been looking for!" Nabis chuckled to himself.

"Woahh!" Lincoln yelled as he lost control while he tried to land. He caught himself as he hit the dirt hard rolling to a stop. He was up quickly dusting himself off.

"Are you ok?" Matias asked, trotting over. "Yes." Lincoln said panting, completely out of breath. "Did you see?" "Yes," Matias replied with a proud grin as he helped dust him off. "Watch me this time." He exclaimed a twinkle in his eye. "Don't grab." Nabis warned, but Lincoln hadn't waited to hear him. He leapt and then ten feet later lept again, he took off but he wasn't concentrating, and didn't have his balance. The power hit him and he grabbed instead of letting the power lead him, he went flying through the air out of control, hitting Agrius in the chest with a thud, and dropping like a sack of potatoes landing in front of Agrius' metal feet. The assembled congregation ran to him.

"My Prince!" Nabis exclaimed. "Lincoln!" Matias yelled. Lincoln was lying on his back, looking up at the huge robot as the others came running over, he was laughing. "Are you ok?" Matias asked. "I am fine Uncle," he said. "Just a little bruised." Agrius' servos and gears whined as he looked down at the boy. "Very good my Prince," he boomed metallically. "Like a ...bird?" he questioned. All of them burst with laughter. "Yes my big friend, like a bird," Lincoln said as he was helped to his feet. After the laughter died down Nabis looked at him. "Lincoln, you are gifted; you have been chosen to do this. I have never seen anyone take to flight so quickly. The application alone is remarkable. Tell me how did it feel?" "It was as if I can feel the air, the power surrounding me. I don't know, it felt easy to hold, but powerful."

"It was good, Lincoln, who am I kidding it was great." Matias said. "True Commander. You have the touch Lincoln. Do you feel like trying once more?" Nabis asked. "Yes." Lincoln said ecstatically.

"Good, now this time concentrate, take hold and remember what we have gone over, take the principles and use them to guide you." Lincoln nodded. He took a sip of water, and when he was ready he went back to his stance, closing his eyes. He stood still moving his feet to be in perfect starting position. His hands came to his sides and he pushed down breathing deeply as he raised his forearms until they were parallel to the ground. He flashed his right hand down in a motion then his left moving them out. Slowly he started to shake and then he squeezed his fists together throwing them downward. He exploded up like he had been launched from a cannon, the dust kicking out all over Nabis, Matias and the other guards as they shielded their eyes. He was about twenty feet off the ground and looped then soared for a few seconds. The crowd below was in awe. Even Matias was surprised at just how fast he was learning.

Then Lincoln started to lose control. He yelped, but regained himself, righting himself arms at his sides as he turned and sputtered toward them. He pulled up and eased himself slowly to the ground. He was completely out of breath his face reddened and covered in sweat. "How, was ...that?" He asked, sitting down in breathless pants, sucking in the air as he tried to catch his breath, a huge grin on his strained face. "Amazing." Nabis said, "You have the power Lincoln." Lincoln looked up at Nabis and Matias standing over him and closed one eye as the sun's glare was in it, he smiled, his head dropping between his knees.

* * *

The day had finally come, and all was ready for the trip to White City. Yesterday's events at flying had been the highlight of the trip so far for Lincoln. He was excited to learn more, though his ego had grown slightly after the praises Nabis had lavished on him. Lincoln was standing on the columned balcony of the Acropolis watching the workers load the last of the supplies in to the hold of the mighty Gryphon, the propeller zeppelin Man O War airship. It wasn't a zeppelin with a balloon so much as it was more of a propeller driven air ship, the balloon deflating once in the air. It had five propellers, two on each of the sides and engine thrusters that were steam powered, the hot air giving it lift; on the main deck was a larger propeller to help it stay aloft. It was an amazing piece of work. Bor had told him, it was a rare ship that was still in the air after the wars. Lincoln thought the Gryphon looked like an old 48 gun Man o War from the pirate stories he had been told as a small boy. Though the stern was larger and raised to allow for the Councilor and guest quarters. This ship however had been re outfitted. It was trimmed in gold and its transom had been reinforced with pillars covered in runes of silver. True to the look it did indeed have 48 guns, and looked to have more from what Lincoln saw with the huge cannons poking out the sides. His eyes were pulled from the loading when he saw the Wartrak driving up into the aft ramp of the airship, Agrius following it, the last of the cargo to be loaded. Matias was below him on the steps leading to the launch pad and waved him down. He waved back and let go of the railing jumping to the floor and headed to the stairs. Once outside he weaved through the people to stand beside Matias, Greal never too far behind him.

"There you are." Matias said his hands behind his back as he watched Lincoln walk up. "How was the view?" "Busy," Lincoln replied. "Wait till you see the White City," Matias told him, "It is amazing, everything is floating, the Islands themselves suspended in midair." "Really?" Lincoln asked. "Oh yes, the stones are made from the Valum rock, it has magnetic properties, they float in midair and don't move. It's quite amazing. The whole city is like that, the bridges and air walks, that's the area of White Cloud. It's one of the most beautiful places on Partha Terra, and you get to train there." "Uncle this is going to be so awesome." Matias chuckled as Lincoln, continued to talk and ask questions. Off to the side a worker cloaked in a brown hood was holding a box. He was walking toward Matias, and stepped a bit close, Matias felt him and turned. "Sorry, excuse me," said the Commander. The man looked out from under his hood. "I am sorry sir," he said winking. Matias continued, "Not at all, I should have seen you a few seconds ago and moved, please continue." The man nodded his thanks and boarded the ship. Matias watched for a second, before talking to Lincoln again. "So what where you saying?" he asked.

As the man holding the box walked it up to the freight elevator he set it down and quickly ducked in a small side closet. There he slipped out of his hood and put on a shirt of one of the security officers on the ship. When he was sure he was presentable, Le Kai stowed his gear and slipped back out the door.

Air ship Gryphon, 400 miles from Kansa City, close to the outskirts of the Pallance

The flight had been easy. The takeoff was fun, the ship rising in to the air, and Matias enjoyed watching Lincoln's reaction to the whole spectacle. It was a nice send off for the Councilor, but rough for Matias. He wasn't sure who to look for, even though he knew that no one in the crowd that had gathered to watch knew who the real cargo was, or that Lincoln, the Prince of the continent of Ultima Thule was even on the ship. If they did, it would have been a different situation.

The takeoff was uneventful, and the last few hours had been a pleasant ride. The view of the land below amazing to see in person, and the time was passing without incident. Matias was standing on the top deck of the ship; the wind slightly wisping around his head.

The invisible Res shield was in place, keeping the wind from blowing all who were standing on the deck. It was a piece of technology acquired from the Razium during the truce, which had been fitted to the railings around the ship, and used so that glass or walls didn't need to be added. It was very helpful and elegant, allowing the ship to maintain its classic look, but not lose the protection of reinforced glass. Though a small bit of wind still came over the edge every now and again. Matias watched as a security guard was heading toward him. "Good day sir," the man said, stopping to talk. Commander Matias, who was garbed in a combat shirt sleeves rolled up and fatigues addressed him back. "Hello to you as well, it took you long enough to get over here. Well what did you find?" "Sorry sir, loaded my stuff in the trak. A lot actually. Our Nabis has been linked to mostly good people, but there are rumors." "There are always rumors Le." "True, I have more, but we need a better place to talk. As for Orson, well no one knows for sure, but I have a good lead that thinks he will be in Royal or Navarre."

"Royal?" Matias questioned. "That cesspool? I would say Navarre is a better spot to hide, but either would be sufficient I guess."

"I have already sent a message to Mac, and let him know to look there, if possible." Le finished. "Good job Le, when we land I want you back with us, understood." Le nodded. "Also, Commander, we might have more players in this, the Dru Nar." "Alright, we need to talk more, and I will address the Council when we get to the city; I have heard only seven of the twelve are there now, so I will request a meeting during which I will introduce them to Lincoln." "Yes sir, sounds like fun." Matias nodded, and Le started off.

About 20 feet from Matias, Le felt a tremble, and looked back over his shoulder at the Commander who had himself gone back to studying the lay of the land below them. Matias didn't move, and Le dismissed it as turbulence, the hot and cold air making them shake. He looked around the ship and couldn't see anything. The clouds had become thick, though he could still see patches of ground below them. He put his hands behind his back and started to walk again. He felt it again and this time he knew he felt something. Looking at Matias and the others on the deck he realized he wasn't alone and started for the Commander. He had only taken a few steps toward Matias when the ship shook, and he was tossed slightly. A blast rocked them and the ships propeller farthest from them sputtered, black smoke coming from its steam engine. "Lincoln!" Matias yelled, "We have to get to Lincoln!"

From the clouds around them came the roar of turbines as two Razium craft sped past. "We are under attack!" Matias yelled, as a Spear fighter started a strafing run, its cannons punching into the side armor of the airship. Most of the hits were deflected by the shield but not all as the baroque armor was punctured and torn. The engine that had been hit moments ago was almost lost and the ship was starting to tilt. Matias grabbed the crewman nearest to him. "Stabilize that engine soldier," he yelled to the man. "Now, GO!" Yes sir, was all he could make out as Matias pushed him toward the engine. A mechanic had ran over with a wrench to try and fix it as well. The ship shifted again as Matias and Le Kai ran across the deck toward the cabins.

More fighters zipped past the sides of the ship, one exploding as the Gryphon's cannons opened fire roaring to life. The Captain of the Gryphon, De Mallo, was a good man. He was a man that took his ship and cargo serious, and Matias was thankful he had him on this ship. Matias ducked inside a cabin as the ship took more fire. Le was right behind him. Once inside he tapped his wrist gauntlet. Lincoln wasn't responding. He switched channels, "Bor where are you!"

"I'm in the hold sir; if this ship goes down we need a way out. The tank is almost ready; I made sure to put shoots on her in case, hone on my position, over." "Good man Sergeant, I'll get Lincoln and we will meet you there, out."

Matias and Le Kai were moving down the corridor to the guest cabins when the ship shook again. A door in front of them flew open and they were met by Greal, holding one of his pistols in one Magnus tattooed hand, and Lincoln in the other; the runes on the edges of the Blazer pistol alight with magic. "Uncle," Lincoln yelled running to Matias hugging the tall Commander. "Good, you're safe." Matias said hugging him back. "Alright we need to get to the hold, Bor is waiting for us. Le, lead the way." "Nice of you to show up Le," Greal joked as the party moved back the way they had come. "I do what I can," Le responded smirking as they ran down the corridor. Above them a voice came over the speaker, it was Captain De Mallo. "Attention, we are being boarded, we are being boarded." Greal yelled from the rear of the group, "Boarded? How? We are a two thousand feet up?" "I don't know." Matias replied, "Maybe those fighters, but I haven't seen a transport that could climb this high." Matias paused, then asked, "Greal, have you seen the Councilor?" "No sir, not since take off." Matias frowned and they kept going. They were located in the between section of the craft, leading from the main cabin to the hold of the ship. They had made it past the door they had come from leading to the outer deck and were about five steps down toward the hold when a yell from the outer deck brought the group to a stop. Matias held up his hand. "Wait. I need to see who or what we are facing, and if we can find Nabis. Stay with Lincoln, both of you. I will be right back, keep your wrist coms on." Matias went back up the flight of stairs to the door. As he placed his hand on the door handle, he felt something. Le Kai was at his back, and had taken his officer shirt off. He had on tight fitting armored shirt with his knife bandolier over the top. "What are you doing, I told you to stay put." Matias saw his knives. "You know Greal is more than enough to stop any thing we are going to encounter here," he said, "And beside who is going to pull your old ass out of trouble?" Matias rolled his eyes. "Fine let's make this quick, get Nabis and back down. Got it?" Le nodded. "Good." Matias opened the hatch door and started out to the deck. He was in shock when he saw what they faced.

The ship was in disarray to say the least. Fire was on the upper decks and engines, and the crew members were fighting for their lives against dark creatures. "Astrals," Matias spat, "How did they track us?" Le's hand shot up behind Matias, a runic bladed dagger left its holster on his bandolier and flew following his hand motions until it hit, piercing the creature that was materializing in front of them. The creature exploded with a shriek, the runes of its flesh glistening as it faded. Matias wasted no time running through its combusted remains to find Nabis, Le close behind, blades out.

The crew was getting ripped apart, some were trying to shoot the smoke creatures that seemingly appeared from thin air, and others had blades out swinging wildly, blocking the dark blades the monsters carried. In the corner of his eye Matias caught a flash of light. Magic, Nabis!

Nabis was between three of his guards his hands alight with power. Matias signaled to Le Kai, and they made their way toward him. Multiple creatures started to materialize around him. They were coal black things, holding long swords and barbed weapons. Their eyes were alight with dark energy and their bodies were hard to look at, the strange colors blazing over them. The Astrals were cold to the touch from traveling through their portals, frost appearing where they stepped. These were not like the weaker ones that had attacked Anstone, Matias realized. No these had an evil magic helping them stay in true form, and that magic was close.

Razium Techs, Dark Surgeons or Necromantechs, were some of the names used to refer to the Magicians that used science to harness these abominations. Though Matias didn't see any, one of them must be aboard. Three newly emerged Astrals converged on Nabis and his guards, the middle one moving with a speed that was hard to follow, as it floated through the air solidifying beside the guards. It cut one down, the man not able to block fast enough. Power flared from the Lok, as Nabis launched a ball of light from his hand exterminating the creature. Its shriek was deafening, and Nabis stumbled back giving the other creatures pause allowing Matias and Le Kai to strike. One of the creatures by Nabis turned to screech but instead exploded, as a glowing runic dagger flew through its torso, whipping around flying back to Le Kai's Magnus tattooed hand. Le took out four more of the runic metal blades, tossing them in the air, and with easy hand motions he launched all of them. They flew toward the others causing them to disappear to smoke, only to reappear at other places on the deck. The things knew what Le was and the magic he had in his weapons, and they were staying out of his reach until numbers could be brought to bear. "Master Nabis!" Matias yelled slowing as he reached him. "We have to get you out of here." Nabis looked at him in shock. "Commander, what is going on, where did these things come from?" He asked breathlessly. Nabis was sweating and tired from the use of his magic.

"These are the things that attacked us at the Fortress! Lincoln, they want Lincoln, and we need to move!" the Commander yelled back, lifting Nabis to his feet. Matias threw Nabis's arm over his shoulder and they ran across the deck, Nabis remaining guards following. Le Kai covered their escape. His daggers returned to him, flying back behind his back circling him before he launched them with only motions from his Magnus covered hands. The blades tore through the immaterial substance of the Astrals and they shrieked before exploding, dissipating into dark nothingness.

The Magnus was flowing through him and his weapons, his hands open palms upturned. The runic knives flew through the air a whirling slingshot of power floating around them for protection; the flying blades not allowing the Astrals to get close enough to them. Le was stalling them with his death wall controlling the movement of the knives, while Matias led the others to safety. One of the guards lagging behind was slashed by an Astral blade. As he fell the creature grabbed him throwing him over board. Nabis lashed out with a blast of power for revenge, sending the creature screeching back to the shadow. Matias had made it to the door, when it was thrown outward, Lincoln stumbling through it, Greal behind him firing his weapons back down the hall. "What happened?" Matias asked as Greal slammed the door closed, his face covered in Magnus marks and sweat. "We were compromised and without someone to help with the Prince, I didn't want to risk the journey." Greal said. "I could have helped," Lincoln pleaded. Matias stopped him. "No, you are too important, they can lock on to you and follow your power." Lincoln looked down, saddened. Greal continued, "Those things made it down stairs, some evil force is letting them materialize at will. They normally can't go very long on this plane, I have never seen so many of them! The magic holding them here is powerful indeed. We have to find what's controlling them sir. I don't know what or who it is, but these things are getting stronger. We can't let them get a hold in this world and become solid, if they do then they will be able to bring the bigger ones, Evolutors."

The word died in his throat as a massive beast landed behind them. It was hugely muscled, its upper mass three times the size of one of them. It stood on small but muscled armored legs its long arms hanging, one helping to hold its mass up on the floor, the other holding something that started to become huge a black blade. It wore what appeared to be an armored glyph covered mask that covered its nose with eye holes that allowed yellow glowing orbs to peer through. It scanned them with those evil eyes, grinning with drool running onto its chest.

Another engine was blown, and the ship rocked and shifted causing the creature and everyone else on the deck to be thrown to the floor. In the moment of respite from the explosion, Matias took control. "Get Lincoln out of here!" he yelled to Le and Greal. "I will hold it off." "No Uncle!" Lincoln yelled, "I will not lose you too." Lincoln was trembling, his hands starting to glow and Nabis immediately felt his power. "Hold young student," he said causing Lincoln to fade slightly.

"Don't worry, you will be able to show your mettle, but not now," Nabis pleaded, then turned from Lincoln to the Commander. "Matias, I have an ejector pod. I will take Lincoln and get off the ship, he will be safe that way."

"No, there is no way me or one my men will not always be with him!" They lurched again; they were losing altitude and gaining speed heading toward the ground, as the fighters still zipped around them; battling with the cannons on Gryphon. With a thump the monster was back to its feet. Matias cussed to himself. "Alright Nabis, take him. When we get an opening go." Matias finally relented. The Astral looked at them as Nabis and Lincoln were held to the back of the group. It was watching Nabis, or it could have been Lincoln, but Matias knew one of them was its target. Greal was to the right of Matias and pulled both his pistols his eyes starting to glow, the black tattoos of the Magnus moving over his hands up his muscled arms forming patterns around his eyes and cheeks as he took aim. Le Kai had taken a stance on the left, his hands open in tiger like stance of guard and attack, the dark marks of the Magnus on them. His knives floated in circles around him. "We will meet this together brothers." He said.

Two more Astrals appeared behind the large one. It looked at the group and when it laid its eyes on Nabis they brightened with power. It spoke in a deep evil voice, "My master sends his regards, thank you for the young one." It smiled from under its visor mask, the drool still coming from its mouth. The air was tense as either side waited for the other to strike.

The floor beside the huge creature exploded outward, sending splinters and wooden shards in all directions! A huge metal hand grabbed the floor section and Agrius climbed from the rubble, its left arm clacked and turned as its weapons aligned, and then unleashed hell.

With thunderous detonations, Agrius, WarGear of Anstone and protector of the Prince of Ultima Thule released its payload. The bullets instantly killed the two smaller Astrals, their dark rune covered bodies exploding into mist as the runic ammunition tore through their forms. The bigger one that spoke was getting chunks of it ripped off. The pieces disappearing to smoke as the creature was pushed back from the onslaught.

"My Prince!" Agrius bellowed in his robotic voice. The Spartans needed no other persuasion, and were already fighting amongst the multitude of other creatures that had turned from the crew to help their dark brethren with these new challengers. Le and Greal were cutting them down with the runic weapons. Matias had Lincoln beside him. Nabis was with them as well, using his magic to shield them and launching blasts at any who got too close. "Commander, the ship is still going down!" Nabis yelled. The words thudded in Matias' head. The ship he thought. "Lincoln stay with Master Nabis. Protect him," he said to the Councilor. "With my life," Nabis replied. Matias looked at Lincoln, nodded then turned running from them toward the bridge of the ship.

He had to reach the bridge to try and stop the ships descent or it wouldn't matter about the fighting on the deck. He opened the hatch leading to it and dove to the floor, as weapons fire tore through the bridge and surrounding areas. The Razium fighters that started the attack had returned. After the heavy guns of the Gryphon had stopped firing, the Razium had retreated, though now they redoubled their efforts launching another attack against the airship. The resilient thing wouldn't go down, however this last run had proven too much for its shields and the weapons of the Razium had hit home, shorting the shields and blasting through the armor of the ship. It was only staying aloft with the main middle rotor and one other on its starboard side, the other three engines only smoking turbines.

Agrius had destroyed the huge Evolutor beast, but was still in the midst of the Astrals attacking him. "Agrius, we have to move, make us a way below!" Le yelled to the construct. "Affirmative." Agrius' cannons started to fire, the rounds chewing through any in the way as it blasted a path to the cabin door.

Le and Greal lead the way toward it. They needed to get to the lower decks to the trak or the ejector pod to get Lincoln to safety. They were almost to the door when the ship rocked, and everyone was knocked form their feet. Nabis and Lincoln were smashed to the floor. The whole ship tilted, as its weight had displaced and Lincoln slid down the deck toward the railings. Nabis held out his hand trying to grab for him but wasn't able. Lincoln yelled his name as he slid!

Nabis was horror stricken. "No, Lincoln!" He yelled, and time slowed. Nabis looked for anyone to help, Greal was too far away, as was Le Kai. Nabis watched the boy slide away from him in slow motion toward the edge of the ship! Nabis didn't know what to do. Then it hit him, he yelled, but he didn't know if Lincoln had heard.

Lincoln had his hands out trying to grab something, anything! He was scared and he missed Matias, his family, he started to cry as he slid faster toward the edge. Nabis was reaching and yelling! Lincoln was trying desperately to hear anything, what did he say, he thought as he looked at Nabis yelling. His face was calm, then Lincoln heard a voice in his head, you have the ability, use it, it told him. He faintly heard Nabis in his mind and his eyes started to glow.

Nabis yelled, his hand open to grab Lincoln but he watched in horror as Lincoln slid off the side of the ship!

CHAPTER 19. THE MAN HIMSELF:

The city of Royal, Outskirts of the Dragon Wastes, above the Confederate of the Pallence, Southern Flat Iron Mountains

Colonel and his small group led Walker back through the city; on a nicer and easier route than he had come. They had left the church and as they walked the structures and areas improved dramatically. The streets were clean and the buildings tall. The group turned down a side ally, and when they came out they had entered the richer district of the city. The people walked with mostly no weapons and shops were busy as if they had not a care in the world. Walker watched a very attractive woman walking in front of him, holding a parasol and wearing a very nice flowing dress. She did have two armed guards behind her, but she seemed untroubled by the group that passed. That and the fact that he looked the way he did and she didn't seem to notice the group made him uneasy. "Don't worry sir," Colonel said as he saw his face. "These wonderful people are used to us and our monsters." He said with a chuckle.

"Follow me." He directed the group with his hand, leading them to the end of a beautifully paved road with walls on each side. There they met another burgundy dressed man who was waiting for them in a steam truck outside the gated road. As they got into the truck the gates opened and they drove down its length. A guard or gun turret was located about every hundred feet down the driveway. As the truck was nearing the end of the small road, Walker noticed another set of gates opening as they arrived. They went through, and it led them to a large castle type house. The road circled back on itself in a roundabout, with a high flowing fountain in the middle. The small fortress was amazingly designed. It had a tall tower at its rear and off to the side was a large landing pad, with what looked like a strange bucket that had propellers on its top, and another larger airship beside that. Walker couldn't see all the airships on it however. The battlements on the tops of the walls were armed with small cannon type weapons nestled in their crenels. The front was a bastion that led into the upper arched entranceway. They got out of the truck and walked toward it.

The arched entranceway lead to huge metal doors of the house that were closed and guarded. The place itself was very nicely constructed but what made it stand out were the statues, situated on the tops of the buildings in the fountain and off to the sides of the roundabout. They were detailed and it looked as if some were made of marble, and others bronze or solid gold. All this and they were still inside the huge citie's walls. A fortress in a fortress, Walker thought as he was lead in through the large metal doors. A butler in a black suit, a monocle on his right eye greeted them. "We shouldn't keep him waiting, he is expecting us." Colonel said to Walker as he gave the butler his fine coat. The metal shoulder guards clinking together as the servant draped it over his arm. The butler went to ask for his hat. "No thank you sir, I will keep my hat." The butler nodded and left them. "Follow me," Colonel said leading him into the castle. The other soldiers stood around, or wandered to other parts of the house. Walker looked for the woman that had been with the group at the church, but he didn't see her. He had felt a strange sensation when he had locked eyes with her earlier. Her eyes, something about her eyes, he thought trying to put a finger on it, but dismissed it as he followed Colonel.

The first room and the hall seemed about right. Grey stone and brick, with little more to look at than the walls and placing of the dense rocks, but as they continued the decorum changed. The beautiful dark cherry hard wood floor met them as they turned a corner. An armed guard stood watch as they passed under an arched doorway and into the amazingly crafted living quarters. The walls were light lacquered cedar, and were hung with paintings and portraits of what seemed like the same man doing different things, and in different battles; that Walker knew he couldn't have partook. In one he was conquering a horde of Ice Trolls, another he fought at a battle in Spartan armor with no helm. It was bizarre, the man was truly vane. Walker scanned around remembering the way he had come, as he kept pace with Colonel. The bottoms of the walls were inlaid with a gold trim that went around the boarder of the rooms, and the hall they walked through opened into a vaulted foyer that lead to doors that went to different rooms and to a stair case that went up and into other areas of the house. It was a magnificent architectural design. Colonel turned left and walked to a large set of oaken doors, where he was met by a guard of two muscled Ulthwan. The creatures opened the doors for them as they walked in.

Walker entered a large vaulted room with dark wooden shelves and relic looking items. The room was filled with books, view screens, files and what had to be this mans favored thugs. In the center of the back of the room was a one stepped dais, where a very exquisitely dressed bald man of average height was standing beside a huge desk. As he looked at the man he realized it was the man from the paintings. Two attractive young ladies stood beside him as he watched Walker enter. He was filling a crystal glass with a mahogany colored liquid. He turned to them as the pair walked in. Straitening his gold breasted burgundy long coat, and setting the decanter down he addressed the newly arrived pair before taking a sip from his glass. "Mr. Walker, welcome." he said. He had the look of a fighter, as if he knew how to get his hands dirty. Walker liked that. "Care for a drink?" he asked as he held his hand out toward the bar.

"Yes, that looks good," Walker replied, nodding to Dillion's cup, "I'll have one of those." "Good man," boss Dillion said. "Never turn down good liquor when offered." Dillion was waiting and then looked to his girls who stood smiling at Walker. "Get him a drink." He told them annoyed. The surprised girls moved hurriedly to get a glass and one of his stooges hurried to the bar, pouring Walker the same thing as the Boss. Dillion rolled his eyes as he moved closer to Walker. "Good help is, well you know, and that brings us to you sir." He said sitting down in a chair much more suited to someone of Walkers size, though Dillion seemed to take to it anyway. "Well as you probably know, I am the man behind this," he paused, letting his finger move about in the air looking for the word. City." He finally managed with a smile. "You can call me Dillion, and I have a proposition for you my large friend." One of the girls had walked over and handed Walker the drink. He put his nose in the glass; inhaling the aromas he watched Dillion, then upending it in one gulp. Dillion's eyebrow went up surprised, and then he continued pointing at the Colonel.

"The Colonel here tells me you're good, real good. You trashed Earl and my boys that patrol the street real hard and real fast." Earl the Ulthwan enforcer was in the corner of the room his arm wrapped in bandages. He flinched at hearing about his defeat. "Didn't even use a weapon I hear," Dillion continued, then paused putting a finger on his chin in contemplation. He looked at the painted motif of himself on his vaulted ceiling, then back at Walker. "I could use a man like you. As cliché as it sounds, why don't you join my... ah group here." He made a motion to the warriors and assassins in the room. They chuckled as he did. It was a motley crew to be sure, but all the warriors assembled looked as though they were good at what they did, providing that what they did required killing and punching things. Walker looked at them and then back to Boss Dillion. "Let's say I do, what's in it for me?" Dillion smirked. "Ahh, what's in it for you? Well, I could say if you don't, we will kill you." He stood up from the large chair and held his pointer finger up. "But, I don't think you would respond to that very well." He then started pacing and mumbling. "And I like my room and don't want blood all over it," he said loudly. He stopped pacing and looked at Walker.

"Then I could say that I will give you anything you want. Name a price. But, once again, I don't think you are that type of man either mister Walker. No." He strolled back toward his large upholstered chair. "I think that like me you have a certain thing that drives you. What is that thing, I wonder?" He asked putting his finger on his chin then shaking it. "Well if you do work for me, I want you to know, you will be helping the people of this great city, like uh, your friend the Dwarf, Master of mead. Or the other people in this city, a certain paper boy perhaps... There are many things," Dillion said dismissively. "But while you're in this city, you have to choose and choose you will sir. Yeah and don't leave the city, I mean that's bad too. Am I right?" He asked looking at everyone in the room, smiling. "So even though you don't really have ties, I think that you sir are a hero at heart, and you want to do the right thing, you want to help right?" He asked sitting back down, his hands out.

Walker thought for a sec, not answering. "Help with what?" He asked, not wanting to give his feelings away. "Why to be rid of these accursed Elves of course!!!!! They are stinking up the place!" Dillion yelled as he jumped out of his chair, holding his arms wide. "I lose money on the deals they do. They have been a pain in my ass for far too long, and recently have been too quiet for my liking. Oh and well yes, if you don't help then we will kill you, and if you do, I will give you all the money you could want and help you on your way." He smiled.

"Soooo...what do you say?" Dillion just looked at Walker expectantly, hands open and arms thrown out from his sides. "Well?" Dillion asked, holding his empty glass out, glancing at one of the girls. She realized it was for her, and grabbed it as he let it go, immediately filling it again.

"He will do it." Said a voice to the side of the room. Everyone turned and looked at the new player in this game of choose your fate. "I know his type, he is a hero." The new arrival said thickly. Dillion chuckled. "Yes, let me introduce you to your recruiter, I guess you would say. Mr. Walker. This is Tasha," he said as he held his hand toward the other side of the room.

A woman walked from the shadows of an oaken book shelf. She was the one in the back of the group he had seen after the confrontation with the Ulthwan! He noticed her then but now she seemed different. She was beautiful. Her hair was blonde with a dark streak across one side, and she was clothed in tight fitting sparing type material, with knee high boots. Her long coat and the boots were trimmed in gold, and a sword hung on her side. Her figure was very easy on the eyes and she had a very strong confidant gait. Looking at her he noticed those eyes, her light colored eyes. Magnificent, but troubled. They had slightly dark circles under them, which spoke of sleepless nights. Though it could have been she just finished sparing, by her dress; she was tired, or any number of other reasons in this place.

Dillion continued. "Tasha is one of the toughest people I have had the pleasure of knowing, and someone, I, almost trust." He said with a smile. She will show you to your room to discuss the contract of your service. We will meet tomorrow to discuss our arrangement, nice to make your acquaintance Mr. Walker." With that the Kissar boss of Royal walked out. His muscled Ulthwan and service girls in tow. Colonel tipped his hat, before he turned joining his boss and the girls.

Walker looked at Tasha and the other henchmen who remained in the room. She was amazing he thought, he didn't want to take his eyes off her. Then he felt something else, he started to remember. His thoughts were interrupted as Tasha cleared her throat. "Are you ready? Walker?" She asked slightly sarcastic, but friendly enough, as she gave a little twitch of a smile afterward. "Yeah, I'm ready, please lead the way." "Follow me," she said turning, her voice rich, and easy to listen to.

They walked out of the room, through a hallway and toward what he only assumed were the sleeping quarters. Four guards in burgundy red jackets that all Dillion's people wore had followed them. After they walked through part of the huge house they came to the long corridor that led to where Walker would be staying. Tasha turned to her entourage, "I am fine with him, wait here." They paused, one looked as if he was going to speak, but didn't. They stood off to the side of the corridor and waited for her to return.

Tasha walked down the corridor with Walker. It was a few seconds before either spoke, Walker starting the conversation. "So you rode past me this morning," he said to her. "Why didn't you stop then?" "We were busy, besides I knew you would get here soon enough. So what took so long?"

Walker smiled, "I didn't think this is what I would find here." He said. "And what would you find? This place is where one goes to get away or get killed, not to vacation, so why are you here?" She asked.

Walker quickly deflected the poking question, "Well you don't look as if you belong here either, I would like to know that story first."

"There is not a lot to tell, some things just happen and I happened to land here," she finished looking at him sideways as he shrugged. Neither of the pair was willing to give any information and the casual flirting only made the tension stronger. They walked in silence for a moment before Tasha spoke rekindling the conversation. "So, how does a veteran of the Confederates and a great warrior no doubt find himself here? I know most of you are in the service of the alliance of Confederates, although I have heard of groups northwest of here that are for hire. "Really, a group," he asked?

"Are you part of these groups Walker? Are you a great warrior, a hero, a Spartan?" She asked, though it was supposed to be a rhetorical question, it had an undertone that made him think she truly wanted to actually know the truth about him. That and she knew he had been a Spartan Paladins suggested she knew a lot more than she was saying. Maybe she could help him, but for now he was going to play it safe. "You flatter me.

I was indeed in the wars, but a great warrior, a Spartan, no; I was a good soldier and nothing more." She turned on him. Looking up in his face, her eyes grew hard. "You are lying, that is a lie. I need to know who you are," she said almost losing that cool demeanor she had kept. He looked to see if any of the guards she had left had heard and then looked back to her, studying her face. It changed slightly as she was getting frustrated. She looked away from him to his clasp, her face softened and her hand caressed his chest and moved up to the clasp. Her pointer finger tracing the emblem of the chevron and then back to his chest, and she smiled as she slightly pushed him back to the wall. He let her and then resisted a little. She pushed him anyway and he hit the wall a little harder than he thought he would. "You're strong," he said as he tried to move away from the wall, but she wouldn't let him. He looked in her eyes and she in his, he saw it, what he had been feeling. The animal magnetism she put out. "You're a Warp." He whispered. He saw it in her eyes as they widened. "How did you know," she stopped pushing, regaining her confidence as she moved away from him, he closed the gap. "What am I getting into here?"

Walker knew that the only way to deal with a Warp Changer was to be strong and not let them smell fear. He had no fear, but he wanted to know more about her. He stood tall using his size as a means of intimidation. Tasha stood her ground. "And you are a Spartan," she said with pride as if she had found him out, though it was surprising for her to say it so confidently as she moved back toward him. "I'm no..." he stopped uncertain of what to say next, but didn't have to say anything as she continued. "And this, is your room." She said slightly moving him out of her way, and lowering her hand to the door knob behind him. "We will talk later, it seems we have lots to discuss Mr. Walker." Tasha had regained her cool demeanor acting like nothing had happened. "Get washed up." She said looking at his beard and hair. "I will have someone bring you something to wear for tonight." She glanced at him slightly and then turned away and walked down the corridor. He watched her go, following the silhouette until she turned the corner disappearing from his sight. She didn't look back. He ran his hand through his hair as he let out a big breath. Then looking around in disbelief, he walked into his room closing the door.

The room was average size. It had a rocking chair in the corner, and a basin that had piping coming from the back of it, leading to the wall to his left. Beside it was a razor and other items for grooming. There was a rug on the floor and other pieces of dark stained mahogany furniture. Off to the side of the room was a door that he figured led to the bathroom. There was a large bed and a place to hang weapons and clothes beside it. Convenient he thought, weapons always close. He scratched his beard and rubbed his hands, realizing how filthy he was. He thought back to his conversation with Tasha, and the way he had felt. She was a Warp, a changer. The shape changers he had known were difficult to read indeed, and always close to the edge. In times of frustration they could take on the form of a wolf like creature with the strength to match, and their senses uncanny. Tasha though, she seemed different than any other changer he had ever met, and it seemed she could control her aggression. It reminded him of a friend he knew. Another changer who could do that as well. He thought about her eyes again. So amazing. "What have I gotten myself into?" He said aloud.

CHAPTER 20. TRUE POWER:

Airship Gryphon, Attack

"Lincoln!" Nabis yelled as he watched the prince slide over the edge. The Councilor was in shock.

The ship had leveled out slightly, one of the engines sputtering kicking out black smoke and coming back to life. Greal ran to the edge looking for him, "Lincoln!" He yelled looking for any sign of him. He grabbed a rope and was about to jump off to see if maybe he had been able to grab something on the side of the airship. Nabis had made it to the edge and looked over. He was blown back from the force of Lincoln flying past, a blue power trail cascading behind him.

"Woo hoo, yessss!" Lincoln yelled, laughing as he flew. He felt alive as the power of the Tempest flowed through him. He had never been able to grasp it so well. Lincoln soared over the ship looking down at the chaos on the deck. He saw the creatures that attacked had been thinned by Agrius, though others on the deck were now looking at him, his power like a beacon drawing them. Lincoln yelped and almost fell as he lost concentration, but quickly regained it. With a roar he flew toward them, both hands on fire with the Tempest magic!

His first pass he blasted all the Astrals he could see, anything in his path was sent screeching back to its smoky abyss from the bolts flying from his hands. He felt like a King, like a warrior, undefeatable, like a Lok. He remembered Anstone and was enraged. Aggression and blind furry took him; on his next pass, he slowed hovering above the deck. Nothing could stop the flow of power as he unleashed it on them. He could do anything, he blasted one of the Razium ships from the sky as it passed. Then he saw Matias, Nabis, all of them watching him. On the edge of his mind he knew Nabis was calling to him, but the power felt too good to listen, the power too amazing to give up. The Astrals were almost completely destroyed, and he was going to finish this now. Slowly he started to feel it, then he started to see black spots and his power receded. He had drawn in too much power. With his rage pushing him he had gone too far and he started to feel he was losing focus, his vision went black.

There was light from a door that opened in his mind. He saw the Labrynthian gate, a face with horns, but he didn't know it. He couldn't control the Tempest now and the storm had taken him, the face turned in to a black mask of pain. Not understanding the power had drained him, he spasmed. Releasing all his energy in a brilliant flare he passed out, falling out of the air toward the ship. Le Kai saw him lose his power and ran to the edge to the ship, using the Magnus he caught Lincoln in midair before he hit the deck. Slowly he pulled him to his arms. With the power binding them gone, the few remaining Astrals slowly dissipated, leaving the remaining crew and Agrius with no one left to fight. The Razium fighters slipped away just like the Astrals, breaking off the attack.

With most of the engines coming back on, the Gryphon had slowed but not enough to pull up. It was still headed for the ground at a fast pace. Le Kai handed Lincoln to Agrius to hold. "We need to get tied down it's gonna be a bumpy ride."

A voice blasted over the intercom, "All hands, prepare for a nasty landing!" It was Matias, he had made it to the bridge and was trying to steer them down! "I have one of the engines on again but another is about to go out, strap in," he ordered. Matias had taken control of the ship as he had entered the bridge and come upon the unconscious Captain lying on the floor, the bridge window blown out. So far, and with the help of what was left of the command crew he had been able to slow the momentum, but that wouldn't be enough to get them down safely. After a quick look at the ship's emergency systems he came up with a plan, it might not work but it was their only choice. He prepared the crew and had the operations officer pull the emergency landing gear, and four flat bottomed bilge keels popped from the lower part of the ship.

When the crew was ready the Boatswain hit the impact button to brace. He stepped to the console looking at Matias for the signal. He monitored the distance as they were getting closer to the ground. Matias held his hand up to hold the release. The Boatswain continued to monitor the distance, then looked to Matias. He wiped sweat from his face. "How far?" Matias asked. "200 feet," he replied.

"150... 100 feet," Matias waited a moment longer. "Now!" He yelled. The Boatswain hit the large button and the emergency landing thruster normally used for water landings, erupted from underneath the ship. The burst was intense, shaking the ship, as normally the water would be there to buffet the engine. With a defining blast, the ship slowed jerking all on it with a lurching sensation. They had slowed the descent and changed the ship's trajectory, but it was still moving over the ground and fast.

The thruster finished its burst and with a thud the ship came down landing very hard in the earth. It chipped the bilge keels with the weight of the craft, as it ground into the dirt; sliding on the landing gear. The stress of landing was so hard it bent the keels as they slid sinking them further into the surface, tearing huge ruts in the ground like a plow would a field. One of them was ripped from the bottom with the force of the earth pulling on it, but it only helped to slow the massive airship. A few hundred yards later it finally came to rest, snapping to a sudden stop.

All was silent except for the creaking of the downed airship. The dust and dirt swirled around it, as if one of the great dessert sandstorms had erupted from nowhere to cover its mass. Matias was covered in sweat. He picked himself from the floor as he looked around the bridge. He felt like he had just been punched. "That was a hard ride. Good job," he said smiling and nodding to the crew as they were picking themselves up; smiling as well.

* * *

Bor had unloaded the Wartrak and it was revved and ready to go. The ship had come down hard but even with all the damage it had sustained it was in decent shape. There was a trail of four routes about fifteen hundred feet behind it and some of the hull and landing gear was strewn about as well, but it could and would be restored. Matias was walking from the still somewhat majestic vessel; he had just left from his talk with the battered Captain De Mallo and Master Nabis. Nabis called after him. "Commander, are you sure you won't wait, it is not far from one of my Bannerman's homes. We can be back to Kansa by nightfall." Matias had turned from his path and stopped to listen to what the man was saying. "No lord Nabis, thank you but that is quite alright, we need to go. I can't have the most important person on this planet in the middle of nowhere, especially now that my enemies know where we are and the state we are in. They will be back, and I can't jeopardize that boy." Matias nodded good bye turning away, and continuing toward his tank. "Commander," Nabis pleaded, "Please allow me to go with you, or to offer some assistance." Matias turned on him standing to his full height. "Lord Nabis," he said matter of factly. "First I don't know how those things tracked us. Second, I don't trust where we are or how long it will take your men to find us, and third, I don't know why you keep delaying me from reaching my destination! If you have a reason tell me now or so help me I will treat you and your men as hostiles, do I make myself clear?" The look he gave Nabis was hard making the man shrink inside.

"Now Councilor, your reasoning!" Matias demanded. Nabis looked as if he had been slapped. Then his face softened. "No, you are right, I am sorry. I just...I was very excited, selfish even. He is more important." Nabis paused. "I will give you a rear guard, Commander." he said holding his chin high. "Do what you must, they will not follow. My men have coordinates on the small ships, they are close, but I promise they won't get through us." Nabis extended his hand, Matias look changed slightly and he took it, shook, and nodded to him. "Thank you, Master Nabis." He said. "I will see you in White City soon. Let them know we are coming, and give my regards to the Council. I thank you for your help." He turned walking toward the tank; Bor was waiting at the ramp. Nabis watched him go.

"We are cloaked sir." Bor told him. "Good, where are we?" Matias asked as he sat in the chair in the cockpit behind Bor. Bor touched a button, a screen appeared on the back of his seat, and Matias adjusted it with his fingers enlarging it so he could see it better. "We hadn't even cleared the Pallance yet." Matias stated. "Well?" Le Kai asked entering, "We are close to Royal, at least it's not too far out of our way. Let's look for Orson on our way to the Hole, we can stop there first." He sat down in the other seat opposite Matias and continued. "After, depending on what we find, we can meet the others." Matias looked at him. "Yes, that is a good option I think. Set our course Bor." Matias said, and then turned back to Le. "How is Lincoln?"

"He had a rough bout, but I consulted Nabis' doctor before we left, he needs rest, he just pulled on too much power, good thing he let go. He is fine though, just sleeping now." "Good." Matias said sighing heavily, "That boy means everything." Le Kai looked off staring blankly. "I haven't seen that much power displayed in quite some time," he said still staring. "I asked Nabis, and he was shocked when he felt Lincoln's power. He was well, speechless. We do have a hope at this don't we." Le stated grinning that rascal grin he had. "We do." Matias replied.

Nabis had watched the Trak drive away. The sun was up and beating on him as he still stood there, a hollow look on his slightly sunken drained features. The trip had taken a lot out of him. The Sergeant leading his personal guard walked up beside him and stood, chest out, straight back, arms behind him. The emblem of Nabis house on the breast of his armor shined in the light of the hot sun. He stood waiting for Nabis to acknowledge him. Nabis finally realized he was there. "Yes Sergeant?" He asked flatly. "My Lord. The Razium ships that attacked us sir. They are withdrawing; I do not feel we will have another attack."

"Are they following the Trak?"

"No sir the cloaking on the Trak is very hard to track without the correct instruments sir. They have moved out of threat range and appear to be withdrawing completely." The sergeant finished. A look crossed Nabis' face, it was almost unnoticeable, but if the sergeant would have been looking at him he might have seen it. Nabis turned, "Yes, the Trak was unexpected. Excellent sergeant, thank you, and the Gryphon?" "We are making progress sir. The foreman is having trouble with the main engine but it should be finished soon, and other help is on the way." Nabis shook his head, "Thank you sergeant. I would like to see to this personally." He said as he walked passed him toward the ship.

"Yes." Nabis said instructing the foreman of the small army of his crewmembers that was gathered around the Gryphon. "Do what it takes; I want us up and operational as soon as you can get us there!" His normal cool calm demeanor gone replaced with an unsurety of purpose, and that translated into anger, rage. He was furious; the whole day had been a waste. He was grateful that the stupid creatures hadn't done more damage to his flag ship and that he hadn't lost any more men on the trip, but it had finally sunk in that he had lost the Prince. The most important being on the planet of Partha Terra had just slipped through his fingers.

He was going to be the victor, bringing the boy in to the Council but now he was only the one who let him go, the scapegoat. It ate at him; he was seething with rage about to boil over. "Yes sir." the foreman said, hastily leaving the Councilor to his own devices. It was a good thing too, Nabis was about to explode. "Second tier, ahhhhh!" he yelled, the frustration finally boiling over. All around the workers looked and then hurried back to their jobs. Most knew about the man's temper. It had been docile and he had been very laid back the last few months, but now he had let it out.

His sergeant came walking toward him again. "Yes, what is it?" Nabis asked, the annoyance in his voice not hidden. The sergeant stood with the same proud rigidness as before and plainly stated. "Sir you have a call waiting." Nabis looked at him uneasily, though the sergeant didn't seem to notice. "Thank you sergeant, carry on here. Continue with the repairs, and make sure to alert me when our ship gets here." I must go communicate with the Council." "Yes sir, thank you sir." The Sergeant said and rounded on his heel heading back to where the Gryphon rested.

Nabis made his way across the open area to a command tent that had been set for him after the crash. He paused before entering, and looked to the guard outside his door. The man was well built, and armored. He was holding a rifle, and had a pistol at his hip. "Do not let anyone in, the sergeant will let me know when our mechanics arrive, understood." "Yes sir," the guard replied not moving. Nabis eyed him briefly as he walked through the door, shutting it behind him. Stopping inside he closed his eyes. The tent it was cool, dark, and quiet. That helped but he was still enraged.

"DAMN!" He yelled pitching a fit and grabbing some of the pillows and other items in the tent tossing them un-athletically. He stopped, composed himself then stood tall, dusting off his robes. Though they needed no dusting, he did it more out of habit than any need. Nabis had mastered his anger for the moment. He took a breath and then made his way to a large chair in front of a small but very ornate desk. He sat. Then ran his finger along the lines of the black topped desk, stopping at a small smooth surface. He touched a spot on the area. The flat area lit up glowing, small runic picts appearing on the desk running along the lines of the top outlining a screen. Then the three dimensional screen raised itself to face level. Nabis paused and then touched another rune.

A green hued face appeared on the screen though the features couldn't be made out. "Master Nabis, I've been expecting you, for some time." It said the annoyance in the voice clear. "So, the boy is safe?" he asked.

"Yes, my lord," Nabis replied back. "Well where is he? I would like to see him." Nabis burst into a sweat even though the room was cool. "My Lord, he is not here." He said somewhat stuttering. "We were attacked and we were not able to get him off the ship." Nabis was interrupted. "You mean YOU were not able to get him off," the voice said with blame in its tone. "Yes, I was not. The Commander had two Paladins with him, one I knew about but the other was aboard already; he was hidden. Matias had him planted."

The face chuckled. "I told you the old Commander was a smart one, you underestimated Matias." "Yes I did my lord, but that isn't." Nabis voice faded, and he sat, finally he whispered something. "What Nabis?" The face asked. "The Prince showed power." Nabis paused remembering the feeling of insignificance he felt when Lincoln had used it. "I have never seen that much expended by someone so raw, so much, he tapped deep into the Tempest for that power. He wielded it and he survived. The Labrynthian opened to him. It was only a split second but." He stopped talking thinking of how it felt. "Really, and that surprises you Nabis. That the most powerful Lok on the planet could do something like that?" Nabis stammered. "No but." The face continued. "He is that powerful, that is why we wanted him, that is why he is so important, the worth of the Confederates, the world." The green face paused, "The Galaxy perhaps? Nabis, the Paladins with him, what did they look like?"

"Look like? The one that stowed away was tall but slender, he." The face on the screen interrupted him, impatience in its voice. "Were either big, giant even, very muscled, or carry a sword?" "Sword, no my lord, neither was what I would consider big or giant."

"No. Hmm good, we have time then. Alert your men, I have intel that one of the ex guards has escaped Ice Well, he might be able help to them." "What! Escaped Ice Well? Lord, that is impossible." "No Nabis, it appears not." "You're serious?" "Of course I am, I do not joke about this!"

Nabis immediately cowed. "Yes my lord of course I will. Forgive me." The face waited a few seconds.

"Nabis?" The face asked, waiting for him to give his full attention. "Find the Prince."

"I will Lord, I know the way they are traveling to the White City, and I have their trust. If I can," the image cut him off mid-sentence. "Find him NOW, track him, call who you must do what you must, or are you of no use to me?"

"No Lord," Nabis said straightening, finding his courage. "I will put all my effort into his safe return."

"Good, I would hate to have to find another to help me." Nabis's cheeks flushed with embarrassment, and slight anger. "Nabis," he continued. "You can erase this failure."

"Find the boy, and when you are finished," he said with a slight annoyance in his voice, "I am sending you to Lord Nemsor. I feel you might be of use to him, after we take care of this." "Yes Lord," Nabis said trying not to show his chagrin at having to lower his status for Nemsor. "With the boy on the move and the Council soon meeting, it is time. Contact the Elf, and make sure he is on schedule as well, we do need that device." "Yes Lord." Nabis said, and the image in front of him disappeared.

Nabis sat in the chair silent. What to do, he asked himself. He stood and walked to another table where sat a decanter with water. He poured a glass, and started to drink, the water was cool and amazingly refreshing. It was derived from the desert beast called a Rangor, and he needed some of the elixir liquid to bring him back from his day. He took a long gulp then another. After the drink, Nabis immediately felt better, he closed his eyes as the cool liquid went down his throat. Then, he started the chuckle and then to laugh as he opened his eyes, an evil gleam in them. "I know how to solve this conundrum." He said skipping in the air, landing and taking the last sip of the Rangor Water, holding up his glass. "I'll deal with the Elf, but first, I need to hire me some Cowboys," he said in a fake southern accent as he continued looking at his glass. An evil grin split his face as he chuckled.

COWBOYS

Springhill, Water town outside of Lang, Part of the Pallance Confederate below the Dragon Wastes

It was hot, and dusty, the wind picking up the desert dirt and throwing it in all directions. It wasn't hard enough to hurt, but it was hard enough to get stuck where it shouldn't, and just be annoying. A gust of hot wind whipped around a building tossing the sand on its foundation and around the post in front of it. There was a sign hanging from the building post, flapping back and forth in the wind. The scraping of its rusty hinges had been making a small squeaking sound for most of the day. It was annoying, real annoying, that would be if anyone was listening. The dust swirled around the hot dessert ground picking up its pace blowing dust on the boots of a man standing outside of the building. The sign kept swinging in the wind and another gust hit it, the squealing stopped as one of its hinges finally popped, and left it hanging limply in the hot air; twisting in the arid wind. The man stood under the sign. He was covered in dust and looked to be made of the stuff, except for a streak of crimson around his waist flowing out from under his shoulder armored duster. It was a sash that marked the man as a Cowboy, bounty hunter, officer of the Pallance.

Cowboys were known as a lot of things, mercenaries, bounty hunters, lawmen, and the best monster hunters you find below the dead wastes of the Dragon lands. Though now most people called that desolate place below those lands, the Pallance. It's an honor to be a Cowboy to some, though others say it's a curse. Those same people say they are thieves and bandits, using their power for personal gain. Some are right, but Cowboys keep the laws of the lower mid territories of the Pallance Confederate, and their government. The council member that sanctions the law of this place

226

knows the area, and the type of mean people in it. It is wild in the western wastes, and the Cowboys are a needed part of it. The thing about Cowboys is their brand of justice is a little different. They have their own code, and are given leeway for that law by the Governor, under the Council. You know a Cowboy by the red sash or scarf they wear. Most are gun Loks or gun wizards, and the worst or best kind. They can control bullets, making them hit harder and able to shoot impossible shots. Some are so good they can spread bullets around like the roto and torrent cannons of the Gears. They say you never want to meet a Cowboy if you're on the wrong side of their brand of law, and it's true.

The road leading out of Lang was dusty and long. It led to the highway that stretched three hundred miles to the west and then tapered off until it got to the city of Angels. If you're on this road somebody might find you, too bad the soldiers of Fort Baxton were not. They were five miles south east, in a place called Springhill a small homestead outside of Lang. It was a poor farmer city that made its money from growing crops and mining water and selling them both to the other places in the area. Royal, Biloxi, and Santa Anita, were some of the many cities and small towns that bought the goods. The day was dry and the dust was blowing again as a small wind swirled as it swept through the dry plain. The dust whipped around covering the bodies of the men on the ground, and swirled around the three that were standing. Above them the vultures were circling in anticipation of the meal below.

It was hot, damn hot and the six stinking dead bodies didn't make it any better. The two surviving soldiers, a sergeant and private named Neck, were all that was left of the soldiers sent to investigate the killings at the water farm of Springhill. There the soldiers had found most of the farm people butchered and the few women and children that were left homeless and scared. It had looked like a Rangor attack. Damn beasts caused too much trouble, but their water is too valuable a resource to let go unattended, gives energy and some say youth. Poachers look to catch or kill them for this substance, and when the Rangor pride had been spotted the fort had sent some of the soldiers stationed there to check it out and protect the people. The bad thing was most survivors were women, and they had almost been violated by the same soldiers that were supposed to protect them. The Cowboys were called in after the soldiers hadn't checked in on time. The upper officers suspecting them of poaching the Rangor. They say you never want to meet a Cowboy if you're on the wrong side of their brand of law, and the three Cowboys standing now were no different. Actually, they're worse because they're the best at what they do. They kill.

The man by the broken sign looked up squinting reading the hanging piece of wood as it rocked back and forth. This way for a drink, it said. He snickered at the irony of it, then spit a glob of phlegm and walked toward the sergeant and private lying on the ground.

Cobb, leader of the Cowboys stopped walking and stood over the sergeant. Cobb's big mustache covered his top lip and almost his lower. He wore a big red scarf and sash that flipped in the wind as the dust blew back and forth in the hot air. His long, armored grayish brown duster hid the two firearms he was most famous for, although normally he never had to draw more than one. His dark brown diamante fur blend hat had seen some wear, but it still did its job as the brim cast a shadow over his face, hiding his steely blue eyes, killer's eyes. That gaze could pierce a man's heart as well as his nerves and it was doing just that as he looked down at the man lying in front of him. Cobb looked to his right. Tex, a burly man with a fighter's nose that looked as if he'd been on the wrong side of some good punches, was surveying the scene and looking at the man Cobb was standing over. He was dressed the same as Cobb, only he wore a vest with his large arms hanging out, and in his right hand he held his ten gallon hat. It was a cream color weathered white from the sun on the top and sides, and he had a blazer pistol on his left hip, a huge bowie knife on his right and a large scattergun type weapon on his back. The runes of the weapons were starting to glow as he waited for the sergeant to answer Cobb's question. Cobb wasn't waiting anymore; he walked over to Private Neck, who was moaning as he clutched his right arm. It was broken, and he was bleeding from the gash in his side that one of the women had given to him with a large kitchen knife.

Cobb looked back to the sergeant. The sergeant looked up sweat rolling down his beet red sun burnt face, as Cobb looked down at him, his shadow rolling over the man's features. Through cracked lips he said, "You can't leave me here, others will come." Cobb continued looking down at him and then looked to his left, Randall the third member of his party slowly walked towards them. He had the same grayish duster that the other two had; only he was slimmer and with smaller pads of steel on each shoulder, and all three had armor over the breaches. Randall's sash was tied tight about his waist and his clean features looked smooth and cool as if the heat wasn't bothering him at all. His slightly longer brown hair fluttered in the dusty wind, as it continued to swirl around the men. The hard brim of his black hat cast a shadow over his face and he had a toothpick that his gloved hand picked out of his mouth and flicked in the air. Cobb looked back down, his voice a rasp of intelligence and control. "I'm not going to ask you again, you tell me where they went, where the Rangor went and where the money here went." The sergeant didn't say anything, his crusty blistered lips couldn't manage a word. Cobb looked at Randall; Randall pulled his gun so fast that it wasn't even visible and shot Neck, killing him dead. The sergeant whimpered. Randall holstered his gun with a twirl on his finger, just to show off. In a hoarse voice the sergeant said, "I had two other soldiers take the money back to our barracks and that"...

Cobb drew his gun and shot him. He stood there holding his gun in his hand looking at the sergeant. "I can't stand the man who hurts a woman," he said as he holstered his runic pistol. The weapon, a pearl handled quad Blazer, shined in the sun, the runes on the sides fading as he slid the weapon back in its holster. Before this the Cowboys had taken the soldier's horses and given them to the women who were alive. They had sent them to the next town with the authentic seal of the Pallance, which meant they would be safe and under the Cowboys protection. This would ensure that no one would give them any trouble, lord knows they had enough already.

Loading up the rest of the supplies and checking the logs of the town for any other relevant information they could get. Cobb checked his wrist com and their next destination. They were about to mount up, when a dust cloud came up the road. A full twenty five mounted armed men in uniform of the soldiers they had just shot were riding toward them at a fast pace. As they reined in they circled the three Cowboys in a ring of horses, guns and soldiers. The Cowboys were in a triangle pattern in the center.

The lead soldier had captain's bars on his shoulders and a small cropped mustache. As they closed in on the men he held up his hand for halt. The dust settled around them as they stopped. "By the authority of the Regent of the Lower Mesa, I arrest you. You...Cowboys." He said it with a sneer as if the very mention of the name Cowboy made his stomach churn.

"You are out of the Pallance Jurisdiction and you have killed soldiers of the Republic of Mesa."

Cobb studied him; the Captain was a younger man most likely of a noble family who got his position through money and bullying. He was probably there to get his rocks off. Cobb looked up at him. "We have jurisdiction here, you know that, and we don't want trouble with you. These men were in direct violation of treaty 402. They stole money n' they paid the price. If you don't stand down and quit hampering our investigation, we will have to kill you."

The Captain smiled a bright white smile. "Are you serious?" He asked his pompous perfect pronounced words arrogant with disgust. "I have twenty five armed men and you are surrounded, the numbers and the odds are in my favor," he added, opening his hand. The captain leaned over his horse and pointed at Cobb. "You put down your weapons and come with me or I will kill you, old man." Before the captain could turn to look at his men who were chuckling, the Cowboys drew their side arms. The runes of the blazer weapons were on fire as they flashed to life. Blue streaks of light were everywhere knocking the men from their horses. It was as if the soldiers could not move the Cowboys were so fast. In less than five seconds all twenty-five soldiers were dead with shots through limbs, heads, and were already knocked off the horses and lying on the ground. Most of the horses reared and ran. The cocky captain was the only one left alive, lying on the ground having been shot through his lung and his gun hand. He was trying to move and lying on his back whimpering in disbelief. The Cowboy's guns were smoking, and Cobb was only holding one of his, the other had not even been pulled. Randall twirled his weapon around and holstered it with a series of specific tricks, while Tex's large scatter weapon folded in on the sides, with clacks and turns of cogs. The sides that had flared out returned the laser weapon to its stored position. He then holstered the large weapon with a clack and looked around at the men on the ground, checking to make sure they were all done. Cobb walked to the captain, the sand crunching beneath his boots as he did, gun still in hand. "What are you?" the captain asked terror in his face. Cobb looked down and pointed the barrel at him. "Sorry sir, but you're in direct violation of 402 also."

* * *

A mile outside of Springhill, Randall walked down the ramp of the Cowboys' large sleek air vessel. He and Tex had loaded the horses, and Tex was in the cockpit setting their next coordinates. Randal walked up to Cobb as he was finishing his conversation. Cobb was on a hill looking over the plain as the sun was going down. The sky was a beautiful reddish color.

"Over," Cobb said and pulled his coat sleeve back over the com on his wrist, the blue light of the hologram blinking out. "Where we heading?" Randall asked. "I just got a message, Cobb said, "Looks like those soldiers at the barracks are gonna have to wait, but Mira is sending others to retrieve the money. We got a new assignment. I don't like it. We got to head in to the cities." Cobb spit before he continued. "Some Council member has just hired us. Seems we gotta track someone, a boy."

"A boy?" Randall exclaimed. "What's a boy got to do with us, don't they have nannies for that. We hunt." Cobb just stared at him. "Are you finished?" He asked, rubbing his mustache down. Randall just looked at him blankly not knowing what to say. "Good," Cobb said. "I'll fill you in on the way. Just hope it isn't who Mira thinks it is, or we are going to be in some crap." Cobb looked back at the plain before turning to leave, the wind blowing over him.

III

"Some call us mutants, others monsters, and sorcerers, but in the end they will all call us GODS!!!"

-Tusho Lord of the Elves of Dru Nar-

The Dru Nar Elves of Royal

-Summary of Dru Nar of Royal, lesson to Young Scholars of the White
Tower-
-Recorded in a book of intellectual records-

The Elven race is not inherently evil. At one time they were a semi
ally to the Confederates and King Agesilaus. The King of the Elves, Moncul
Orophan Silimaurë Sea Dru Nar, joined forces with King Agesilaus when
the Razium attacked Partha Terra during the first Razium war. He was
instrumental in helping turn tide of the war and then win battles that had
been lost, as if he knew how the Razium would strike and could counter
them. Moncul, again helped during the Affinity wars. Sharing particular
secrets of Dragon speech, though he didn't share all his knowledge, and was
reluctant to fight against the Dragons who his people share a close kinship. It
was during these battles that he and his people retreated to their sacred lands
and closed the doors to all except those truly worthy in the Elves' eyes. The
Elven King is an honorable Elf, but his son the Prince, the Chaos Maker, the
Harlequin of Knaves, the Betrayer, Elerossë Tusho Dru Nar, is not.

The story of how the Elves of the Dru Nar came to be among us is a
harsh one. The Dru Nar originally part of the Sea Dru Nar, the King's royal
line; were exiled. The King's son, betrayed them. They have lost their name,
a very important thing in Elf society, and are pariahs of their own people.
When they were cast out, Tusho, their Prince, sought a way to get revenge
on humanity; who he blamed for his fall. Cutting a swath through any
competitors who dare oppose him, he came to the city closest to the
Dragons, the mercenary city of Royal.

Now they own half the city Royal, which makes it a very rare place
indeed. It is one of the only places you can find an Elf that isn't on one of
their island Kingdoms. Those secret palaces of knowledge and lore are
heavily guarded, and hidden from the eyes of the other races. These lands

are not on the mainlands of Ultima Thule, Ultima Prime, or even on the other smaller continents. They are west of them, past Maelstrom, and east toward the Flame Geysers. Their kingdoms are not on mainland for good reason, but that is another lesson.

At the time the Confederates were at war, so the city became of little consequence. Instead of sending resources to take the city back, the Governor decided to take bribes to stay out of the conflict, and let the Elf scum fight the Kissar for the city. The Governor hoped it would lead to both wiping each other out, leaving little for his forces to clean up. That didn't happen. The Elf Prince had different ideas. After much bloodletting, the Elves and Kissar came to a semi truce, and divided the city. The Elves constructed the wall or Hem, that separated the two sides, and they both prospered.

Tusho cared not for the fighting of the outside, for he only wanted the city as a way to strike back at the Humans. He hated us, and blamed them for his downfall, and what better way to destroy them than to give them the means to kill themselves. Provide them with violence, drugs, sensuality, gluttony, or any of the other numerous ways to hurt the race he so hated.

The Elves disdained other races as well; ones they claim had weakened them and pushed them out of power. The Razium, who they reviled but seemed to be too familiar with, the Dwarger that they have never agreed with but none as loathed as Humans. Not because of anything other than they seemed jealous of them.

Humanity has a special place in their blackened hearts. Hominid or Imperfect, were words the Elves used to describe humanity. The Humans had risen to prominence, claiming to make the planet safer and better, and in doing so pushed the Elves from their supposed seat of power as the strongest people. So now these outcast Elves scorned the Human race, no matter if Lok or normal. They didn't care for race or creed, they hated and blamed them; and their twisted Prince loathed them the most.

Tusho is why the other Elves remain in their own borders, and was exiled after he shown his true face was a face of evil. In his jealousy for the Humans, for the Loks of the Confederates and the power they possessed, he betrayed them to their enemy; giving the Razium the weapon to defeat them. With the Humans out of the way, Tusho would take back what he thought was his.

CHAPTER 21. THE ELVES OF ROYAL:

The Hem, Lithatl

The night was wet, the last few days bringing with it heavy rain and storms, which was normal for this time of year. Lately however, they had been getting worse as if the weather itself knew a change was coming. It had let up slightly in the last hour or so but still there was a slight drizzle falling. Most of the people of the city of Royal were inside for the night, though not all. A figure wearing a dark sea blue cloak walked the streets, staying close to the shadows. The cloak was thick and gave away nothing of its wearer, but on the left breast it had a small emblem of a boat and a dragon, stitched in gold. Most people wouldn't have even seen the lithe graceful creature moving through the night, her movements almost undetectable. Most wouldn't have wanted to anyway. She was an Elf, and most knew to keep their distance from the deadly but almost mythical creatures. She kept moving looking around herself, checking to see if she had been followed.

The rain increased, the pattering of its large drops on the stone street was all the noise anyone, even under cover could hear. Rain however was nothing to an immortal like her. She was a member of the Harlequin's Court, the sick twisted Prince's personal entourage of most dedicated or deceitful followers.

The Elven girl opened her hand holding her slender pointer finger out to catch the large drops of rain. One hit the tip of her finger sending cascades of feelings through her. The rain was a cleanser to these Humans, the people of this infested city thinking it would wash their sins away, she thought to herself. The Humans hide and shy away from the water, but she knew what the rain was. She was a being that had lived for centuries, she enjoyed the life that the cold liquid gave to this world. She loved the rain. Still though, it wouldn't do to keep his highness waiting, even if she did enjoy the basking in the cold of Mother Nature. She sighed, the last of the feeling leaving her saddened. Then the feeling was gone and so was she. She quickly made her way through the streets toward her destination, the Western side of the fortress city, Lithatl.

The wall, called the Hem, that separated the two halves of the Royal was high but thin, especially compared to the larger walls that protected the megalopolitan city from the outside. The Hem was a smooth grey color, which blended to an eggshell white on the lookout towers the Elves had constructed across it.

The Elven girl wasn't looking at either of those now though. She was looking at the wall in front of her, the classic brick and mortar of the mongrel Humans. The Kissar wall had two small entrance gates, one on either side of the large gate that was centered in the middle, used to cross to the Elves' side, and all were almost always locked. Only special days did the Elves and Humans do any trading, and those days seemed to be getting scarcer by the day. The doors of the large middle gate had been made by the Elves. They were huge pieces of functional artesian craftsmanship that didn't skimp on the decorative nature of the beings that had built them. They depicted tall Elven warriors in battle helms carrying trumpets, glaives, and other Elvish stylings with glyphs around them. They were so well crafted that the figures looked as if they could walk off the doors. The material they were made from was smooth with the texture of marble and cold to the touch. The arch above the doors was also covered in Elvish runes and glyph carvings; statues stood on either side of the main entrance. Stones that dimly glowed in the night air were set by each of the runes. Their worth, priceless. Most in the city were not foolish enough to actually attempt to take another of them after the first thief had tried, failed, and was still failing. If the rumors of that were true, the Elven Ol'ea magic had taken him, and one doesn't come back from that. However, every few years another thief foolish enough does come around to try.

The hooded Elven girl looked at a point of the closest tower, her keen vision seeing clearly what most would pass over. She trotted to one of the towers close to the gate. Like a cat padding to its next meal, her muscles smooth and fluid in the movement. The tower, unlike the Human wall, was completely Elven. It was tall and smooth, the color alone setting apart from the Human built sections, much less the shape and texture. She slowed as she closed on the smooth eggshell white tower. The tower was one of eight that the Elves had constructed when they had claimed their part of the city, and were fashioned around and used to monitor the Humans when they built their wall. They were distributed evenly down its length, and had been used as watch posts in days past but no longer. Most had been left, abandoned now and used only when the Elves wanted to make a show of themselves. It made the Humans nervous, those towers gazing on them. Who knew what creature could be looking out from the towers? She smiled at the thought of the scared Humans, knowing her lord liked that as well.

Bending close and checking the area, she looked at the wall then to the ground, seeing the overturned dirt, and scuff of the wall. Something had happened, but who would be so stupid? We have let the Humans alone for some time now, why would they try and break in? She stopped her thoughts as she saw slight traces of blood though nothing else. A look of disdain crossed her face as she thought about the Humans and how they had tried to get into the towers, long ago. As she was thinking on it she looked at the smooth structures and tall edifices remembering how they had fought them here. She touched the surface of the tower, feeling its cold texture, then it felt warm to her. Home, she thought. They couldn't get in then, and now was no different. She moved to the other side of the tower allowing the shadows to overlap her. With her cloak wrapped tight, she was almost invisible as she stood in the dark shadow beside the amazingly crafted spire. She stopped moving, hearing a figure in the distance as he ran across the street in the other direction paying her no heed as he was trying to get out of the rain. She watched him go under the light of the street lamps and vanish from sight. When she was sure no one else was close she moved to a spot on the tower. With a smooth motion of her long white fingers she touched a pattern on the towers' surface. There was nothing on its surface, not buttons or even runes. It was smooth like glass and it seemed as if she had just tapped the wall with her fingers. A faint trace of bluish light outlined the keypad she had just pressed, and with a small release of air that made little sound, the tower opened revealing a small door. With a turn of her head to double check she wasn't seen, she slipped in and through to the other side of Royal, to Lithatl.

Lithatl, underneath Royal

The Human man was sniveling, sucking snot up his large nose as he lay on the ground, his face red from the flush of blood. He had been struck hard, and was scared, the dark spot on his pants showed that. "Please," he was begging. "I'll give it back, don't keep me here, please." He wept quietly. The creature standing over him was in the shadow. He couldn't see it now except for its tall lithe outline, and he was glad he couldn't. The thing was terrifying. The man was in the lower part of Royal, Lithatl. It was a dreaded place to go if you were not invited, and the thief lying on the ground surly was not. It had been raining and the dripping of the water in the background was the only thing that could be heard in the lower section of the city, that and his sniveling. The drips of the cold wet water echoing in the shadowy depths of the sewers they were in.

The large figure he had been afraid of slowly stepped out of the shadow, and the man was struck again, this time not physically but visually. The figure wasn't what he had seen earlier, it was the same but somehow it had transformed, the monster was gone. This creature before him was a beautiful thing. It looked like the most perfect of beings, a woman. Its body and face a white cream color, and its features flawless like a statue. It stepped into the light and revealed itself to him. The thing was perfect, so graceful, sensual he thought as he watched it move. Though as he did, he realized it looked as if it was made of marble or bone. The thief forgot about the monster that had been there, being caught up in the beauty before him. He thought it was an Elf at first but it wasn't. It was entirely alien compared to the Elves, just as an Elf was to a Human. It watched him, and he saw its eyes had no iris, only the same cream color as its body. He looked at it, and it looked back, cocking its head. The thing saw the light in his eyes, he was mesmerized. He started to smile, and reached his hand up toward hers. She did the same, then his eyes widened in terror. The beautiful creature transformed, and he screamed!

Once in the tower, the Elven girl had made her way through the tunnels and hidden doors to far below the Elven side of the city. She hurried down the corridors, the cloak draping her, not able to hide the smooth action and movement of her graceful bounds. It was cold below the surface and the corridor was not spared the chill, a continuous breeze ran down its length, her breath misting as she ran.

If seen in a normal light the corridor would have been crowned an achievement of its builders, and they would have been famous for their work. The artist responsible for its creation would have been tasked with creating a monumental piece of artisanship for the entrance to an amazing castle, promenade of a Champion's den, or Governor's palace. For the Elves it was just another of a series of tunnels, though the craftsmanship was almost unparalleled. Especially for only tunnels that reached far below the surface of Royal. Though these hidden tunnels led to a special place, a place that would have shown off the grandeur of its splendor if not for the disgrace of how it came about, and the Prince who caused it.

She made her way to the end of the tunnel that led to another, warmer corridor. The oval shaped corridor was smooth, and had circular patterns of runic devices that carved the length of it. The runes were outlined in gold and they sparkled as the figure hurried past them. The light that bathed her hurried form was a smooth dim blue. It gave the corridor an eerie feel, but one she enjoyed. The light came from smaller versions of glow gems like the ones at the Elven gate. They were mounted every few yards on each side, each giving off the perfect amount of light to see but not too much as to show more than was needed. Well, to other eyes perhaps; not her eyes. She was an Elf after all, and her people's vision was amazing at day, and some would say better at night. She wasn't there to look at the craftsmanship, no she had been summoned to see her Lord, the ruler of this realm, and she hurried to obey. Looking over her shoulder, she checked again, making sure she had not been followed. It was very unlikely, but Elves were Elves and trusted no one. She continued on, quickening her pace as not to be late for her Lord Prince.

She thought about him as she ran. Prince Tusho was famous, though now more infamous and most knew his name, most feared it. The Humans spoke it in whispers, as a plague, a story and not wanting him to be real. The Red Dragon, Chaos Maker, the Harlequin of Knaves, the outcast

Prince, Ruler of the West of Royal, Son of the Lord of the Mists, Elerossë Tusho Dru Nar had many names, and all were hated even by his own people.

Tusho had made a deal with powerful forces, dark forces that he had no control of. In his arrogance he was betrayed, and the Elves lost half of their race in a battle that should never have been. In the aftermath, Tusho was cast out by his father, shamed his house, and was stripped of his titles. He had half his locks shorn from his head, and he and his were branded with the mark of the Solitaire, to be forever alone. He left with all who followed him, his people disgraced and forever banned from the world they knew, lived, and loved; never to be welcomed home. He became sick and twisted, not in look, but in mind. He became what he wanted most. Hate, for those he blamed. Humanity. Tusho swore vengeance on those responsible. He would do anything to get what he had back. She remembered that, as she neared her destination.

She was loyal to him, and his army was loyal to him. She would bring the gift to him that would start his climb back to power, their climb back. Her Prince would take the first step to reclamation, and she would be by his side. The blue glow continued, as did the Elven girl's thoughts of power with her master, smiling to herself as she hurried down the corridor, the light of the gems catching the menace of her eyes.

* * *

Tusho, the Prince of the Elves of Dru Nar, reclined like a large feline as he sat on his massive throne. The throne itself sat toward the back center of the room. A room that was of the same design as the corridors that led to it, though much more elaborate, perfect in fact. Instead of inlays there were golden statues of Elven figures and mythical creatures, the biggest of which was a huge twenty foot golden dragon that rose behind his throne. It loomed over the room, its head sticking from the shadows. There were many other beautiful items and weapons off to the sides as well, treasures of the highest value in most kingdoms, but seemed no different than the fruit dishes or goblets here. The room itself was an eggshell beige and trimmed in gold and platinum on all surfaces, the perfection of the angles a thing to boggle one's mind. It wouldn't have looked real to the eyes of most mortals, but to an Elf it was the single minded perfection that they were used to, it was home, born of the angles of their long lives. The room was immense, its four main pillars creating a perfectly equidistant square in the middle. They dominated the area holding up the massively impossible arched ceiling, the top lost in the dim shadows above. In between the pillars vassals danced for their liege, dressed in bright and colorful outfits, make up, and costumes. The lithe creatures were moving and playing out some tragedy in the interpretive dance, the beauty of it breathtaking to see.

Prince Tusho stood as he watched them dance. So breathtaking he thought. He was garbed in deep purple robes trimmed in gold, with necklaces and trinkets that hung around him and over his black tight fitting body suit. The colors starkly contrasted with his pale skin, almost the color of the years first snow. All his kind had the light colored skin and usually it was flawless. His was as well, only more pale than most. His hair also white and cut short almost to the scalp on one side, which meant he had been diminished or shamed. The other side was long, tied in braids and pulled back over his ear. Small fetishes of jewels and beads were braided into the lengths. His lips were a dull red, the lipstick he wore enhancing his strange look. He was being entertained by beautiful vassals of his court; three were standing with him on the stairs that lead to his dais throne. Beautiful they were, as were the others dancing the story for him between the pillars. He had sat back on the throne and continued watching them as his food was being brought to him, and served. He was the Prince after all, all should serve. He was given meats and fruits and was drinking a cup of his homeland's finest wine. When he had left his homeland he was too attached to the drink to not have brought some with him, his gluttony of it bordering on addiction. He supped the drink while the dancers lept and teased, giving some of the liquid to his vassals that stood with him. Skouro Aima or Dark Blood, the Elves called it. It was made from a strange fruit indigenous to the Elven lands alone. It was exquisite to taste and it enhanced the senses tenfold. Its only down fall was drinking too much. It would turn anyone who did into a happy but mindless puppet until they passed out, which he did often, to others, for his pleasure and theirs. He didn't have to worry about the side effects though, his tolerance was too high and it would take too much for him to get to that state. Still he was enjoying its qualities.

From the side of this amazingly grand room, a secret marble covered door opened. A thing stepping from the shadows of the secret entrance, a tall and gruesome half marble half monster Golem. It tread softly for a being so big, and moved through the shadows with a grace that it shouldn't have possessed. In its marble like hand hung the limp form of a man, a thief.

The thing held the man by his leather studded jerkin. He hung limply, arms dragging the ground, the goggles around his neck dangling back and forth. He stunk, and the immediate presence of the man was sensed by all in the grand room. The dancers slowed and then stopped. Tusho turned his head lazily to look upon this offensive intruder, staring at the Golem through his lilac eyes. "Well, well, well what have you found?" His voice caring and sweet as he asked the Phenii the question. It stopped in front of him dropping the lifeless form of the thief. He landed with a thud, the jolt waking him and he groaned. The Phenii looked at Tusho with the evil grin its created face held, and then the face of its smaller self, the marble maiden was pulled up from its storing area over its smiling grimace. The pretty doll like face covered the evil clown like visage it wore. It then tilted its doll head to the side, its girl like features looking so innocently at the Lord of the Dru Nar. He watched as the rest of it enclosed upon itself, where before stood the hulking armored plated monster, now stood the tall slender figure of the marble maiden. "Oh," Tusho said to it. "I see, you like this toy." Tusho grinned and gave the Phenii an evil mischievous look. Stepping down from his perch on the throne, he glided down the steps to the floor.

As he passed the marble Golem, he touched its face with his slender finger, running it down the perfectly smooth side of its cheek to its pointy chin. Tusho stood a few feet away from the man on the floor, not wanting to get any closer and inflict anymore pain on his nostrils from the stench of the man's piss.

The thief had started to come to; and realize where he was; and that he needed to find a way out of this predicament or they would surely kill him. When he was sent on this mission he didn't except to see the Lord of the Elves himself, and to be here in this secret place. Many would have paid a fortune for this information. His mind stopped racing and came back to the mess he was in. He was only supposed to have reconned the area and then report any findings to Dillion or Tasha, but his greed and pride had gotten in the way after he had made it through the defenses of the Elven city. The changing device that he had been given had worked amazingly, it had worked too well. He had made it through the streets attracting no attention, and had worked his way in to the stronghold of the Elves. Once in, he stumbled upon the plans of the Elves working with the Razium, and the weapons they had been trading. He had reported back to Dillion, and his Gangster Boss had sent him in again, promising wealth and power. Only this time he had to get more information and leave a message, whatever the Elves had, the Kissar could take.

Dillion wanted to make them feel vulnerable. Take them down a notch. The thief had made it to the Palace and had found much to report, but after using his info to find one of the Elves prized treasures, he had accidentally found a wealth located in a hidden cache. The value of the items he had found was too much to leave, and his greed had overtaken his better senses. He had to have some of the treasure for himself, he deserved it, was his reasoning. But, how would he get it out? He looked at his disguise realizing he couldn't carry much without giving himself away, and then he saw it. On the top of one of the chests was a dagger of exquisite beauty, the jewels alone small fortunes. He took it, he knew someone he could sell it to, a collector of such things and with the dagger he had taken he would have never had to work or worry again. If only he could have gotten it out. He snapped out of his trance realizing that the Elven Prince was staring at him, and he had better think quickly if he wanted live. It hit him, information. He could barter the information he had for his freedom. He shoved down the strange nausea he felt, and stood.

Standing, he was still not nearly as tall as Tusho and he felt little next to him. He was about to say something, but Tusho held up his hand for silence. "Why are you in my house? And why have you taken my things?" Tusho asked, his voice a thing of dread sorrow.

It was all the man could do not to start crying and say he was sorry, fall to his knees and beg forgiveness. He almost did, but something stopped him, maybe Dillion's wrath, who knows, but he was able to control himself. Unfortunately he caught Tusho's eyes, and he couldn't help but stare. The Elven Prince looked sad, his large purple irises illuminated by the lights of the room. Tusho held his hand out, holding it toward him, beckoning him.

He couldn't stop himself, he was Tusho's puppet. The thief's legs moved without thought, and he walked toward the prince. As he did, the guilt hit him as he peered into those eyes. He reached in to a secret place in his jerkin pulling an exquisite sheathed dagger from it. It was so well crafted, its like had not been seen in a century. He gently handed it to the Prince, and stepped back. A beautiful Elven girl swiftly moved to her lord's side and gently took the blade. Tusho had taken his gaze away from the thief, and looked at the dagger, his face still full of sorrow, as though his memories of it were unbearable. After the Elf girl had taken it, Tusho slowly looked back to the thief. The thief almost had to look away from those eyes. "Thank you," Tusho said quietly, though his facial expressions overemphasized the words. His grief once overflowing seemed to leave his face with relief and stiffly he turned from the thief walking slowly back up toward his throne.

The thief stood there, not knowing what to do. He felt awkward with the gaze off him, but maybe he would live, there was a chance. "Am I free to go?" He squeaked, braver than he felt. His legs felt like they were made of lead. Tusho turned so fast the thief barely saw him move; there was no sorrow now, only maliciousness. "Go? Go?" The Elf asked pausing. "Go where?" Tusho spat, the gaze of the Elf penetrating him to the core. The thief felt a chill up his spine and he was afraid but he had been in difficult situations before, and the mocking tone in the Elven Lord's voice was turning his fear to anger. No one treats him like this; the Elves thought he was trash. He had broken into their impenetrable palace, and taken a dagger, that obviously had value. The thief was gaining a small amount of confidence; maybe they were not so powerful if he could break in to their palaces.

Tusho could tell that his demeanor had changed. "Ooooo," the Elf said slowly and sarcastically, "You want to hurry back to your master, and tell him the goodies you have found out, is that it?" He asked looking hard into the thief's eyes. "No? I don't think so either." Tusho continued, "You want to live; I mean leave, don't you." His cruel sarcasm making the man lose more of his frayed nerve. With the phrase he had turned the man's anger back to fear, and his fear was growing into terror. Tusho read him like a book. He continued. "Your Human soul, you don't deserve such a thing, the power of it," he said trailing off as he looked at this trash in front of him slowly walking back toward him. The thief started to panic. "My lord, I won't

244

tell him, I swear!" He was stammering almost crying, "I can tell you much of our secrets, I can show you secret entrances, I can."

"You can what," the Elf Lord asked mockingly leaning out toward the man, cocking his head slightly so he could hear him better. The thief began again, trying to find his backbone. "I can tell you of plans to conquer your side of the city." He stated boldly, "And ways around your security."

"Can you now?" Tusho asked mildly intrigued, "Well, I would be very interested to hear them, if I wasn't going to destroy the city myself," the Elf said smiling holding his hands out to either side palms up, the evil grin returning. Tusho was standing tall looking around the room as if addressing an army. "You see, Homin Apo Deka tipota." He said emphasizing the Elven words, meaning the thief was less than nothing. "I don't care about this place or the things in it. I will destroy it all, and when the Razium are through enslaving your people, mine will rise from the ashes. I will awaken our kin and lead them to victory. I will do that which my near sighted father could not; the God of Sorrow and Laughter has shown me. As for the Razium. They and their Zajust masters are nothing. I will not have to worry about them anyway. I will kill them and take it all, then climb the throne as the new Lord of this world!" He finished, hands raised, his voice a triumphant jubilation, as he stood at the top of his dais. Then he returned back to nonchalance taking his seat again, flopping into the thrown as a tired child would after a day of playing. His servants immediately brought him his wine. After Tusho sat, the thief stared in awe at the monster before him. Tusho noticed. "I know," Tusho whispered, smiling and taking a sip of his wine, as if the man was basking in his radiance.

"You're mad," the thief said trembling.

"We all go a little mad sometimes." Tusho returned as he waved his hand around nonchalantly. The Elf girl returned with the now polished dagger, and handed it to her lord, along with a pour of the Dark Blood to his goblet. He looked at her, smirking as though they were sharing a small joke, and she returned his gaze. Lustful wonder was in her big sparkling eyes, then she also drank. The thief watched them, seeing the amazing dagger in Tusho's hand.

The thief asked. "So, you are going to kill me?" Tusho looked away from the girl, the strange connection broken by the man's question. He looked at the thief's puzzled face and answered. "Kill you? Kill you?" His voice rising, "No, of course not," he said somewhat jokingly, chuckling. "That my friend would be too boring." He finished talking, his voice lowering as he tilted his lowered head up to look at the man from under his pale brow. "And this will be much more fun," he said lowering his voice. The Phenii behind the thief came from the shadows transforming from the marble maiden into the monster as it moved. It grabbed the man dragging him screaming into the shadows the way he had come in. All watched.

All was silent, the thief's screams still echoing before the secret door closed. When they were gone Tusho looked back to his vassals, "So where were we?" he asked. At once, they started to dance seductively, music playing in the background as if nothing had happened. "Ahh, yes." He said, reclining raising his eyebrows.

"My lord?" One of his young very attractive vessels asked. Without looking Tusho raised his hands, "Oh what is it now?" He rolled his eyes and turned to look at the Elven girl. "Well," he said after looking at her. "Who are you? It is no matter, what is it?"

"Sire," she said sweetly, bowing to him. "You have someone for you lord, a Human." She said holding her hand toward his throne console. Tusho narrowed his eyes to the girl, a sly grin on his mouth. "I'll see you later," he said flirting with the attractive Elven girl. She smiled and bowed. Then with a push of a few buttons his throne turned, the large chair sliding silently around and back a few feet. A three dimensional screen appeared from a projection below it, as a few of Tusho's court gathered behind him. He clicked it on, Nabis' face appeared. "Lord Nabonidus of the Council." Tusho said annoyed rolling his eyes, "To what do I owe this pleasure?"

"Lord Tusho." Nabis replied, his dignitary heir was apparent as he spoke. "I hope all is well with our transaction. Have you had any complications, thus far?"

"Well, well with me? How nice of you to ask. Yes I am fine thank you, and our, ah transaction. You mean the item, yes it is in good hands I assure you, and no nothing out of the ordinary is stalling us." Tusho cocked his head to the side. "Although, I am rethinking some things. The Tempest is in flux you see, and the time isn't right for the device to be forced. So."

"What!" Nabis interrupted. "No, Tusho you will do this, I have kept the governments off your back, we could take that damned city from you, for the resources there if we wanted. We have helped you, don't you think the

Kissar have friends in the Confederates and abroad as well? They are getting ready to move on you Tusho! The magic is in flux! Don't give me that, I'm a damned Lok, I know what is happening and I know why the currents are changing! I don't know what you're playing about with your fool games, but you need to do this and now. The Labrynthian will be opened again and soon, and..."

Tusho held up his hand silencing him. "Yes I know," he said softly. "That is what I was telling you," Then paused. "You see Nabis, I know the Labrynthian. I of my kin can control the Tempest, better than most." He waved his hands around nonchalantly. "My people, we own the magic of this world, be lucky you and your Lok brethren can even use it, in your unskilled way." He pointed at the screen and then dramatically touched his head with the back of his hand, bending over looking at the floor.

"Listen you crazed Elven clown!" Nabis was livid. "You take up your damned crusade against the Humans and Loks another time; you're in your mess because of yourself. If you hadn't have taken that," One of the Elves of Tusho's court that had been listening to the exchange spoke up. "How dare you talk to our Lord in this manner! You will learn your place Human."

"Shhhhhhh," Tusho said extremely loud to the Elven guard behind him, holding his hand up looking up from his seated bent over position. He continued shushing the guard before finally standing, putting his pointer finger to his lips. He continued shushing, the spittle getting on his finger as he pressed hard against his lips. Then he stopped, and stared at the Elf that had spoken out of turn. His eyes where huge. "We don't talk about that," he finished as he took the finger away from his lips stepping to the Elf and pressing his wet finger to the Elf's lips. "Shhhhh." He said softer, his face a mask of concern for the Elf, and then he slapped the Elf in the face knocking him to the floor.

"That is so you will remember your place!" He yelled at his guard who had gone to a knee holding his face, a trickle of blood running down his lip. Tusho's face was a mask of rage. "Now get up, and run along." He said, as he instantly changed back to his nonchalance, flipping out his robes and sitting again.

"Lord Nabis, please, continue." Tusho said as if it wasn't out of the ordinary to do what he had just done. Nabis, not believing what he had just witnessed, tried to remember what he wanted to say. "Ahh yes, Tusho. Also,

I have talked with the master; they are sending a Zajust to meet with you. To make sure all arrives safely, as a precaution. Protection if you will." Tusho looked at the screen, not saying anything. Nabis continued. "Make sure it is done, we need that shipment to be at the right place, at the right time. Are we understood?" "Yes Nabis, we are. Tell your master I am his, for now." Tusho smiled and started laughing. Nabis nodded and the screen dissipated.

* * *

The actual entrance of the Prince's lair was a set of huge steal trimmed burn wood doors. They were relics from another time, from the architects and builders of the things long gone. In the many years they had stood not one scratch had been put on their dark hides. Though they were actually brownish red, they looked black in the dimmed light of the room. They were massive, hinged and hydraulically operated with pistons off to each side. The silver mechanics of the doors cogs and gears large enough to keep almost anything out, or in, depending on your taste. Still though, they had heavily armed and armored guards stationed on either side, the sigil of their Elven Prince on their cold grayish breast plates.

The large doors mechanisms clacked and the doors opened. An Elf armored in the same color as the guards walked in, bowed and saluted his liege as Tusho's throne had returned to its original spot. The Elf was wearing his grey and silver colored armor, helm, and purple cape with the sigil of a mighty ship and Dragon on his breast plate. Tusho made a gesture and the vassals stopped their dancing, scattering, making no sound as they left the center area. Their movements fluid, reminding the newly entered Elf of lithe deer when a predator grows close.

He strode across the onyx and marble checkered tiles, and continued to watch the exciting mass of servants and vassals as they melted into the shadows and went to their private chambers. As he walked he touched his gauntlet, the facemask of his helm slid back and his gorget retracted behind his neck and to his shoulder, allowing his face to be seen. He lifted his smooth helm off his head, his perfect features regal as he walked. He was older for an Elf, though most who looked at him couldn't tell, but upon closer inspection one could see the lines at the corner of his eyes and the slight creases that had started to mare his perfection. His close cropped white hair was half shorn, shaved on one side, and his goatee trimmed. Setting his helm in the crook of his armored left arm, he turned back to gaze at the steel wood doors he had just come through, and hit his breast plate twice with his right hand.

Between the doors walked a monstrous troll. The thing was massive. Its skin was green grey in color and it was heavily muscled. Its front lower canines were protruded from its mouth, the points ending below its cheeks, and it had earrings and fetishes in its long braided hair. Its dark goatee was tied in the same manner, swishing back and forth like a pendulum of a clock as it lumbered in the room. The troll was clothed, wearing a vest of sea blue, and dark brown breeches. In his huge arms he was carrying a chest the size of a small calf, with no strain on his brutish features. His thick forehead and small inset eyes lowered as to not look at Prince Tusho directly.

The chest was another example of Elven craftsmanship, though not because of beauty, but of indestructibility. It was dark in color, resembling the armor of the Elven elite, and had silver inlays and black clasps that chinked as the Troll stepped. On its front it bore a mark, the mark of the Dru Nar, a boat and a Dragon made of gold. The Elven general that had entered spoke. "My lord this is the last of the cases. It is ready for your approval." Tusho stood from the throne, and motioned for the Troll to set it down. "Bring it," he whispered as if it didn't matter, as if nothing mattered. Reaching the bottom of the dais before the throne, the beast slowed. He set the huge chest down gently, with no strain on his corded muscled arms, then stepped back. The general opened it. Tusho looked at him, as the light from the treasure highlighted his regal perfect features when it hit his face, then he spoke.

"Than, my friend. I need you to accompany this shipment, make sure that it arrives and that this chest goes to our..." He paused searching for the right word as he rolled his hand around in a circle. "Benefactor." he finally said smiling sarcastically. "I will be behind you, soon. This one chest will start my ascendance back to the throne of my people. Our people," he said putting his hand on the general's pauldron as he stood. Tusho had the dagger that the thief had tried to steal in his belt. He pulled it and showed it to the general, who acknowledged the knife and Tusho set it in the chest. "Now the pact is complete by our laws."

"Yes lord," the General agreed and motioned for the huge Troll to close the chest. "My Prince, she is here."

"Send her in." Tusho said with anticipation in his voice. Than turned and held his hand towards the massive doors that hadn't fully closed. The guards moved aside to reveal a slender figure draped in a blue cloak, a gold embroidered Dragon and ship on the breast. The lithe Elf entered the room, walking through the guards unhindered. The dark doors closed behind her with a hiss and click as they locked. Her steps were smooth as she came towards them. It was as if she floated to the front of the throne, rather than walked. She stopped before Tusho and bowed, pulling back her hood to reveal a young attractive face. She had big eyes and short cropped colored hair with braids on the side. The prince awkwardly walked to her, touching her cheek, running his slender pale white finger around her jaw stopping at her small pointed chin. He slowly, gently lifted it up. His voice was soft. "What do have to tell me little one?" She stared up at him, her iris's turning black as she raised her face, her thin lips curving into a smile. "My Lord," she said, "I have procured the Key." Tusho smiled, sickly. "I don't think your rival will miss it," she said, producing a black velvet bag. She opened it, the glow from within washing over them. The crystal inside bathed them in a liquid blue light. It was breathtaking.

"The warmongers want the power of the Labrynthian, do they? They think they know. Oh, but they do not know its power. The Tempest is a difficult mistress." Tusho finished speaking and held the Key looking at it. "General, as per the arrangement, make sure this gets to the Razium." Tusho could tell Isabella, the seer that had brought the key to him, disapproved. He looked to her. "Yes?" he asked his voice echoing in the vastness of the room. Her voice was rich with power. "You read me, my Lord, as always."

"Say what you will my seer."

"My Prince, I cannot see it, the future of this endeavor is clouded." "Do not worry. I don't," he said turning back to his general. "Than?" Than snapped to, tall and proud. "Yes my Lord." Tusho became serious. "They have sent one of their dogs, a Zajust warlord. Do not trust the Za, they are conniving and warlike, the little ones are the worst. He will betray you."

"They have no honor," the general stated, "I am Dru Nar, we pay no head to such trash. Once this is concluded and our allies secure, I will kill the thing personally." Tusho smiled at his friend. "Good, now go." Than nodded and the Troll hefted the chest turning to leave.

As they left the room Isabella's gaze followed them, then she looked to her lord Tusho as he watched them go. She spoke. "The key will give us the edge, it was wise to trust the general with it. That I know. It may be the key to control of this war, though the path is still black to me." "True my seer, beautiful seer," Tusho said caressing her cheek. "It may be." "Also, I need him alive if it goes awry. Than is loyal, he will be able to tell me what is happening with the Zajust mongrel. I mean knowledge is power after all."

CHAPTER 22. MEMORIES OF WAR:

Northeast confederate of Essex, York region the city of Massal

The Tower of Thrones was a vast walled citadel located in the middle of the busy industrial city of Massal. The basilica palace was an impressive work of ancient craftsmanship, and artistic vision. The walls were high and impregnable, and its flying buttresses lead inward to its center where a grand spire rose over the city poking almost into the clouds. The sky around its pinnacle was filled with air traffic. The airships, fighters, and zeppelins of other cities coming for trade and export of their goods, at least those ships that had managed to get trade authorization. The Razium had seized York, the capitol of the north eastern Confederate, and now controlled the areas air travel and exports to and from the city.

The Tower was a very impressive sight, even its name was impressive. Originally named by one of the first founding Confederate Kings long ago, the Tower of Thrones had always stood as a symbol of hope for the people of the region. Now however, it wasn't a symbol of hope, freedom, or democracy but, of pure power. Lord Nemsor Vaul, the Iron Knight, had made it his personal fortress. No more were the days of celebrations and parties, now it was a place of dread and sorrow.

The Razium had imposed their will upon the people of the region, and they took or rather recruited the sons and daughters of the land to bolster their army. Some joined because they had no choice and were forced, some joined because they had families to feed and needed money, and others because it was easy money. The Zajust gave you a choice, help the cause, or be the cause, and after too much bloodshed, the people of the northeast slowly relented.

* * *

The huge Zajust Lord Sinagog, entered the dark corridor leading to the battle chamber of the Tower. His steps thumping in rhythm with the clinking of his chains as he walked. He had been summoned by Nemsor Vaul and had come with haste, arriving at Massal just this morning. He and his retinue had docked their space cruiser on one of the upper landing platforms the Razium had built for resupplying their craft. Dismissing them when they had landed, the giant Zajust had come to Nemsor's chamber by himself. He came to deliver his account to Nemsor personally. It is how the Zajust did things. It was all about might. The mighty won a warrior's honor on the battle field. If you didn't have that, you were nothing as a Zajust. He was seething at his failure at the city of Anstone and wanted to atone for it. He didn't fail though, he thought, he was tricked by Matias and his Spartans. Tricks had no battle honor, and he hated them. He was getting angrier, breathing harder, his green scared cybernetic face contoured in rage as he thought how the boy had been stolen from him at the last moments of the battle.

The Razium grenadiers guarding the way to Nemsor's chamber, moved as they saw Sinagog. They knew his temper and when to be away from it. As he came to the entrance of the chamber he paused, looking down at the severed helmet of the Wargear Talos. It clinked on his thigh armor when he stopped. At least he had a new trophy, he thought. His head snapped up hearing the noise of battle. He listened as he peered through the shadows and into the chamber.

The chamber was located in the most defended part of the spire. It was a large room, big enough to accommodate a sizable audience. It had once been used for the most elaborate celebrations and coronations, even Agesilaus himself had used it to bestow the award of regent to the old Governor. Now it was different. After the Zajust had taken it, it had been re-outfitted for the sparring and torture sessions it so regularly held. Might was everything to the Zajust, and that meant feats of strength and combat.

The chambers arena was circular with flat openings opposite each other. The openings that used to allow poems and plays to be displayed had now been altered to allow combatants to enter. There was a large mezzanine overlooking the whole room; and the fighting area itself was lowered compared to the main floor. It was a way of allowing the audience to watch the action from comparative safety, while not losing the thrill of the fight.

The walls of the room were stone block and there was a stair case in the middle of the arena that led from a throne down into the bowels of the fighting pit. There was a red circle painted in the center of the pit, with a combination of ancient and alien tribal writing on it, while hanging on the walls every fifteen feet or so were weapons of various design. They ranged from simple axes and many bladed spears, to firearms, and strange alien ballistics; which the contestants could use in the matches.

Sinagog stood in the shadows of the room. He had found the noise that caught his attention, it was a fight in the arena. The huge Zajust switched his stance as he watched, causing the chains around his wrists and waist to clink together. He watched his brother Zajust jockey for better position. Sinagog squeezed his huge cybernetic hand as he watched the fight play out in front of him.

Moore, the Blade, the Savage was covered in sweat. Moore had been sparring for the last hour and was breathing heavy. He was in the middle of the arena and was almost finished with his last sparring session. Moore was tall, thinner than most of his race. He was garbed in his dark cloak, its hood down as usual, and was holding his war mask, a metallic skull face with no jaw guard. His head was covered in black tight fitted nanocellulose material, like a mail coif of a knight of the old stories. A long dark ponytail with dyed red streaks ran down his back.

Vangel, the Berserker, was there as well. He also wore his black cloak, though he stood defiant while he watched Moore fight. He was readying to challenge his brother Zajust. They always fought amongst themselves. That was the Zajust way, grow strong or lose position. Sinagog saw the interaction, and it made him think of war. He saw Moore tensing, readying himself for the coming confrontation. Sinagog enjoyed the fights they had. He savored the fights, the war, and the battle to come, as did their entire race. Battle was everything, testing one's mettle and worth with might was what made life good. They were warriors and conquerors, only now these last few years, had he ever had to wait to fight, to conquer. He remembered when this wasn't the case.

He remembered his home, it was not like this. Battle was his life. Landing on worlds across the galaxy, taking what he and his brothers wanted. Duels with great warriors and battles with vicious creatures across the stars. That was what he loved. Each victory making them better at killing and

254

taking, even defeat made them stronger, though defeat was rare. He missed the wars, wars that strengthened his people; only through war would the weak be cowed. The Humans, Elves, Dwarger, Ulthwan and all the others on this planet were weak. He hated the sniveling and the bureaucratic, them and their pathetic efforts to rule through subterfuge. Strife, pain, work, and war. These are the traits that create greatness he thought. He was a master of these things. The battles he had fought near limitless, the people and species killed meaning nothing to him. They were only trophies on which his battle prowess had fed on. He squeezed his massive hands, open and closed, with contempt and idleness, the rage of that idleness starting to come to the fore. This world was weak, he thought, and when they gained the boy, the Labrynthian would be open to them. War would rule this world, then the galaxy once more. His race would thrive as they always had, fighting, always ready for another go.

The war to get this land had been a good war, he thought. The Dragons were good enemies, and hard to beat, but they too were ultimately defeated by him and his people; and the Spartans. He grimaced at the word. He hated the Spartans. They took his glory. He respected them as he enjoyed fighting and killing them, but hated them as well. The former King actually thanked us for our help. Thanked us, the monster thought. We could have taken it all, and would have if not for his Spartans, and his damned pet Dominus. Sinagog was fuming with anger at the memory of the Spartan. Dominus slew the Dragon Lord, then backed us down; we would have taken this world that day if not for him and his sword. It should have been me, he thought. I should have killed him then, but he is dead now and the sword lost.

We were relegated to nothing after that. It was our tech that built the Wargears and Constructs that won the day; they couldn't have won without us, even with their powers. He remembered the King saying he wanted no more hostilities. No more war! He was weak; he offered land and peace, the fool. That is why Nemsor rules now. Agesilaus was a fool; the summit showed that, the day he died. The day I watched him die. Sinagog remembered what they had done to get here. The betrayal, the day he watched the death of the alliance, the fall of the King and the making of the Zajust as a power once again. The day he had killed all in Gimralta, the day he had started his war again. Sinagog Vaul watched and savored the death of the ruler and the free world, just as he savored the conflict he watched now, he relished it. Just as he would watch and savor his triumph when he found the boy. He had been close before, but he would have him soon. He knew that was why he had been summoned. Remembering that feeling of conquest, simmered his anger. A movement from the arena broke him from his thoughts. He watched from the shadows even though the ones he watched knew he was there.

Moore, spared with three bots of intricate design. Moore had slid his mask on and blinked, the red lenses of his helm opening the spectrum to allow more colors through into his optics as he readied for his attackers. The skull face mask he wore was bright white, though as he moved the full color spectrum could be seen and the mask shifted colors, seeming to match the environment it was in. He tensed as the first of the three robots came at him from the rear. A double sided pole arm was raised high above its head, the robot spun the weapon; bringing it down in a slashing motion. Moore didn't have his weapons in his dark green hands. He didn't need them. The speed was amazing as he moved when the attack came, he blurred, and suddenly the bot was disarmed. Moore lashed out with a kick that caught the bot in the rib section, sending it sprawling on the floor with sparks, wires dislodged. He then pulled his twin single edged serrated blades, blocking the other bot that had rushed him on his flank, its sword drawn. As he did he evaded the third of the amazingly designed robots, its spear thrust missing the small of his back by inches. He kicked out, sending the rushing robot stumbling forward and past him. As he did he turned the sword of the other into itself, jabbing it under its armor, turning with his blades he knocked the still reeling form of the first into the spear of the last. It burst through its chest with sparks and smoke. Moore had won and all three were down. He held both blades in his hands at the neck of the bot holding the spear. Then he spoke, "Finished, decompress." With a hiss of steam and sparks, the bots stood and bowed to him. Moore flicked his blades as if there was blood on them, a habit more than a needed movement.

He held his swords while he controlled his breathing, a technique not practiced normally by his barbaric berserker kin, as they just looked for the next kill. No, he was different. He was still Zajust, the green skin race of warriors that ruled the Razium, but unlike his kin he was a thinker. A Dokx in their rough native tongue, meaning smaller and cunning. He watched the bots limping out of the room, then heard clapping from the side of the arena, "Very good," the guttural voice said. "The simborgs are not your equal, are they cousin?" The voice had a sarcastic and jealous undertone.

"Gell." Moore said, grittily, his back turned as he checked his blades. From across the arena walked the other Zajust Lord that had spoken, Vangel. He pulled his cloak back, unclasping it as he walked. He was tall as most Zajust were and had large broad shoulders that tapered to a thin waist that could be seen through his brigandine and the thin arcanium lined hauberk. Underneath his tight fitting armor were bands of grayish black with dark greens. He had pistols at his hips and knives at his waist with two twin brutish axes sheathed in dark leathers on his back. His face was covered as well, in a silver mask that contoured around his chin, lining his huge jaw with two huge tusk points jutting out underneath its sides. The front under the nose was a metal plate with spiked studs down the middle. It looked over sized for the face plate, and had no mouth, but there was a slash of red under the left eye.

The helms voice box was deep. "I could show you how to take care of those evil bots. Ha, I could even show you how to use those weapons you have there. Such power wasted." Moore twirled his swords sheathing them. He still hadn't turned to face his cousin. After his weapons where stowed, he pulled his cloak over his shoulder and looked back, "Really, care to test that theory?" His gruff accented voice was ripe with anxiousness, knowing he was goading his insane cousin in to a fight. Moore slowly turned to face his kin, cocking his head, as if seeing a pathetic creature, instead of his equal. "Maybe," Vangel spoke slowly. Then reacted to the challenge, in one fluid motion of power he pulled one of the blades at his belt and bounded toward Moore.

He was fast and had he been fighting anything or anywhere else he would have killed his prey, but not him, and not here, in the Tower of Thrones. Moore had not moved, standing completely still, still covered in his long dark cloak waiting as Vangel charged. Vangel leapt and Moore stepped back, blades out, so fast as almost not to be seen, but stopped.

The deep voice of Vangal's battle cry was cut short as the big creature was stopped in mid leap. His blade fell from his hands, as he was held in midair by a powerful force. He couldn't move or breathe. From the mezzanine above, four hulking Anusiya warriors formed the Vanguard of

Nemsor Vaul. They moved aside for their lord and stood awaiting his commands. Nemsor walked through his cyborg guard, his hand raised as if he was gripping an invisible fruit. He opened his hand with a flick, the Magnus force hurling Vangel against the wall of the tower where he smacked it with a metal clank, falling to the floor.

Nemsor's Vanguard walked down the stairs to the staging area and stood at the bottom awaiting their master. Sinagog, who had watched the whole scene play out from the shadows walked from beyond them and into the light of the chamber. The lacquered armor of his immense shoulder guards gleaming in the light, his chains and skulls clicking together as he stopped. Nemsor's hand turned up as his power coursed from him. He floated off the side, using the Magnus to guide him as he floated down from his viewpoint. His armored boots touched the floor so soft they almost made no sound.

"I know you want to fight, but if we fight for blood amongst ourselves we are beaten. I need commanders who will be strong. No weakness." Nemsor said as he walked toward Vangel and Moore. Sinagog grunted as he nodded his agreement with Nemsor, looking at Vangel. Vangel was on all fours lifting himself off the ground. He growled his acknowledgment, not wanting to challenge the larger Nemsor, but trying not to lose face after being disciplined for his outburst toward Moore. Both of them had their blood up growling at each other like wild dogs in a challenge. Abruptly they were cowed; their noises were cut off by a strange voice from behind.

"Yes, very good. Aggression is the key to domination. To dominate is to cause fear, to cause fear is to rule, and to rule is power." The shape of an older man appeared before them, projected from a small disk that hovered only inches from the floor, the 3d image floating to the side of Nemsor. The figure was deliberately distorted, and looked humanoid, but his features were green, hazy, and hard to make the face out. The power radiating from him was easily felt though, even though he wasn't in the room or even near the city.

"Nemsor," the image said not looking at him. "Your generals show promise, though they have been shackled too long it appears." Vangel had stood and retrieved his weapon, standing at attention. "Yes, I agree master Agmon." Nemsor said. "I look forward to their successes, when unleashed."

"Good. I as well, and that time will not be long, but for now leave us." the figure stated. The warriors and elite guard started to go. "Sinagog, not you, nor Vangel." The huge Orcs stepped to their masters.

"Vangel, I have an assignment for you, and it might even allow you to release some of that anger, get you back in Nemsor's favor." Vangel had taken his helm off, his green skin and light blue tattooed face draped in shadows, though he moved his incredibly massive jaw closing it with a snap. He stood tall in front of Nemsor and the image of Agmon. "Anything my Lord Agmon." He said breathing heavy. "Good. You are always the Berserker. This endeavor I think might need your skill, but I need some diplomacy from you first. You will be an emissary for your lord to the Elves. Make sure my trinket arrives here for me. Do this and be rewarded. Understood?" "Yes." He said.

"Good, now go, you will be briefed shortly." Vangel slammed his huge fist to his armor and turned leaving the room. Sinagog watched him go, the chains on his armor clinking as he turned to Nemsor. Sinagog dwarfed the huge lord of the Zajust even as big as he was, but he knew and respected the power of Nemsor. He was dedicated to him. Anyone who would lead him to war he would follow. His eyes glow had not dimmed. Nemsor looked at the huge warrior beast in front of him. "Follow, but go undetected. I will reinforce you with a small company. Do what is needed and return to me with the Key, if Vangel cannot. Do what you must, and do not fail." Nemsor finished emphasizing the word fail. He knew Sinagog would take it as a slight and work all that much harder. Agmon started again, "Yes, what you must. We have intel that might benefit us, and I don't think your brother can handle this alone. A war is coming, do you understand?" A deep growl came from the evil giant. "War," he said. Nemsor nodded, "Yes." Sinagog turned to leave. He would not fail, he thought, and as he thought of the war to come Sinagog did something he hadn't done in a long time. He grinned.

Nemsor and the hologram of Agmon walked from the arena, the figure flickering slightly as it floated beside him. They walked until they were alone, the décor changing from the bitter warlike aspect of the Zajust to a more suitable royal attire. The walls were covered in tapestries and art, statues of nobles and kings of the past running down their sides. The marble floors reflecting the evil warriors walking on them.

They made their way to a large foyer, servants and other Razium scurrying out of the way as they walked. When they were alone, the image of Agmon spoke to his general. "Things are going as planned. We will find the boy. He will make himself known. There is nowhere to go now and once we have the west, the rest of the Confederates will be powerless, assaulted from two fronts. They already argue amongst themselves. We sow the seeds of mistrust, my friend." The figure laughed. "Ahh yes, this country as we know it will fall. With the progress we have made across the ocean, and the Aun Ka as our allies we can't be stopped, and once we have the boy and the Labrynthian, we will have the world. We will unleash the Zajust on them. We will unleash the Zajust on them," he repeated chuckling. Nemsor was silent. "You do not share my sentiment?" Agmon asked puzzled. Nemsor took a second to reply. "I feel something. That we have overlooked, something."

"Fear not," Agmon said. "They rely on the Council to lead them, Speakers and Loks. They have no real power. As long as we don't let them have a figure to unite them, to lead them. These people are as pathetic as any other conquered, I should know. I have already staged the takeover of the Golden City, Nabis flies there to meet you. As for the boy, well, he is being tracked. I have received word that he is in good hands already. This will be the last piece to the puzzle, and the Labrynthian will be ours once we have those pieces. Once we have them, this Nation will fall to us, after that there is no one else strong enough. The Isles will fall and the Elves as well. Nemsor, I trust you my friend, go take what is rightfully yours, and we will crush these insignificants. Then look to the stars."

"Report to me when you have Angel City secure." Nemsor nodded. "And Nemsor," said the image, stopping him from walking out of the room. The Iron Knight looked back. "Be discreet. I don't want the surrounding cities rallying to the capitols aid. This needs to be delicate." "Agreed." Nemsor replied.

CHAPTER 23. SECRETS REVEALED:

The sewer tunnels under Royal

The group was under the city in a tunnel that led down into the bowls of unknown territory. It was a tunnel few knew about and none used, unless you counted the rats and vermin of the soiled city above them. Tasha looked over the assembled warriors with her, checking her soldiers, making sure they had their gear and understood the operation they needed to accomplish. They were a small reconnaissance force and under the watchful and beautiful eye of their commander, they had found what the Elves had been up to, and why the city of the pointy ears had been so quiet recently.

The Elves had a secret lair underground that was below even the sewers, ancient ruins that they had rebuilt over the years creating a place for their insane sire to conduct his transactions in peace and private. The Dru Nar had been able to smuggle arms and armor out of the city unnoticed. That wouldn't be so bad except it was during war time and the Razium were making a push toward the center of the continent. After finding out this information, Tasha had been chosen to stop it. It wasn't war or a government that had made this small handpicked force she lead possible. No, it was Dillion. The fact that he wasn't making money on the operation, and the Elves were, left a bad taste in his mouth, and he wasn't going to have that. He had Tasha take a team of handpicked soldiers to investigate, steal and to sabotage if needed. They were more like mercenary warmongers, than soldiers. They worked for a crooked gangster warlord and had come from all over the continents, some fresh from the Boer War, or the battle for the Isles overseas. Others, local thugs, but no matter who they were or where they were from, they were here for one reason. They were here for the money. Luckily, Dillion had loads of it.

Walker however was here for a different reason. After a week with the soldiers and guards of the Kissar, Walker knew how to judge them, and they had come to respect him as well. He had beaten the best fighters they had in sparring contests and made a good show in the drinking challenges. The thing Walker enjoyed but didn't understand until recently was Tasha. She made no sense here. Her demeanor, her knowledge and the way she distanced herself from the others, it was as if she wasn't a part of this group at all. She was a warrior alright and was trained in the art of stealth. Trained well in the art, and until she had let her guard down it had made no sense.

The Truth of Royal

Neither Tasha nor Walker had talked much about the hallway when they had first met or how he knew what she was, but both knew they had a connection. Though what type was still to be decided. Over the week they had grown fond of each other, training together, small smiles and playful taunts only increasing the magnetism between them. She had explained the reasons Dillon needed him, familiarized him with the compound and the do's and don'ts of the city, and had divulged information preparing him for the mission ahead of them. She really hadn't completely come out with it, but she had alluded to getting into the Elven side of Royal, and that it might be dangerous. That is why they needed the extra muscle, experienced muscle. Walker allowed himself to be lured into the mission and she appreciated that. The last two days they had been inseparable, to the chagrin of some of the other mercenaries, who were obviously jealous of their blossoming relationship. Two days ago, Walker had tested her mettle to see what she was made of and try and get more out of her, or so he thought. It could have been that she was testing him. Either way it had worked. Walker had found out why he was really at the compound and why she needed him so badly.

"On your guard," Tasha said smoothly, walking around the center of the training mat to stand directly before Walker. He was dressed in boots, fatigues, and a tight fitting shirt that covered his arms, though emphasized his muscle. She wore training fatigues as well, and boots, with a tight compress type shirt that emphasized her upper body. Her hair had been pulled into a ponytail. She held a staff clutched behind her back, both hands reaching back to grasp the weapon, one high over her back and one low. She stood tall, a beautiful temptress, legs slightly crossed and feet bowed in a T, ready to strike. The soldiers of the Kissar had heard she was sparring and wanted to see who was dumb enough to step in the ring with the woman. They gathered around to see how fast the new recruit was going to get beat.

None of them had been able to best her; even Earl and some of the other Ulthwan had not been able to best her. Tasha had a reputation, she ruled the combat arena, and that somewhat explained her ascension to lead this troop. She never lost. A few of the assembled chuckled while Walker smirked at them then her. The betting started. Most were in favor of Tasha but after the odds were given Walker had a few takers. In his last match he had easily dispatched Dahl, one of the better warriors, and Tasha's second in command. The mercenaries knew he had skill, the question was how much. Walker stood across from her. He set the small blade he had been using on the ground and slid it across the floor toward the rack. Dahl stopped it with his boot, picking it up and racking it. Then took the staff racked above his head and tossed it to Walker, who caught it. Nodding his thanks, he tested its weight in his hands.

"Are you ready?" she asked. "For what?" Walker was asking, but was cut off as she advanced toward him. She was fast, too fast, and he knew he needed to disarm her before she started in on him, and he really had to fight. He high blocked, just in time to stop her staff from smashing his head in. Walker pushed back, and she was tossed slightly, a feeling she obviously didn't like. With a small grunt and cheers of the assembled she was back on the attack, her blows getting stronger. Walker blocked a low blow aimed for his midsection and then took a shot in the leg, then blocked another. He could tell she was taping into her Warp power, and he needed to end this now. Tasha turned and spun the bo, bringing it in an overhead strike toward Walker's shoulder. He blocked letting it roll off his staff catching it, pulling it and its wielder to him. She tried to spin out. Walker dropped his staff and used her momentum to turn her into a rear choke. She was obviously taken by surprise that she was getting choked. She stopped struggling and contracted her muscles surging them with power, the force knocking Walker back. He tripped over his staff and landed on the floor. Tasha was angry now and slightly losing control.

She snapped the staff over her knee, tossing the pieces to the side and turned to the weapon rack behind her, grabbing a huge ax that was way too big for most, but especially her. The muscles in her arms bulged with strength as she lifted it. She spun, twisting the huge weapon around in arcs and 360 patterns. The soldiers watching were stunned, they had never seen her lose control before. Walker was on his knee from where he had been knocked back; watching her grab the weapon. Her instinct was to win and she was right on top of him to do just that. Dahl yelled her name and tried to stop her, but it was too late. She didn't hear him; she was in a beast like state. She swung at Walker, and he tried to jump back, but fell instead landing on his back. Tasha swung the pole arm around her in an arc bringing the huge axe blade down toward Walker, right at his head. The blade stopped a few inches from him. She stood over him sweating, panting, looking at him; his hand was open and held up to his chest.

"Well done, ha ha, well done." A voice came from the side of the room. "I thought you had her there Walker, for a moment, but she is a tenacious one isn't she?" Boss Dillion had come to view the battle slipping in mid-way through. "I like this, a good investment." He chuckled, holding his glass out. It looked as if he had been out for a stroll the way he was dressed. Black slacks and a long double breasted coat with large buttons pulled tight over his turtleneck. His monocle hung loose by the upper pocket. A pretty girl moved up right away filling his almost empty wine goblet, another putting a cigar in his mouth. "Thank you, my ladies." He said taking the unlit cigar out of his mouth stepping toward Walker and Tasha. Tasha's cheeks flushed and she lowered the weapon. Walker put his hand down, dark black marks of the Magnus receded into the skin on his hand, though no one had seen them. As the boss walked in to the sparring ring, Tasha turned and racked the weapon, then quickly left the training arena.

"Good show," Dillion said, as she walked past him to the locker room. Dillion shrugged, looked at Walker and continued. "I'm having a thing tonight; Tasha will give you the details." He said, waving his hand around while watching her leave. "So it's a business thing?" Walker asked. "Don't ask me about my business Mr. Walker, I will tell you about my business," he said coldly and then shrugged his shoulders. "But yes, since you asked, it is about business, the business that keeps me going." He paused for effect and looked up, hands and arms moving out. "Killing the Elves that plague my city. So yes, and hey I know you have your whole big thing going," he said motioning his hands back and forth at Walkers chest and shoulders. "But get cleaned up will you?"

"Good," he said turning on his heel not waiting for a reply. Colonel who had been behind Dillion the whole time, tipped his hat and he and his guards followed Dillion out of the room.

The rest of the spectators had left or were leaving grumbling about the fight. It was awkward and Walker knew why. Tasha lost her cool, and that was a very rare thing. He dried his face with a towel and looked to the readying room where Tasha stood by herself. She had dried off and was getting ready to leave when he came in. "I'm impressed, you almost had me," he chuckled. "Really though, you have great moves."

"You are an amazing warrior." She looked at him, embarrassed. "Thank you," she finally said, "I'm not used to being tested."

"I can tell," he said back grinning. She looked at him. "I lost control and I" ... .she stopped talking. She knew this man might be able to help her. She liked the feeling she had around him, and felt she could trust him, but she didn't like the feeling of being beaten. But she craved more, the power he projected, it had to be. "Go on." Walker said, snapping her out of her trance. She knew this was it, why she had been sent and she took her chance. She found her confidence and smiled a dazzling smile.

"You are not one to mess with, Walker." She said changing the mood, her amazing smile holding his gaze. "You say that like you didn't just almost kill me." He joked. "You are the one that needs to be kept in check."

She walked toward him, "I need to tell you something. Meet me at seven in the main hall on the other side of the complex, before the party." She brushed past him rolling her eyes. "Ok," He said. She flipped a towel over her shoulder before she walked out of the training room, looking back at him she said, "We both know I couldn't move that axe head, Spartan." He smiled and was impressed, she had tested him. She had baited him, and he took it. Then a thought hit him, "What if I hadn't been a Magnus user?" He asked her. She walked out without another word. He had never met anyone like her before.

Later that evening Walker arrived at the end of the main hall that lead to the main foyer and entrance to the party. He was clean shaven and dressed in a light cream colonial style shirt and dark officer's coat that did little to hide his bulk. He wore a pair of dark brown boots and army trousers with suspenders and pouches around his waist. The long hall he was walking through was exquisitely crafted. He thought it looked like an indoor cloister, the way the small arched openings ran down its right hand side. It reminded him of the outside colonnades he saw when he had been brought to the fortress.

Also, like the colonnades, every few openings had a sculpture, or some other type of very expensive looking art piece in them. He noticed these pieces were amazingly detailed, and every one had Dillion's face on them. Walker chuckled "Really," he asked and wasn't sure if he had said it out loud. Embarrassed he looked around, though he saw no one close enough to hear. He followed the vain art down the hall, looking at the pieces as they led him to the main foyer that was the entrance to Dillion's massive vaulted grand assembly room.

The main foyer had a staircase leading both ways down from its upstairs summit, and directly below the stairs centered in the wall of steal and gold was what looked like an assembly room, as if it were fitted for a King, and made more like a bunker than a room. The huge decorated doors that lead in had an attendant guard at each and were held open. Walker could see in and it was filled with guests. After scanning the room and not seeing Tasha, he studied the guards.

They were wearing the burgundy cloak of the house of Kissar and Dillion's eagle head emblem was on each one's shoulder. Both wore metal plates and armor that attached to the legs, knees, and shoulders. They were holding long spears, small swords, and pistols rested on their belts and hips as well. Also, in the back of the assembly room by the stage, stood a smaller Wargear construct. Its head moved back and forth as it monitored the party guests, searching for threats. Walker smiled at seeing this marvel. Those machines had been crucial in the defeat of the Dragons, and more than once he had owed one for bailing him out of a jam; despite his powers. Remembering, and the nostalgia kicking in, he thought about one of the battles and flexed his hand. He knew that some of the machines were still around, though most had been destroyed with the Razium conflict. They thought them too powerful, and made it a mission to destroy as many as they could, lest they were turned against them. They were almost impossible to reproduce without the Tempest resources and runes.

He wasn't surprised that the Dillion had one of the Gears, heck he wouldn't have been surprised if Dillion had more than a few in this puzzle of a house. Looking back to the front of the foyer, he saw more guests entering the party. They walked in on a red carpet that led from the outside where they had arrived. The carpet took them up a flight of stairs and through the large front doors, continued through the foyer, between the guards and right into the assembly room.

It was getting busier and the guests were arriving by the handful. Still not seeing Tasha, Walker made his way over to see exactly who was coming to this soirée. As he looked outside he noticed the outer complex was lit up with lights on the sides of the colonnades that lead up to the entrance. The lamps on the drive in were dimmed to create a magical glow. Walker took a glass of white wine off a tray as a waiter walked by, and made his way to the front doors looking out across the grounds. "Wow." He said aloud while he stood looking at the show the Boss had put on. He could see artillery cannons of all sizes, amazing vehicles of various types, steam tanks, and an assortment of military items on display outside the compound. All the weapons had been put on display close to the walls. The walls themselves were covered with Dillion's armed guards. It was as if Dillion was daring the Elves to challenge him. Boss Dillion was known for his extravagance, but usually his brass displays didn't show his power like the one tonight. Tasha had explained to Walker much of the gangster over the last few days, but he wasn't sure why she had, or why she had shared so much. He had also found that she hadn't been there long herself, only a year or so, and neither of them knew the extent of the crime lord's narcissism. Of course, this soirée was a meeting of the higher ups in the city and even more powerful people had come from beyond its walls in support of the man, who appeared to be running for Governor the way he was campaigning.

Boss Dillion was very well connected in all the major cities of the Confederates, and this was a way to gain more influence with the recent silence of the Elves. It also allowed Dillion to show off his power and wealth, which he loved to do. He had invited the top rich families in the cities. Traders and merchants from other city governments were in attendance as well. He was trying to win people to his cause against, what he called, "The Dru Nar Elf menace."

Walker stepped back from the tall windows of the foyer and waited in the hall for Tasha. He continued watching the guests arrive, getting out of newly designed steam cars, long sleek pieces of metal with pipes on the sides, and puffs of steam coming from the vents. Some came in classical carriages and others in balloons, landing on the platform on the back of the fortress. They came in top hats and tuxedos, gowns, close fitting dresses, and corsets. It seemed only the truly wealthy were at this event, with the styles he was seeing. He began to think he was under dressed.

He walked back to the to the main foyer lobby toward one of the huge paintings on the wall by the stairs. It was a masterpiece of art, a general riding horse as it reared. He was holding a cavalry saber, pointing in the direction of some unknown enemy, and yet again it was Dillion's face on the painting. Walker smiled, chuckling at it and then felt something, and it wasn't his drink. He knew she had walked in. He turned finding her with ease. She was radiant. Her locks flowing freely over her taught shoulders. The dress she wore, burgundy and tight fitting, emphasized her curves. He walked to her. "Good evening mam." He said adding a bit of southern twang in his voice to be charming, he took her hand and kissed it. "You look incredible." Tasha blushed slightly. "Thank you, Mr. Walker, and you aren't too bad yourself. I almost didn't recognize you. You clean up rather nicely." Walker's dark hair had been cut shorter and combed, though the front was a little messy. "I like the shave, makes you look younger." He grinned, "Yeah, younger," he playfully teased, but then thanked her. "Let's go inside." She motioned as he took her arm in his and went under the stairs to the ball room.

Dillion was in the front of the room as they had come in, and was surrounded by what could only be politicals and the wealthy. Dillion saw them enter and excused himself, making a beeline toward them. Tasha saw him coming and took one of the glasses of white wine from a passing server, downing it. "Here he comes," she said. Walker had already seen but nodded anyway.

"So, how do you like it Mr. Walker? All the money and power one could want, ehh....No not for you I suppose, warrior." Walker looked down at the Boss. He was wearing jodhpur pants that puffed out on the sides, and had an exquisite maroon jacket, the right shoulder armored with a clasp that had his familie's crest of a small Eagle or birds head on the edge that held a cape hanging off it. The jacket was buttoned with eight golden buttons on each side, and a pair of ornate looking steam goggles hung out of his jacket pocket. "No," Walker replied, "I rather like it. The energy in here is electric," he said loosening his shoulders. "You know very powerful people Mr. Dillion. The Councilor over there," Walker nodded, "and I see one of the generals from the Confederate army. I am impressed with the show. The Dru Nar have been a thorn in the side long enough." Walker finished and took a drink of his wine. Dillion's eye raised at the unexpected interest Walker showed, and knowledge he had of the guests.

"Good, it seems a man after my own taste. After this," he paused his hands moving in circles as he searched his slightly tipsy brain for the word. "Thing." He finally blurted out. "You and I need to talk Walker." He finished, slapping Walkers massive shoulder. "Enjoy the party, though do be careful of that one," he said nodding at Tasha. "She's wicked." Dillion made a clawing motion like a cat. Walker laughed, "I think I might need a leash." Dillion burst out laughing, "That's good, Walker. That is funny," he said as he turned walking back to his guests, his finger waving in the air. In another place little man, Walker thought disgusted as he glared at him. No, now is not the time for thoughts like that, he will get his. He turned from the gangster and looked to Tasha.

The glare Walker got was anything but nice, and he blushed slightly. "A leash, oh so now you're a comedian, huh?" She asked, rolling her eyes and walking away from the main press of people. He followed. "I am sorry, but you are vicious. You almost put me down not too long ago." He said, trying to joke. They walked through the crowd smiling and mingling. Tasha pulled him aside, and looked up at him. "I was testing you with that axe, but there is no doubt of what you are." She stated getting serious. "I couldn't move it Walker, and you know my strength. You are no ordinary soldier, no matter what you say." She finished looking away from him.

He moved to face her. "You are strong Tasha, I have never met anyone like you. The first day we met I knew you were special and not for your powers," he said gazing in her eyes.

"I have to be strong. To be on top. To lead these mongrels, there can be no weakness. I have to bust them and keep them in line, but I don't feel that way with you." Tasha said. She was nervous, though for some reason she felt she could open up to him. Walker listened.

"I hate Dillion and those like him. I am disgusted with the wretch, and if not for my power I would have been made into one of those." She looked to where Dillion was about to give a speech. He was close to a stage that had been set up and ten or more girls were swooning over him. "I," she started but stopped herself as she caught Colonel looking at them from across the room. A microphone speaker went off with a squeal.

"Oh, ha ha, I am sorry, you would think with all this money I could afford some speakers." Dillion said laughing into the microphone. A chuckle went through the crowd.

"Let's get some air." Tasha said taking Walker's hand, leading him out of the room. Dillion had started into his speech. Colonel watched them leave, then turned his attention to Dillion, and laughed at one of his bad jokes. A cute lady walked by him, smiling, taking his mind off Tasha and Walker.

Dillion finished his speech of welcoming and all the guests applauded him. "Now enjoy yourselves," he said as he stepped down from the stage. He thanked a few of his guests as he was stepping down; Dillion had caught Colonel's attention and nodded him over. He had seen Tasha lead Walker out as well, and he didn't like it. Colonel came up to him as he was shaking hands with one of the high ranking officials from across the sea. "No, no ... Thank you for coming." He told the man. "Now if you will excuse me." Dillion said, stepping away from him and his family to talk with Colonel. "Yes sir." Colonel replied, the twang of his accent thick. "Tasha and Walker. Watch those two, I don't know what or why, but," he didn't finish.

"Could be she has someone she likes?" Colonel stated. "Two alphas? Just watch them." Dillion said, "I need a drink." He motioned to one of his girls. "We are too close now, and I am being paranoid," Dillion finished gulping down the wine, shaking his head. "I'll watch them sir." Colonel tipped his hat as he blended with the crowd.

Walker and Tasha had made their way out of the press of the guests, and as they went outside Walker grabbed two full wine glasses from a passing server. When they were outside he handed her one. "For you." he said.

"Thank you." She took the glass in her slender hand. Walker found himself alone with Tasha on the balcony of the fortress of Dillion. They were there in silence, looking into a wondrously clear night sky. He glanced at her, he didn't know what to say and didn't want to make it awkward. "So, what should we toast to?" He asked nervously trying to start a conversation. "You do look wonderful." He said after she didn't answer, trying desperately to end the awkwardness on the terrace. She looked at him and her hair fell in her eyes. "Walker," she said, letting out a long breath. Then realizing what he said she blushed. "Oh, thank you."

He smiled. She smiled back and pulled the hair from her face then took a long sip of her wine. She set her glass down on the terrace edge and moved closer. "I know who you are." She said. Walker looked at her, surprised she was so blunt, but the Warp in her sometimes took over. He looked deep in her eyes thinking there was no way she could ever be cruel with those eyes, and asked slyly. "Oh really, who am I?" "You are a soldier, and you are a Spartan Paladin, a hero, and I need a hero." She finished coolly.

"What makes you say that?" Walker asked. "I feel it." She said. "I don't know everything about why you are here, but I know there is something about you Walker. You calm me, and that has never happened." Not wanting to feel to exposed she continued. "I know what you have been up to as well." Walker looked at her unsure about what she was going to say. "You have been asking questions. I visited the Dwarf at Hans. I talked to the man, I mean Dwarger, Snorri, and he told me you were old guard." Walker's face hardened as he looked at her, baffled she had gotten that from the old Dwarger. She read his reaction, and kept going not wanting to play her hand too soon. "Don't worry your secret is safe with me, that's why I am talking to you now. The boss has had you tailed; even right now Colonel is trying to find us. I smell him." She said smiling.

"Dillion is getting too anxious, and he doesn't trust anyone, though you he likes. He suspects you are more than meets the eye as well. He has had you watched and I know you saw some of the men tailing you when you first got here, but you never saw me," she paused. "Also, I know who you are looking for." She knew what? He thought. Clearly she could read the weariness in his face. "Orson," she said, "he is who you seek." "Why are you telling me this?" He asked.

"I think I can trust you. I need to trust you, we need each other." She looked over his shoulder. "We are going to run out of time here. Damn." she said frustrated. "Meet me at your room in twenty minutes, then we can talk and I will explain everything. Wait a minute or two until I leave and then go to your room the long way. Ok? Meet me, please?" Their eyes meet and she took his hand. "Alright," he said. She pulled her hand away and left him on the large terrace.

He lingered for a few minutes finishing his wine, trying to get the feelings he was having in order. His face was flushed, and the cool air felt good to him. "How do you like the view?" A southern accented voice asked him. "I'd say it was robust." Walker said as looked up at the starry night sky. He turned. "Colonel." Colonel was standing dressed in all white and brown, which included his hat. "Yes, Mr. Walker I would agree with that summation. I would be carful though," he said nodding the direction Tasha had left. "That one is a handful, she bites." "That's good advice, though I have heard it before. Lucky for me, I don't mind blood." He said to him, and handed Colonel his wine glass. "Here you go, thanks, now if you will excuse me. Nice party though." He said to the annoyed southerner, and walked inside.

Walker had mingled for a few minutes, and then he took the long way back to his room. He had been very careful to make sure he hadn't been followed. He came to his door, and after a quick glance around to double check he hadn't been followed, he walked in. It was dark but seemed just as he had left it. Weapons still hung on the rack and everything seemed to be in place. "Hello." she whispered stepping out from the shadows. Her muscular form could be seen in the tight fitting body suit she now wore. She walked to him and drew close. "I am glad you came." She whispered to him, slightly leaning in and then without warning, kissing him. It was a deep kiss, and it felt right. Walker flushed and started to kiss back, but then she pulled away. "Sorry." She said, quickly moving away and walking passed him to his table before he could say anything. She did not look at him but produced a small tube wrap, pulling out a map and rolling it out across the table. It glowed slightly. It was enchanted, and was able to light itself to show the topography better.

He stepped behind her looking at it over her shoulder. He wanted to touch her, but stopped when she started talking as if nothing had happened. "Here," she pointed. "Look here," touching a spot on the map by the city. The map came to life when he made contact, and it turned the whole thing in to a 3D rendering of the area she touched. "Elf magic," He whispered. She looked at him, and nodded excitement in her eyes. Walker studied the map not being able to read the Elven writing on it, but saw it led out of the city, an unknown area. "Where did you get this?" He asked, walking around the table.

"A thief Dillion hired got it when he was in Lithatl, but that is irrelevant, but what it is isn't. This." When she touched it the area became a hologram like rendering of the tracks. "It is a track for a bullet steam train that leads out of the city; it doesn't ever join the normal trains that bring goods in. However, further out it joins the main line and heads west, towards the west coast. It leads to Angel City, Walker." She paused, knowing it was a gamble to talk but she knew this was her chance. "I need to trust you." She said in earnest. "I will give you the man you want, if you help me. Will you, help me?" She asked her eyes on fire with feeling. He wanted to say yes, but he had so much riding on this as well. He didn't know what it meant, and the kiss earlier, what was that? Walker was looking at the map, then raised his head looking in her beautiful eyes. He needed to find Orson, and get to the Prince, he was wasting time and he didn't have much more to waste. Duty outweighed all, even if he did have feelings for her. "Yes I will, but you have to tell me how you can help me."

"Ok." She nodded then swallowed hard. "I am an agent of O'cea. The Governor, Hector, has sent me to infiltrate the Kissar and find who has been supplying the Razium with weapons and armor, and how close they really are to war."

"What! You work for the Governor of O'cea?" He asked dumb founded. "Yes, we don't have a presence here, and the Governor of the Pallance is crooked. With the war to the east there is too much bad intel. I was sent here to find out why and how the Razium are being supplied."

"But the western Confederates are united, and the Council is in control. They fight overseas, and are holding off Razium to the north."

"No, Angel city is being invaded secretly, and the military presence is being bolstered by the Dru Nar, here." She told him. "Yes they are fighting in the North but the Razium have gotten to someone on the inside. Someone on the Council, and that person has been able to circumvent them. The Elven Lord Tusho is in support of the Razium and could turn the tide of war in one blow." Tasha stopped talking and let this news sink in. "Why hasn't O'cea reacted and helped? Their army is substantial. They have the Myrmidons."

"They can't." She said. "They are still looking to the western ocean borders as they always have, but the Governor's hands are tied now, his daughter Tessa has been taken as a bargaining chip. He will not do anything until she is safe. I was sent to find a way of stopping them and finding a way to get her out. I think I have found that way," she said looking to him. "It's you."

* * *

Walker snapped out of his thoughts, as he saw Tasha looking over the mercenaries, the cool of the tunnel bringing him back to the present. He had gotten sucked in to a mob war that could finish the real war. All he knew was he needed her to find Orson. He would help Tasha and do it as soon as possible, and hopefully be able to answer some of the other questions he had in the process.

So here he was with a small group of mercenaries, about to assault an underground Elf fortress, to stop a bullet train from delivering goods to the Razium; who were secretly taking over the Capitol. I've had worse odds, he thought, chuckling to himself as he looked at the grey clad outfit he wore. They had even been able to find a suit big enough for him to be garbed the same as them. Walker looked at Tasha, why was he so drawn to her he wondered as he watched her checking her soldiers. Dillion had given them the means and the man power. Now it was up to them to use it. His mind wandered for a second, remembering what he had told Snorri, the last time he was at Han-Fords. He wanted to make sure he would deliver a message to his brother Glorin in Navarre. Snorri assured him he would get him the message, and then wished him good luck and told him he was sorry for telling Tasha everything, but she was persuasive. They both smiled and laughed at that. Walker thanked him for his trouble, telling him he owed him a drink next time he was in. The sound of removing the manhole cover brought him back to the tunnel and the mission. What a game he found himself in, he hoped he could win it.

CHAPTER 24. DISCOVERY:

Outside of the Pallance, below the Dragon Wastes, close to the outskirts of east Royal

Lincoln watched in awe as the large warrior walked toward the stairs. He was immense in his sculpted armor and horse crested helm. He had a huge sword sheathed at his side and an animal pelt over his shoulders. He was smiling at him as he was waving to the gathered crowds, their cheers thunderous in appreciation and admiration. He looked like a champion or great hero of the stories Lincoln had been told as a child. As Lincoln watched this warrior walk to stand with his father, he felt his chest swell with pride. "Ohh, there you are," a voice said from behind him. Lincoln spun and smiled seeing an older man, who smiled back. Though he knew who he was he couldn't remember his name. The man was bald with a thick white mustache and goatee. He was in robes that were a crème color and he had a large belt on that had a book clasped by his hip. "Well come on," the man waved, "Your brother is getting his accolades again."

The old man waited for him to run over, then turned to go outside and watch the celebration. Lincoln made to follow, he was walking toward the doors with the man, but the man kept walking and Lincoln couldn't follow. He couldn't move! He called out to the man, and the man said something but he didn't hear what he said. The old man stopped walking and turned to him. He had a curious smirk on his warm face. He said something again and smiled. Lincoln still couldn't hear him, something was stopping him from hearing, and then it started getting dark, fading, where had the man gone? Why was it dark? A dark shape stirred close to him. Lincoln woke with a start, and a bump. He was in the Wartrak. He caught his breath, sweat on his brow. "A dream." He said aloud. Rolling over, he sat on the edge of the small cot bed, trying to calm his nerves. When he finally felt better he stood and walked out.

Matias turned as the door slide open, and Lincoln drug himself through. "Hello, well the dead rises. You have been asleep for sixteen hours. How do you feel?" Lincoln's eyes were sleepy still and he nodded sitting down across from Bor. "Sixteen, wow." He said to Matias as he yawned. Bor was sitting at the table looking at the pieces of the chess game, and Greal was in the corner sipping a hot beverage. "Playing War Chess again?" Lincoln asked trying to perk up. Bor looked up. "I think, I have you. The pieces are still the same, as when we left them and it's my turn. Wanna play?" He asked a twinkle in his eye. "Don't rip his arm off about it, let him wake up," Matias said sipping his coffee. Bor just looked annoyed. "Lincoln how do you feel after such an ordeal? How did you sleep?"

"Good but restless at the end. I had a dream. It was weird," he replied to Matias with a frown.

"About your father?" "No, this one was different." He shook his head, thinking. "Bor, go ahead, I feel like playing." Bor perked up, "Alright," he said gleefully, and made a move.

"Well, do you want to tell me about it?" Matias asked. Lincoln nodded. "It was a celebration for my brother, though I didn't see his face, he was armored with a huge sword, and an older man was there. I knew him, but I didn't remember him." "What did he look like?" Matias asked eyeing Bor. Lincoln had gotten something to drink, and sat back down across from the large sergeant. Then he moved one of his own pieces across the board taking one of Bor's. Bor looked down and frowned at Lincoln, clearly not seeing the move, then stared hard at the board. Lincoln looked back to Matias. "Well he was average size, older, and bald. He was wearing robes like Nabis only more adorned, and he had a large white mustache and goatee." "Really?" Matias asked. "Yes why?" Lincoln looked puzzled when he asked. "Lincoln, the man you described in your dream matches the description of Orson." Lincoln almost spit out his drink! "The Lok Master Orson?" he asked. Matias wiped the water off his arm and chuckled. "Yes, the Lok master. I think he might have tried to reach out to you mentally. This dream only furthers the fact that we should try and find him. I hadn't been able to tell you yet, but we are on our way to Royal to try and find Master Orson."

"So that was the man in my dream? I have read his books in the study, he was the Master for my father, the greatest of the Loks, but do we even know where to look for him?" "We have a hunch." Matias said. "We don't know where yet, but we will, this is a sign. After what I saw you do on the Gryphon, it's the best way to help control your powers." Lincoln looked discouraged at the mention of the battle and his powers. Matias saw his expression change when he mentioned the battle, it wasn't a reaction he expected. "Hey, what you did saved us all, don't get down on yourself. It doesn't matter if it is Master Orson, or the Masters of the White Tower, you will be able to learn about your powers. Don't be discouraged. You were amazing. You feel ok?" He asked.

With a sigh Lincoln answered. "I am ok. I wish I knew more. I am thinking of home, Eric, my friends. I hope everyone got out after ok. I miss our home Uncle, and now my power, this situation with Master Nabis." He tossed his hands up as he spoke. "He says I have the power to do whatever I want, but I'm not sure I can. It's so much to take in."

"I can only imagine. Lincoln what Nabis said is right, about the power that is, but we have to keep you safe for the good of the people. Without you, defeating the Razium might be impossible." Matias finished with a huff, finally letting his usually guarded demeanor slip. "I miss home too." Matias told them. "We all do," Bor agreed, "But don't worry Lincoln, you are what is needed and you're safe with us." Lincoln looked at both of them. "He is right you know," Matias said his usually bravado coming back. "We now have a chance in this war and you will give the people hope. We will unite the Confederates, and end the tyranny that the Razium have been causing." Linc still looked unsure and uneasy. "I don't know if I am worth that much, and we might not even be able to find Orson." Matias chuckled. "Oh you are and we will, I know that old man pretty well, but don't worry about that now." The intercom came on, interrupting the conversation. "Commander, I picked up something on the sensor. I am not sure, but I think you need to see it." "What is it Saul?" Matias asked. As he did, Bor went back to studying the board.

"I think I have something," Bor said excitedly. Matias held up his hand to quiet him, as Saul came back on. "Sir, it's an energy signature, its well...." Matias was curious. "What kind?" he asked. "Magnus signature sir."

Right as Saul said it, Bor exclaimed, "I knew I had a move, ha your Lord is now mine." "I'll be right there." Matias said looking at Lincoln then to Bor. "Let's go. Linc you might want to come with us too, it might prove to be interesting?" Lincoln nodded. Matias exited followed by Lincoln. "But the game, we will never finish at this rate." Bor said and huffed as he stood. Looking at Greal who had been sitting in the corner, he said, "You see that don't you." Pointing at the place where he was going to move. Greal just looked at him not knowing what to say. Bor sneered and left with curses on his breath.

The cockpit door slid open and Matias walked in. "Where is it Saul?" he asked as he looked at the monitor. "Well its faint sir, but it's out there. It is toward Royal on the west side, the Dru Nar side." "The Mercenary city?" Lincoln asked excitement in his voice. "Yes the very one. Thugs, vermin, and treachery waits at that hole." Bor said coming in behind them, "Among other things." Le Kai added, smiling from the copilot seat next to Saul. "There sir." Matias eyes widened as he read the readings. "It can't be, lock onto that signature, and head for it." Matias was in shock almost. "What?" asked Bor. "If that's right, we might have just pulled off a miracle." Lincoln looked at him, "What is it Uncle?" Matias looked down at the young man. "Hope."

As he was looking away he noticed Lincoln's wrist com. It was glowing. He kept it to himself, but Matias knew the other things the wrist com was able to do, and it was a good sign, especially so far away from the city. The night was setting in and cold was creeping up outside the venerable vehicle and its crew. The engine of the war machine revved as it made haste on its course towards Royal.

Lower Lithatl, under Elven Royal

They entered the tunnels leading to the Lithatl from a tall smooth tower that paralleled Dru Nar property, Midwest of the city. It was easy to get to and what little resistance was given was easily dispatched. Tasha's intel had proven effective, though the under city was in more disrepair than she had expected. Some of the tunnels they had found were flooded or damaged, and they had to double back, but as they went deeper under the city it was apparent the information was correct. The architecture improved and the resistance started getting better as well. They had dispatched two small Elven perimeter squads and now had located the third.

The mercenaries were tucked around a corner that led out into another drain tunnel. Walker was on point. He had his back against the wall, his bare Magnus covered hand touching it. He felt vibrations through the stone. An Elven guard was walking toward their location and was now only a few feet away. He felt the vibrations of the Elf as he grew closer. Nodding to Tasha and Dahl who were behind him, the big Spartan made his move. He was like lightning around the corner, grabbing and smashing the Elf against the wall knocking him out instantly. Dahl was next taking out the other guard from behind, and the rest moved in stowing the bodies as they did.

Normally Elves were impossible to sneak up on, but with Walker and Tasha to locate them, and the gear they had been wearing to hide them, it made for an easier task. The team wore their utility belts, packs, and weapons over cloaked gray body suits, goggles with helmets, and cloaks. They were body suits new to the war, even though Walker had seen similar items when he had served. The gray suits were Razium in origin and very hard to get. Dillion had some funding for sure to get his hands on these. Grays was a military slang word for the tight fitting dark gray camo suits that the elites of the Confederates had used, and these mercs now wore. It was a Kevlar type material that could deflect small caliber bullets and could have small armor plates attached if needed. The material was also light and durable. The best attribute of the suits and the reason they were so valuable was that the material would slightly bend light, making the wearer blend in better with their surroundings. They were not invisible but very close, and they had been used to full effect on the Elves they had encountered so far.

Walker was still point man as they moved down a smaller tunnel. Tasha was beside him, and tried to move past getting caught between him and the wall. "You would make a horrible thief," she whispered. "Now move over." He grinned sucking in close to the wall allowing her to pass. They came to the end of the tunnel and stopped, looking through an opened grated culvert cover. Tasha stared down the dark opening that looked like one of the subway tunnels of York more than an abandoned depot underneath Royal, but these tunnels were much larger and more elegantly built. She could tell it was a newly built edition compared to the ancient architecture of the old parts of the city. Which for their age were in amazing shape, but this was Elven, and it was unmistakable.

They opened the grate and continued through the tunnels a few hundred feet that took them to a dark gunk infested and grimy looking dead end. It was anything but. Tasha motioned a mercenary up and one of the soldiers from the rear moved beside her. She slid her huge wrapped weapon from her back so she could get a better stance. The soldier handed her a smooth light colored stone as he took her weapon. She took the stone and motioned around her in a pattern. She then rubbed the end of it in another pattern and waited, watching as the end of the stone melted away with a dull glow. Runes that were not visible seconds ago lit up faintly, as did places on the ceiling and floor that were marked with the same pattern. The runes continued to light up as the tunnel grew longer in front of their very eyes. Walker had seen this weapon used in the wars, a Latent stone. Its powers were used to uncover concealing magic. The runes of cloaking covered the walls around them. As Tasha held the stone out in front of her, they continued to light up in a bluish hue, and as they did, the slime and debris of the filthy tunnel disappeared. It was an illusion, and such a good one that it seemed real, even to the senses. Tasha slowly walked the tunnel, and the magic in the runes continued to be undone as the spell lifted. The gunk and slime covered walls slowly moved back turning with her, turning into the clean smooth architecture of the Elves. Tasha smiled, and walked carefully toward its end while the magic fizzled out around the edges.

The glow gems along the corridor activated as she moved past them. The stone had revealed a now perfectly clean carved tunnel of amazing design, the end of which was covered with a large round metal grate. When she reached the grate she looked through its bars and down at the mass below them, the others moving up behind her.

"A rail depot," she whispered. Walker looked as well, hearing the bustle of people working, cranes, and steam engines. Whistles were sounding in the background as the train was being readied to depart, and Elven guards were stationed everywhere. There were massive columns on both sides of depot that attached to borders that ran one hundred feet to the semi circle shaped ceiling that went the length of the loading dock, roughly four hundred yards. It was breathtaking, and seemed to reach forever. The bricks and rocks that made the secret place, looked as if they had been carved by master masons. They were shaped and marked with ancient Elven workmanship, perfect in every way. The angles of the architecture a matchless beauty; with gold and colored stones that covered its walls. The symmetry was perfect; it looked more like a painting than a real life place.

Tasha looked below at the movements of the crews. The loaders operated cranes and hand carts, taking crates and boxes of ammunition, armor, and weapons to the cars. These workers weren't Elven though; they were Human, Troll, and another almost tree like people, with occasional small Gnome creatures that seemed to be overseeing the loading. Tasha studied the train. It was a masterpiece of steam and electric technology. It was silver in color and it had smooth dark iron pin stripes that ran down the sides of the first two cars, the engine and the carriage. They had side steps and gold trimmed hand rails the length of both as well. The train itself was long and smooth like a Massel passenger train in York only larger, the edges and footholds worked so well they seemed to be invisible. What separated these cars from the passenger carriers of the northern Confederate, was that these gun metal gray cars were wider allowing them to hold more; perfect for carrying goods and weapons. Also, the armor on its sides looked thicker as well.

As pretty as it was it could take a beating, Tasha thought, looking down its length. Along its sides were silver rails for soldiers or guards to stand if needed. The thing that really made it look different though was the engine. The engine was huge, silver, and round like a bullet, but the front had the look of an old style Boiler, and one headlight on its nose. It had the same silver rails, only the ones on the engine were smoother, and thicker. The back of it had two massive covered electric coils pointed skyward at forty five degree angles. The train was able to harness steam and electric power.

It was a hybrid of the classic steam trains that had been reinvented to use the new electrical energy as needed to pull its load. The speeds it could get too had never been achieved before by conventional rail trains. "The perfect getaway car," Tasha said aloud. She watched its cars being side loaded with weapons, supplies, and all types of crates. She couldn't help but marvel at the creation, and hoped she didn't have to destroy it. "Tasha." Called Dahl, her second in command and one of the mercs recent from the Boer War overseas. He had brown hair and was taller than average with the muscular build of an athlete. He wore a gun on each thigh and had a pack full of demolitions on his back. The man preferring to shoot first and talk later if caught. But like the rest of this team, he had been trained in the art of stealth, and so, was perfect for this job.

"Where are they likely holding the Key?" Dahl asked. She motioned him up and Walker moved back. Dahl slid beside her and pulled a pair of field binoculars, out of a pocket on the side of his pack. He held them to his eyes and looked down. These glasses had extensive modifications and were able to go to lower resolutions if needed. They also had an electronic device that magnified an area giving clarity as if you were only a few feet away. The technology definitely Razium in origin but looked as if crafted by Human artificers, with the icons on the sides. "Tough cookie to crack." He said looking through the lenses at the cars and spotting two areas likely for the item to be stored.

The first was a car toward the front that seemed heavily guarded by the troops loading in it, and the second a similar car in the back of the train a few cars from the rear. Dahl pointed them to Tasha and handed her the glasses. She looked at both cars, and saw they were loading a chest in the later of the two compartments. "I think I found it," she paused scanning the dock where a large black robed figure was walking. He was flanked by armed Grenadiers of the Razium. They were heading toward one of the few Elves overseeing the load. "Razium," she whispered. Dahl looked at her as he took the glasses. He looked down spotting who she was talking about, looking back to her after seeing the hooded figure talking to an Elf.

"Not just Razium, I have seen his kind before only once, overseas, when I fought the Aun Ka. He is a Zajust, he is a killer. I don't think we can handle this." Dahl finished shaking his head.

"Nonsense," she said, trying to instill confidence in the rest of the group that was listening, but seeing the look in his eyes she realized he was losing his nerve regardless. "We have you, and Walker. Plus, he isn't getting on the train." She said as she saw a squad of Elves fully dressed for war heading toward the cloaked Zajust. They were elites of the Elves. Tasha knew this by the weapons they held. The Elves were called, Elio Knights. They wore full armor, chest plates, shoulder pads, and greaves, though they were light and easy to move in. In their hands each held a large curved gun blade and all had daggers and other weapons on their hips. The weapon each carried was a sword type weapon that was combined with a shotgun style barrel, the handles holding the trigger. Elves where amazing fighters as it was, but with these weapons they were able to engage a foe that outnumbered them three to one and come away victorious, though their range was limited.

The weapons the Elves carried had been designed by the Dwarger of the Glorn clan, and when the Glorn Mountain city of Nee Brak'ah had fallen during the Battle of Fire, the Elves and their Dragon allies had the pick of the spoils. For the Dragons it was a number of things, mostly treasure. But for the Dru Nar it was weapons and knowledge. That is what they wanted. They took sacred building scrolls and tomes, along with some of the best weaponry ever designed. Elio Knights is what they were called, and to see them along with a Zajust was like seeing a lion converse with a pack of wolves.

Tasha was afraid this alliance might happen, but she had to get the Key. It was what she had been sent for. It was to go on the train is all she knew, but her thief and contact hadn't returned from his last entry into the fortress. He had been missing for a few days so she hadn't found out all the details. Like why the Zajust was there. She had to find out what else was on the train and warn the Governor of O'cea, and that Key was what she needed to carry out that mission. She turned and looked at her small contingent. "Ready your weapons and be on high alert. We must carry out this mission and when we do, we will all be rich and drinking by this time tomorrow." She flashed her sparkling smile at them, and then looked at Walker. He saw through her false excitement, and she knew it, though the others seemed appeased. She got a few nods and grins from the men, as they readied their weapons and gear. Tasha knew the mention of money would get their minds off of the strength of force they were about to face, and on to the mission at hand.

Getting on that train, finding what she needed, and getting off alive to spend the money that Boss Dillion had offered, was all they cared about. Plus, though they didn't want to lose anyone, they all knew the cut was bigger for the ones that returned, so danger, and luck were part of the mercenary game as well.

Tasha moved out of the way, "You're up tiny." Walker looked at her shaking his head. He moved past her putting his left hand on one of the huge bars that covered the tunnel they were in. He tested it, and then grabbed another with his right, testing its weight again. "Hand me a line." He said, and he was given a small corded metal rope that he latched to the grate. "Hold this taught, don't let it slack," he said and handed it to one of the mercs who passed it back to the others. He put his finger to his lips to be quiet, and then Walker put his hands in the bars of the gate. Making sure he had a good grip he slowly pulled turning, then pushed outward. The noise he made could barely be heard with the commotion coming from the equipment and hustle of the figures below them. With a final grunt the grate popped out, and the mercs held the cord tight.

Walker's huge arms bulged with its weight and he slowly lowered the grate to the wall. Making sure it was secure; he jumped out of the sewer pipe landing in a crouching position on the stacked crates below it. Walker was in the shadows, and clothed in the grey camo was almost invisible; even as big as he was. With the Grays on it would be very hard to spot him unless he was directly looked at, even with the armor he wore. They lowered the grate down and Tasha had the last soldier tie it off on a bolt in the tunnel, to hold it.

They moved away from the grate, and down toward the floor, spreading out as they went. Slowly the force moved to the crates of the lower parts of the depot. "Plant the explosives," Tasha had told them before they had descended down. "And get ready for my signal." After Tasha had navigated through the boxes and crates, she found where she wanted to enter the train. Looking back to her troop, she began giving quick hand signals of where to start. She looked over to Dahl and Walker, a wild gleam in her beautiful eyes. "We have a train to catch." She said, the train's whistle erupting as she did.

CHAPTER 25. TO CATCH A TRAIN:

Hidden Depot of Lithatl, under Royal

The Elven General Than, walked proudly toward the hooded figure of the Zajust and his guard. The Elf's steel eyes seeing the thing in front of him for what it was, a war dog. Someone's pet. Disgust marred his perfect but slightly older features as he looked at the Orc. Than was wearing his grey and crème colored armor with a light blue cape, the sigil of a mighty ship and Dragon on his breast plate. "Commander." He said with a slight hesitation. "I bring you greetings from Lord Tusho, he will be joining us in time. For now he is preoccupied, talking to your master." The Elf General was trying to hide his disdain for the Zajust as he spoke.

The Zajust was cloaked completely in black, a pelt of some beast on his large shoulders, though the dark ridges of his armor could still be seen, his large green jaw jutted from under his hood. Than knew who and what this thing was and what it did for his sire. For a creature such as this to defile the sacred lands of the Elves, even outcast such as his own house, was unthinkable to him.

However, Than was here to do his duty for his Prince and his people so he bore this responsibility. He had vowed to set Tusho on the throne again and regain his birth right, if dealing with this scum meant that, then he would stomach it a little longer. "Thank you, General." Was the deep gritty reply. "Please, you don't have to mask the way you feel about me, don't patronize me with the corgal deguot of your people." He said in very broken Elvish, cocking his head to the side. "You know why I am here. You and your knights are not to task, but," the Zajust Vangel held a thick green finger in the air. "Do not worry, I will make sure your Lord gets what he deserves." The General held his tongue, as rage built in his soul, his eyes hardening. "Good, you have learned to keep that tongue of yours silent, there is hope for your race after all." Vangel noted, his taunting voice almost causing the general to lose his temper. Before the Elf could retaliate he was hailed from the yard master.

The train was almost loaded and a whistle blew in the background, they were making final preparations to depart. Than nodded to the yard master and turned on his heel, guards in tow. "Follow me," was all he said. Vangel followed. "Right," he said gutturally as he and his two armored Anusiya guard followed. From behind the crates twenty yards away, Tasha watched them walk out of sight.

* * *

Elerossë Tusho Amn Drannar, Lord of the Sea Dru Nar outcasts, was talking to the glow of the holo screen mounted on his elegantly carved wall. He was in the tallest tower of the Elven fortress on Lithatl. He was a few feet from the screen gazing away out a large amazingly crafted window, seeing the huge mountain city below him; not really caring what was being said. "Yes, Nemsor, I know," he said back nonchalantly, not looking at the person on the screen who was speaking.

"I have sent my envoy, he will ensure your items reach me intact. I don't want any interference from the gangster or his cohorts. Do you understand?" The cruel voice spat. Tusho turned stepping back to the screen. He wanted this to end so he would appease Nemsor, for now. "Yes, I will see to it myself." Tusho replied. "See that you do." Nemsor methodically said. "I want my plan to be fully developed when we attack the Palace." "Alright Nemsor." Tusho replied with a hint of sarcasm in his voice. The vid screen blinked off. Tusho sat for a moment in silence. Then mimicked the last remark from the Zajust Lord. "I want my plan to be bla bla..." he said making a face. Then yelled in frustration, slapping a cup beside him. It flipped and landed with a clang, its contents spilling on the marble floor. Tusho was standing in the middle of the room. He started to spin around, turning in circles his arms out to his sides like a child in the rain, the beautiful colored silken robe he wore opening like a dancer's dress. He stopped spinning, slamming his arms down to stop the fabric. "Who does he think he is?" He flailed his arms for a moment, annoyed. Then composed himself, standing tall. "I will have my throne and my father will see me rule. These aliens will bow to me!" He said, his eyes getting a clouded look of purpose about them. Then he laughed, and turned to regard the huge thing that had stirred in the corner of his exquisitely large chamber.

Much like the throne room below the city, this room was just as extravagant, if not more so. It was covered in gold and platinum trimmings, colorful tapestries were draped all around the beautiful alabaster columns and the furniture, statues, and treasure around the room would be that to rival any king. He watched the huge thing lying on the floor. "Won't they, my friend?" He asked walking toward the shape, its scales the colors of violet and blue gleamed in the dim light of the room. He heard a rumble. "Are you hungry?" Tusho asked the giant beast.

The Prince walked over and opened a metallic ice box, the blue light inside the box enhancing the frosty wisps floating out of it; he reached in taking out a huge flank of some large beast, blood dripping off it. "Yum," he said as he tossed it to the dragon lying on the floor. Faster than it should have moved for as big as it was, the flat head of the dragon drake lashed out, grabbing the meat before it hit the ground. It bit down, snapping the bone that was in the meat with a sickening crunch. "Bone voyage," Tusho said. The horrible pun making him snicker, as he watched the young drake devour the flank. "Eat up my friend; I will need your strength soon," he said as he walked around his room. He stopped, stood still and listened eyebrow raised. He felt a vibration. He looked at Saphron, the dragon, who was still busy eating. There was another tremor. Tusho's eyes narrowed. He was rocked slightly. "What is that?" He asked aloud, still looking at the Saphron. The tremors started to increase, the next getting stronger. He quickly walked toward his screen, almost losing his footing as the next vibration jarred him. He grabbed his screen, touching it, "What is going on!" He yelled at it as it came to life. He looked at the screen eyes wide and anxious, he received no reply. The rumbling continued. One of his priceless urns fell to the floor shattering. Then a goblet fell to the floor as well, spilling the wine inside all over the cut marble tile. "What was that?" He screamed, fully enraged, the screen finally coming on.

An Elf appeared on the screen; behind him was chaos in the depot below. "My Lord, we are under attack." "What!" Tusho yelled at him. "All around us Lord, crates are exploding and we," He was cut off as a piece of the ceiling came crashing down, crushing him. Another Elf took his place and was pushed aside as General Than stepped into view. "My lord, we are compromised, saboteurs. The train is moving but we are being undone."

"Than, you twit!" Tusho yelled, balling both hands into fists, "How do we get attacked at a secret base below my own city! Get that train moving now, I will be there to deal with this shortly!" He slammed his hand down on the monitor and it blinked off. Swiftly he walked to a small but elaborately wood carved entrance way on his wall, making annoyed faces and sticking his tongue out as he did. Touching a button, the carved door slid open to reveal a tunnel leading out of the luxurious room. He made his way down it to his armory. He loved his armory. It was an overkill of swords, guns, and armor that could outfit an army, with weapons from hundreds of battles. What he loved the most was the blood red armor that stood in the middle of it. The armor dominated the room, a light from overhead showcasing its amazing craftsmanship. It was muscled, and scaled, with a long black cape, the scrollwork on the breast plate depicting dragons breathing fire. As he entered, Tusho's servants came running in, bowing to their liege, while others went to saddle Saphron. "Quickly now, I mustn't keep this soon to be dead person waiting," he said happily as they helped him with his armor. His slaves moved as fast as they could, not wanting his temper to fray any more that it had, he was already on edge.

Once done, he flexed his hands, the scales of the red catching the light. The armor moved with his body. It felt good. His helm was the shape of a dragon's head, and his weapons black like its claws. Sheathing his dagger and attaching a folded hilted device to his hip, he took the last piece of his puzzle, his Laser Lance. The weapon was a long black pole that ended in a cruel six inch white point on the end, the tip of a dragon's claw. Small etched devices with the heads of dragons coiled around the lance, and along its round surface. They ran from the large flaring guard to the dragon claw tip of the expertly crafted weapon. Tusho, the Red Dragon, walked from his armory to the top of his tower.

It was a marvelous and ingeniously made glass encased tower lantern above his upper chamber. The walls were a crystal glass of Elven make, and two huge doors of gold and crystal stain opened onto a landing that lead out about thirty yards to look over the city. The landing was rectangle in design and its cornered ends had two dragon gargoyle statues that hung from its textured sides.

The doors leading from Tusho's chambers opened and he stepped from them, one of his servants followed holding his helm. He walked toward Saphron, who was in the middle of the glass room. The drake had been saddled, and there was a huge pool of blood on the floor beside the beast. Tusho saw it, rankled his nose, and then noticed that the other Elves had backed away. He shrugged and climbed to the back of the mighty Drake, taking his helm from the servant who hurriedly scurried away from the Dragon.

"Nak Nak?" Tusho asked, waiting for an answer from his retainer. He looked at the servants that had backed away. "My dragon trainer, Nak Nak, where is he?" One of the servants spoke up. "He is dead sire, Saphron ate him." The Elf who spoke pointed to the pool of blood. Tusho looked annoyed. "He did? Saphron liked him. Oh well then, I guess no one's there," he said chuckling. No one else laughed. "Get it? Nak Nak. Who's there? No one," he said to them. "Because he died?" He looked at the cowed Elves shaking his head that no one got the joke. "Never mind, it was a bad joke anyway."

The drake Saphron roared. "That is right my friend, these insects will feel my power, I have suffered their existence long enough." He touched a rune on his gauntlet; the huge glass doors leading out of the room opened. Saphron walked through them, the wind whipping around them both as they surveyed the mountains around the city. The view was breathtaking. They neared the edge of the landing, then with a grunt Saphron leapt off. As they fell the dragon spread his enormous wings catching the mighty updrafts, and shot skyward. Tusho sighed, and with a gesture only a true Dragon Whisperer of the Realm of Mists could create, he guided the dragon higher into the air. It flew above the city to glide. Then with another small gesture from Tusho, Saphron tucked his wings and dove. The dragon sped toward the ground below, the giant beast taking aim at the city. The acidic saliva in its maw warming. The liquid a dragon could make had been used as fuel for certain creations long ago, and when alight it could burn through almost any substance on the planet; if the dragon was old enough. The older the dragon the more potent was its flame. Dragon's breath is why Royal was originally founded so close to the inhospitable lands. Hunting dragons was a dangerous but prosperous business back then.

The drake was closing on the city below it, Tusho sitting atop it in his saddle, laughing and goading the large monster on. Saphron opened his wings and started to slow as he drew in a breath to create his fire.

The Human people of Royal had felt the vibrations as well. Most were still looking around, checking for injuries, while vendors looked over their merchandise. Everyone in the square seemed to be alright, minus the occasional cry or complaint of being hit by debris. There were no serious injuries, and all seemed to be settling back to the normal. The chatter of what had happened or what it could be was the focal point of most conversations.

A shadow crossed the busy streets of the Kiss as Tusho flew over the city, and slowly headed toward the east side of the huge metro. He would have his revenge, and it would start now.

One of the women in the market noticed the shadow slowly moving over the city. Thinking it was a low flying zeppelin or some other wondrous air machine she slowly looked up, expecting to be amazed. She seized at what she saw, horror stricken she couldn't talk, or even move. Only her child pulling on her dress broke her trance. "Dra...Dra....Dragon!!!" She finally screamed, as the poor thing realized what was flying at her. She grabbed her daughter and ran. All the people around her burst into terror screaming, as they too saw the magnificent horror that was descending upon them.

"Vengeance is mine!" Tusho yelled as Saphron flew towards them! The beast opening his mouth as he came low. Flames erupted, pouring from the dragon's maw. The sound it made was a crack as the heat from the mixture exploded breaking the sound barrier. The flames engulfed the buildings, people and everything else too close to them in the orange red of death. Tusho flew through the streets of Royal, unleashing the blazing heat of the monster. Glass shattered, metal burned or melted, and the buildings hit with the infernal liquid slumped against one another as their solidarity was tainted. People ran for cover, but there was little to be had for them. The dragon fire exploded carts as it streaked the city with flame. Saphron opened his wings and rose over the wall then turned back for another dive. "You will learn who your master is!" Tusho yelled. The people ran, scattering, trying to hide as the drake's flames continued burning the city.

Saphron landed on one of the taller buildings his mighty claws crushing into the brick; as he roared his triumph.

Tusho surveyed the destruction of the main square. "Good job my friend," he said patting the dragons scales. Tusho nudged the beast and Saphron's huge wings opened. With a mighty flap the beast took to the air once more. Tusho guided him and they flew west toward the train tracks, where he would make sure his train was successful in departing this dreadful city. Then he would come back and finish what he had started. The city would fall and he would take what was his.

Outside the city of Royal

The Wartrak drove over a small hill rounding the mountain road a few miles southeast of Royal. "Commander, we are three miles away from Royal, your orders, sir?" Saul asked. Matias looked at him. "Do you have a reading?" "No sir we lost it, I haven't been able to pick it back up in the last hour. Interference, or maybe in a secure place." he finished. Lincoln looked at Matias from his seat in the cockpit, eyes wide. "What is it Linc?" Matias asked. "I feel something, I don't know how, but it's familiar. I have felt it before. I feel it, no not it." He said somewhat taken aback. "I feel a him."

"What do you feel, how?" "I don't know, but Uncle," Lincoln held up his wrist com. "Look, I didn't know it could do this."

The wrist band was glowing and the runes were lit; bright blue light radiating from them. Lincoln pressed the largest middle rune that was blinking. The bracelet opened and a glowing three dimensional sphere appeared above it. He recognized it, it was the planet, Partha Terra. It grew larger, locations and beacons all over it soared into being, the three dimensional images were coming to life all around the cockpit before their eyes. Then it narrowed to a continent, then to a place in the middle, then to a location, it looked like a city. Then it narrowed to the city itself. It was honing in on a signal. It continued until it showed that there was an item in the city. Well under it, and it was moving and picking up speed, it was in some sort of vehicle. "Uncle?" Lincoln asked alarmed. "It is leading us Lincoln, it's a map son. I haven't seen it work like this since." Matias stopped himself and then said, "It is heading west. Head to the west side of the city. Lead us down the mountain, find a way." Matias ordered. "Aye sir," Saul responded punching the throttle.

The tank took off heading west. Matias checked Lincoln's map. "Keep this course, just follow that signal." "Uncle what were you going to say?" Lincoln asked. "Well," he said thinking of the right words. He didn't want to say that he hadn't seen it work since the King's death, but he didn't know what else to tell him. The tank sped around the bend, the huge walls of the city became visible in the distance. "What is that?" Saul asked pointing. Before the commander could speak, he looked out the cock pit glass toward Royal. Lincoln right beside him. What they saw had not been seen in years. The city was burning, and above it was a dragon, a dragon flying above Royal.

CHAPTER 26. PATHS MERGE:

Train depot under the Lithatl side Elf city Royal

Dahl crouched behind one of the larger crates close to the dock. He took five round explosive spheres from his pack. They were munitions that had been a fairly new tool in the war, about the size of a very large grape or small plum with a primer switch on the side. Grenados is what they had been called, but the mercs referred to them as grems, or palms because the size. Dahl was a sapper. He loved the explosives, and he looked at the small round bombs in his hand. He smiled as he thought about the destruction that these little things were about to unleash. Priming them, he opened his hand and rolled them toward the train. The rest of the squad had followed Tasha's signals and snuck into areas of cover, around the crates and loaders, getting as close to the train as they could. They did the same with their supplies of explosives, rolling them under, and setting them on crates and by munitions. The primer would give them enough time to get back to their hiding places. Then they were to get to the train in the confusion of the explosions and take the items Tasha had instructed were the targets. She had hoped they didn't have to fight their way out. It was a good plan, but it was only good till first contact.

One of the mercs rolled a grenado toward a crate but it stopped short as it hit the boot of a Troll, the beast lumbering through the station way with one of the last caskets to be loaded. The mercenary froze, eyes wide. The stupid beast was about to step on it. But it didn't. One of the little Gnome creatures yelled at the Troll and pointed back toward the train. The lumbering creature must have remembered something and it turned and looked. The huge beast turned back and grunted a word to the little creature. The mercenary looked over to where Tasha had been watching, she shook her head in relief and they both let out a breath.

Then the beast turned back around, and the other foot fell stepping right on the grenado. Everything seemed to stop, the mercenary stood to run, surprising one of the little Gnome creatures, but with the crunch of the Trolls boot the grenado detonated, and all hell broke loose.

The mercenary and the Gnome creature were thrown through the air as the Troll exploded, showering all within fifty feet in guts and goo. The concussive force knocking the soldiers, loaders, and anyone else in the blast range to the ground. This first one's detonation started the reaction that set off the grenados all over the depot. Tasha ducked behind the crate, as the noise and explosions ripped through the station. "Damn," she breathed, not hesitating she knew she had to seize the moment.

"To the train!" She yelled pulling her weapons, and running into the press toward the engine. The mercenary who set the grenado tried to stand but was deaf for the moment from the explosion, a constant ringing noise in his head. An Elio Knight had seen him. Unsheathing his weapon, the Elio leapt the crate the mercenary was behind. The mercenary pulled his combat blade but was dead before he could use it. The Elf stood over him, unloading the gun barrel to be sure he was gone.

Like a stalking panther revealing himself to his prey, Walker leapt from his hiding place grabbing one of the passing Elio Knights. He took his weapon smashing him in the face with the butt of the gun. Then turned the gun on another as he ran toward him, blasting the Elf. Walker was knocked sideways from a blast. The explosions were ripping through everything. He got to his feet and shook his head looking through the chaos for Tasha. He saw her bolt for the train. Another explosion obstructed his vision, and when he looked back she was gone.

The train had started moving, a whistle blowing in the background. Walker had to hurry, there wouldn't be much time to board before it was out of the depot. He ran to follow Tasha, but was stopped in his tracks by the punch of another Troll. The meaty fist catching him in the head knocking him off balance, luckily it wasn't a solid punch. He was able to deflect it with most of his shoulder but still the force knocked him to the ground, his helmet falling off. Walker rolled and was up immediately on the defense as the creature advanced upon him. He pulled his halberd that had been sheathed on his back. He flipped the switch and its handle shot out elongating the weapon. The Troll bellowed and charged but was blown off the station dock, as Dahl came running behind it. He had tossed a grenado at its feet, blasting the beast from the planet. Dahl ran passed, "You coming!" He yelled unloading his pistols at other Elves. "Yeah," Walker said nodding and running after him. Together they fought down the dock, cutting through a few Elven soldiers and another of the brutish Trolls. There was little to stop the giant warrior and the sapper in front of him as the pair left a messy path in their wake.

Another of the mercenaries; a man named Ford, had joined them during the fighting, and the three man wrecking crew had almost reached the back of the moving train. Walker was looking for Tasha. He hadn't seen her since she ran toward the train, but he knew she was already on. She had to be, he thought. Ford had caught up to the rear of the train. He jumped to the platform of the back car; catching hold and pulling himself up.

"Hurry!" he yelled, waving them on, trying to give them some cover fire. Dahl made it next, grabbing a hand rail. An explosion from the side rocked them, and Dahl almost fell. He grabbed for a rail, but lost his grip on his pistol as he caught it. The well-crafted shooter fell to the platform that Ford was standing on with a clank. Dahl cussed, and pulled himself up, then slid over to get the weapon.

Ford kept firing at the Elves closest to the train, and was waving for Walker to jump. "Come on," he yelled, holding out his hand. The words died in his mouth as he was launched backward by a bullet to the chest. Dahl ducked for cover. Solid slugs from Elven snipers on the columns above had taken the other man out, he had slid off the rear of the train before Dahl could grab him. Another slug hit the railing as Dahl ducked back behind the bars trying to reload. Walker was running behind the train shots hitting the ground at his feet. He jumped, catching one of the railings and pulled himself on, as Dahl stuck his gun over the rails firing at the snipers' pinning them down. They both had managed to get to the last car, but didn't know who else had made it. It had been a bloody mess. The grenados going off early had messed everything up. Walker helped Dahl up. "Come on!" he yelled as he kicked in the door of the rear of the car, both running through as shots whizzed past them.

The train was picking up momentum, and was almost clear of the station. Walker slammed the door shut after they barreled in. As they sped toward the darkness of the tunnel, Dahl looked out the rear window of the car seeing another of his small force get cut down. An Elven commander in a light blue cape stood over the mercenary. He was yelling orders and pointing at the train. The depot was in flames behind him, the explosions growing. It was the last thing Dahl saw before the tracks bent and the tunnel took them.

The train was moving fast down the tunnel, it was dark at first but the glow gems on the insides of the cars lit up, giving off a smooth blue glow. Walker and Dahl looked around the caboose; there was no sign of life. The respite allowed them to catch their breath, and Dahl reloaded his pistol as Walker shortened the length of his weapon; so it was more manageable in the smaller space. All that could be heard was the fading explosions as the train carried them from the now not so secret station of the Elves.

The train entered a wider section as they moved through the tunnels, echoing noises coming from above. "New passengers?" Walker asked looking at the ceiling. "I'll go up top, meet you in the middle." Dahl said as he pulled back the slide of his gun. Walker nodded in response as Dahl went out the back door, climbing the ladder on the back of the car toward the roof. Walker was left alone. All he could think was he hoped Tasha was on board, but the thought was replaced as he felt something. It was something strange, magical, but very familiar. He had felt it before, long ago. He blinked it away as he heard a noise coming from the next car. He walked through the caboose to the next car's door. He put his ear close listening intently. He couldn't hear anything and it seemed as if the passengers, wherever they were, didn't know he or his friends were aboard. Surprise is a good weapon, he thought. He stepped back and counted to himself. One, two, three, then kicked through the door.

* * *

Tusho flew above Royal watching the smoke rise from below him, a sadistic grin was plastered on his face. He had flown back over the east side of the city just to watch it burn; see the destruction he had caused. He knew he needed to go, but something in him yearned to see the beauty of the chaos he had wrought on the Humans below. He had waited too long to see that sight. He passed over the fires in the square, the yelling and panic music to his ears. He circled once more to savor the small victory, then flew over the Hem, into the west side of Royal.

From here he would turn Saphron southwest and fly over the huge walls of the city, then over the mountains. There he would meet his silver beauty as it came out of the tunnel in the lower regions. Tusho's vision was amazing, and from the back of the mighty Saphron he would be able to see the silver streak come out of the mountains; where the large cliffs joined the lower plain. Then he would deal with anyone that wasn't supposed to be on his train. Soon, he thought, and he looked at the monitor on his wrist. It was tracking the train, soon he thought again. With a slight tilt, Tusho turned Saphron toward the mountains. The creature spread its wings, flying over the huge walls of the city.

The crack boom of cannon fire broke the silence of Tusho's flight, and a beam of light raced past as Saphron bucked. "What? What is shooting at me? Who dares!" He screamed, adjusting himself in the saddle, trying to find where the blast had come from. Another blast sounded. This one grazed Saphron's belly and the dragon roared in pain. Tusho was furious. "Who dares?" He was looking around them frantically. Then below them by the city walls he found the culprit.

A tank was following them, a Wartrak! The spire breachers, he thought! He knew what type of machine it was. A dragon killer. He needed to close the distance lest that cannon kill his pet. "Ooden daya Despas!" he yelled in Elvish tongue, meaning, No one shall, and turned Saphron back toward the war machine. "I will kill you insect!" He screamed as he and the drake dove toward the oncoming tank.

Saphron inhaled, his throat readying for the lava like heat that was his breath. As they closed on the tank, Saphron unleashed the fume! Tusho laughed as they passed over it. Tusho nudged Saphron and he circled back around making for another pass at the venerable war machine. Tusho was astonished, on second glance the tank was still on fire but it was barely harmed and the flames were dying out. Tusho snarled under his helm and lowered the laser lance firing its beam weapon.

The tank swerved evading the blast by inches. Saphron sped past, and the tank sped up to match the dragon's speed. As it did, what little remained of the fire blinked out. The Wartrak's automatic .50 caliber weapons opened fire, launching a barrage on the drake. Tusho knew what they were going to do. He leaned Saphron in to a spiral, the control phenomenal. Saphron followed Tushos every move as if they were linked somehow. Saphron dodged and turned, the shots missing him entirely but blew chunks out of the walls of the city as they raced passed them. Tusho brought the dragon low to the ground. Its massive claws tearing a long rut and throwing the dirt in the air to cover its flight. The tank turned suddenly to miss the newly tilled soil, driving parallel to the deep trench the creature had just created. Bor had been driving and couldn't see where it had gone, but the tank continued to fire, hoping he might hit the beast.

"Bor, can you see anything?" Matias asked. Trying to find something to target in the smoke and falling dirt. "Nothing, sir," Bor came back, "I can't see anything in this dust." The targeter was triangulating, but couldn't lock on. The beast had vanished. A button on the console blinked. "Sir, the signal of the item is stronger now," Saul told him. Matias looked at Lincoln's wrist com, it was glowing brighter. "Its leading us to a." Matias stopped. "What Uncle!" Lincoln almost exploded as he asked the question. "A Key, son, it's taking us to a Key." Any sign of the dragon, Bor?" "No sir." "Then follow the Key." Matias finished.

CHAPTER 27. ENEMIES:

Mid-western plains

The train had gotten up to speed and was barreling down the tracks, though its turbine coils hadn't been engaged yet. It had made it out of the tunnel, under the mountain and now the sun reflected off its silver surface, glinting in the light of the day. It was beautiful, a silver bullet streaking away from the mountain range and heading to the sandy brown of the open plain. The reflective colors shimmered, dancing on its silver surface like a moving rainbow. The hues rippled and then darkened as a shadow from overhead descended on the train.

Saphron was gliding low, its large wings beating to keep up with the silver streak that was the train. "Get me closer my pet, I must make sure all is well. I will not let my ascension be ruined now!"

Tusho had realized the Wartrak was stalling him and Saphron had been hurt in the exchange. As much as he hated being bested, he knew he needed to get to the train, before the tank got lucky. He had pulled Saphron up over the walls and away from the Wartrak as the cover from the dirt hid him. The Key was most important, and he had to ensure it made it to the Razium, or his plans would be hampered as well. He hated having to rely on the forces of anyone other than his people, especially the damned Razium, unfortunately he had no choice. He needed them for the moment. He whispered to Saphron and the dragon pulled in its wings to dive towards the train. As they neared, one of the rear cars buckled outward, the force knocking metal free from its side. Saphron growled and reopened his wings to pull up out of the way just as a piece of the train's outer wall flew by them. Tusho screamed, "Someone is on my train, they will suffer!"

Digging his heels in to the mighty beast, he pushed Saphron closer; a sneer on his pale lips. "And now they will die." He said, the dragon flying straight at the car unleashing its flame.

* * *

Walker kicked the door in. It flew open, and left Walker staring at twenty Elio Knights. "Crap," he said. Elio Knights were supreme warriors, best on horseback but no slouches on foot either. The armored warriors had all turned, staring at Walker, surprise on their slender angular faces. He saw over them to the front of the car, and the cloaked figure that was behind them. The Zajust!

"Kill him!" The Zajust yelled pointing at Walker. As one they raised their gunblades and started to fire. Walker hadn't used his powers much since being in the company of the Kissar, but the time for secret and concealment was over. He pulled his small blade as he raised his other hand. The Magnus felt strong as it flowed into him, stronger than usual, it let him feel both their auras; and the metal of their weapons. With a flick of his wrist all the barrels lifted as they fired, the powerful guns blowing chunks out of the ceiling, though none penetrating the armor of the car.

Walker wasted no time and charged them. He caught them off guard and was already among them before they could regain control of their weapons. His pole arm blade was shortened and he was using it as a sword, hitting one in the midsection and then smashing another to the wall with his backswing. He had two down as he shattered the armor of a third with his open palm, the Magnus blowing a hole in the metal and throwing the Elf against the wall. As he reached the forth, the Elf dodged out of his way and unloaded his gun at the charging Spartan. Walker had to drop his pole arm to repel the shots as they ripped through his grey suit. He had almost been too slow. He flexed his hand sending the pellets flying back toward the Elves who were trying to close in on him. Using the Magnus he made the Elf that had shot the weapon slam the blade he was carrying into the other beside him! The Elf fell to the floor, allowing Walker to smash the other to the ground with a back hand to the face. Another of the Knights rushed him, Walkers eyes had changed to a golden yellow, and on his arm where his Greys had been torn open from the shot; the Elf could see the Magnus marks had flowed over him. The Elves eyes widened in alarm and he tried to cry out, "Spart..." but his alarm was cut off as Walker's hardened fist buckled his helm. The others rushed him, not seeing his marks through the tears in his Greys.

Walker slammed his fists together unleashing a Magnus ripple, the force throwing the Elves from him, their armor splintered as they hit the walls of the car. The car buckled outward from the energy of Walker's power. Walker made easy work of the others that hadn't been caught in the impact. He blocked punches, and blasted Elves from him with hand movements, sending them sprawling on the floor. He glanced to the front of the car. The Zajust was gone. He had made it out the door and exited to the next car. "Enough!" Walker shouted, smashing the last few of the Elves that were in his way. He made his way toward the front of the car to follow the Zajust. He threw open the door of the next car hand up. It was empty. He was close though, and watched the door on the other end close with a click of the handle. He ran toward it determined to catch the creature that had eluded him, but stopped halfway in the car when the door opened and more Elves entered. They were garbed differently than the Knights. They had high collars folded down and what looked like short, tight, darkened leather pea coats over their torsos. Walker tossed his small cloak to the floor, throwing out his hand toward them to launch them back with the Magnus, but they barely moved and steadied themselves.

The coats they wore suppressed the magnetic fields around them making them somewhat immune to his power. Two of the Elves came at him, jumping, flipping, and landing one to each side. They pulled small elongated blades from their suits, and simultaneously attacked.

Walker dwarfed both in size, but they were fast, and very good with their blades. He turned his skin hard, blocking with his hands. He watched their fighting pattern, and threw an elbow catching the Elf in the collar bone, breaking it and dropping him to the floor. The other pressed his attack, and Walker only barely blocked a thrust, then another and another.

The Elf found a way through his defense and one of the blades hit home. He felt the point bite in to him and knew he was in for trouble if he kept trying to fight. He had to end this quick or bleed out. Whatever these weapons were made of was magic in origin, and could pierce even his hardened skin. He smashed the Elf in the face laying him out, but another took its place coming at him with its blades. The new enemy slit him again, then he felt another prick from another that had come from his back. They had not been engaged for more than a few seconds and he had been cut multiple times.

In a feint, he lashed out grabbing the closest one punching him in the gut; he felt the crack of ribs as the Elves air left his lungs with a grunt. It was the first sound that any of the things had made. The others came at him. He blocked a kick from one and used his momentum to take the Elf into his partner knocking them into each other. Then in the struggle snapped the first one's neck, ending him, as the second regained its feet. With a jolt they all lost their footing briefly as the cars rocked back and forth. An explosion a few cars ahead had almost derailed the train. Walker stood, he was wasting time and needed to be done with this nonsense. The Elves were fast, but Walker was in no mood for mercy. With a renewed frenzy, he kicked and punched, smashing faces, breaking noses, and arms. He caught one of the Elves under the chin, the crack from his blow was deafening and the Elf lay still. A front kick sent the last of them through the door of the rear of the car. Walker paused catching his breath; it had gotten hot in the car, too hot. He looked up panting, the ceiling above him was getting red and slowly starting to melt, parts of the car catching fire. One of the Elves he had knocked out earlier had come to and started to laugh, "Dragon fire, the Red Dragon comes for you Spartan," it said as it pointed.

The heat was suffocating as the melting roof tore away, the air whipped in from the speed of the train, clearing the smoke from the melted car. The sun shone in and Walker had to shield his eyes from the glare of the sun. He saw a shape but wasn't sure what he was looking at, then realized there was a dragon flying above them! The thunder crack he heard gave him chills. He had fought these beasts and knew what the noise meant; it was going to spit more flame! Walker also knew he was not at his full strength, and would not be powerful enough to last the heat.

He and the Elf looked at each other. They had to get out of this car. Turning simultaneously, they ran. Walker looked back to see the beast inhaling for the blast of the white hot fire. He grabbed the Elf and pulled him back, using the momentum to launch himself toward the next car. The Dragon breath hit the car, torching it; incinerating the Elf. Walker dove crashing through the door of the car. He landed with a thud, turning, and kicking the door shut behind him.

It was cool and dark in the new car. He stood, coughing; he was smoking from the heat of the dragon fire. He took a moment to get his bearings, and dust himself off. His sight hadn't adjusted to the darkness of the room yet. He realized he had lost his pole arm and most of his other gear. The Grays he wore were tattered, and his massive arms showed through the cuts the Elves blades had made. He still had his belt though, the runic enchantment protecting it. His sight was adjusting slowly, but he noticed this car was different than the others. It was dimly lit by illuminators on the ceiling. He paused as he felt a presence, someone was here! He spun to see a shape he had missed in the corner. The large cloaked thing stepped toward him lowering its hood. It was the Zajust he had seen earlier, though its green face was still hard to make out in the gloom.

It spoke. "So you think to ruin my chance at glory warrior? You are impressive, but today is my day, and you will be my trophy." The Zajust had a deep rough accented voice, which was getting deeper as he talked. He put on his helmet and threw his cloak to the floor, stepping towards Walker, the room slowly illuminating. The Zajust was tall and had broad shoulders covered in dark armor and ornamented with talismans trinkets and trophies of his battles. The width of the armor only helped to emphasize his small waist. His helmet was a silver skull type mask that contoured around his face, lining his huge jaw and jutting out underneath. The front under the nose was a metal plate spiked with studs down the middle. It looked oversized for the face plate and Walker remembered where he had seen this mask before; knowing who its bearer was. He was the berserker, Vangel. Vangel reached behind his back and unclasped two huge hand axes, testing their weight one in each hand. He dropped them on his cloak. The shoulder guards, he took off and let them fall on the cloak as well.

The undersuit he wore was similar to Walkers. As he stepped into the dim light he continued to talk. "This is your end hero." Walker did the same standing to his full height not giving an inch to this creature; he wanted it to know who it faced. Though the creature was corded in a lean muscle, Walker was thicker. Vangel looked at him. "You're big, I see that, but no matter." his voice had deepened to a baritone as he started to laugh, and then he started to grow. Vangel grimaced as he started stretching, the suit stretching with him, though only just. He grew, until he was slightly bigger than Walker, but still not quite as thick through the chest; laughing as he did. "Now die!" he yelled as he charged.

The Zajust threw a punch that would have shattered a boulder, but it was blocked and countered as Walker used his momentum to throw the beast off balance. Vangel was quick and recovered easily. He launched a feint and, as Walker avoided it, a second punch connected, blasting Walker in the side. He felt that blow, and as he lost his breath momentarily, Vangel moved in close. Walker caught his kick, twisting the ankle, and tossing him away. Losing his balance, Vangel growled and came back at him with a flurry of blows. Walker blocked the first and threw a punch of his own, catching the helm but was hit again in the ribs, then kicked in the side, though was able to deflect the blow slightly. Vangel seemed to be getting bigger, and was now taller and thicker than Walker, but Walker noticed he was trading power for speed. A huge fist just missed his face and connected with the wall behind him, denting it outward. Vangel yelled, "Stand still little one!" Walker realized that he needed to be done with this quickly. He countered a punch from the brute, and then turning his powers inward hardened his fists to stone. Vangel threw a finishing cross; Walker countered, turning his hand in to the others, crushing Vangel's fist.

Walker's other hand shot down to catch him in the leg. Then while he was momentarily distracted, Walker launched a hard jab right to the ribs catching the Zajust and doubling him over to his side. As the monster was going down, Walker punched him in the face and then hit him in the throat. Vangel grabbed for his windpipe and then Walker hit Vangel in the side of the knee and crumpled his joint. The beast's knee almost gave completely and he yelled in pain as he went down. Walker moved in to finish him, but the train rocked slightly giving Vangel a moment of respite. He pulled a blade from his belt and lunged up at Walker, jabbing it into his side. It bit into a weak part of his armor, and pain flared over him. Walker's Magnus skin protected him from most of it but didn't stop it all, causing him to fall back a few steps going to his knee.

Vangel saw his opening to finish the Spartan warrior. He stood up chuckling thinking he had won as he limped toward Walker. Walker knowing he had to regain control of the fight, shook most the pain away, and he channeled the Magnus to reinforce his wounds. Walker drew him in, allowing him to think he had done more damage than he had. Vangel limped close and Walker surged to his feet, head butting the approaching Zajust warrior catching him under the chin. Vangel's head flew back with a crack, blood spurting; the force of the blow pushing his mask into his nose breaking it. Vangel yelled reaching for his mask to adjust it. He swung wildly;

attempting to prevent Walker from following up the hit. Vangel tried to focus looking around as he cleared his vision. He opened his eyes in time to see the kick to his face, breaking the mask, the blow knocking him into the wall of the car. The Zajust warrior bellowed as he tried to get his bearings. The face guard was broken off, and with a yell he pulled off the rest of the broken mask, growling at Walker. The dark green, red blood mix ran from his small piggish nose down his face to drip on his chest. He reached up to touch the liquid he felt running down it. Standing in the light of the illuminator he pulled his hand away staring down at the blood.

He looked like a brute. His green face had blue tattoo lines and runes scrawled over half of it running from forehead to jaw. The huge over extended jaw had two yellow white fangs jutting from the bottom, and piercings in his eyebrow and ears. His head; set between a hugely thick neck, was completely shaved on the sides, though the blue tattoos of his face ran in a pattern down the side of it. His dark hair was in a ponytail that was pulled tight, braided to his lower back. He was cut, bleeding, and mad. "No Human harms me, I am immortal. You will pay for that." He said tossing his helm down with a clank. He talked tough and wasn't backing down but Walker could tell he was losing his nerve. Vangel was the Berserker, in a field of many with his warriors to cheer him he would have been trouble, but without the slaughter or ego to feed him he could be beaten; he could get no bigger, and would ultimately lose.

Walker studied the mad beast before him, clenching his jaw he spoke. "You don't recognize me, but I know you... I have fought you and your brothers before, when there were more of you. I won then, and I will win now." Walker finished and paused letting the complexity of what he had just said sink into the head of the brute he now fought. Vangel raised his eyes; he looked at the warrior in front of him, as if seeing him for the first time, the black marks on his neck and face receded. "No, it's not possible," said the green skinned monster, his deep voice losing its tone, "You are dead..." Walker only smiled and said. "Yes."

Vangel yelled and charged Walker with the force of a rhino. Walker under hooked his arm around Vangel's neck as he ran into him, and pulled down driving Vangel's head into the car wall behind them. It dented out, the silver of the outside domed from the impact. Vangel was woozy from the blow but still enraged, throwing another punch that Walker blocked. Then he cracked down with his elbow hitting Vangel's wrist with a snap, breaking it. He followed with a left hook, and then a right uppercut, catching the already hurt creature in a flurry. With a crack the beasts head shot back, and he slumped down the wall. He reached up as if to feel if his jaw was still intact. "That was a good shot whelp," he spat, and greenish red blood spittle flew from his mouth. "But my kind never loses, you know that." He slurred. Walker saw the look on his face and grew wary. Vangel knew he couldn't win, he was hurt, and almost spent. He had shrunk back to his normal size, and had taken too much damage, his power dissipating. He touched his wrist and Walker could see a small light appear. Vangel smiled a bloody smile, "Let us see how good you really are, Spartan!"

CHAPTER 28. TASHA AND THE TRAIN:

The Silver train

Tasha had made it onto the train. After the crate had exploded and Walker and Dahl had caused such a ruckus, she had knifed an Elf and stole his cloak.

Blending in with the rest of the crew she hurried aboard during the chaos. After that, it had been easy to find or fight her way to the middle of the train. She had been through three cars already and there was a line of dead to prove it. Tasha was in front of the door that lead to the next car. She paused sniffing the air, knife in hand, the large axe weapon on her back ready to be pulled if needed. She counted to herself, "One, two, three," then kicked the door in.

There were two figures in the car. The first dressed in the creams and blues of an Elf, but harmless as he had the look of a clerk, just like the last car. The other was tall and muscled completely covered in black armor. Pipes hiding coils and bundles of wire wrapped around its torso between the muscled neck and shoulder guards making the thing look very thick. Anusyia, she thought! Both turned at the crash of the door, terror on the Elve's face. The Anusyia reacted immediately. The thing held its left arm up, the power shield on its wrist gauntlet humming as it activated, covering his left side in a purple hue of electric protection. In its other hand a laser blade came to life as well, the edge of the weapon glowing as its core was activated.

Tasha was a blur as she moved, sheathing her knife she dropped to a crouch position pulling the axe weapon from her back. It was enormous, slightly serrated, and had old runes carved into its large blade. There should be no way a woman her size no matter how muscled could lift that weapon, but she held it now perfectly balanced. The blade was close to her left hand that was open, extended toward the cyborg guard. The shaft crossed her back her right hand holding it, the bottom slightly pointed to the floor of the car. She was bent to strike. There was a pause, both sizing each other up.

The Anusyia advanced on her with a speed hidden by the bulk, his laser blade shimmering and humming in the air. He swung at her, a perfectly executed slash. The sound of the burning air wisping toward her, but she was already gone. She had adopted a defensive stance on his side. Turning, he came at her again launching three quick thrusts; she evaded all three and hit him in the helm as she moved. She swung her blade again. His shield blocked her blow, allowing the monstrous cyborg to punch her in the mouth. She stumbled back, catching herself on the wall. Her lip started to bleed.

She watched the metal monstrosity that was her prey, licking the blood off her lip almost seductively. Her eyes shined and changed color turning to a deep blue, the pupils changing shape to that of a beast. The Anusyia gripped his sword and came for the kill. The yell of battle she gave was ear shattering, as she launched herself at him, changing into the beast she was. In two steps she had warped. Her muscles bulged and her beautiful features contoured into an animalistic face of rage. As a beast she was huge. She blocked his swipe with the back of her axe, spinning it out and up over her head and bringing the blade down with both hands cutting the guard from shoulder to groin. Sparks shot out from his robotic gears that had been severed as it fell to the floor in sparks and sputtering oil. The clerk screamed. She silenced him smacking him against the wall with a quick backswing of her fist. He flew through the air like he was a child's doll, hitting the wall with a thud. She was panting and her features softened slightly, but her head whipped around as she heard gun shots. Her instincts took over, the animal inside her longed to be released. With a roar, she tore her blade from the floor by the Anusyia and bound through the next door, ripping through it like paper as she charged. The Elves in the car had their backs to her. It would be the last mistake they would ever make.

* * *

The roof of the train was melting off. With curiosity, Tusho watched a large warrior and a Dru Nar assassin turn to look at him from the glob of melting steel that had once been a silver masterpiece. So that is who is going to die, he thought to himself touching Saphron's scales.

At the touch the dragon's neck heated and he sucked in his next breath. Prince Tusho started to chuckle. He watched as the warrior grabbed and pulled the Elf past him, the momentum launching him through the door of the next car. "Nice move. That is what I would have done." He chuckled.

Suddenly his humor ended, and he sneered. "But that is my train. I will rip out your insides and pull them through your eyes warrior!" Again Saphron lit up the train; the extreme heat of the Dragon fire had melted the metal of the hull and it was dripping through, burning the inside. Even though he was not a full grown dragon, still only a drake, Saphron's fire mixture was very powerful. Powerful enough to melt most metals. His bigger kin could do more damage with less effort though; legends stating that some could burn through Arcanium laced steel. An explosion came from one of the other cars ahead, shrapnel was blowing in to the air, and one of the pieces clipped Saphron. The beast roared and opened his huge wings, catching the air and pulling out of the danger. Tusho looked to see if the drake had been hurt. "Are you alright my pet?" he asked. "If not, I don't know what I would do without you." He told the beast, truly saddened. His face in anguish like he had been hurt, and there was a tear in his eye. He rubbed Saphron. "Mother, I miss you." he said pouting his lips from a memory. Then his face changed and he glared down at the small streaking train below him. "I don't know who dares but I will kill them with my own hands," he gritted through his teeth. With a motion, Saphron's wings flapped and he gained speed matching that of the train below.

* * *

Vangel laughed as he pulled his finger from his wrist device. Behind him the car's door opened as two of the huge Anusyia stepped in. They pulled long single edged blades. Flicking switches on the weapons they thrummed to life; the light of a laser beaming down their keen edges. They activated their wrist shields and the glow illuminated the room. "Your time is ended, Spartan," Vangel cursed through broken teeth, trying to regain his confidence. He laughed holding his broken ribs and crushed wrist, limping behind the Anusyia as they flanked him one to each side. Walker readied to meet them, reaching to unbuckle the runic edged compartment on his belt. He wasn't going down without the sword in his hands. Before the door that the Anusyia entered had fully shut, 4 small balls the size of large grapes rolled into the car. The Anusyia both looked down watching the grenados rolling between their legs. Vangel lost his grin, "What?" Is all Walker could make out before the explosion!

Walker was already moving, diving for cover as the car exploded. Fire engulfed everything in the blast, the force blowing out its hold. Walker was thrown from the car. He reached out to grasp onto something, anything. He almost missed it as the light from the outside filled his vision, blinding him as the sun flowed in the train. He saw a flash of metal before it was too bright and reached for it, managing to grab hold of the broken silver rail that ran the length of the car. He held on for his life, using the Magnus to stabilize himself.

The train shuddered and rocked, Walker only had one hand on the rail, and almost lost his grip, as the train raced around a turn in the tracks. They were almost completely out of the mountainous area now and were heading west toward the flat lands. He managed to grab the rail with his other hand and pull himself up, using the Magnus to float the rest of the way into the car. He landed with a thump.

Walker looked at the remains of the car. He could see the Anusyia guards were in pieces, their black armor scattered everywhere. Of Vangel there was no sign. Walker wondered if he had been blown to scrap. No, I am not that lucky, he thought. I've seen the green skins survive more than a few grenados. He looked over the edge of the destroyed car, then down its length. The cars behind him were mangled and melted. Only the frames remained, and they were in bad shape as well. Some still had flames on them flickering in the racing wind. Squinting, he saw the dragon was still above them, and he knew he needed to find cover. He was already wounded, and this ride wasn't over yet.

* * *

The Wartrak had been pushed to its limits, to catch up to the Key. After they had lost the dragon at Royal they had continued to follow the Key's signature. Lincoln's map had led them to the train, and as luck would have it, right to the dragon as well. Matias didn't want to lose either again, so they had stayed cloaked as they followed them. The cloaking mechanism took power from the cannon coils, but that was a risk Matias had to make. They would remain cloaked until it was the right time to strike, and then the time for hiding would be over.

The tank jumped a hill landing hard, rocking back and forth as its tracks dug in the ground, dirt flying high in the air. "Buckle up back there!" Matias yelled. "It's gonna be rough!" The dust flew past the tanks speeding tracks as they were pulling closer to the train, continuing to monitor the dragon that flew above them. "Get behind it and stay out of its sight, I am going to line up a shot." Matias said as he stood and left the cockpit. He made his way to the weapons bay and took command of the Dragon Cannon. Checking the power gauge, he knew he had full power for the shot. He activated the coils and the cannon came to life. Locking on the dragon he found his target, a softer part of skin under the wing on the beast's flank. In his youth he had a lot of practice taking these beasties down, and he knew the best spot to aim for maximum damage. He was about to pull the trigger when an explosion erupted from the side of the train, pieces covered the ground as the train shook. The Wartrak swerving to miss the flying debris. Matias looked in the scope trying to see what had happened! He could see nothing from the smoke and debris coming from the exploded car.

Bor was at the helm, swerving as a huge chunk of what was the inside wall of the train flew past them. Matias turned the cannon back on the beast, but he had missed his chance to take the shot. The Dragon ascended higher, dodging the debris. "Damn," he said, turning the scope back to the train. Through the smoke and debris he saw something; he was in shock as he squinted. A big man was hanging from the side of the exploded car. Hitting the com button he asked, "Lincoln, what do you feel? Is the power you felt earlier close?" "Yes, it is right here, I can feel it, and I feel stronger myself. It's empowering me. Uncle, my wristband is honing in on the train. I've never seen it do anything like this." He replied back.

"Touch the middle Rune," Matias told him. Lincoln did and the blue light locked on to the man that now pulled himself into the car, then to another source that was a few cars ahead of him. Once it locked to the item, runes and counters flashed in the air before Lincoln. "Uncle, its going crazy!" He said as 3d images floated above the device, circles and runic letters scrolling in midair beside the things it had locked onto. "Bor," Matias said over the com. "Describe it to me, what is the thing saying?" "Sir, you are not going to believe this, but I think we found another Spartan, the Key, and something else." Bor replied over the com. "Get me a place to stop Bor." "Sir?" Bor asked confused. "Just do it. A safe place. I will explain, just hurry!" Matias looked back through the scope of the cannon to the train. He was squinting trying to see through the smoke. As it cleared the man was gone. "I have a place commander, there is an outcropping not far," Bor said reading his monitor. "It is close to the turn in the tracks ahead." "Go there, and double time it." Matias said clicking off the com. The Wartrak turned toward it, as Matias watched the damaged train pull away from them. He powered the cannon down. The stakes of the game had just changed, and Matias smiled to himself as he went to explain to his sergeant what he had seen.

CHAPTER 29. FINISH THE MISSION:

The Silver train, the plains edge

Walker was holding his side, and breathing heavy. Looking at the next car he saw it had been damaged by the explosion and the door was leaning open. He walked over and tested its weight, then pulled. It slid open the rest of the way. He walked in the car and closed the door locking it behind him. He concentrated, using the Magnus to heal himself quicker. He almost puked, the power taking its toll on his body. The explosion from the grenados had dislodged something inside and it hurt, he might have a broken rib or two he thought. He let out a breath as the pain subsided and sat for a moment. He felt strange, like that feeling you get when someone is watching you. Something had entered the car. He slowly stood.

On instinct, he held his hand up stopping a blade in midair. A gesture sent it flying back toward the shadow it had come from. The black clad creature that had thrown it, flipped out of the way; the blade hitting the wall were it had been only a second earlier.

It pulled two swords from sheaths at its sides, they were just like the Elves weapons earlier. Walker tried to use the Magnus to control it, but it had little effect. It came at him, a thin curved Katana in each hand. It swung the first, then the second, again and again. The Magnus coursed back over Walker's body, his marks becoming black. He blocked the first strike with his forearm, then the second, third and fourth. They kept at it, sparks flying from the blades meeting his steel hardened flesh. The thing kicked him, and bounced off. Walker moved in getting close; he was in no mood for games. He felt strong for some reason; even though he had used so much of his power. Something from outside the train was helping him, strengthening him. He used the strength and in three moves he was in the Elf's guard.

With a palm to the chest, he knocked the thing into the wall. It hit with a crunch, rocking the car, the impact so great the Elf dropped his blades as the wind left his lungs. Walker grabbed his mask and pulled, ripping it off of the Elves head. He saw the mark of the Dru Nar underneath the half shorn head, and the black veiled garb it wore. This Elf was not like the ones he had already faced, this was an assassin or Kain, and he had seen it's like before. These Elves where magically protected, which explained why the Magnus had no effect, and it could take so much damage.

They would stay hidden until the appointed time, killing their prey before they ever knew they were there. The killing of the Zajust must have brought it to the fore; to fight a greater foe. Walker realized, this was going to be a double cross! The Elves had planned to kill the Zajust, and pin it on the Confederates!

"Se moy nia soo," the Elf spat as he lunged at Walker, who missed with a punch as he moved to intercept it. The Elf rolled under the swing and jumped kicking out, catching Walker in his hurt ribs. He grunted with pain.

The door leading to the other cars cracked with a ramming sound. The shouts Walker heard were in Elvish. The assassin had back up on the other side, and Walker was running out of time to find Tasha. The assassin launched himself at Walker with a flurry of punches and kicks. Walker blocked and countered the assassin, smashing him in the face; the Elf stumbled back grabbing at his nose. With a crack the door flew open, Elio Knights stepped through with guns aimed. Walker turned launching them back through the door with a gesture of his Magnus powered hand, then was kicked by the Elf assassin. He took the blow bending over. It hurt, but not as much as Walker let on. The Elf moved closer to finish him. Walker caught the mistimed punch, surprising the assassin. He squeezed the Elf's hand, crushing the joints and dropping him to his knee as he winced.

Walker looked over his shoulder as the Elio Knights were coming back through. With another gesture he slid the door closed before they entered, then pulled the assassin to him hitting him in the face again. The Elf's eyes watered as he swung with his free arm trying to release himself from Walker's grip. Walker dodged the forced move and let go of the Elf's fist, countering with a solid strike to the Elf's solar plexus, knocking him back. The Elio Knights were trying to get through the door. Walker looked over his shoulder at it, and opening his hand toward the door, he closed it into a fist. As he did the lock on the door turned in on itself crumpling the metal grinding together crushing it. The Elves on the other side pounded harder. Walker popped his neck and stepped towards the assassin to finish the fight.

* * *

Tasha danced the death dance as a dancer would perform ballet on the biggest stage. She was in the air flipping, landing, striking, all while dodging gunfire and the slashes of the Elio. She stepped to the side dodging a sword slash aimed at her shoulder, her axe haft crushed the Elf in the face, and then flew from her hand splitting another's armor open. Tasha was in her battle fury, and the Elves couldn't stop her. She was a wolven avatar of destruction, her anger turned towards them in a tide of blows and reposts none could match. She had retrieved her axe, landing in a low crouch after she had flipped away from the Elf she had engaged. She blocked a blow from the last one standing, and with a flick of her wrist disarmed him, turning she hit him with the flat of her axe poles haft. He flew to the other side of the car, hitting the wall and landing in a heap. No one was left.

She was standing in the middle of downed Elves, panting powerfully. She was trying to calm herself before she was completely lost to the beast inside her. Calm down, she told herself. You still have a job to do; you have a mission she thought, trying to concentrate on releasing her power. Her ears beat like drums, the blood pumping through them. It was hard to let the power go, the rage was intoxicating as the blood kept pumping. There was no one left to fight, she needed to let go of the beast. She used her training, her guidance that could keep her in check. It had made her the warrior she was. She was trusted, respected. She remembered Princess Tessa, she was the mission. Slowly her thoughts cleared.

Tasha's breathes were slowing, the blood slowing as well. She could hear it in her head as she looked around the car. It was dim with blue lights around the ceilings edges. The lights were calming, and she started to shrink. Her eyes turned from the almost purple back to her normal green blue. She was gradually losing size. Some of the bands of her Grays had popped, but the ones that were intact were getting less constricting and shrinking with her. As she returned to normal she wondered why there had been so many guards in this car. She was still woozy from the shock of being in Warp form so long.

She took a moment and gathered herself, then noticed the door at the end of the car. It was different than the others, thicker. She went to it, touching the pad on the door. It was locked. She looked around seeing a clerk on the floor. She hadn't noticed him in the fight. She lifted his hand to the door putting his palm on the panel. It unlocked with a beep, pulling back to reveal another door of the same make that opened as well. She dropped the Elf and went through the air lock connecting the cars. After she entered, both doors closed behind her. In the middle of the car there was a chest on a raised pedestal, a light from the ceiling shining on its amazingly crafted top. There were other caskets as well, all around the sides of the car. She was holding her axe, alert though still weakened from the transformation. The car was cold, and she felt it even though she was still sweating. She let out a breath, seeing its warmth frost in the cold of the car. She stepped to the chest in the middle. It wasn't the main chest that they had loaded; the one she had seen. No this was smaller and incredibly intricate. The lock mechanism was finely detailed, the shape of a dragon carved on its surface. As she got closer she noticed just how intricate. The dragon looked as though it might move. She studied it for a second while she continued to calm her nerves.

From a pouch on her belt she pulled a small black device. Holding it above the chest it beeped and she smiled. This was the one she wanted, her intel had been correct. She pulled another small black item from a compartment on her belt and set her axe down, leaning it against the chest's pedestal. She stuck her tongue out, as she started to pick the lock with the item she had pulled. The jewels around the lock lit up, their color changing from a green to red. She paused, still sweating. She touched it again and slowly turned it. The colors changed back to green. Then she turned it again, her other hand touching a rune on its center. The lock clicked, then another click. She was concentrating so hard on opening the lock, she almost didn't feel the change in the room. She stopped, her hackles rising as her blood froze. Someone had entered the car and was now behind her. She stared to panic, she was still weak and she wasn't holding her axe.

* * *

The assassin hit Walker in the ribs, causing him to grunt as he took the blow. Walker caught the Elf's wrist, pinning it with his elbow, then punched him almost knocking him unconscious. He could hear the Elio Knights on the other side of the door, he had to finish this before they broke through. The assassin tried to fight back, but Walker blocked the Elves weak jab slapping his arm out of the way.

The Elf couldn't get free; he had lost and he knew it, but he would take this trash with him, it was all he had left. He glared at the Spartan through his black bruised eyes. "I will live forever, but the Dragon comes for you," he coughed, as he clicked the detonator on his wristband to kill them both.

"Not today," Walker said pushing him back, front kicking him in the chest sending him flying through the back door of the car. The assassin looked surprised as the device detonated taking him with it. The force of the blast knocked Walker back but he stayed upright.

The Elio knights finally busted through the other door. Two Elves holding gun blades stepped over the threshold and opened fire. Walker spun dropping to one knee, thrusting his hands out toward them using the Magnus from across the car. The power ripped the guns from their hands. They flew to Walkers' hands. He caught both by the handles and started shooting. He continued firing at the others behind them, not stopping until there was no one left standing. Holding a smoking gun blade in each hand, he stood and looked around. "No one else?" he asked himself letting out a deep breath. He was exhausted, and blackened after almost being blown from the train. His many cuts from the Elves and battle with the Zajust were finally starting to register. He relaxed and dropped one of the guns, as he grabbed his side. He was hurt. Then he thought of Tasha.

"Tasha," he said aloud.

"No, but we need to find her," said someone behind him. Walker spun pointing the gun at the person who had spoken. "Dahl." Walker sighed, lowering the weapon. Dahl was standing there bleeding and cut in a dozen places as well. He was limping and looked in rough shape. "Yeah, I made it." He said holding his side, red staining his grey outfit. "I was hoping the grenados were helpful with that Zajust earlier." Dahl looked up at Walker, "You look horrible." Walker smiled, "I feel worse, and yes they did help, thanks. Let's move, if I know Tasha, she has already found that case, and probably trouble."

* * *

The Wartrak was running hard. It had had finally caught back up to the train, though had used over half its coils for the power to do so. Saul, the more accomplished pilot and racer, had taken the helm of the tank by Matias' command, and had used his skill to catch up to the train. He down shifted catching the momentum from a hill they had just peaked, and the engine roared, the tank gaining speed as it launched practically flying off the crest and over its base.

"Commander, we are coming up on the train now sir." Saul announced over the intercom. "Good, I see it. Could you watch the bumps soldier." Matias said back. "Aye Commander sorry, she can move sir." "No worries, just get me there son." Matias replied with a chuckle. Saul shut the coils down, slipping the tank into cloaked mode as it drew near.

"I have a visual Saul, take us closer." Matias told him while watching the dragon in the scope of the cannon. Saphron was flying above the train, slowly descending toward its silver hull. The dragon's claws splayed open as is he was going to land on it. "That is close enough, keep us steady, turn cloak off." Matias said as he maneuvered the cannon attempting to lock on to the beast. "Got you now," he whispered as the cannon locked on. The barrel of the powerful weapon lit up, burning the air around it. The blast tore through the sky hitting the flying dragon. The beast screeched in agony and pulled up wildly, the rider almost thrown off, but he was able to hold on.

Tusho turned in the saddle lifting the long pole lance he held, and pulling up shot Saphron skyward. Then turning the dragon as a rider would turn a horse, Tusho came back directly at the tank, yelling in Elvish. He lowered the lance and fired, its laser bolts streaking over the tank. Saphron maneuvered back and forth, as Matias tried to line another shot. They streaked over the Wartrak, Tusho unleashing a volley of laser blasts as he did. Saul outmaneuvered most except for a few scattered shots that glanced off the shield. Then Saphron started to slow. Tusho looked down at the drake.

Saphron was hurt, the beasts hide had been pierced, the shiny blue and green gold scales had been knocked loose and it was bleeding thick black blood. Tusho looked at his pet, "My baby no... They will pay for this," he muttered gritting his teeth. As he patted Saphron's hard scaled flesh. "We will have revenge my friend but not now, I am sorry. I must do something first." Tusho had turned Saphron and was steering him toward the train.

Saphron landed on one of the middle cars, ripping into its top with his claws. It roared then reopened its mighty wings and took to the air again. "What is it doing?" Saul asked over the com. Matias wasn't sure. "Just keep it steady soldier," was all he said back. Saphron swept back overhead, diving right for the tank opening his mouth!

The fire was unbearable as the beast hovered above it, showering the vehicle in hot liquid death. Saul jerked the controls, just able to dodge most of it, but it had come back too quickly and he couldn't maneuver out of the way completely. Its claws reached out grabbing at the tank, ripping into it to dislodge one of the armor plates. The claws digging into the metal.

Matias was trying to get off a shot from the canon, but at such close proximity he couldn't get a good lock. It was then he noticed the rider was gone, the dragon was acting alone. We have to get free, he thought. "Saul the static button!" Matias yelled over the com. Saul looked over the console and slammed his hand down on a button. The tank came alive with blue waves of electric power, shocking the dragon. With a roar of pain, it released the tank, leaping off of it into the air, its wings catching the current. Another explosion came from one of the train's cars some distance away as it was speeding on, smoke rising from the mangled car.

Saphron stretched his claws, getting the feeling back from the shock it had just taken. The beast looked at the train below and the Wartrak following it. Then opened it huge wings beating them to gain speed, and soared back to the train and its master.

The silver streaking machine had sped up. The electro coils on its engine working overtime for the speed. Small lightning flickered and cascaded between the coils, giving its turbine more power as it zoomed over the plains. Saphron dipped down closing on the front cars. Suddenly the Dragon shook, swinging its head back and forth as if it had been cut, roaring in pain. Its wings folded out and it glided back to the rear cars. The beast wasn't trying to dodge or run, it was truly hurt; shaking its head pawing at its eye. It punctured a car, with its claws, digging into the metal. It wanted in, it was roaring and frustrated, but then it finally relented.

What is it doing? Matias thought. The tank sped up, gaining on the train, as Matias was lining up his shot. He had to make this one count. If they kept this game up they might not be able to catch the train. The tank was running hot as it was, the coils overheating from the speed they had to maintain and the recharging of the Dragon Cannon. "Saul, keep it steady, I have it now." "Aye sir," the young man replied. The tank pulled closer, as Matias took aim.

"Gotcha," he said as he squeezed the trigger.

The blast erupted from the cannon, smashing into the Dragon hitting the creature below its left wing. Saphron couldn't get his left wing moving again to maintain flight. A huge chunk had been blown from it and without the wing; Saphron spiraled out of control. He smashed down hard onto the top of the train, landing on the smooth silver roof denting it, and sliding slightly. The impact of the huge beast tipped what was left of the rear cars as it clawed for a hold, the claws tearing a long gashes into the metal as it slid. One of the claws sunk deep and finally caught, stopping it from sliding off the side of the car. Then the train exploded!

CHAPTER 30. REUNITED:

The Silver train, the plains edge

Tasha didn't know who was behind her, only that someone was there. She smelled him, and knew she had to get her axe. She paused before she moved. Like lightning, she pivoted to grab the handle. Her vision exploded in light as she hit the wall with a thud. She stumbled trying to get to her feet, just barely dodging the next punch of the tall red armored thing behind her. The blow crushed the wall next to her. She dodged again, and he swiped with his dagger, cutting her cloak.

"You can't run from me forever little beast," he said the contempt in his voice more of a slap in the face than the words themselves. "I will kill your kind starting with you, pretty little slut!" he yelled. Her vision finally cleared and for the first time she saw her attacker. Tusho, the Red Dragon himself!

"You're Dillion's little pet thief aren't you? Yes, your thieving companion told us much, before he was taken by my Phenii. I will enjoy this." He sheathed his long dagger, then touched a button and his helm retracted. The long braids of his hair spilled out from underneath as he lifted it clear of his head. He let it fall to the floor, and he smiled an evil smile, licking his lips as he walked toward her. Tasha had finally found her bearings during his monologue, albeit just. With the speed of a cat she lunged rolling through his sweeping grab. Landing beside her axe she moved back, letting her momentum carry her as she grabbed the axes' handle. Tusho followed her methodically walking to get his prize. "What games we play..., where are you going?" Tusho asked, cockiness oozing from him. He knew he was the master here. This creature was nothing to him. He would have some fun, before he killed her. He smiled and lunged at her, at the exact moment she exploded up with all her might; thrusting from an awkward position. It was fast, too fast and caught him by surprise. The tip of the axe head caught his cheek running up to his eye; ruining his perfect flesh. He screamed smacking the blade away, the force knocking her back to the floor. Tusho flailed yelling and screaming, "My eye, I will flay you for that!"

She heard a muffled roar of what sounded like a dragon on the outside of the train, and then the car shook. Tasha looked up, as claws dented the metal bullnose styled roof.

Above the train Saphron felt Tusho's pain and tried to claw his way through the car, the claws almost penetrating the ceiling armor. Tusho fell to his knee, holding his eye, while Tasha listened to the scraping above them, then it stopped. Tusho looked up still holding his face and started to laugh. "Oh, oh, this is one <u>eye</u> won't forget." He paused, "Get it, one eye?" as he pointed to his ruined face. Tasha didn't laugh, she was crouched holding her axe, and still stunned from his previous blow, and now confused as well. The Elf was insane. "Not a fan then?" He asked her lowering his head, the blood flowing over his hand. "I will still enjoy this," he said to her without looking up, his hand closing around the hilt of his dagger as he started to rise.

An explosion took both by surprise and the door behind Tusho was blown open, throwing him across the car to land in the corner. Tasha moved as he flew past her. Luckily she was far enough away not to be caught in the blast, though she felt the heat. She looked up as the smoke cleared. Walker and Dahl entered, the smoke silhouetting them; making them look like heroes of old as they walked over the threshold into the car. The auxiliary door closed behind them. Walker looked at Tasha, then the chest, and then the Elf Lord that had slumped to the floor. He hurried over to her, lifting her sagging form. She smiled at him, staggering as she tried to get to her feet. "Are you ok?" He asked, gently lifting her up to stand. She nodded, rubbing hear head. Dahl was already at the lock of the chest, and was fiddling with it. He looked up. "Glad to see you too," he said to the pair as they came toward him. "What happened to him?" Walker asked as he looked to the armored Elf on the floor in the corner.

"That is Prince Tusho. He almost had me, but I was able to help him see the light." She said smiling then winced grabbing her waist. Dahl took out a scanner device from one of his pouches. He held the thing toward the chest. "Dahl, stop," she said. He looked at her puzzled. Tasha held up her hand. "Remember, Razium cases are trapped. See the runes? It has a code; I hadn't been able to get in yet, but almost had it a few minutes ago." Dahl backed away, as Walker helped her over to examine it.

"Let an expert do this," she joked as she limped past Dahl. Her grin was intoxicating as she looked at him through her black eye. She turned back to the chest and the black lock device she had left on it earlier. Touching a pattern she had rehearsed in her practices, it clicked and the latch opened. "I have it." She stated aloud. Tasha winced slightly as she stood up. Placing both of her hands on either side of its superbly crafted top, she slowly opened the box. As she cracked its edges, a light started to shine from the inside. The three of them peered into the chest as she opened it; the light illuminating their faces. Tasha pulled her hands away. It was beautiful. It was a Key to the Labrynthian, one of the almost mythical devices that could open the magic portal again. It was set in a red velvet inlay. The Key however didn't look much like a key for a door; it was gold with intricate and amazingly detailed patterns and designs. The shapes alone boggled the mind at the craftsmanship of such an artifact. The real beauty came from the perfectly cut Arcanius crystal, set into the middle of the Arcanium and gold laced item. Its inner light glowed with the power of the universe. It was mesmerizing, the way the main crystal floated, suspended in the middle of the artifact. The gates to the universe. As they peered in, Dahl's mouth was open. He looked at them. "Wow, its more beau..." He was lost for words as he grinned and shook his head. "I have never," he started again, and stopped abruptly, then started jerking and shaking.

"Dahl?" Tasha asked. He spit blood as a sword blade was shoved through him from his back, the blade pushing through his chest. Tusho stepped from behind him as he pulled his blade free letting Dahl fall to the floor.

"See the light," he said pointing at his mangled flesh by the blood dried to his eye, and referencing the joke Tasha had made at his expense earlier. "That's funny, and I thought you didn't have a sense of humor. Oh was I wrong," he said sarcastically.

"Also," holding up one finger and then pointing to the Key that was now in Walker's hand. "That is mine," he said in a slow ragged breath, as he glared at them with his one good eye. Walker grabbed Tasha sliding her behind him and opening his other hand, defensively. The train rocked as something big thumped the rear cars and the whole line shook. All three tried to stay upright and keep their footing with the impact of whatever it was.

The Elf prince flexed his body and bent to keep his balance. He paused, the rumbling of the train passed, then he opened his free hand palm up. "Well, give it to me." He said expectantly. "Come and take it, Elf." Walker said, daring Tusho to fight him. Tusho was tall, close to Walker in height, and was covered in lean corded muscle, but he was nowhere near as big as the Spartan he faced. "Alright then pig!" Tusho spat, and moved toward him. Walker looked disgusted, he pushed his open hand toward Tusho, hurling him back with the Magnus. The Elf was repelled, but stayed on his feet landing gently from the push. Unlatching the folded device fastened on his belt, he pressed the bottom of its hilt. It transformed, lowering a hilt guard over his hand. A long blade unfolded flipping out from its side, and clacking together; its razor sharp edge glistening with malice. It reminded Walker of the blades the Elves had used against him earlier, only much bigger. Tusho took it in a two handed grip, pointing it towards them. "Oh I see, you're a Spartan Paladin, a magnetic wielder. Hmmm, how quaint," he said with contempt. "I didn't know there were any of you left?" He added mockingly. "How cute. Hey you don't have a large sword by chance?"

Walker's eyes narrowed. "What?" he asked. "Nothing, you won't be around to use it even if you did." Tusho's now open hand started to glow, causing the air in the car to freeze, and a swirling white mist was pulling to his palm. "He is a Lok!" Walker said while tucking the Key in to one of his belt's compartments. He pulled both hands to his sides facing Tusho, daring him to try and take the prize. Walker had to survive this, he flexed pulling all the power he could, his eyes golden as the marks running along his face, arms, and body darkened from the Magnus power. Tasha was still weak and wasn't sure what to do, then a movement caught her eye. She looked down and saw Dahl lying in front of Tusho. He was holding his chest, the blood on his hand. They locked eyes and then he grinned. He held out his other hand and it was full of grenados.

He mouthed, "Go," and winked. Tasha nodded, her eyes widening, then looked at Tusho. "Another time then Elf." She turned grabbing Walker pulling him to the door with the last of her strength. "What are you?" Walker yelped confused, then saw Dahl and the rolling orbs by his smiling face. Walker's eyes widened in alarm and he turned, grabbing Tasha in his large arms, hefting her and running to the door of the car. "What?" Tusho asked puzzled as he was expecting to fight the giant, but instead heard the gurgling laugh of the man below him. He looked down seeing the small balls rolling across the train's floor. "Damn," was all Tusho could manage as the explosion rocked the car blowing it from the tracks.

* * *

Saphron hit the train with a thud, it was trying to fly but its wing too badly damaged, and was sliding about to go over the edge its claws not able to find purchase. The beast was scratching with all it had, as the ground sped past. Its claws finally found a hold stopping it from flopping off the top, but it was for nothing.

The train exploded, and Saphron was tossed in the air as the whole thing derailed coming off the tracks. The Wartrak was following close, and had to swerve as the dragon's body hit the ground rolling, a great hole rent in its flank. The tank was able to dodge the dragon but had to pull away from the train or get sucked into the destruction of the thing. The cars had turned and started to roll, flipping as each detonated, blowing the train to bits.

Walker and Tasha were thrown as the force of the blast launched them through the door of the car, his Magnus covered body protecting Tasha as they flew. The ride wasn't over though, the train's screech was deafening as it derailed. The cars were coming off the tracks one by one, the momentum too great to stop. The cars that had broken free had already started rolling, pulling the rest off the tracks. Explosions took the carriages, engulfing them in flames! Treasure and weapons spilled out flying all over the ground, while Walker and Tasha were launched out of the cars, a maelstrom of sound and fire engulfed them. Walker held her close, his huge arms around her. He used all the power he could muster to try and break their fall, but he was hit as one of the cars slammed into him knocking her out of his arms. "No!" He yelled reaching for her as Tasha was pulled out of sight, the dust filling his vision. He felt a thump in the back of his head, everything exploded into color, and he lost consciousness.

The Wartrak drove up to the wreckage of the train, the smoke and dust clearing. Saul had seen the man fly out of the train, and was looking for where he landed. The huge war machine pulling to a stop with the sound of gears winding down and release of steam vents. The hatch of the Wartrak opened to the hiss of hydraulics, the only noise to be heard, besides the rumblings of the settling train; explosions in the background.

Matias stepped out with the twins. "Establish a perimeter, I've got this one. Search for any other survivors." The twins saluted and jogged off following his orders. Matias walked slowly toward the large warrior lying face down in the dirt. "Well I'll be damned." He said smiling as he turned him over. Blood was spattered on him and he had many cuts and scrapes, but he was alive. Matias watched as the remaining traces of the Magnus receded into his flesh. His body and face still blackened by the explosion.

Walker looked around, the air had just gotten cool and everything was so bright. He was wearing his helmet, the back tail of his horse hair crest hitting his neck in the wind. He was in his armor, the silver and gold resplendent in the sun, he saw his brothers. They were in battle formation. The Spartan Paladins, his people were arrayed for war. The red and grey banners where flapping in the wind, the breeze hitting his face as he removed his helm. He stood over the warriors, realizing he had given a speech. He felt confident and saw his friends, but he ached all over as if he had been fighting for days. A dark skinned Spartan asked him a question. What, Kree? He thought, not hearing what the man had said. He ached, why did he ache? He looked at his gauntleted hand, the armor, the Arcanium runes shined. Kree, the man beside him was smiling and the warriors around him cheering, fists in the air. The sun was coming up, why did everything look so strange? There was no color everything was in sepia, and why now was it getting brighter, the sun was beaming brighter, why so bright? A dream, he was in a dream. The sudden sensation ripped him back to the present. The train!

Walker took in a gulp of air, coughing as his dream image faded. He cracked his eyes. The sun was shining down on him, and he realized he wasn't alone. Crunches of dirt alerted him to where another had stepped close. He tried to move, but only grunted as he did. The man stepped over him. "Are you alive?" The voice asking sounding amused. Wait, that voice, what? Walker thought. He recognized that voice. It could not be, there is no way that voice is here! Walker finally opened his eyes looking up, squinting at the man above him. The man reached out his hand and shielded Walker's eyes for him. "Matias?" He croaked, in a tired voice. "Aye, it has been a long time my friend," he said almost tearing up. He held his hand out; Walker clasped him at the wrist and was slowly helped to a sitting position. Matias bent down hugging him. "Matias it is you, but how...How did you find me?" he asked exhausted but smiling, overcome with joy.

"It's a miracle, I thought you were dead!" Matias told him, "It has been too long. What happened? How are you here?" Walker interrupted, "Oh my head," he said. He was still woozy and lifted his hand to the back of his head to steady himself. He felt a big lump and it was slightly wet with blood. "Whoa there big fella; I'm sorry." Matias said, "It's just you're here, and there is so much to talk about, but you need to rest first."

Walker grinned. "It's good to see you Matias, real good." Matias laughed a huge grin on his face. "I saw you fly out of that thing," he said motioning to what was left of the once amazing silver bullet train. "If it wasn't for the Magnus you would have been ripped apart, one of the cars hit you in the head." Matias said as he put a hand on the big warriors shoulder to further steady him. "Thank the creator we saw you, and it is good to see you. Where have you been, we thought you were dead all these years, we had heard rumors." Walker chuckled. "I have been through quite an ordeal." "I have a lot to tell you." Matias looked at him. "Yes, you do."

After a check of the immediate area, Saul and Ian headed back to the Commander to check in. Walker heard them coming and when they were close, saw they wore the emblems of the house of Sparta. They looked like they were young soldiers in training. They were twins, or at least close enough to look very similar. Matias smiled at the soldiers that had questioning faces. "Come to the Wartrak, let's get you cleaned up." Walker nodded. "Ok. Man, it is good to see you," he said again, shaking his head as

Matias helped him to his feet then addressed the twins. "Gentlemen, come and meet a true war hero." Matias was saying as they walked up. "This is..." Walker cut him off. "Walker, just call me Walker." Matias looked at him, puzzled but nodded. "Yes, this is Walker. We served together in some of the greatest actions the wars have ever seen." The twins grinned. "These are two of the brightest house soldiers we have, though our pickings have been slim of late," Matias said jokingly. They all chuckled. "They are both already Hoplites, and soon I hope full Paladins." Walker looked at Matias, "New recruits, that's good, from what I hear we really need them." He and Matias shared a look. Matias nodded.

"Walker, this is my first Corporal Saul," Matias said introducing him. Saul was young, He had a solid slender build and looked as if he was growing into his newly found muscles. His hair, a lighter dirty blonde was cut short. "Soldier" Walker nodded, "Hello sir," Saul said. Matias nodded, and continued. "This is Ian, his brother if you couldn't tell." Ian looked similar but had darker hair and was more slender with keen eyes that spoke of intelligence. "I would love to hear some of your stories sometime," he said to Walker. "I will have to tell you some, especially about this crazy Commander you have here." Walker replied back, pointing to Matais. He stopped talking as the banter reminded him of why he was here, though his head was still pounding.

"Matias, where's Lincoln, are you still with him? What happened, is he alright! Am I too late?" "How do you know all that?" Matias paused. "No not too late, it was close though, and yes he is ok. In seven years I have never left his side. You knew that though. We need to talk in private." Walker nodded.

Matias looked back to the twins. "Anything?" He asked. "No sir Saul reported, "We found nothing, alive. There are prints that lead off to the west but they disappear after only a few yards. All the others are dead sir, and not much left with the fire." "Alright, thank you." Matias said. "Were there any signs of a girl, or a Zajust?" Walker asked alarmed.

"What?" Matias interrupted, "A Zajust here?" "Yes," Walker replied then looked at Saul. "Wait soldier, did you say the tracks disappeared?" "Yes sir." Walker felt around his belt and pockets. "Damn," he complained. "What is it?" Matias asked. "I had a Jumper. She must have taken it." "She?" "Yes she, I will have to explain later. She took the jumper, but not the Key." Matias' eyebrow moved up quizzically. "You have the Key?" He asked, with excitement in his voice. "Yes," Walker replied, "That is what she wanted; when I was out she must have taken it, mistaken the jumper for it in her haste."

Walker shook his head; not believing Tasha would do that to him, then looking at his friend. "Wait how did you know about the Key?" "We do have lots to talk about," Matias said. "Let's go inside. I imagine the shock is still with you, especially with that knot on your head. Even a Spartan is still human. We will get you cleaned and fed and we can talk." They turned and the four walked to the tank, up the ramp, and went inside. The tank started up and drove away from the wreckage as the sun was starting to set. A few miles away they stopped to talk.

Walker had gotten cleaned and dressed. The compartments on his belt carried more than just a magic sword. He had his old cloak and coat, and Matias had a shirt that fit; though it was a bit tight. They sat, ate, and talked, swapping stories of where each had been, and the events that had lead them to each other. They were laughing just like old times. "She really said, show him the light. I mean a catch phrase in the middle of that. Ah, she must be something. Sounds like you found a spark plug," Matias chuckled.

"Matias I can't believe I have missed so much," Walker sighed his face serious. "Me either, it's been too crazy my friend. I am just glad you are alive." Walker paused, taking a deep breath. "Matias, I need to know something." Matias looked at him over his coffee. He knew what Walker was going to ask. "Ask," he said. "Tell me the truth about Blood Night." Matias frowned. Then nodded, and told him all that had happened.

When Matias finished they sat for a few minutes in silence. Matias looked at his wrist com. "Time flies doesn't it, I need to check in with Bor's camp. Would you like to talk to Lincoln?" "Not yet, I know he is safe, that's enough for now." Walker told him. Matias nodded, touching the screen. Bor's face illuminated it. "Matias!" Bor's voice was booming as usual, Walker grinned, and sat back in his seat processing what he had heard. So much time he thought. His mind drifted; to the King, the wars, and then to Lincoln. He hurt inside, thinking about it all. He had to make it right. He hadn't been listening to Matias, but noticed he had stopped talking. Walker looked up.

"Lincoln is fine, and I told Bor we would see them soon." Walker nodded. "So, going by Walker?" Matias asked. "Yes, for now." The big man shook his head. "I've let too many people down Matias. So for now, it's Walker." "Ok." Matias replied. "At least it's a good name," he said. "Hey what's that supposed to mean?" Walker joked back. They were both grinning and then sat together for a few more minutes.

The hatch opened and the two friends walked down the ramp. It had gotten dark, and the huge moon was out, the light casting all around in a pale glow, behind it the second moon was visible as well. They had stopped talking, admiring the amazing view. "Are you sure you don't want to go with us?" Matias asked breaking the silence. "No, not yet. Lincoln is safe and you are right, finding Orson is still the best course of action." He said as he put the tracker that Matias had given him in one of his belt compartments. "I will head to Navarre and look for him. Who knows, maybe I'll get lucky." Matias nodded. "Alright, then I will meet you at the Hole and get the others, then we will go to the White City together. It will be good to reunite after all this." Matias' voice trailed off. He looked at Walker reaffirming what they had decided to do. "Yes, that will be good. I will see you in a few days time, you just keep Lincoln safe."

"I will, find the old man and we will see you soon. Use the tracker if you need. Remember the wards around the bunker will dampen it." Matias reminded him. "Either with it or on it." Walker said extending his hand. Matias grasped him by the wrist. "With it or on it." Matias returned. Walker turned from his friend and Matias watched him go.

CHAPTER 31. COWBOYS TRACKING:

Royal

Smoke was rising above the huge fortress city of Royal as the sleek craft approached. It was about a mile off when they slowed. "Put us down here Tex." Cobb said, turning from the cockpit and walking back to the hold of the ship. Randal stood by the large bulked Mustangs. "We are riding in," Cobb told him. "Readings telling us there was a fight, air traffic has been stopped, and seems the city has had riots. I would rather not have to shoot my way in to that mess. So we are riding in, get ready." Randal nodded.

They were about four hundred yards outside Royal when they stopped. It was cool as the mountain air blew around them; it was the only sound they heard as they looked at the mess they had stumbled into. After a few seconds of watching the goings on around the huge city walls, the lead rider Randal, spoke. "I would have liked to have seen this." Cobb reined in beside him. "Yes, but they didn't do this." "Well at least not all of it," Cobb said through his large mustache. "Looks like they helped finish it though," said Randal.

"Yes it does, look at those blast shots in the walls." Cobb was pointing toward the edge of the city seeing the clear patterns of fighting and bullet fire on the flame blackened walls. Rubble was strewn around the outside of them, and there was a crew filling in a huge rut where it looked as if something had ripped the ground up. There were horses and steam tractors pulling the bigger pieces of wall sections to a wagon to be dumped. Several small cranes were helping lift the largest loads, as workers were clearing the debris from the area. Cobb looked back to the last rider. "Tex, get me somthin' to go on here." Tex nodded. "We need to get a lead, that boy is close I know it."

"Randal." Randal looked at Cobb, "Let's go say hi." They rode toward the huge walls of the city and as they closed Tex broke from them riding toward the workers by the cranes. Cobb and Randal rode to where a group of workers seemed to be on break. They were standing and listening attentively to a man in the middle of them. The Cowboys rode up listening to what the man was saying. He was a braggart for sure, and half of what he said probably wasn't true. Talking about an escape from a castle and how he had seen tanks and robots. They had destroyed his vehicles but ran from him, then he found a ride here from some merchants. It sounded like crap to Cobb, but then he heard something that caught his ears. Cobb rode over and looked down at the man. "What was that last part, I didn't catch it?" He asked.

The others listening to the story quieted, staring and moving away from the new addition to the group. Dust flew from behind the mounted man, flapping the long duster he wore. Mounted, he cast a large shadow over all of them. The man talking was full of himself, but noticed all the people around him had gotten real quiet; he turned to tell off this rider for interrupting his story, that was until he saw him. His eyes widened and he squeaked.

"A war tank sir".

Cobb stared right through him. "Go on," he said. The man looked at the sash at the rider's waist, and the guns on his thighs and realized he could make this into something, or end up dead. "Well, a Trak, a Wartrak to be precise, from the old wars. It did all this and headed west, after the dragon." He said waving his hand at the damage around them. "It was a tank I had been following, blew up my trucks."

"That's what I thought you said." Cobb replied. He looked at the man; he immediately noticed the pants he wore were from the uniform of a Razium soldier. "What's your name?" The man realized he might be on to something, and might not die today. He smiled to himself, looked up to Cobb squinting and said, "Ike sir, the name's Ike."

* * *

The Wartrak had driven off, and it had gotten darker as the night set in. All was quiet save the fires that still burned and crackled, as the last of the once innovative and revolutionary silver train was returning to the nothingness from which it had been born. With a screech of metal, a piece of the train was pushed back, breaking the silence. A figure crawled from the wreckage. He could barely see through his good eye, the other still a mangled ruin as was his red burnt broken body. He came from under a piece of metal debris that had been thrown from the engine as it was pulled off its tracks by the combined weight of his now dead drake Saphron, who laid a few hundred feet away on the dirt beside the train tracks, and the explosion of the damned Humans weapons.

Flames were still burning from the wreckage as the figure crawled, the fire crackling in his ears. Saphron he thought, my friend, my pet. Have to get to you. The once proud beast's flesh had already begun to crystallize and crack. It was the way the dragons died, and returned home. The dragon's body would turn to a crystal dust, catch a current from the east riding the wind, and float to its proper home on the mount of dragons, just as it had always done.

The explosions that had ripped through his locomotive throwing it from the tracks, throwing him from the tracks, continued in the distance. That stupid girl, he thought. He winced, he ached, and hurt. He burned, and could barely see. "Agghh," he grunted or screamed, he couldn't tell, he hurt so badly. The figure crawled, and crawled. He had been crawling forever it seemed. "That stupid girl and the warriors with her. I know them. I do know them. I will know them again." He kept telling himself, his hate fueling him giving him purpose. "I will know them again!!!" The red claws, his claws kept pulling his mangled form. He had lost his eye in the fight with the Warp creature. "I will make her lose an eye, a beautiful eye, yes she will lose two," his deranged mind was telling himself. His already mangled brain was becoming crazed with his thoughts of torture, the pain and hate giving him the will to pull, to kill, to go on.

"No, my baby," he said, as he finally made his way to the drake's carcass. He crawled into it, snapping out of his mad rant. He had to hurry. Not long now, he thought. "There you are," he croaked, through shattered cracked lips. He crawled through the carcass, every inch breaking off pieces of the beast that turned to dust and magically floated around him. The reddish gold dust started to float away in the wind. He crawled through the leftovers of his pet, its crystallized form breaking now more easily, the sparkling dragon dust floating all around. He had made it to the middle, to the heart of the beast. The dragon's heart; it pulsed with the power it gave off. It could save him from death.

The volcanic red glow was warming to his cold dying body. It was one of the most powerful items one could hold, and few had ever held a dragon's heart, or knew of its revitalizing power. He broke off a piece of the inside of the heart. Slowly with all he had left, he put it in his mouth and chewed. It broke bitterly in his mouth as he chewed, puffs of dust leaving his lips. He swallowed and his vision spun. He stuffed the rest in his mouth and forced himself to chew. He swallowed hard and choked. He could do no more and his head fell to the ground. Darkness took him as he swallowed the hot dirt.

He didn't know how long he had been out, or if he was even awake or dead, but as he opened his eye a cool breeze hit him. His head was in darkness. It had come to take him. He felt this was the end, but stopped himself. This was no dream, and he was alive. He managed to open his eye and look around. The sun was at his back and almost down. He was headed east, flying. There was nothing below him. Then he heard the wings flap above him; a monstrous set of wings. He was being held in a huge dragon's clutches. The wind was zooming over his face. The blood was gone; he reached up to his ruined socket. He felt it. He had no eye, but his split features had healed. The heart had healed him. He Tusho, the Red Dragon had found his current and he was going home. He laughed, and it grew louder and louder till he was maniacally cackling. He would get his revenge he thought, just as he had always done.

EPILOGUE

Hard rain played across the dark streets of the large port city of Navarre. The sound of it echoed off the citie's rooftops. The tall buildings crooked awnings, giving off a mini defining sound to all who cared to listen, or were out in the torrent. Mud was the order of the day for anyone venturing out; the stench of everyday life hadn't quite been washed away even though rain like this cleaned the massive river port city once or twice every year. It was needed but not wanted, at least not in this capacity; as the water was coming down in buckets, harder in the last few hours. It filled the streets and ran into the narrow alleys toward the pier, rolling over the cobblestones and emptying in the river that had risen, running as fast as it could beside the huge city. A bell chimed in the distance. The city clock had struck and another hour had gone by. The sound of the bells barely audible over the smacking of pouring rain as it strengthened.

Off to the side of the streets in a pitch black alley way, a rat sniffed the air. It was hold up under an empty barrel of beer watching the water go by, unsure if it should run into the liquid or if it was too deep. It was sniffing the air for food, and was trying not to get dumped on by the storm. Its nose caught something, and twitched as it realized it wasn't alone. Something was behind it. A bolt of lightning lit up the night sky, the light showing the silhouette of the huge man standing behind the barrel in the alley. The rat squeaked and fled the alleyway, jumping across a puddle to a piece of trash, then to the wet ground. It landed awkwardly almost getting itself crushed by a few passersby. They were huddled under an umbrella and were trying to flee the deluge of rain themselves.

The woman holding the umbrella squealed as she saw the rodent. The soldiers walking with her jumped at the scream, looking for what had scared her. She pointed and yelled, "Ew, rat!" They all burst out laughing, and one of the men kicked at it. "Filthy vermin!" he yelled. His boot splashing more water than actually hitting the rodent, but he protected his dignity. "You showed him," said another, as they all continued laughing. The rat was gone and they tried to squeeze back under the umbrella the lady was holding, hurriedly walking toward a large tavern. The man in the ally watched them pass. He was still in the shadows watching the tavern from under his drenched hood. The Fat Pig is what the Tavern was called. He was studying it, waiting for his move, then he saw something. It was on its roof, and it was big.

The Fat Pig was a local Tavern bar, and one of the more expensive and notorious hang outs of thugs, pirates, and anyone looking for mischief in Navarre. It was also one of the best places to eat. Always full of young rich idiots trying to show off; guards who wanted a good drink, and a place where people generally of higher status that were up to no good, went to play. The main reason the Pig did so well was that they served the best Glorn, or Dwarven Ale in the city. After a few tankards of that golden liquid, anything sounded great, nothing seemed impossible and any treasure could be found. Glorin Goldfinger, the owner and benefactor of the Pig, made sure he stayed stocked. He was of the DwaVergear, Dwarger, Glorn or Dwarf race as most called them, and Glorin was well known throughout the Confederates. Long ago he was a runic advisor to the King's artificers of the north, and had retired setting up the establishment after service to him during the wars.

He got the land cheap after the wars, and had built the establishment and a lot of this part of the city from the ground up. He was tall for a Gwarger, with a great beard that went to his belt, and a kind attitude, even though he tried to play tough. He was sitting in his chair in his office doing what his kind liked most, drinking and counting coin. Glorin looked out his second story window, having been interrupted by a scream from outside his tavern. He saw a rat flop in the rain and soldiers laugh and help a lady turn toward the Pig. He resumed counting his money, thinking, more customers to please, and laughing to himself as he took a sip from his pint. The rain continued pouring down outside his large window. He heard a bump on the roof and looked up.

The soldiers finally made it to the door, where laughter dancing and music could be heard coming from within. A huge pair of doormen waited to make sure they were acceptable to enter. The soldiers were in their green dress uniforms buttoned up in the front and had their hats off, and the lady was in a very exquisite gown. It looked more appropriate attire for a ball or royal function than this tavern. The doormen checked them and let them in.

A few hours ago the tavern was empty, and its very best customer, an old man no one but the owner cared about, had been sitting in his normal booth in the corner. He was enjoying his nightcap and smoking his pipe as he did. Normally, he left when the rest of the city showed up, but tonight he had had too much to drink and was now singing and enjoying the revelry with the rest.

The atmosphere of the tavern was electric and loud. The old man was sitting at his small booth in the corner enjoying the last of his dinner. I guess it isn't so bad, he thought to himself as he looked around. I should stay out more often. Heck, I could put on a show for these people, ha ha, like I used too. He took another drought of his large tankard. Then thought about what he was saying, the alcohol not helping him think clearly. Bah, that's all changed, he thought, and burped. Oh well, that's good for me anyway. These people wouldn't know a good show if it hit them in the face. He chuckled to himself at his joke, looking at the last morsels of his meal. He picked up a small piece of aged Swiss with his left hand and his tankard in his right smiling to himself. Ale, he was thinking as he looked at his three quarter full stein, head still around the edges and frost still on the rim.

These thoughts and a dozen others were floating through Orson's ale soaked brain. He was drunk; seems the ale did make everything better. He took another drought off his stein and slammed it down. Orson, or Ol' Hedge as most in the area knew him, was sitting at his favorite table in his favorite bar and talking to himself. He was a man of average height and slender build though had put on a few pounds these last few years, probably from the tavern food. He had a round head and a good jaw line, with a white short trimmed goatee and a bushy mustache under a distinguished nose; which he scratched, and pushed his small reading glasses up. His hair was a short cut to the ears and trimmed around the sides, but he was balding on the top. He wore robes of brown and cream and had on a deep blue tunic. His order was that of Lok or wizard, well hedge wizard is what he had told this town. He always moved from city to city, keeping his head down, making good friends, and gathering information but never staying long. He was known for his elixirs and tricks at kids parties. Most only thought of him as an old healer or street conjurer, not one of the regal or distinguished Loks or members of the Council. Those great men led the White City and kept the Razium at bay. No, he was just an old vagabond here for enjoyment and

338

fun, but then again, he had never been asked where he had come from, only what he could do for others.

It was a busy night and people, cooks, soldiers, and the like were making a great if not noisy atmosphere, and Orson was taking it all in smiling to himself; watching the people pass from his table. He took the rest of his bread socked up the last of the gravy of his meal, stuffed it in his mouth with a few chews and washed it down with another swig of his ale. Crumbs covered his tunic, and even his dark brown cloak which was hung on the back of his chair wasn't spared. As he chewed the last of his meal, with mostly amber liquid filling his mouth, he thought that the room seemed to be getting louder. The change in the noise pulled his attention from the delight he was having. Some soldiers and a young lady had just entered through the door and Orson looked over at them. The room had indeed gotten louder, and he knew it.

He looked at the girl with the soldiers. She is pretty he thought. Red lips not quite full but nice, and long brown hair. She wore a deep blue dress that marked her as some sort of wealth, and that pulled her already adequate bosoms up more. Of course she was with the soldiers. He looked down at his stein. Oh well, he thought, the ramblings of an old man. Orson you are drunk, what have you become, he chuckled to himself. Then looked down to his over exaggerated time piece. Hmm, he mumbled, trying to remember what he was thinking when he looked to his watch, the large cogs turning. Then he smiled and took another gulp. He stopped mid swallow and started to feel a tingle.

He knew this feeling, he had felt it before. He looked at the door where the soldiers had just entered, it wasn't them. I think I've drank too much, he thought. No, not that, something else from somewhere, but he couldn't quite place where. Then he looked up realizing what he had felt, and almost lost his mouthful. He panicked! Then calmed himself using his training to help. He stood and tried to leave but he had gotten up too quick and his head started to spin. He looked around the room, as all the people spun. The tang of magic had entered his mouth and he ran into something, grabbing the nearest item to steady himself. His head stopped spinning and he looked into a pair of beautiful eyes. He was holding the girls right shoulder in one hand and a mug of ale in the other. He guiltily smiled.

"Sorry," he managed and pulled his hand down. The woman blushed, and was about to say something back when a shadow passed over them.

The room had quieted and the rain had stopped. Orson looked up in time to hear, "Ah, you're that Wizard aren't you?" Orson tipped slightly as he looked at the man from behind about a barrel of ale rolling around his eyes. "Yesh, that would be me." He slurred drunkenly to know one in particular. "The one and only greatesht," he reached for the chair he thought was there to hold him up and with a crash and roar of laughter from the patrons; he lost his balance and fell to the floor. He had dropped his stein and watched as the last of his wonderful amber contents washed all over the old wood floorboards, some of the liquid spilling on the boots of the cocky guard. The man looked down on Orson with disgust. "Ha ha ha," he roared sarcastically. "You're about as good a wizard as I remember. Ha ha ha."

Orson knew something was wrong. Magic was here and getting stronger. He needed to leave this place now; he was feeling sick and it wasn't the ale. Orson was trying to regain some of his dignity and get to his feet at the same time. He found the back of his chair, and the wood felt good in his hand, solid. As he lifted himself up, he looked at the laughing soldier as his other hand started to glow.

Suddenly the guard's laughter slowed, the soldiers all seeing Orson's hand glow stopped laughing. Their eyes got wide in amazement as the Wizard started talking as he stood, but slightly sliding on the wet floor. "I shummon..." Without another word Orson's foot hit the ale and he slipped. With a curse, he was on his backside and from nowhere a blue flower appeared in his glowing hand. When it did, it made a little popping noise and fairy glitter sprinkled all over the ground. The tavern erupted in laughter again, and as the laughter died down the arrogant soldier stepped over the ale and bent down still looking at Orson in disgust. Kicking Orson's cloak into the ale he said, "Nice trick fool, I'll be back so you can clean my boots. Now give me that." He ripped the flower from Orson's hand. "I know a Lady who deserves it." He finished, stood and straightened his uniform, then turned and walked away a fake smile on his face.

Orson looked around. The background music had started again and people were ignoring him, going back to their tables murmuring and chuckling. Orson was sitting in his ale, he hadn't felt this type of magic in years. Not since the wars. Luckily the wards he had just set as he had made the flower, had given him some defense, and hopefully some time. Though the people thought it was a trick, he might have just saved them all. Better to get made fun of than to start a real spell in the middle of all of them, it would be hysteria. His head shot to his right to see the soldiers and the patrons, nothing yet but he had to get out of this bar now! He hoped his show had bought him some time. He started to rise but couldn't, he was too late! The Scion was here!

A Scion was a Lok assassin used by the Razium. The things were a type of alien that could track magic users with their own Lok signature. They were perfect hunters, able to blend in with the surroundings, and appear as if from nowhere. Also extremely durable, the only way to really kill one was to burn it, or they would come back to hunt their prey; arcanium magic weapons did the trick as well. At least that was the rumor. Orson looked up. It was here, the beast had made it into the main room. Where? He tried to look, but it was locking him down, paralyzing him with its magic. Only the strongest willed people could break the terror hold, as it had been named. The individuals that can break it, get a massive headache and feel nauseous. Orson was feeling nauseous now. The patrons were starting to feel it as well and the Fat Pig had slowly quieted. The people in the pub knew something was wrong and were looking around. One of the door men walked into the main room, a strange look on his face.

The Scion appeared dropping from the ceiling, smashing the big doorman to the wall. Its strange skin hard to see as it moved faster than most in the bar could follow, leaping from the doorman, to the wall, then right toward Orson. The tall soldier that had kicked Orson's cloak was in its way. The soldier had seen it appear and grabbed for his weapon, his eyes giving away the terror he felt. Orson tried to yell at the man not to engage that monster, but he couldn't. It seemed as if all time was in slow motion. The people, doorman and soldiers frozen for that moment. Then the Scion moved. Instantly time sped, so fast.

With its right hand the Scion spun grabbing and squeezing the soldier's hand, breaking all the bones in it. The soldier yelled and crumpled to the floor in pain. The Scion hit the second soldier in line with a back fist strike; breaking his nose, the force sending him flying. The people started running in panic and the beast had already taken down another of the soldiers. The Scion couldn't be stopped. He had dropped three and about to smash his fourth in as many seconds, when the other door man pulled his dagger and thrust it into the beast's back. The Scion turned knocking him to the floor, stepping over his prone form looking for Orson. Orson had tried to leave, but the terror hold was strong, and in his drunken state he couldn't shake it. Most of the patrons had run from the tavern, leaving Orson to face the thing alone.

The creature slowly walked toward him, locked in the mental game of magic with the Lok Master. Orson's mind was on fire, beads of sweat poured down his face, he couldn't defend himself, and it had almost beaten his wards. He was still more powerful than the beast though, and was resisting, but it was taking a toll.

The creature glared at him with contempt and a dark blade appeared in its coal black hand, as it raised it over him. Orson slowly lifted his hand trying desperately to stop the blade. He almost had a spell if he could only hold on.

The blade never fell, the thing couldn't move. It looked frozen as if an invisible force held its arm in place. A huge flash of Arcanium steel from the right caught the creature in the neck, its arm dropped. A huge pair of hands grabbed its head and its body as it started to slowly topple over. The large warrior holding the pieces jumped over the soldiers on the floor, landing in front of the hearth; tossing both body and head in the fire. They melted to ichor, then puffed into black smoke and were gone.

Orson was still on the floor. He reached up to his temple, the thumping in his head had started to subside with the death of the creature, but its mental assault had almost been too much for him. With a wretch he puked all over the floor. The man standing by the hearth looked over his shoulder at him. "You know you have to burn the parts, or they will come back for you," Walker said with a sarcastic grin. Orson just looked sick, as he stared at Walker, the fire silhouetting the huge man in front of him. Walker was holding an unfathomably large broad sword in his hand, along its center Arcanium etched runes of power were fading. "You're late!" Orson said smiling and wiped his mouth on his large sleeve.

Glossary

Dramatis Persona
Alphabetical order-

Spartan Paladins-
Agesilaus- the King of the confederates
Bor- Granken Bor Blu Ordin, or Bor- Veteran of the Spartan Paladins, mechanic
Dominus Tor - Commander of the Spartan Paladins, the Bull of Sparta
Greal- Spartan Paladin, Gunman, pistoleer
Ian- Hoplite, twin of Saul
Le Kai- Le Haw Kai- (Lee hawk Eye) - Spartan Paladin, marksman, scout
Macguyar- Mac, Spartan Paladin, Centurion, swordsman
Matias Layne-ex-Commander of the Spartan Paladins, farmer, protector
Orion- Monk, Spartan Paladin, Old Guard, Warp
Saul- Hoplite, twin of Ian
Steerpike- Spartan Paladin, Centurion
Walker- Spartan Paladin, mercenary, brawler, traveler

Razium-

Anusiya- Elite Cyborg personal guard of Zajust

Agmon Goth – Lord of the Razium

Derus- Captain of the Lord's Wrath under Norn.

Phalayon- Razium tech and biological overseer, Artificer

Stren Norn- Senior Captain of the Lord's Wraith, Shipmaster

Xylor- Admiral of Air Navy

Zajust-

Orc or Yrch- Green Skinned

Anx- Second in command to Pale, assassin, Dokx

Moore- Zajust Warlord, the Blade Master, the Savage, Dokx

Nemsor Vaul- Zajust Overlord, General of the Razium

Pale - Zajust assassin, Astral Master, the shadow Lord, Wyrd

Sinagog Vaul- Zajust Warrior, part machine, huge, the Monster, the Beast

Vangel - Zajust, the Berserker, can grow stronger when in battle

Loks-

Lincoln- Lost Prince of the Confederates

Nabonidus or Nabis- Council member of the Outer Circle

Orson- Master Lok, Wizard

Zen- Master, Lok Master and high seat of the Council

Kissar-

Colonel- Southern commander for the Kissar guard of Royal

Dahl- Mercenary of the Kissar

Dillion- Boss and leader of Kissar in Royal

Earlinom- Ulthwan guard for Dillion

Tasha- Commander of the Mercenaries of Kissar, Warp

Cowboys-

Cowboys- Bounty and monster hunters, Lok assassins

Cobb- Cowboy Leader, one of the fastest Blazer gunman ever.

Ike- Hired hand for the cowboys, ex member of the Black Legionaries of the Razium

Mira- Blazer Cowboy, commander (Half Elf)

Randal- Cowboy, fast draw gunman

Tex- Cowboy, big brute, mechanic, Warp

Elves-

Tusho- Elerossë Tusho Amn Drannar, Elven outcast Prince, leader of the Sea Dru Nar of Royal

Isabella- Elven Seer

Moncul Orophan Silimaurë Dru Nar- Monoro- King of the Elves

Phenii- Elven construct, made from Elf grown substance, bone or marble

Saphron- Dragon, Tushos mount

Than- Elven General, second to Tusho

Others-

Agrius- Wargear, construct, machine, Guardian of the Castle of Anstone

Bally and Martin- A café owner that has a secret and his son

Decker- One of the Leaders of the Rogues of Erach in Kansa, clan guilds

De Mallo- Captain of the ship Gryphon- Kansa

Edmond Haight- Governor of Angel City

Glorin Goldfinger- Dwarger owner of the Fat pig

Morain- Governor of Kansa

Paper- Paper boy (Teen) of Royal

Rogues of Erach- Clan of Gunmen, Le Kai used to belong to

Rulik (Snorri) Goldfinger- Dwarger Tavern Owner Royal

Talos- Wargear, Guardian of the Castle Anstone

Tessa- Princess of O'cea

Other Information

Anusyia- Zajust guard- personal retinue, deadly fighters, usually armed with power blades, chain blades and heavy fitted armor. Cyborg or robotic.

Aryonic Disks- Disks usually silver in color that enhances the bearers ability's for metal manipulation. Found on Spartan Paladin armor.

Astrals- Shadow assassins magic, Shadow Punches, spirit, dimensional

Aun Ka- Necromancers on Ultima Prime- Allies of the Razium

Black Legion- Legionnaires- name of the normal Razium troopers- These are comprised of peoples of other races as well

Blazer- Runic projectile weapons that can be enhanced by magic, also slang for wizard gunmen. Usually a pistol.

Destroyer- Nemsor's blade.

Elio Knight- Elven elite, uses specialized weaponry including Gunblades, laser swords and power lances

Estomagnetics- magic and study technology of metals and magnetics

Dwarger- Dwarf, DwaVergear, Glorn

Governor- Leaders of the confederates

Grimox- Cross between an Ox and Elephant. Has tusks or horns that curve.

Havoc- A huge broad sword, most powerful weapon ever crafted. Made of pure Arcanium. Lost

Jotunn- Ice Giants from the northern regions. Jormunger the Tyrant, was their Lord.

Kissar- Northern people, gangsters that own half the city of Royal.

Kiln- Heat magic

Labrynthian- A series of gates or doors that act as a portal, to transport the wielder to a desired location. Also part of a powerful realm where the magic of the Tempest originates.

Lin Nae- nation of the east

Lok- Wizard or manipulator of the Labryinthian.

Lord's Wrath- Razium battle ship (Desolater pattern), Lord Nemsor's command ship. Space worthy vessel.

Phenii- Undead constructs, guardians of the Elves

Magnus- Magnetic waves of energy between all things, most powerful in the elements of metal and flesh with magnetic properties

Mariners- O'cea guard, soldiers

Mechanican Titan Wargear – A huge version of a Wargear

Myrmidons- O'cea Elite guard. Amazing soldiers

Old Guard- A term for a Spartan Paladin that was the King's selected guard. The best of the best of the best

Old Line- People who had the Magnus gene in them

Pallance- A confederate, area outside republic or confederate boundaries.

Phalanx- The perfect fighting formation, mostly used by the Spartan Paladins. If correctly executed, it cannot be penetrated.

Praetor- A leader and councilor- usually a Master Lok.

Rangor- Cat with scales, can hold water under its scales. The purest water drinkable.

Razium Ranks- Anusiya elite guard, Zajust, (sometime Anusiya will lead squads of grenadiers.) Grenadiers elite soldiers, Legionaries Black Legion, common. Troops, that can compromise many races, hired soldiers

Rike- Title

Sao Lin- A Monk.

Scion- Magic tracking assassin, Astral strange skin armored and helmed.

Spartan Paladins- Greatest known fighting force in history. Have been scattered and reduced. Few left but still powerful, by themselves. Lead the forces of the Confederates.

Tor- Honor Name, Title

Ulthuan- Ogre Craftsman. The greatest builders, Honorable people.

Vaul- Title for superior warriors. Razium, Zajust

Wargears- Gears- Robot constructs with enhanced original design to fight the dragons in the Wars. Most destroyed, but some wealthy merchants and lords have them for guards

Warp- A person who has the ability to change, shape usually into a large wolf or cat type creature. The person is far stronger and faster, retaining some level of strength in human form

Young scholar- A Lok in training. A student or apprentice.

Zajust- the leaders of the Razium. Orcs or Yrch, A different warlike race. All have the Vaul title mostly green skinned.

Places

Angel City- Capitol of the Southwestern Confederation- Seat of power in the Southwest

Anstone- Castle Fortress city where Lincoln lives. Hidden South

Confederates- City States on the continent of Ultima Thule

Dragora- Court of Dragons- Home of Dragons. Midcontinent, in the wastes

Dragonion Spires- Dragon houses of the North

Fat Pig – Popular Bar in Navarre

Flame Geysers- Eastern area protecting Elven lands

Fort Braxton- Fort for soldier in the lower territories.

Gimralta- Meeting Summit for all nations

House of Swords Sparta- training grounds for the Paladins

Kansa- Confederate in the mid-east

Kansa City- Kansas Capitol- Acropolis of Nabis Councilor

Lang- city in the Pallance territories- a farmer city that made its money from growing crops and mining water and selling- sold to Royal

Lafourche- Southern city, known for its black magic, swamps, culture, and parties

Maelstrom- Western lands and sea protecting Elvish Kingdom

Massal- industrial area of York

Mesa- Territory leading south

Navarre- Large port city

Nee brak' ah- destroyed hold of the Dwarger, Dwarves

O' Cea- Lowest main Southwestern city in the confederations- The pearl of the South West- A port city that has a lot of culture and a strong but small military force. Has been reluctant to open borders to people for help. Only economic trades

Partha Terra- The Planet

Royal– City of Crime on outskirts Dragon Lands

Skaga Foss- Place of the Ice Giants- Jotunn

Sparta- Palace of the King

The Isle- Islands across the eastern sea. Magic heavy, currently involved in wars

The Hole- secret bunker built in a mountain. For the Confederate commanders to use a staging area for battle

The Round- Huge City with walls in circles aqueducts

The Tower of Thrones- Personal fortress of Nemsor Vaul

The White City- A city that hovers on the rock of Valum. (Magnetic Rocks- where Magic is taught, Learning place of Loks)

White Tower- School of Mages

Ultima Thule- Continent the Confederates are located. Western Continent

White Cloud- Where White city is located

York- was the capitol of the North Eastern most Confederate

Things

Affinity wars- War Confederates and Razium were allies

Boer War- Current War over seas

Dark Hand- smaller Razium space going vessel

Dragon Wars- Confederates

Glow gems- stones that glowed when a specific person is near. Some think they were Dragon eggs

Hover Blades- Two to three man crafts, hover ships of the Razium. Used on the ground, and midflight

Ice Lock compressors- Coolant systems for the Gear weapons and engines. Super-fast. Taken from the Jotunn science

Spear Fighter- small crew ship, space traveling vessel used for missions on earth as would a bomber of the confederates

Typhos class Warbirds- Huge space going vessels of the Razium

T-300s- Truck designs. Model T's, old chassis

The Anvil- A Special order of the Paladins

Terror Hold- mental barrage

Tryonic fields- Shields over a city- protection and helped to hide form scanners. Taken and reengineered from Razium space craft

Wars of Fire- Glorn and Elves

War of the Isles- Current Stalled war, Ultima Prime, Boer

Wolfsburg Castle- Place of kings assassination (Original Name)

Wrist com- Wrist mounted communicator or radio

-A verbatim copy of an induction speech given to new pupils of the
White Tower, recorded in a book of intellectual records-
Master Omno

Class, let us begin. Please look at your notes. The Razium. A purple
skinned alien people, whose unending wars destroyed their own worlds,
took what was left of their armada and fought their way across the stars to
find a new world they could inhabit. They settled here: Partha Terra.

Our planet was in a time of peace and recovery after the Dragon
wars, an arcane world we were just coming into our own steam powered
industrial revolution. The Razium and their Zajust masters thought us a
backwater planet populated with savages, and felt that even in their war
ravaged state we would be easily conquered.

Agesilaus, King of the Confederates of Ultima Thule, the most
powerful continent of our planet was a magic user, War Lok or Lok in the
common tongue. As you know, as you are all trying to become one.

A Lok is able to control the power of the Tempest. That power
allowed our King to use the doorways of the magical gates of the
Labrynthian, to meet this new threat on their own ground. As the Razium
Warships entered our atmosphere, the King acted. To the surprise of the
Razium, he led an armored guard of Spartan Paladins to the bridge of their
flagship, he and his warriors stepped directly from the Labrynthian gate onto
the bridge of the ship itself.

The leaders of the Razium, now wary of the King's power asked for
parley, which he granted. After the meeting with their leaders, the King
agreed to a truce. Both races prospered from the knowledge that was shared;
us from their technology and them from our magic and runes.

For a time our peoples coexisted, but we were deceived. What the
Razium wanted wasn't peace, but power. They wanted the

Labrynthian, having seen its ability; they coveted its power. Magic clashed with high technology, neither able to overcome the other, both forces being weakened in the conflict. The magic however, started to overpower the technology and as the Confederates gained the upper hand to finish the war, both sides were beset by a new enemy. The Dragons had returned.

The large beasts launched a brutal attack against both weakened forces. With little other choice, the King offered another truce to fight a common enemy. The Zajust Warlords agreed and the Affinity War began. Using their technology and the magic of the Tempest, the two forces combined to defeat the Dragon Lord at his spire. This was where Dominus Tor, greatest of the Spartan Paladins, killed the Dragon's leader with a runic sword forged from the rare and magical metal, Arcanium. With their leader gone the Dragons and their allies were scattered and defeated. For a time after the war the truce continued. Though there was peace, the Zajust secretly resented the King for how the war had been fought, feeling he had cost them much of their technology and glory in the final battle.

With resentment, war never sleeps long.

Now open your texts, and we will begin.

To be continued in book two
Lok and Key

ABOUT THE AUTHOR

Tommy Rice is the author of The Lok, book one of the Partha War series. He has been seen in White Dwarf miniature magazine, weight lifting magizines and has appeared in short movies and commercials. He is an ex-football player, weight lifter, and comic geek. This is his first book.

Tommy is a husband and father and lives and works in Washington State, in Northwest USA.

Made in the USA
Middletown, DE
21 November 2017